'*City of Miracles* . . . ends the story of The Divine Cities with style, grace, and beauty. This may be the last we see of this world, but if it is, all the more read on, and treasure these divine tales'
Barnes and Noble

'Sigrud, a stellar protagonist, conflicted, haunted, and struggling to come to terms with his past is sure to become an avatar of the futuristic epic hero readers will cherish and never forget. *City of Miracles* is highly recommended'
Rogueski Reads

'There's just so many good things about *City of Stairs* that it's hard to ignore, and you'll be blown away by just how awesome it is'
The Founding Fields

'Seriously, if you liked the first two books in the series, at all, you have to read *City of Miracles*. It was so so so good. Five out of five stars, and my unconditional recommendation'
Mental Megalodon

'Robert Jackson Bennett's books succeed in creating believable places filled with suspense and thrills to astound and amaze . . . Certainly one of the more talented science fiction/fantasy writers around'
Raul Chapa at BookPeople

'[Bennett] has said that he hopes his readers learn something definite about the world from his books; he's succeeded in his aim . . . A murder mystery, spy thriller, fantasy adventure and philosophical treatise rolled into one. Highly recommended'
SciFi Bulletin

'*City of Blades* has really left an impression and however much I try to write I feel like I can't do the book enough justice. It is so much more than just another fantasy novel with gods, war and mystery'
Draumr Kopa

Also by Robert Jackson Bennett

City of Stairs

City of Blades

7/3/18

'One of the most brilliant and extraordinary fantasy series

'*City of Miracles* is perfect from start to finish and will be one of the best books to come out in recent memory'
The Quill to Live

'Does [*City of Blades*] live up to the Locus, World Fantasy, British Fantasy and GoodReads Choice Awards-nominated *City of Stairs*? Allow me to answer with an emphatic yes . . . Robert Jackson Bennett is one of the most talented authors writing in SFF today and this is his finest work to date'
Fantasy-Faction

'Invigoratingly ambitious . . . an absorbing and mature work, with some fantastically creepy monsters'
SFX

'One of the finest fantasy series of the decade is getting its conclusion'
Fantasy Review Barn

'[*City of Blades* is] a very sharp portrayal of a political powder keg, complete with fantastic, fantastical action and hugely likeable characters. You're going to want to read this'
SciFiNow

'The Divine Cities is one of the most important works of this decade. Bennett . . . has created a genuine world and works out the issues through complicated, original stories with characters who are appealing, complex, flawed and who often show different facets of themselves to different people'
Fantasy Literature

'Bennett has probably written the perfect blend of fantasy and crime fiction. Everything works . . . one of the best books of the year. A must read'
Civilian Reader

'Well written and deeply evocative, *City of Stairs* is an intriguing and clever fantasy adventure'
For winter nights – A bookish blog

'A refreshing fantasy that takes risks that pay off in spades . . . It's accomplished, bizarre, horrifying and imaginative – I can't wait for more'
Wilder's Book Review

CITY
OF
MIRACLES

ROBERT JACKSON BENNETT

Jo Fletcher
BOOKS

First published in Great Britain in 2017
This edition published in 2018 by

Jo Fletcher Books
an imprint of
Quercus Editions Ltd
Carmelite House
50 Victoria Embankment
London EC4Y 0DZ

An Hachette UK company

A CIP catalogue record for this book is available
from the British Library

PB ISBN 978-0-85705-359-6
EB ISBN 978-0-85705-390-9

10 9 8 7 6 5 4 3 2 1

Printed and bound in Great Britain by Clays Ltd, St Ives plc

Typeset by CC Book Production

To Harvey:

Hello, baby. Welcome to Earth. This place is pretty swell, and I recommend you stick around for a while. You never know, it might even get better. Maybe. We're trying, at least. We're trying.

I.
Fallen Trees

All political careers end in failure.

Some careers are long, some are short. Some politicians fail gracefully, and
  peacefully – others, less so.

But beloved or hated, powerful or weak, right or wrong, effective or irrelevant
  – eventually, eventually, all political careers end in failure.

— MINISTER OF FOREIGN AFFAIRS VINYA KOMAYD,
LETTER TO PRIME MINISTER ANTA DOONIJESH, 1711

The young man is first disdainful, then grudgingly polite as Rahul Khadse
approaches and asks him for a cigarette. It's clear that this is the young
man's break, his chance to relax away from his duties, alone in the alley
behind the hotel, and he's irritated to have his moment violated. It's also
clear that the young man's duties must be something serious: one just has
to glance at his dark, close-cut coat, his black boots, his sun-darkened skin,
and his black headcloth to see he must be military, or police, or some
enforcement arm of some authority. Perhaps a Saypuri authority, or perhaps Continental – but someone paid to watch and watch carefully, surely.

Yet the young man does not watch Rahul Khadse with much care, only
polite contempt. And, indeed, why would he care about Khadse? Why
would he care about this old man, with his smudged spectacles, his tattered
briefcase, and his headcloth so musty and poorly arranged?

'All right,' says the young man, giving in. 'Why not.'

Khadse bows a little. 'Thank you, sir. Thank you.' He bows again, lower,
as the young man complies with his request, reaching into his coat to fetch
his tin of cigarettes.

The young man does not notice Khadse glancing into his coat, glimpsing the butt of the pistol holstered there. The young man doesn't notice Khadse gently setting down his briefcase, or his right hand reaching back to his waist as he bows, slipping out the knife. Nor does he notice how Khadse steps very slightly forward as he accepts the cigarette.

He doesn't notice, because he's young. And the young are always oh so foolish.

The young man's eyes spring wide as the knife smoothly enters the space between his fifth and sixth ribs on his left side, spearing his lung, tickling the membrane around his heart. Khadse dives forward as he stabs him, placing his left hand on the young man's open mouth and shoving his head foreward, the back of the young man's skull cracking against the brick wall of the alley with a dull *thud*.

The young man tries to struggle, and though he's strong, this is a dance Rahul Khadse knows all too well. He steps to the right of the young man, hand still on the handle of the knife, his body turned away. Then he slides the knife out of the young man's chest and steps away, neatly avoiding the spurt of blood as his victim collapses against the alley wall.

Khadse glances down the alley as the young man gags. It's a rainy day here in Ahanashtan, foggy and dreary as it often is this time of year, and very few are out and about. No one notices this fusty old man in the alley behind the Golden Hotel, peering over his spectacles at the streets beyond.

The young man chokes. Coughs. Khadse sets down his knife, straddles him, grabs him by the face, and slams his head against the wall again and again, and again and again and again.

One must be sure of such things.

When the young man is still, Khadse pulls on a pair of brown gloves and carefully searches his pockets. Khadse tosses away the pistol after unloading it – he has, of course, brought his own – and rummages about until he finds what he needs: a hotel key, to Room 408.

It's quite bloody. He has to wipe it off in the alley, along with his knife. But it will do just fine.

He pockets the key.

That was easy, thinks Khadse.

Yet now comes the tricky part. Or what his employer *said* would be the tricky part. Frankly, Khadse has a lot of trouble figuring out which orders from his employer he should worry about and which ones he should ignore. This is because Rahul Khadse's current employer is, in his own estimation, absolutely, positively, stark fucking raving mad.

But then, he would have to be. Only a mad person would ever send a contractor like Khadse after one of the most controversial political figures of the modern era, a woman so esteemed and so notorious and so influential that everyone seems to be waiting on history to get around to judging her so they can figure out how to feel about her tenure as prime minister.

A person made of the stuff of legends. Both because she seemed to come from legends, and because it is public record that she, personally, has killed a few legends in her day.

Perhaps Khadse was mad to take the job. Or perhaps he wanted to see if he could do it. But either way, he means it to be done.

Rahul Khadse walks down the alley, glances around the Ahanashtani street, and then turns right and climbs the stairs of Ashara Komayd's hotel.

The Golden Hotel remains one of the most lauded and celebrated places in Ahanashtan, a relic of an era when the nation of Saypur was free to intervene in Continental affairs as it wished, throwing up buildings and blockades and embargoes on a whim. Walking through the doors is like walking into the past, a place where all the imperial grandeur of the Saypur that Khadse used to know has been impeccably maintained, like a stuffed bird in a wildlife exhibit.

Khadse stops in the lobby, appearing to adjust his glasses. Marble floors and bronze fixtures and palms. He counts the bodies: the doorman, the host of the restaurant, the maid at the far corner, three girls at the counter. No guards. None like the one he just killed in the alley out back, at least. Khadse's an old hand at this, and he and his team did their homework: he knows the guards' schedules, their number, their stations. His team has been watching this place for weeks, arranging every step of this delicate ordeal. But now the final deed is Khadse's alone.

He mounts the stairs, his dark coat dripping with moisture. It's all going very smoothly so far. He tries not to think about his employer, the man's mad messages, and his money. Usually Khadse would delight in thinking about the money on a job, but not this time.

Mostly because the money is unimaginable, even to Khadse, who's very good at imagining lots of money and in fact spends much of his free time doing so. This isn't the first job he's done for his employer, but this payday is an order of magnitude larger than the last. Enough money to make a man worry.

But the wardrobe requests . . . that's odd. Very odd indeed.

For when Khadse went to pick up the most recent instalment of his payment, he found the money came with a folded black coat and a pair of black, well-polished shoes. Both came with strict instructions: he was to wear these articles of clothing whenever he performed his contracted duties, with absolutely no exceptions. The instructions suggested that if he did not do so, his very life would be in danger.

At the time, Khadse simply thought – *All right. My new employer is mad. I've worked for madmen before. It's not so bad.* Yet then he tried them on, and found that both the coat and the shoes fit perfectly well – which was very strange, as Khadse had never met his new employer, let alone told him his shoe size.

He tries not to think about it as he climbs the stairs to the third floor. Tries not to think about how those articles of clothing – so neat, so dark, so perfect – are of course what he's wearing right now. He tries not to think about how spectacularly strange all of this is, or about how his employer specifically requested Khadse go alone for this job, without his usual team in tow.

Khadse climbs to the third floor. Very close now.

I wouldn't even be doing this damned job, he thinks, *if it weren't for Komayd.* Which was fairly true: when Ashara Komayd came to be prime minister, oh, seventeen years ago or so, her first order of business had been clearing out all the hardliners from the Ministry of Foreign Affairs. Hardliners like Khadse, who saw a lot of action in those days, plenty of it very nasty.

He can still remember her memo, ringing with that self-important, priggish tone Komayd was always affecting: *We must remember not only what we do, but how we do it. As such, the Ministry will be going through a period of reorganisation and reorientation as we make adjustments for the future.*

Ashara Komayd was cleaning house, cutting everyone recruited by her aunt, Vinya Komayd – and Khadse had always been a favourite of Vinya's.

And suddenly, there he was. Cut loose in Ahanashtan after a decade of service, and promptly forgotten. He tried to find some pleasure when Komayd herself was booted from Parliament, what, thirteen years ago now? But politicians always have their parachutes. It's the grunts like Khadse who have the harder landings. Even Komayd's personal thug, that lumbering, one-eyed oaf of a Dreyling, even he'd gotten a plum retirement, some kind of royal position in the Dreyling Shores – though he'd also heard the fool had found some way to cock it all up.

I'd be doing this for free, Khadse thinks, seething. *Twelve years of service, and then so long, Rahul, good-bye to you, good-bye to you and all you worked for, all you fought for, all you bled for, I'm off to spend the Ministry's coffers on worthless idealism and leave the intelligence world a smoking crater behind me.*

He walks down the fourth-floor hall. Another guard, a woman, young and trim and dressed in black, stands at attention at the corner. As Khadse expected.

Khadse shuffles toward the young guard, his face the very picture of doddering befuddlement, holding a smudged piece of paper with a name and a hotel room on it. 'Pardon me, ma'am,' says Khadse, bowing low and emanating obsequiousness, 'but . . . I seem to be on the wrong floor, perhaps?'

'You are,' says the guard. 'This floor is off-limits, sir.'

'The fifth floor is off-limits?' says Khadse, surprised.

The guard almost rolls her eyes. 'There is no fifth floor, sir.'

'Oh, no?' He stares around himself. 'But what floor is . . .'

'This is the fourth floor, sir.'

'Oh. But this *is* the Golden Hotel, yes?'

'Yes. It is.'

'But I . . . Oh, dear.' Khadse drops the piece of paper, which flutters to the guard's feet.

The guard, sighing, reaches down to pick it up.

She doesn't see Khadse step lightly behind her. Doesn't see him whip his knife out. Doesn't have time to react as the steel bites into her jugular and severs it wide open.

The spray of blood is phenomenal. Khadse dances away from it, careful to avoid any spatter on his clothing – he reflects, very briefly, that avoiding bloodstains is one of his oddest but most valuable talents. The guard falls to her knees, gagging, and he dances forward and delivers a devastating side-kick to the back of her head.

The guard collapses to the ground, pouring blood. Again, Khadse puts down his valise and dons the brown gloves. He wipes and sheathes the knife, then searches her. He finds a hotel key – this one 402 – grabs the guard by the ankles, and hauls her around the corner, out of view.

Quickly now. Quick, quick.

He presses his ear to the door of 402 – they're all suites up here – and, hearing nothing, opens it. He hauls her in and dumps her body behind the couch. Then he wipes off his brown gloves, pulls them off, and exits, delicately picking up his valise on the way.

He almost wants to whistle merrily as he steps over the bloodstains. Khadse always was good with a knife. He had to learn to be, after an operation in Jukoshtan when some Continental took objection to the way he was walking and tried his damnedest to slit Khadse's throat. Khadse walked away from the experience with a lurid scar across his neck and a predilection for working close and dirty. *Do to the Continentals*, he used to say to his colleagues, *as they would do to you.*

He walks to Room 408 – which is, as he expected, right beside the King Suite, where Ashara Komayd has set up her offices for the past month. Doing what, Khadse isn't sure. The general word is that she's managing some charity or other, something about locating orphans and finding homes for them.

But from what Khadse's employer said, it's a lot more than just that.

But then, thinks Khadse as he silently unlocks Room 408, *the mad bastard also said this hotel was covered in defences*. He opens the door. *But I don't call two soft young eggs like those a very rigorous defence.*

Again, Khadse tries not to think about the coat and shoes he's currently wearing. Tries not to think about how his employer suggested that such articles of clothing would serve as tools against Komayd's defences – which, of course, would suggest that Komayd's offices are covered in the sort of defences Khadse cannot see.

That, he finds, is a very disturbing idea.

Horseshit, is what it is, he thinks, shutting the door behind him. *Mere horseshit.*

The hotel suite is empty, but its arrangement is deeply familiar to Khadse, from the weapons on the distant desk to the security reports on the bedside table. Here is where the guards prepare for their assignments, there is the telescope they use to watch the street from the balcony, and here is where they doze in between their shifts.

Khadse stalks over to the wall and presses his ear against it, listening hard. He's almost positive Komayd's over there, along with two of her guards. An unusual amount of security for a former prime minister, but then Komayd's received more death threats than almost anyone alive.

He can hear the two guards. He hears them clear their throats, cough very slightly. But Komayd he doesn't hear at all. Which is troubling.

She should be in there. She really should. He did his homework.

Thinking rapidly, Khadse silently pads over to the balcony. The doors have glass windows, veiled with thin white curtains. He sidles up to the windows and glances out sideways, at the balcony next door.

His eyes widen.

There she is.

There sits the woman herself. The woman descended from the Kaj, conqueror of the gods and the Continent, the woman who killed two Divinities herself nearly twenty years ago.

How small she is. How frail. Her hair is snow-white – prematurely so, surely – and she sits hunched in a small iron chair, watching the street below, a cup of tea steaming in her small hands. Khadse's so struck by her smallness, her blandness, that he almost forgets his job.

That's not right, he thinks, withdrawing. *Not right for her to be outside, so exposed. Too dangerous.*

His heart goes cold as he thinks. *Komayd is still an operative at her heart, after all these years. And why would an operative watch the street? Why risk such exposure?*

The answer is, of course, that Komayd is looking for something. A message, perhaps. And while Khadse could have no idea what that message would contain or when it might arrive, it could make Komayd move. And that would ruin everything.

Khadse whirls around, kneels, and opens his briefcase. Inside his briefcase is something very new, very dangerous, and very vile: an adapted version of an antipersonnel mine, one specifically engineered to direct all of its explosive force to one side. It's also been augmented for this one job, since most antipersonnel mines might have difficulty penetrating a wall – but this one packs such a punch it should have no issues whatsoever.

Khadse takes the mine out and gently affixes it to the wall next to Ashara Komayd's suite. He licks his lips as he goes through the activation procedure – three simple steps – and then sets the timer for four minutes. That should give him enough time to get to safety. But if anything goes wrong, he has another new toy as well: a radio override that can allow him to trigger the blast early, if he wants.

He dearly hopes he never needs to. Triggering it early might mean triggering it when he's still too close. But one must be sure about such things.

He stands, glances out at Komayd one last time – he mutters, 'So long, you damned bitch' – and slips out of the hotel room.

Down the hallway, past the bloodstains, then down the stairs. Down the stairs and through the lobby, where all the people are still going through their dull little motions, yawning as they page through the newspapers, snuffling through a hangover as they sip coffee or try to decide what they'll do with their vacation day.

None of them notice Khadse. None of them notice as he trots across the lobby and out the door to the streets, where a light rain is falling.

This isn't the first time Khadse's worked such a job, so he really should be calm about such things. His heart shouldn't be humming, shouldn't be pattering. Yet it is.

Komayd. Finally. Finally, finally, finally.

He should walk away. Should walk south, or east. Yet he can't resist. He walks north, north to the very street Komayd was watching. He wants to see her one last time, wants to enjoy his imminent victory.

The sun breaks free of the clouds as Khadse turns the corner. The street is mostly empty, as everyone's gone to work at this hour. He keeps to the edges of the street, silently counting the seconds, keeping his distance from the Golden but allowing himself a slight glance to the side . . .

His eyes rove among the balconies. Then he spies her, sitting on the fourth-floor balcony. A wisp of steam from her tea is visible even from here.

He ducks into a doorway to watch her, his blood dancing with anticipation.

Here it comes. Here it comes.

Then Komayd sits up. She frowns.

Khadse frowns as well. *She sees something.*

He steps out of the doorway a little, peering out to see what she's looking at.

Then he spies her: a young Continental girl is standing on the sidewalk, staring right up at Komayd's balcony and violently gesturing to her. The girl is pale with an upturned nose, her hair crinkled and bushy. He's never seen her before – which is bad. His team did their homework. They should know *everyone* who comes into contact with Komayd.

The gesture, though – three fingers, then two. Khadse doesn't know the meaning of the numbers, but it's clear what the gesture is: it's a warning.

The girl glances around the street as she gestures to Komayd. As she does, her gaze falls on Khadse.

The girl freezes. She and Khadse lock eyes.

Her eyes are of a very, very curious colour. They're not quite blue, not quite grey, not quite green, nor brown . . . They're of no colour at all, it seems.

Khadse looks up at Komayd. Komayd, he sees, is looking right at him.

Komayd's face twists up in disgust, and though it's impossible – From this distance? And after so *long*? – he swears he can see that she recognises him.

He sees Komayd's mouth move, saying one word: '*Khadse.*'

'Shit,' says Khadse.

His right hand flies down to his pocket, where the radio trigger is hidden. He looks to the pale Continental girl, wondering if she'll attack – but she's gone. The sidewalk just down the road from him is totally empty. She's nowhere to be found.

Khadse looks around, anxious, wondering if she's about to assault him. He doesn't see her anywhere.

Then he looks back up at Komayd – and sees the impossible has happened.

The pale Continental girl is now on the balcony with Komayd, helping her stand, trying to usher her away.

He stares at them, stupefied. How could the girl have moved so quickly? How could she have vanished from one place and suddenly reappeared across the street and four floors up? It's impossible.

The girl kicks open the balcony doors and hauls Komayd through.

I'm blown, he thinks. *They're on the move.*

Khadse's hand is on the remote.

He's much too close. He's right across the street. But he's blown.

Nothing more to do about it. One must be sure about such things.

Khadse hits the trigger.

The blast knocks him to the ground, showers him with debris, makes his ears ring and his eyes water. It's like someone slapped him on either side of the head and kicked him in the stomach. He feels an ache on his right side and slowly realises the detonation hurled him against the wall, only it happened too fast for him to understand.

The world swims around him. Khadse slowly sits up.

Everything is dim and distant. The world is full of muddled screams. The air hangs heavy with smoke and dust.

Blinking hard, Khadse looks at the Golden. The building's top-right corner has been completely excised as if it were a tumour, a gaping, splintered, smoking hole right where Komayd's balcony used to be. It looks as if the mine took out not only Komayd's suite but also Room 408 and most of the rooms around it.

There's no sign of Komayd, or the strange Continental girl. He suppresses the desire to step closer, to make sure the job is done. He just stares up at the damage, head cocked.

A Continental man – a baker of some kind, by his dress – stops him and frantically asks, '*What happened? What happened?*'

Khadse turns and walks away. He calmly walks south, through the streaming crowds, through the police and medical autos speeding down the streets, through the throngs of people gathering on the sidewalks, all looking north at the column of smoke streaming from the Golden.

He says not a word, does not a thing. All he does is walk. He barely even breathes.

He makes it to his safe house. He confirms the door hasn't been tampered with, nor the windows, then unlocks the door and walks inside. He goes straight to the radio, turns it on, and stands there for the better part of three hours, listening.

He waits, and waits, until finally they begin reporting on the explosion. He keeps waiting until they finally announce it.

. . . just confirmed that Ashara Komayd, former prime minister of Saypur, was killed in the blast. . .

Khadse exhales slowly.

Then he slowly, slowly lowers himself to sit on the floor.

And then, to his own surprise, he begins laughing.

They approach the tree in the morning, while the mist still clings to the forest undergrowth, carrying axes and the two-man saw between them, tin helmets on their heads, their packs strapped to their backs. The tree is marked by a single blob of yellow paint that drips down its trunk. They survey the area, gauge where the tree should fall, and then, like surgeons before a delicate operation, they begin.

He looks up at the tree as the others scurry about. *To convince this grand old thing to fall*, he thinks, *is like carving off a piece of time itself.*

They begin the face cut with the two-man saw, he on one end and a partner on the other, ripping the saw back and forth, its curved teeth slashing through the soft white flesh, peels of wood speckling their hands and arms and boots. Once the bottom of the face cut is established, they chop at it with axes, swinging like pistons in an engine, down and in, down and in, hacking off huge chunks of wood.

They pause to wipe their brows and consider their work. 'How does it look, Dreyling?' the foreman asks him.

Sigrud je Harkvaldsson pauses. He wishes they'd use the name he gave them – Bjorn – but they rarely do.

He kneels and lays his head sideways in the face cut, vaguely aware of the several tons of wood suspended directly above his skull. Then he squints, stands, waves to the left, and says, 'Ten degrees east.'

'You sure, Dreyling?'

'Ten degrees east,' he says.

The other men glance at one another, smirking. Then they resume with this slight adjustment in the face cut.

Once the face cut is complete, they move to the opposite side of the tree and begin again with the two-man saw, slicing through the wood in agonising strokes to grow close, but not *too* close, to the face cut.

When the man at the other end of the saw tires, Sigrud just waits, silently, for someone else to take up the other end. Then they resume sawing.

'I damnably do swear, Dreyling, are you an automaton?' says the foreman.

He says nothing as he saws.

'Were I to open up your chest, would I find naught but gears?'

He says nothing.

'I've had Dreylings on my teams before, and not a one of them could work a saw like you.'

Still nothing.

'Youth, perhaps,' the foreman muses. 'To be as young as you, aye, that's the ticket.'

Still Sigrud says nothing. Though this last statement troubles him deeply. For he is not a young man by any stretch of the imagination.

They pause periodically in their sawing, listening: listening for the deep, complaining cracks, like a shelf of ice collapsing. He is reminded of an argument, an old friend reluctantly coming round to your position: *Perhaps you're right, perhaps I should fall . . . Perhaps I should.*

Then, finally, they hear it: a *pop-pop-pop* like massive harp strings snapping. The foreman screams, '*She falls!*' and they scatter away, tin helmets clapped to their heads.

The old, groaning giant tumbles over, branches snapping as it ploughs to the ground, sending up a great plume of soil. They creep back down to it as the dust settles. The pale circle of wood at the truncated end is bright and soft.

Sigrud looks at the stump for a moment – the only thing that will mark this tree's decades of existence here – and notes its countless growth rings. How odd it is to think that such a colossus could be eradicated in a few hours by a handful of fools with axes and a saw.

'What are you staring at, Dreyling?' says the foreman. 'Are you in love? Start buckling the damn thing, or I'll scramble your brains even more than they already are!'

The other loggers chuckle as they straddle the fallen tree. He knows what they think of him: that he is slow, demented by some childhood accident. That must be, they whisper among themselves, why he never talks, never takes off his gloves, and why one of his eyes is never quite looking *at* anything, but rather just to the right; that must be why he never tires at the saw – surely his faculties must not *register* that he is fatigued. No normal person could silently withstand such punishment.

He does not mind their chatter. Better to think less of him than too much. Too much attention draws eyes.

He raises his axe, brings it down, and shears a branch off of the trunk. *Thirteen years moving from little job to little job.* He does not relish the idea of moving yet again, nor does he wish to alert any authorities to his presence. So he stays quiet.

He focuses on thinking the same question to himself, over and over again: *Will she send for me today? Will today be the day she tells me to come alive again?*

The logging crew bags their quota, so they're all in high spirits come nightfall when they start the journey back to the logging camp, the campfires visible from halfway up the mountain. They make their way down through clear-cut forests, stark wastelands pockmarked with sullen stumps, their tool cart clinking and clanking over the bumps. They hurry as they grow near. Their logging range is not too far outside of Bulikov, so the sack wine is decent even if the food is abominable.

But as they near the camp, the air is not filled with the usual shouts and songs and raucous cries, celebrating the survival of another day stuck to the handle of an axe. The few loggers they see are clumped together like visitors at a funeral, sharing whispered words.

'What in all the hells is the matter tonight? Ahoy, Pavlik!' says the foreman, calling to a passing logger with a drooping moustache. 'What's the news? Another casualty?'

Pavlik shakes his head, his moustache swinging like the pendulum of a long-case clock. 'No, not a casualty. Not a casualty here, at least.'

'What do you mean?'

'News came of an assassination in Ahanashtan. There's talk of war. Again.'

The loggers glance at one another, unsure how seriously to take this.

'Pah,' says their foreman. He spits on the ground. 'Another assassination . . . They say such things so gravely, as if the life of some diplomat were worth so much. But at the end of the day they'll all back down again, just you wait.'

'Oh, I'd agree, if it were just some diplomat,' says Pavlik. 'But it wasn't. It was Komayd.'

A silence falls over the crew.

Then a low voice speaks: 'Komayd? Komayd who . . . who did what?'

The logging crew parts to look at Sigrud, standing up straight by the cart. But they notice that his glance seems much brighter and clearer than they recall, and he stands straighter and taller than before – very tall, in fact, as if he's unpacked three more inches from somewhere in his spine.

'What do you mean, Komayd who did what?' says Pavlik. 'Who died, of course.'

Sigrud stares at the man. 'Died? She was . . . She is *dead*?'

'Her and a bunch of other people. News came through the telegraphs just this morning. They blew her up along with half of a fancy hotel in downtown Ahanashtan, six days ago, lots of people ki – '

Sigrud steps closer to the man. 'Then how are they sure? How are they *sure* she is dead? Do they really *know*?'

Pavlik hesitates as Sigrud nears, until the big Dreyling is looming over him like the firs they fell each day. 'Well, uh . . . Well, they found the body, of course! Or what was left of it. They're planning a big funeral and everything, it's all over the papers!'

'Why Komayd?' says someone. 'She was prime minister over ten damned years ago. Why kill someone out of office?'

'How should I know?' says Pavlik. 'Maybe old grudges die hard. She pissed off nearly everyone when she was in office; they're saying the list of suspects goes twice around the block.'

Sigrud slowly turns back to look at Pavlik. 'So they do not know,' he says quietly, 'who . . . did this to her?'

'If they know, they aren't saying,' says Pavlik.

Sigrud falls silent, and the look of shock and horror on his face gives way to something different: grim resolution, perhaps, as if he's just made a decision he's been putting off for far too long.

'Enough of this,' says the foreman. 'Dreyling, quit your damn foolery and help us unpack the cart.'

The other loggers scurry into action, but Sigrud remains still.

'Bjorn?' says the foreman. 'Bjorn! Damn you, get your ass into gear!'

'No,' he says softly.

'What? No? No to what?'

'No to this,' says Sigrud. 'I am not this, not anymore.'

The foreman strides over to him and grabs his arm. 'You'll be whatever I damned well say you a –'

Sigrud turns, and suddenly the foreman's head snaps back sharply. Then Sigrud twists him, turns him, and slams the man down on the ground. The foreman lies on the ground clawing at his neck, choking and coughing, and it takes the other loggers a moment to realise the Dreyling struck him in the windpipe, a single, quick blow that was so fast the eye could hardly perceive it.

Sigrud walks to the cart, grabs an axe, and walks back to the sprawling foreman. He holds the axe out with one hand until the tip of its blade hovers before the foreman's nose. The foreman stops coughing and stares at it, eyes wide.

The axe hangs in place for a long time. Then Sigrud seems to deflate a little, shoulders slumping. He tosses the axe away and strides into the night.

He packs up his tent and belongings before they gather enough sense to come after him. He makes one final stop on the way out of camp, filching a spade from the camp's wares. He can already hear his foreman's shouts echoing over the campfires, his voice crackling like wax paper: '*Where is the bastard? Where is the bastard?*'

He sprints across the clear-cut fields to the lower forests, a scarred moonscape of ravaged trees, pale and grey in the bright moonlight. He slows down only when he falls into the shadows of the firs. He knows these grounds, knows this terrain. He knows how to fight in these conditions far more than the loggers do.

He stops briefly at the top of a gully, boots perched on a coiled root.

His heart is hammering. Everything feels faint and distant and horribly wrong.

Dead. Dead.

He shakes himself, trying to compartmentalise it. He feels tears on his cheeks and shakes himself again.

She can't be dead. She simply can't be.

He cocks his head and listens: the loggers aren't following him, or at least not yet.

He looks up at the moon and gauges his location. He skulks through the forest, all the old tradecraft returning to him: his toes find soft needles rather than brittle, snapping twigs; he keeps to highways of crisscrossing shadows, mindful of any glinting metals on his person; and when the wind rises, which it rarely does, he is careful to sniff the air, searching for any foreign scents that might betray a pursuer.

He spies scarred trees, amputated branches – landmarks he left behind to guide him back to what he left here. To lead him back to the man he buried, or tried to.

He comes to one leaning, dead pine tree, a long, sloping scar on its face. He sets down his pack and starts to dig. He's in shock, he can tell, and he digs faster than he means to, using up precious energy that he should be saving. Still he digs.

Finally the tip of his spade makes a quiet *clunk*. He kneels and scrapes the rest of the soil away. Inside the hole is a leather-wrapped box, about a foot and a half wide and a half a foot deep. He pulls it out, hands trembling, and tries to unwrap the leather, but his axe gloves are too unwieldy. Glancing over his shoulder, he removes them.

The bright, shining scar on his left hand seems to glow in the moonlight. He winces at the sight of the scar, which almost has the look of a brand, a sigil seared into his flesh, representing two hands, waiting to weigh and judge. It's been months since he's seen it, since he's revealed it to the waking world. An odd thing, it suddenly seems, to conceal a part of one's own body for days on end.

He unwraps the leather. The box is dark wood, its clasp still bright and clean. He's moved this package several times, whenever he had to move to a new job, but never opened it.

The trembling in his hands grows as he unclasps the box and lifts the lid.

Inside the box are many things, any one of which would cause his fellow loggers' eyes to pop clean out of their heads – most notably, probably, the seven thousand drekel marks wrapped into tight little bands, probably three times what a logger makes in a year. These he goes about stuffing into various hidden places in his clothing: the cuffs of his shirt, his coat, his pants, the false bottom of his pack that he personally stitched into place.

Next he tends to the seven different POTs wrapped in wax paper: papers of transportation, allowing the holder free passage throughout the Continent and Saypur. He unwraps them, shuffling through the names and identities – all Dreyling, of course, as he can't exactly hide his race, though he has shaved his head and beard in an effort to distance himself from his old life – not to mention purchasing a false eye. *Wiborg*, he thinks as he rifles through them, *Micalesen, Bente, Jenssen . . . Which one of you is compromised? Which one of you will they watch for, after all these years?*

He wonders briefly why he's doing this, what his next step is. But it is easier to just keep moving forward, hurtling through the motions like a stone rolling down a hill.

Beside the POTs is a bolt-shot pistol: a small, crossbow-like device that falls well short of a true weapon of war, but should be capable of a single silent, lethal shot, provided it has held up in the months underground. The next item at first appears to be a bundle of lambskin, but as he slowly unwraps it, it proves to be an old, well-cared-for knife in a black leather scabbard. He carefully folds the lambskin and stores it away – one never knows what one might need – and pulls the knife out of its scabbard.

The blade is as black as oil. It has a wicked sheen to it, the glint of metal that has tasted a great deal of blood.

Damsleth bone, he thinks. He holds up a pine needle and swats at it with the knife, using the barest amount of force; the needle parts cleanly, splitting in half. *Retains its edge*, he thinks, *for decades and decades*.

Though now, he knows, all the damsleth whales are surely gone: some due to whaling, which he himself pursued as a young man, and others either moved away or perished from the changing climate, the cooler waters killing off or dispersing all their food sources. He's never seen another damsleth weapon besides his own, nor has he ever heard of one still in existence.

He sheathes the knife and buckles it to his right thigh. The motion comes back to him in an instant, and it brings with it all the memories of those days in the field, waging silent, shadowy warfare against countless enemies.

And memories of her, the woman who was always by his side for all of it.

'Shara,' he whispers.

They were closer than lovers – for love, of course, is a flighty, mercurial thing. They were comrades, fellow soldiers whose literal survival depended on one another, from the moment she dug him out of that miserable little jail cell in Slondheim to the days of reconstruction after the Battle of Bulikov.

He wilts a little, crumpling over at the edge of the hole.

I can't believe it. I simply can't believe it.

Sigrud had always felt that, despite his long years in fugitive exile, Ashara Komayd – or just 'Shara' to her friends – would reach out to him one day; that she'd somehow ferret him out amidst all the lowlifes and roustabouts he worked alongside, and he would receive some secret message, some letter or a postcard, maybe, saying she'd done her work and cleared his name, and he could come back to her, he could go back to work on one last operation, or perhaps return to his home.

It was a romantic idea. One she herself often warned against. He remembers her sitting at a window in a checkpoint outside Jukoshtan – thirty years ago, probably, working a dull assignment – blowing steam off her teacup and saying softly: *We are neither of us essential, you and I. To what we do, who we work for . . .* She turned to look at him, her dark eyes wide yet hard . . . *Or to each other. If I am forced to choose between you or the operation, I will choose the operation – and I expect you to do the same for me. Our work asks us to make terrible choices. But make them we shall.*

He smirked then, for at the time he'd always thought as such, resigned to brutal pragmatism; but as the years went by he found himself softened, perhaps by her.

He looks at the moonlight reflected in the black blade. *Now what am I waiting for? Whose call do I wait for now?*

He returns to the box. Hesitates.

I do not wish to see this, he thinks miserably. *Not this.*

But he knows he must.

He pulls out the last remaining artefact: a cutting from a newspaper, brown with age. It is a photograph, depicting a young woman standing on the deck of a ship, looking at the photographer with a mixture of amusement and measured disdain. Though the photograph is in black and white, it's clear the woman's hair is bright blonde, and her eyes a pale blue behind the strange pair of glasses fixed on her nose. On her breast is a company crest with the letters 'SDC.'

The caption reads: SIGNE HARKVALDSSON, NEWLY APPOINTED CHIEF TECHNOLOGY OFFICER OF THE SOUTHERN DREYLING COMPANY.

His one eye grows wide as Sigrud takes in the face of his daughter, rendered in the crude stippling of newspaper print.

He remembers the way she looked when he last saw her, thirteen years ago: cold and pale and still, her face frozen in a look of slight dissatisfaction, as if the exit wound in her chest were a source of only minor discomfort.

He remembers her. Her, and what he did to the soldiers afterward in a fit of wild rage.

I was not there to save you, he says to the photograph. *I was not there to save Shara. I was never there for any of it.*

He stows the newspaper clipping away in his pocket, then gives the pocket a reassuring pat, as if ushering the memory back to sleep.

He grips his knife in his other hand. His grip is tight, his knuckles a bright white.

Sigrud lunges forward and stabs the dead pine, his knife sinking in almost to the hilt. A sob nearly escapes his mouth, but he retains the sense to strangle it before it can give away his position.

Wretched is the creature, he thinks, *that is not even allowed to weep!*

He flexes his entire body, trying to push the knife in deeper and deeper, his fingers crying out in pain. Then he relents and hangs there, gripping the tree, breathing deep.

His instincts take over. *It was bad, what you did back there in the camp*, he tells himself. *Cover blown. Again.* What a stupid creature he is, driven by rage and emotion.

Focus. Nothing to do but move on. Move on and keep moving.

He pulls his knife out, sheathes it, and picks up his pack. Then he starts up the hill into the darkness.

Hours of silent stalking, of careful movement through the midnight darkness of the deep forest. When the trees break he looks up, measures the stars, adjusts his course, and moves on.

Somewhere close to daybreak he remembers.

It was in Jukoshtan, he thinks, back in 1712. Someone in the Ministry had been blown and blown quite badly, all of their assets and networks thoroughly compromised by Continental agents, and no one could gauge just how bad it was.

He and Shara were forced to part, for the Ministry suspected a mole within their ranks – and Sigrud, as a foreigner, was high on the list of suspects. *I've made all your arrangements for transportation out of the city*, Shara told him on the last day together during that rocky stretch, *and from there on out you'll be left to your own devices. Which I think should be quite sufficient.*

He grunted.

I'll go back and tell them it wasn't you, Sigrud, she said. *I'll go back and tell them everything they want to know. I don't know if they'll listen, but I'll try. And I'll find you and reach out to you the second everything's clear.*

He listened to this coldly, for he assumed she thought of him as little more than a tool in her armoury. *And if that does not work*, he said, *and if they lock you up or cut you down?*

Then a rare gleam of passion flared in her eyes. *If that happens . . . Then, Sigrud, I want you to walk away. I want you to run away from all of this, run away from this life and go live your own. Go find your family if you can, go start all over again if you wish, but just . . . Go. You've paid enough, you've done enough. Forget about me and just go.*

This surprised him. They had spent so much time together, two lonely people waging a solitary, lonely war, and he assumed she never thought about a life beyond tradecraft – especially for him, her grim enforcer, the one down in the weeds with a knife clutched in his teeth. Yet she was not content to let him go on being her thug.

She cared for you even then, he thinks, standing still in the darkness. *She wanted you to be something better.*

He looks down at his hands. Rough and scarred and filthy. Most of those scars came not from lumber work, but from nasty, brutal battles in the dark.

He thinks of Shara. His daughter. His family. All of them lost, all of them separated or dead.

He stares at his scarred hands. *What an ugly thing I am*, he thinks. *Why did I ever believe I could wreak anything but ugliness in this world? Why did I ever think that those near me would meet anything but pain and death?*

He stands alone in the forest, then looks up at the pale moon above.

What else is there to be? What else is there to do?

He bows his head, and knows what is left.

The fawn is easily tracked, easily caught, easily killed with a single bolt from his bolt-shot. Sigrud was not sure his hunting skills would hold up, but these deer are truly wild creatures up here in the Tarsils, unaware of men or their tricks and traps.

He carries it over his shoulder to the hilltop. He will not eat this creature, for to eat it would be to make use of it. The point of this ritual – one he has not performed himself in over forty years – is desecration and violation, the creation of a terrible wrong.

In the dawning light Sigrud strips to the waist. Then he carefully beheads the fawn, disembowels it, and props its carcass upright so that it appears to be pleading to the sky, begging the heavens for . . . something. Perhaps mercy, perhaps vengeance. His hands are strong and ruthless, breaking open the delicate bones, tearing the tendons, the ligaments. He places the fawn's organs in a pile before its open body cavity with its tiny, beautiful heart on the top.

Then he places twigs and sticks around the organs and body. He lights the kindling with a match and watches as flames slowly crawl across the bloodstained earth around the grotesque scene, the heat scorching the bloody hide of the once-beautiful, fragile creature.

He thinks back to when he last did this, when his father was murdered. *The Oath of Ashes. Do they even know such a thing in the Dreyling Shores anymore? Or am I such a relic of the cruel, ancient days that only I remember?*

The flames begin to die as the sun dawns. The remnants of the fawn are black, twisted fragments. Sigrud leans forward and pierces the moist, hot soil with his fingertips. He takes a clump of the earth there, soaked with blood and hot with cinder, and smears it on his face, on his chest, on his shoulders and arms.

A desecration has been done, he thinks. *And I am touched by it.*

Then he reaches into what's left of the pile of organs and plucks out the charred remains of the fawn's heart. He holds it in his hands, brushing off the ash. It queerly reminds him of the feeling of a child's hand in his palm.

Weeping, he takes a bite of the fawn's heart.

And I shall do more desecrations yet, he thinks. *Until justice is done, or I am spent.*

2.
Bringing Battle

Of the six original Continental Divinities, only four ever bore children — Taal-havras, the Divinity of order and knowledge; Jukov, the Divinity of merriment; Olvos, the Divinity of hope; and Ahanas, the Divinity of fecundity. Despite this limited number, they had quite the constant mess of interactions and relationships, producing dozens if not hundreds of Divine offspring: Divine sprites, spirits, and beings that peppered the whole of the Continent. These offspring were produced in a manner that mortals cannot truly understand — the genders of the Divine parents did not particularly matter, nor did inbreeding seem to have an effect — but we must consider them, for all intents and purposes, to be the children of the Divine.

One of the favourite questions historians toy with in modern times is exactly what happened to all of those offspring. Did they vanish when the Kaj invaded the Continent and killed the Divinities? Divine creatures — beings created by a singular Divinity, much as a Divinity would create a miracle — definitely did not survive the death of their creator. But some Divine children seemed to survive the deaths of their parents, though those who were found were promptly executed.

Did they have some Divine agency of their own, like miniature versions of their parents? Did the Kaj succeed in executing them all? Or did they find some way to hide themselves? We are not sure. But if they persist within this world, they have not announced themselves yet.

— DR. EFREM PANGYUI, 'ON THE LIVES OF THE DIVINE'

The boy's feet pound on the pavement, his breath burning in his lungs. He ducks under an awning, swings around a lamppost, skids across a cobble-stoned street. An old woman carrying her groceries glares at him as he sprints past a display of apples. A shopkeep cries, 'Watch it!' But the boy ignores them, paying mind only to the next turn, the next street ahead, his face dripping sweat as the sun beats down on him.

Faster and faster, as fast as he can go. He's got to lose him, got to.

And he *should* be losing him: the streets of the city of Bulikov are so tangled and labyrinthine that one could get lost just walking home. Yet so far it's proven shockingly difficult to lose this particular pursuer.

A turn, a turn again. Then down the stairs, across the vacant lots, and down another side street . . .

The boy stops, gasping, and staggers into the mouth of an alley. He waits, breathing hard, and pokes his head around the corner.

Nothing. The street is empty.

Perhaps he's lost him. Perhaps he's really gone.

'Finally,' he says.

Then the light . . . shifts. Twists. Changes.

The shadows begin to twirl at his feet.

'Oh, no,' whispers the boy.

He looks up to see an odd sight, but it's one that he was expecting, even dreading: the clear summer skies directly above him are flooding with darkness, as if evening is being injected into the atmosphere, hues of indigo and dark purple and black swirling amidst the pale blue. He watches, wide-eyed, as the darkness curls around the face of the sun, choking it out and painting over it until it's as if the sun had never been there at all.

There are stars in the new darkness, which hangs directly above him: cold, distant, glimmering white stars. The boy knows if he waits longer the skies above him will turn pitch-black, and those glinting stars will be the only luminescence remaining.

The boy turns and sprints down the alley. The skies above him clear up as if he were directly under a thundercloud: the sun returns, and the bright blue sky is visible once more.

But too close, thinks the boy. *Much too close, much too close* . . .

He's getting desperate. He knows he has to use one of his tricks. He doesn't like trying this while running, but he doesn't have a choice . . .

He shuts his eyes, envisioning the city around him, seeking them out.

It takes him a while to spot them – he's not near one of the entertainment districts, so there are very few theatres or restaurants or bars around here – but then he sees one burst into being somewhat close to him, a tangle of something bright and silvery and quivering, quaking merrily amidst all the gloom and sobriety of the city in day.

He reaches out to it. Grasps it.

Becomes it.

The world shifts around him.

He hears the final line in his mind: '. . . and the shepherdess, of course, says, "Well, it ain't look too much like his father, neither!" '

Suddenly the boy's ears are inundated with a glorious, wonderful, happy sound: the sound of men laughing, cackling, real tears-in-your-eyes laughing, absolutely bent-double laughing, and the boy is there with them, giggling merrily.

He has to force himself to remember what's going on. He opens his eyes and sees he's in a fish shanty down by the Solda River, surrounded by filthy fishermen all sipping from bottles of plum wine. None of them have noticed the sudden appearance of this young, pale Continental boy, who has, it seems, popped out of thin air. They act as if he's always been in the crowd with them. One of the drunken fishermen even offers him a sip of wine, which the boy, still snickering, politely refuses.

It's far too early in the day for such celebration. But he's grateful for it. Wine creates merriment, merriment creates laughter, and laughter gives him . . .

The boy looks out the window of the fish shanty. He's about three miles away from the alley where he was.

He sighs, relieved. '. . . a way out,' he says.

But then his brow crinkles. Is it his imagination, or is the sky darkening above him? Just above the fish shanty?

And are those stars shining so coldly and cleanly up above?

He stares as the sky above him floods with solid darkness, like blood leaking through a bandage.

The boy thinks desperately. Another trick, another turn. He doesn't have a choice.

He shuts his eyes, and searches.

Another tangle of silvery joy. This one isn't quite so thick, quite so bawdy, but it should still . . .

The world shifts around him.

. . . work.

He hears a voice: 'Where is Mischa? Where is . . . Mischa!'

Giggles fill the air. He opens his eyes and sees he's in a small apartment. A curly-haired infant is lying on a sofa, laughing hysterically as his mother hides behind the sofa's back and pops out, crying, 'Where is my Mischa? Where could my darling boy have gone? Could he be – *here?*'

Another explosion of delighted squeals. Neither seems to have noticed the boy's sudden appearance, but perhaps it's because they're too involved in their game. The child's laughter is infectious: the mother begins laughing, which makes the infant laugh even harder.

Remember where you are. Remember what's going on.

The boy walks to the windows of the apartment. He's about seven miles from the fish shanty, he guesses. He can still feel that other tangle of laughter out there, the fishermen sharing their bawdy jokes, and he can tell the distance between them. It should be far enough. No one can move that fast that far. And how could his pursuer even know where he's go –

He freezes.

The shadows on the street outside begin to shift. Darkness floods the skies, as if night itself is manifesting right above him.

'No!' he says. 'No, it can't be!'

The mother and infant laugh hysterically behind him. He can feel the joy in her, feel the pain in her stomach from laughing too hard, all her senses flooded over with merriment.

He wants to stay here. This is what he is, what he does, what he loves. But he has to move on yet again.

Farther this time, he thinks. *Go and keep going.*

He shuts his eyes. Finds the next laughter, the next bright spark of joy. The world shifts.

He's in a house on the outskirts of Bulikov. A man sits on the kitchen floor with a giant pot of pasta spilled all across the tiles, the yellow sauce bright against the white surfaces. His face is red with laughter, and his wife stands at the doorway, howling in amusement.

'I told you it was too heavy!' she says, gasping for air. 'I told you it was!'

The boy laughs too, the laughter tasting of shameful glee. Then he shuts his eyes and searches again.

The world shifts.

He's in a dormitory room beside the university. A young woman sits on the bed, nude and convulsing with laughter. Were you to glance at her it'd be difficult to see what's so funny – until you saw the young man's head buried between her thighs, the rest of his body concealed by blankets.

The boy cackles with her. Her laughter is like sunlight and flower petals raining down in his mind. But he knows he must move on.

He shuts his eyes. Reaches out.

The world shifts.

A ball game in an alley, with one young man lying on the ground, clutching his crotch and gasping after a pitch went awry. The other children laugh uproariously, unable to contain themselves, while the young man says, 'It's not funny . . . It's really *not funny*!' but this makes them laugh all the harder.

He smirks. This laughter has a crueller edge to it, the taste of copper and blood. But he knows he must move on.

He shuts his eyes. Searches.

Again, things shift.

He's in a courtyard. An elderly man and woman sit in wooden wheelchairs in the sun, their legs covered with blankets. They chuckle weakly as they remember some ancient story from days long, long gone.

'She really told me that!' says the woman. ' "Hotter than a stiff cock," that's what she said, right in front of everyone. I swear it!'

'I know, I know!' the man says, wheezing but smiling. 'But who could ever believe it?'

Laughter of wistful incredulity, basking in the joy of two lives well lived. His heart sings to hear it, to taste it in his mouth. But he must move on.

I am laughter, he says, shutting his eyes. *I am wherever there is glee. So he can never catch me . . .*

He reaches out. Another tangle, this one sloppy and drunken and warped, the silvery laughter of someone well sotted.

Any port in a storm, thinks the boy, and he grasps it, pulling himself to it. The world shifts . . .

He opens his eyes. He expected to be in a bar or someone's room, but . . . this appears to be a basement. A dingy basement with one table and one chair.

In the chair is a cackling Saypuri man, but it's clear he's not laughing of his own volition: his eyes have a glazed look to them, and there's a smear of drool on his chin. Despite this, he has the look of a soldier to him, as does the Saypuri woman standing over his shoulder, who's holding an empty syringe. They both wear headcloths, for one, which is common to the military, but they're also trim, muscular creatures, people who have made weapons out of their bodies, especially the woman: there's something to her hard, dark face and amber-gold eyes that suggests a history of command and lethality to her.

The boy stares at them. But then the woman with the syringe does something very strange: she *looks* right at the boy, her expression somewhat apologetic. This *should* be impossible – when the boy shifts he becomes laughter incarnate, the spirit of merriment, invisible to mortal eyes – yet the Saypuri woman just smiles at him with a touch of regret and says, 'Hello there.'

'Wh-what?' says the boy.

'He figured that if he kept you jumping you'd come here eventually,' says the woman. 'Just had to keep someone laughing long enough.'

The boy then senses something riddling the clothing of the two people, forces and designs and structures woven into the fabric.

The boy blinks. The two soldiers are wearing protective miracles, Divine miracles – but they're of a type he's never seen before. So who could have made them?

The Saypuri woman looks at something behind the boy. 'Ah. Well. Here we are, then.'

The boy turns around.

Behind him is a wall of darkness – not just shadow but the night itself, a wall of vast, endless black shot through with coldly glittering stars . . .

A voice echoes out of the darkness, a voice as cold as the light of those stars. 'WHERE ARE THE OTHERS?'

The boy screams.

*

A rattle, a roar, and the train emerges from the tunnel.

Sigrud wakes. It takes longer than it ought for him to remember where he is, what's happening. He rubs at his eye and glances around at the other passengers on the train, all relaxed or bored. They ignore him, thinking him to be another shiftless Dreyling dockworker, dressed in his blue peacoat and knit cap.

What an odd thing it is, he thinks, *to don civilisation again as if it were an old jacket, lying unused for years at the back of a closet.* Perhaps civilisation never truly suited Sigrud, but he must feign it now, after so many years in the wilderness. And after what happened in Voortyashtan, over thirteen years ago now, he is still very much a wanted man. As someone who once worked for the Ministry of Foreign Affairs, one thing he knows full well is that the Ministry does not forget.

Nor should they. He remembers that moment as a blur of shadows and screams – he'd been raving mad with grief and fury after the murder of his daughter – but fragments of what happened in Fort Thinadeshi still sear bright and hot in his mind.

Grabbing a soldier's sword, using it to cleave off the man's arm below the elbow. Ripping a bayoneted rifling away from another and thrusting it deep into her abdomen.

I didn't even know their names, he thinks, huddled low. *I still don't even know their names*.

The train rushes on.

Back when Sigrud worked as an operative on the Continent, it would have taken two to three weeks to travel from the outskirts of Bulikov to Ahanashtan. Today it seems you can simply buy a ticket, go to a train station, and all the world will shift around you until you find yourself where you wish to be in but a handful of days.

He focuses on his goal. *Ahanashtan*, he thinks, remembering what he read in the papers. *The Golden Hotel*.

And then what? he wonders. What will he do there?

He looks at his reflection in the window. *The only thing I know how to do anymore*.

Sigrud je Harkvaldsson stares at his reflection. He takes in the scars, the wrinkles, the bags under his eyes. He wonders if he has it in him to do this. It's been years since he worked as an operative – over a decade.

Perhaps this is foolish. Perhaps he's an old dog insisting he can still perform old tricks.

Yet there's something curious in his face, something that's concerned him for a while, something he's tried to dismiss. But now that he's faced with mirrored surfaces time and time again – for mirrors were rare in the logging camps – he can tell something is wrong with his appearance.

The face in the reflection is not the face of an ageing man. He is much how he remembered himself before he went into hiding: middle-aged, scarred, and bitter – but still middle-aged. Which Sigrud certainly no longer is.

Perhaps it is simply the blessing of good lineage. Perhaps that's it.

Then Ahanashtan emerges on the horizon. And instantly, he forgets his worries.

'Oh,' he whispers, 'by the *seas . . .*'

When Sigrud first came to Ahanashtan, over thirty years ago, he regarded it as one of the most impressive metropolises the world had yet produced (behind Bulikov and Ghaladesh, of course). Yet at that time it was still mostly a sea port, devoted to industry and the military – in other words, it was dirty, dank, and dangerous. It had a few skyscrapers then, buildings fourteen, fifteen, even sixteen storeys tall, monumental achievements for architects in those days, and everyone agreed that the future had truly dawned on the Continent.

But as Sigrud's train grows closer to the colossal clutch of towers on the ocean, he sees that the architects and industry magnates of thirty years ago had no idea what was coming.

He tries to count their height. Maybe thirty, forty, or even sixty storeys tall? He can't believe it, can't fathom the massive stone-and-glass structures that stand so still and perfect against the sea, the sun dappling their crenellated surfaces. Some are tall and straight and square, others are like vast wedges, like a cut of cheese made of granite and glass, and still others look like nothing more than gigantic metal poles, silvery and shimmering, with rows and rows of tiny windows riddled in their sides. Running across the countryside to this cluster of structures is what at first seems to be countless rivers or tiny, shining tributaries, but Sigrud slowly realises that these are *rails*: what must be a hundred or more railways weave and merge until they all, eventually, join together in Ahanashtan.

To the northwest is something even stranger: a glittering metal construction that looks almost like utility lines, huge wires mounted on poles, except they're far too tall . . . and it looks like little pods are crawling along the wires. He can't figure it out from this distance.

Sigrud turns back to the metropolis ahead. *And I*, he thinks, *am supposed to find Shara's killer in there?*

He packs up this emotion and shoves it away somewhere in the back of his mind. He has no time for self-doubt.

There is where Shara met her end, he thinks. *There is where she was murdered. And there is where I will shed the blood and break the bones of those who cast her down.*

The gleaming towers of Ahanashtan swell up before him. He remembers something Shara said when they first came here, she seated at a table, encoding a message; Sigrud on the bed, sewing up a rent in his coat. She said, *No one knows what the original Ahanashtan really looked like, back in the Divine days. The historians theorise it was a giant, organic tangle of trees and vines, all of which merged together to create homes and structures. Glowing mushrooms and peaches acting as lights, vines flowing forth with healing waters, that kind of thing. Records suggest it was beautiful. But it all vanished when Ahanas died.* Then she paused, and added, *And good riddance too.*

He looked up from his work. *Good riddance? If it was so beautiful?*

It was certainly beautiful. But Ahanashtan was also the port where the Continent brought in Saypuri slaves. All these beautiful structures, overlooking a bay teeming with human misery . . . Even the most beautiful creations cannot wipe away such corruption.

Sigrud watches as the giant towers loom over him. *Maybe the change*, he thinks, *is only superficial.*

First, logistics.

A room at the edge of town, close to the docks but not too close. He knows the waterfront, knows its crannies and its smoke and the tang of diesel. He wants to have his back pushed up against known territory.

The room is bare-bones. Walls and a bed and a tiny closet with all the soul and allure of a soiled bar of soap. Not a great place to hide things. So he doesn't.

He finds an abandoned restaurant down the block. It's suffered water damage from some past storm, and clearly won't be occupied anytime soon. He picks the lock on the back door and skulks inside. He assembles a cache in the oven ventilation shaft, the dilapidated kitchen ringing with little *clinks* and *clanks* as he works.

Inside he places his handheld bolt-shot, a pistol and ammunition – acquired along the way – and a second, shoulder-mounted bolt-shot, this one much more high-powered than the little handheld one. He stores away his backup POTs, as well: he's Mr. Jenssen here in Ahanashtan, here to look for work, but he might need to be someone else if the situation calls for it. He also stores away some but not all of his money. He knows to seed that throughout his terrain like a squirrel does nuts. But he's been without money before. He knows it's easier to live hand to mouth in the city than in the wilds. Provided you don't mind what you're putting in your mouth.

He slips out the window of the restaurant, then stands in the shadows for a moment, watching the streets. No movement, no watchers. In and out and done.

Now to wait for nightfall. And then to visit the Golden.

Midnight in Ahanashtan. The city is largely electrified now, so the streets are never fully dark. It's a strange feeling for Sigrud, who knows the shadows better than he knows his own skin. He doesn't like it. He doesn't like how the steam and clouds obscure the moon and stars, yet the moisture traps the artificial light of this modern place, smearing the world above with a muddy orange colour.

Or perhaps he just doesn't like being here, being on this street, on this block. Where she was. Where she died.

Sigrud stares at the Golden from a darkened doorway. It is a husk of a building, a corpse, its facade broken and dark. Police ropes, dyed bright red, festoon the streets outside, warning people to keep out.

His eye lingers on the massive rent in the top corner, lined with splintered wood, like broken teeth in a gaping maw.

That was her. That's where she was.

A few patrolmen lurk in the doorways, Ahanashtani officers keeping watch over the site. Sigrud's already spotted them, even the ones trying to remain hidden. The Ahanashtani police know as well as anyone that the death of Ashara Komayd is an international incident, so they must deploy their forces as much as possible to stave off any criticism – even if they aren't quite sure what to do with those forces.

Sigrud slips out of the doorway, satchel over his shoulder. He pads down a back road, ducks through a torn chain-link fence, and weaves down a filthy alley until he approaches the eastern side of the Golden.

He dodges under the police rope and waits in the darkness, head cocked, listening carefully. Nothing. If he's been seen, they aren't doing anything about it yet.

He walks along the hotel's brick wall until he finds a service door. He tries the knob – locked, of course. But after a moment's work with his torsion wrench and his hook picks, the lock springs open, and he slips inside.

Sigrud stands in the darkness of the hotel, listening once more. He can tell right away that the building is broken: there is a curious way that the wind blows through bombed-out structures, one you only hear when segments of the walls have been torn apart.

He winds through the spacious lobby, then climbs the stairs. He has a torch, but chooses not to use it. The luminescence from the streetlights spills through the Golden's many windows, and is more than enough to see by.

He climbs to the fourth floor. The wind is stronger now, bearing with it the smell of chimney smoke and burned fabric. He walks down the hallway, his boots sending up plumes of dust from the soiled carpet.

He pauses at one corner and sniffs.

A familiar, coppery smell.

He kneels and touches the carpet at his feet. He pulls out his torch and flicks it on, allowing a narrow beam of light to dance across the fabric.

Blood. A lot of it.

Someone killed the guard on station, he thinks. *Then slipped down the hall to plant the explosives.*

He stands back up and looks down the hallway. He can see streetlight and faint moonlight spackling the walls outside the ruined rooms. After a few steps, there will be nothing more to explore. Just shattered walls and burned-out rooms.

I must look, he thinks, though he is not sure why. Perhaps it is because he was denied his chance to hold vigil. *I must look and see.*

He comes to the edge of the devastation and looks out. Shara's room is completely gone. Nothing left of it, not even a stick of wood. He can see straight through to the city street below. He read in the papers that her two guards died with her, along with a young couple vacationing in the room below. All dead and gone in but a second.

He thinks about Shara. How she moved, how she laughed, how she hunched over a cup of tea. And though he never really knew the girl, he thinks of her daughter – a Continental, adopted. Tatyana, he thinks her name was. Sigrud only saw her for an instant after Voortyashtan. He'd read in the papers – when he could get them in the mountains, that is – that Shara and her daughter had retired to the countryside to live in peaceful seclusion.

Wherever that girl is, she will now go forward in life without a mother.

He remembers Signe, cold and still on that table in the dark. Leaves in her hair and her collar askew.

What a crime it is that creatures of hope and justice fade from this world, he thinks, *while those like me live on*.

Sigrud stares out at the Ahanashtani cityscape beyond, cheery and glittering with light. He blinks, feeling suddenly very empty, very powerless, very small. There is nothing here for him. But what did he expect from this place? A record, a note, a file, a message? Did he think she would think of him in her last moments? Yet there's only ash and blood.

He takes a deep breath. *Time for a last resort*, he thinks.

He sets down his satchel and begins unpacking its contents. He takes out a glass jar, a bag of daisy petals, and a small tin of grey earth.

I saw you do this enough times, Shara, he thinks, working away, *that I could do it in my sleep.*

He fills the jar with daisy petals, shakes it, then dumps them out. *Daisies. Sacred to Ahanas for their wilful recurrence.*

Then he takes a bit of the grey earth – still moist – and smears it across the bottom of the jar. *Grave dust, the final state of all things*. He waits a moment, then wipes the earth away. Then he picks up the jar and applies its open end to his eye, as if it were a telescope.

He looks through the jar at the ruined rooms before him, and his heart drops. Nothing looks different. This is an old miracle, of course, an old ritual from back before the fall of the Continent. Shara used to perform it all the time: amplify the glass with the right reagents, then look through it, and any Divine alterations to the world would glow with a bright, blue-green phosphorescence. He remembers her saying that it was almost useless in Bulikov, since the walls there glowed so bright that they hurt her eyes and drowned everything else out.

Yet the shattered rooms before him are as dark and shadowed as they were before. If something miraculous was once here in these rooms, the bomb wiped it away as surely as the lives of the people within them.

He sighs, turns away, and drops the jar.

Then he pauses. He thinks for a moment.

He slowly turns back, and applies the jar to his eye again.

Nothing glows in the ruined rooms before him. It's all still shadows and ash. But there *is* something glowing in the streets *outside* the hotel. He can't see much of it – just a sliver of the streetscape is visible from this angle – but he can tell that someone has drawn some kind of line or barrier in the concrete.

A line or barrier that must be miraculous, or Divine – for it glows as bright as a lighthouse at sea.

Sigrud slowly lowers the jar. 'By the seas,' he whispers. 'Someone did something to the *streets*?'

Though this makes him wonder – was it Shara? Or someone else?

His hands are shaking, partly with excitement, partly with shock. He never encountered such a thing once, not even when he worked with Shara in this very city. He turns to go back downstairs and outside, but pauses again, just as he's about to take the jar away from his eye.

He didn't think to look through the jar down the hallway. He didn't think there'd be anything inside the rest of the hotel. But he sees he was wrong.

Sigrud stares through the little glass jar. There are more miraculous barriers here, more designs, more glowing wards placed in the walls and the floors and the ceilings of the hallway. He walks down the hallway and takes the jar away from his eye, and the wards vanish immediately. He touches one panel in the wall, a spot that glowed bright a mere second ago, but he can't see anything there, no device or symbol or totem of any kind. Whatever these miracles are, they must be alterations of a kind so faint and so immaterial that they don't even register to the naked eye.

Which is strange. There is only one Divinity still alive, and that's Olvos. Her miracles all still work – that would be why the miraculous walls of Bulikov still stand – but they should be the only ones.

Yet Sigrud doesn't recognise these Divine alterations to the world. He was no expert on the Divine – that was always Shara's area – but he's fairly sure that, like altering the streets themselves, he's never seen miracles or works of this kind.

He stares at the miracles through the glass jar. It's clear that they're barriers of a sort, running across the threshold of a hallway, or the top of the stairs, or even in the lobby.

This was not just a hotel, thinks Sigrud, lowering the glass jar. *It was a fortress.*

He looks back down the hallway, toward the ruined room where Shara died.

Were you waging a war, Shara? And if so – against whom?

Then he hears it: a cough, a shuffle, and the click of a heel from downstairs. Someone's inside the hotel, someone very nearby.

Sigrud shrinks up behind the corner next to the stairs and slowly slides out his knife. He listens carefully, standing perfectly still.

He can hear them mount the stairs, hear the carpet being crushed under the soles of their shoes. A light springs on downstairs – a torch – and the beam goes bobbing and dancing among the white panelled walls of the Golden.

They're almost at the top of the stairs, just a few feet away. He crouches, ready to jump, to stab them in between the ribs or slash their neck open – whichever is quieter or quicker.

They come to the top of the stairs and stand there for a moment, shining their torch around, just barely missing Sigrud crouched in the corner beside them. It's a man, he can tell by the way the person carries himself.

'Huh,' says the man. 'Thought I saw . . . Hm.' He turns around, shaking his head, and walks back downstairs. Sigrud allows himself a quick glance around the corner, and sees the golden epaulets and badge on their chest – an Ahanashtani policeman.

He waits, listening, until he's sure the policeman's gone. Then he waits more, another ten minutes, just to be sure. Then he finally lets out a breath.

He looks down at the knife in his hand and sees it's shaking.

Just a policeman. No one of consequence, no one of note. An innocent bystander, really.

Sigrud sheathes his knife. He wonders – how many innocent lives is he responsible for? How many have fallen simply because they happened to be close to him while he did his work?

He walks back downstairs, trying to ignore the trembling in his hands.

Once he's outside the hotel and back in the safety of the shadows, Sigrud explores the alterations done to the streets around the Golden. He must look like a madman, standing there with a glass jar stuck to his eye, but there's no one around to see him at this hour.

Whoever made the miracles in the Golden clearly did far more work to the streets outside. There are barriers and lines and invisible barricades everywhere – some hanging in the air, ghostly modifications to what must be reality itself – and it doesn't take long for Sigrud to understand what this is.

If the Golden was Shara's fortress, he thinks, *then these must be its moats, its drawbridges, its outer walls and gatehouses.* He has no idea what would trigger these miraculous traps. They certainly didn't do anything to keep him out, or to harm him. But perhaps they were attuned to a specific opponent. The Divinities could change reality as they wished, so they were certainly capable of creating a miraculous defence that would respond to a single, precise enemy.

But it's still concerning that he's never seen these miracles before in the whole of his career. Then again, he really only knew what Shara knew – and it's possible Shara learned a lot of new things during their time apart.

Who was she when she died? Perhaps she was no longer the woman you knew.

The thought troubles him. Yet Sigrud doesn't think Shara would act too differently. He knew Shara perhaps better than anyone in this world – and an operative is an operative until the day they die.

She must have had some method of communication, he thinks, scanning the streets. *Some way of sending messages to clandestine agents and allies.* And he has no doubt that if she had access to Divine defences, she would have used some of those same methods to prepare a communications system.

He wanders the darkened streets around the Golden for nearly two hours, the glass jar stuck to his eye. He shies away from any early-morning pedestrians, especially police officers, even though he appears fairly harmless – he cannot risk having a common stop escalate into something nasty.

Then, finally, he spies it: it's just a dot, a distant blot on a brick wall nearly two blocks away. But it's there, glowing bright, that same, curious blue-green phosphorescence of the Divine.

He puts the jar away and approaches the brick wall slowly, conscious of any surveillance. If this was part of Shara's communication methods, it might be compromised.

He takes his time, spending two, three hours circling through the streets surrounding the blue-green blot. He sees nothing, but since he now seems to be dealing with something Divine, not seeing things doesn't necessarily mean anything. The Divinity Jukov once stowed the body of his lover in a glass bead or something, if he recalls. An assassin could pop out of the walls and cut him down if they had enough miracles at their disposal.

Yet this does not happen. The closer Sigrud gets, the more confident he grows that this site – whatever it is – remains secure.

Sigrud walks toward the wall and casually holds the jar up to his eye, or at least as casually as one could possibly do such a thing.

One brick in the wall glows bright blue-green. Five bricks up from the ground.

Sigrud walks up to it, then scans the streets. There's no one.

He looks at the brick. Throwing lots of caution to the wind, he touches it.

His fingers pass through it as if it were made of fog, and the instant this happens, it vanishes, leaving a hole in the wall.

Sigrud peers into the hole. There are two objects inside: one is a candle, burning with a strange intensity. The other is an envelope, sealed but unmarked.

He picks up the candle and quickly blows it out, for it's not wise to be lit up like a firework when you're trying to go unnoticed. He thinks, then flips the candle over.

Inscribed on the bottom is a symbol of a flame between two parallel lines – the insignia of Olvos, the flame in the woods.

Sigrud grunts, surprised. He's seen such miraculous candles before, with Shara, in Bulikov – they never burn out, and give off an intense, bright light. But why put one here? Why light up a dead drop?

He drops the candle and picks up the envelope. On its front is a single letter – an *S*.

He pockets the envelope, turns, and takes a long, circuitous walk back to his rooms. He's fairly confident he has no tails, no surveillance. One person happens to walk alongside him for a little bit – a pale, young, Continental girl with odd eyes and a queerly upturned nose – but their paths quickly diverge, and he never sees her again.

Once he's back in his rooms, Sigrud watches the streets for another hour. When he's satisfied he's gone unnoticed, he shuts the curtains and opens the envelope.

It contains two letters, both handwritten, though one is in code. Sigrud reads the uncoded one first.

Shara,

Spotted him again on Neitorov Street, then again on Ghorenski Square.

This was on the 9th and 12th. I am almost positive it's the same man we sighted around the hotel two weeks ago. Small, upper middle-aged, Saypuri, scar on his neck. Clearly a hood of some kind, but not Ministry. And he has a team working for him, I think. Too many familiar faces.

I suspect he's working for our opponent. He's difficult to track – I believe he has been given tools to hide his movements. Highly recommend leaving Ahanashtan with all due haste.

We were drawn here, I think. This city has always been a trap. Now he has our list of possible recruits. We have to act immediately.

As for the little Saypuri hood, and his team – I managed to steal a communication of theirs. I pilfered it from a dead drop of theirs, copied it, and replaced the original before anyone noticed. It's enclosed, but it's in code. Yet codes have always been your kind of thing.

Stay vigilant. He's not the poor child we thought he was. He's broken in more awful ways than we could have ever imagined.

– M

Sigrud rereads the letter. Then he reads it a third, fourth, and fifth time. Then he sits back and lets out a long, slow sigh.

It's clear now that Shara was working a big operation – especially if she was putting together lists of possible recruits. It's not at all clear what they were recruiting agents for, but it must have been something specialised, something sought-after – otherwise, their opponent stealing a list of those recruits wouldn't be such a devastating blow, which this letter makes it sound like it was.

But as to who wrote this letter, and who their enemy is, Sigrud has no idea. Who is 'M'? Could that be Mulaghesh, Shara's longtime military ally? He doesn't think so. Last he heard, Mulaghesh was still serving in Parliament in Ghaladesh, and was enjoying a surprising burst of popularity – he knows her supporters fondly call her 'Mother Mulaghesh,' which amuses him, as Mulaghesh was about as motherly as a dreadnought.

Whoever their enemy is, they penetrated not only Shara's tradecraft practices, but also the Divine barriers she'd put up around herself in the Golden. Not someone to trifle with, then.

And whoever wrote this message was trying to warn Shara, trying to tell her the sharks were closing in. But it never got to her.

Yet the little Saypuri hood . . . That rings a bell.

He rereads that line again and again. Sigrud worked with all kinds of Saypuri hoods and operatives and hardliners in his time in the Ministry.

An ageing Saypuri hood with a scar on his neck . . .

The blood on the floor. Dirty work, silent and close – knife work.

The memory of a face comes swimming up in his mind: a thin, wiry, short Saypuri man, with high, sharp cheekbones, a starved face, and burning eyes. And just below his chin, nearly hidden in his collar, a bright, lurid, white scar, running across his throat.

He remembers the man tapping that scar once and saying, *I got this in Jukoshtan. Fucking Kolkashtani took exception to the way I was walking. Too much pride for a Saypuri, he said. But I survived. Found him later. Gutted him like a pig. Never forgot that he tried to do that to me. Whenever I get a contract for a Continental . . . Why, I grab my knife, and remember . . .*

'Ah,' he says. 'Khadse. Of course.'

Lieutenant Rahul Khadse of the Saypuri Navy. Sigrud remembers him. Nasty little man, one of Vinya's pets. When Shara took the prime minister's seat, he'd been one of the first to go. But if it's him – and Sigrud only has this mysterious testimony suggesting so – then it seems he found a home here in Ahanashtan, practising his grisly trade.

Sigrud puts down the handwritten note and looks at the copy of the coded message. It appears to be a copy of a telegram, which would have been sent through the normal channels – so the date is there in plain text at the top. It looks like it was sent the week before Shara's death.

He sighs and scratches his head. *I thought I'd never have to decrypt anything again*, he thinks, *yet here I am once more*. He rummages around in his room for a pencil and paper. *How I hate codes.*

It takes him the whole morning to decrypt it. He tries some standard methods, but none make any headway. He tries some systems Shara devised, but those don't work either.

I should sleep, he thinks, rubbing his eyes. *I must sleep . . .*

But whenever he thinks of sleep, he remembers the sight of the Golden, its walls ruined and torn, and he has no appetite for rest.

It's only when he starts really thinking about who this message was intended for – Khadse, likely – that he has any ideas.

If Khadse was the hood that Shara's enemy was working with, then he probably would not have his own encryption team. Maybe he would have twenty years ago, when he was still in the folds of the Ministry and had access to resources – but not now. So he'd need something familiar. And what sort of code would be familiar to Khadse?

After one more hour, he stops, thunderstruck.

He knows this. He's used this code before.

He tries out one key.

The first few lines of the original order begin to materialise:

ONCE CONFIRMED KOMAYD HAS BEEN ELIMINATED . . .

'Shit,' says Sigrud. He can't believe it. It's a code that was used by Bulik-ovian partisans twenty-five years ago, when the capital of the Continent occasionally resisted Saypuri rule. He can't blame Khadse for using it – it's an obscure one, one broken by the Ministry long ago, and used in a region fairly far from here. It's likely any contemporary Ministry operatives would be stumped by it. But Khadse likely didn't think there'd be any ageing operatives like Sigrud on his tail.

He decodes the rest of the message, and reads:

ONCE CONFIRMED KOMAYD HAS BEEN ELIMINATED NEXT TARGET LIST WILL BE PROVIDED 12 DAYS LATER STOP

EXCHANGE WILL TAKE PLACE 1300 HOURS 28TH OF BHOVRA STOP

SUVIN WAREHOUSE FACILITY REMAINS MOST SECURE LOCATION STOP

MAINTAIN HIGHEST POSSIBLE SECURITY FOR EXCHANGE STOP

Sigrud rereads the message, then reads it a third, fourth, fifth, and sixth time.

The 28th of Bhovra . . . He has to do some maths, since he usually thinks in Saypuri months, not Continental months – but he eventually realises that's in three days. So he still has time. Not much, but some.

He has a time, a date, and he knows one half of who will be there – Khadse and his team. Likely a lot of them, judging by the last sentence – 'highest possible security'.

He looks down at his hands. Scarred, worn, ugly things – the left, especially, its palm brutally mutilated using a Divine torture method long, long ago. *I was only ever meant for one thing*, he thinks. He slowly makes fists. The knuckles pop and creak unpleasantly. *Meant to practice one art. How just it feels that now I shall do so.*

He goes to bed, and sleeps deeply for the first time in weeks.

The Suvin Warehouse proves to be an old coal facility, situated on a stretch of docks on the eastern end of Ahanashtan – very sketchy, very dangerous, very old and dilapidated. An odd choice for an exchange: usually they'd pick someplace more accessible.

No simple dead drop, then, he thinks. *Whoever is giving this information to Khadse, they mean to make him work for it.*

But if Khadse is being put through his paces, it means there's much, much more to protect. Shara was just one facet of all this, and Khadse was but a tool in a larger game.

I must meet this employer of Khadse', he thinks. *And ask him many, many questions.*

He walks along the perimeter. *Bolts*, he thinks, looking at the niches and shadows. *Radios . . . Rope . . . Explosives, perhaps.* He looks around at the nearby crumbling lots. *And I'll need a safe house. And probably to steal an auto too.*

He has work to do, things to buy, things to make. And not much time to get them.

He returns to the streets to find his way home. But as he does he checks his periphery, doubles back, and performs some quick manoeuvres to see if he has a tail.

He doesn't. But he could have sworn he saw a familiar face: the pale, young Continental woman with the upturned nose and queerly coloured eyes.

He shakes himself.

Time to go to work.

3.
Such Filthy Work

It's silly, but I still worry about miracles. We tell ourselves that they're all dead, but I'm never quite reassured enough.

Pangyui writes that, in some ancient texts, miracles were described not as rules or devices but as organisms, as if Saint So-and-So's Magic Feet or whatever they called it was just a fish in a vast sea of them. As if some miracles had minds of their own.

This bothers me. It bothers me because organisms focus on one thing: survival. By any means necessary.

— MINISTER OF FOREIGN AFFAIRS VINYA KOMAYD,
LETTER TO PRIME MINISTER ANTA DOONIJESH, 1709

Rahul Khadse glowers out the auto's window at the night sky. He shivers. *Just nerves*, he tells himself. *That's all it is.* But he can't help but admit that the evening has a bad taste to it.

He sighs. How he hates this particular job.

His team clutches their coats tight around their shoulders as they sit in the idling auto, as if they could seal out the creeping, chilling damp. It's a hopeless cause. 'How is it,' mutters Zdenic, 'that this damned city gets both the hot summers and the cold winters?'

'Not as bad as a few years back,' says Emil, their driver. 'That was wh –'

'Shut *up*,' snaps Khadse. 'And watch for the other team!'

Silence. Some uncomfortable shifting.

Khadse shivers again as they sit in the idling auto, but not due to the cold: he knows what's waiting for him at the coal warehouse tonight. Just like his coat and shoes – the ones he wore to the Komayd job, and the ones he's wearing now – the coal warehouse has its own strange, specific instructions.

He still remembers his bafflement the first time his employer arranged an 'exchange'. In his day if someone wanted to pass along information, Khadse would just arrange a dead drop, or a precisely timed, fleeting encounter somewhere public. But his employer, of course, was different. Khadse was sent a small silver knife, and an old wooden matchbox filled with matches that had yellow heads. With these came instructions to take the items to a certain room in a certain warehouse, utilising the *utmost* precaution in doing so, and then he was to . . .

Khadse shivers again at the very thought of it. *Will tonight be the last time I do this? Or will I be doing this for the rest of my life – however long it lasts?*

Finally the second auto arrives. They watch as it pulls up to the alley exit across the street from them. The lights blink on, then off.

'Site's clear,' says Emil. 'Proceed?'

Khadse nods. Emil puts the car in drive, pulls out, and starts off toward the eastern end of Ahanashtan, taking a predetermined series of alleys, back roads, and, once, cutting across a vacant lot.

The old coal warehouse emerges from the fog. It looks like some ancient, spectral castle, and reminds him of the ruins he saw when he was stationed in Bulikov, long ago, fragments of a civilisation long since faded.

They park. He sits in silence, surveying the area.

'Matrusk's been here all day,' says Zdenic. 'No one's come in or out or even close.'

'If this fucker didn't have the strangest damned exchange system in all the world,' mutters Khadse, 'this wouldn't be an issue.' He grunts to himself. 'The hells with it. Let's go.'

He steps out of the auto. There's a symphony of *clunks* as the rest of his team does the same, their auto doors opening all at once. He approaches the warehouse, walking with the air of a man coming to collect a debt, his dark coat fluttering, his wood-soled shoes clicking and clacking against the asphalt.

His crew follows him. Stupid to have so many for just a dead drop, but his employer did say to use the utmost precaution. He's never liked how his employer is so paranoid, making requests as if they're being watched *all* the time. It does give one ideas.

When they near the entry he makes a motion with his hand. His team members pull out pistols and begin moving ahead, sweeping from room to room. Khadse knows which room matters, the one at the very top, where the site manager's office once was. A long way up.

They enter the warehouse bays. The rooms are huge and looming, giant seas of shadows. Khadse's team switches on torches and sweeps the rooms with light, revealing giant concrete walls and ceilings, some corners awash in piles of coal and coke.

The torchlights dance over the piles of coal. *Such filthy work*, thinks Khadse.

No one. Nothing.

'Clear,' says Zdenic.

They leave two guards at the entrance, then proceed up the rickety wooden stairs to the next floor. They cross the entirety of the warehouse, then go up a winding metal staircase to the third floor. Everything is dark and dank, sooty and ashen, as if this place was built of the jetsam from some horrific fire.

Up to the fourth. They leave three more guards behind on the third, making it just Zdenic, Alzbeta, and Khadse on the fourth floor, where the site manager's office awaits.

They walk down the hallway, then through the offices to the break rooms, where a sink must have burst long ago, leaving plumes of mould running across the walls and floor. They turn and approach the office at the very, very back. Khadse makes a gesture, and his two remaining team members take up positions: Zdenic at the site manager's door, and Alzbeta at the hall entry.

'Won't be a minute,' says Khadse. Then he opens the site manager's door and walks in.

He turns on his own torch, sending shadows dancing around him. The room is drab and empty, its walls and floors tattooed with scars and scrapes, impressions of absent objects that once spent years here.

Grimacing, Khadse turns off his torch. Darkness swallows him. He fumbles in his pocket, takes out the matchbox containing the matches with the yellow heads. He places a match head on the sandpaper bit, and strikes it . . .

A low blue flame blossoms in the dark. Khadse wrinkles his nose at it. It is not a *natural* flame, not one that a normal match should make. It casts light, certainly, but its light somehow seems to make the shadows harder, more concrete, rather than dispersing them. He's never seen a light that made a room feel *darker* – and yet this is exactly what he feels this match does, even in such a dark room.

He blows out the match. Waits. Then he flicks back on his torch.

He looks down. 'Hells,' he mutters. 'Here I am again.'

At his feet, on the floor, is a perfect circle of total darkness that was definitely *not* there before.

Khadse wrinkles his nose again, sighs, and pulls out the silver knife. 'Well. Let's get to it.'

In the darkness, Sigrud begins to move.

He keeps his lips clamped around the steel tube running up through the six inches of coal covering his form, taking deep breaths before he starts to shift the coal off of him. He picked particularly dusty coal, small particulates, so it creates little more than a soft hush as he rises.

He removes the tube and the cloth from his face, and blinks. He's been lying hidden in the coal for nearly twenty hours now, having sat totally still as Khadse's team searched the warehouse. His head is light with hunger, his crotch damp with urine – unfortunate, but a necessity. He swallows, shakes himself, and goes over what he heard.

Two at the bay door. Six more upstairs. Probably guarding the stairs. Eight total, then, including Khadse.

He listens closely, hears a quiet cough from the bay door around the corner. He slinks off the coal pile and creeps to the edge of the wall. His entire form is shrouded in black and his boots are wrapped in cloth, masking the sounds of their soles against the concrete. He darts his head out and back.

Two, yes. Both with pistols and torches.

Sigrud picks up his handheld radio, turns it on, checks the frequency. He readies himself – bolt-shot at his belt, knife on his thigh – holds up one finger, and taps the receiver, hard.

Three bays over, the radio's mate – which is turned up very, very loud – makes a sharp *tok* sound, which echoes through the darkness.

'What in hells was that?' says one of the guards.

A long silence.

'Maybe some coal fell,' says the other. 'Or rats, probably.'

More silence.

'Khadse would want us to check it out,' says the first guard.

'He also wouldn't want us to leave the door unguarded. If you want to go look at your damned rats, I'll stay here.'

'Fine.'

Footfalls. Not heavy. Light. A small man?

The guard rounds the corner, his torchlight bobbing ahead. He doesn't see Sigrud standing in the shadows. The man is small, maybe five and a half feet. Sigrud takes full measure of him, estimating the way his body will move. Then he slinks after the guard, slipping through the darkness to hide behind the walls of the second coal bay.

The guard walks to the entry to the third bay, where Sigrud's hidden his radio. The guard stops, the torchlight slowly crawling across the piles of coal.

This won't do, thinks Sigrud. *I need you to turn the corner . . .*

He turns his radio back on and taps it again, softer. Another *tok*, but not quite as loud.

'What?' says the guard. 'What *is* that?'

The guard turns the corner and walks behind the wall, out of sight from his partner.

Sigrud slips around the corner behind him, knife in his right hand. When the guard has gone far enough, Sigrud springs.

He worried that he'd botch it up, but muscle memory takes over. With his left hand he reaches around the guard and rips the gun from his hand, and with his right he whips his black knife up and around the guard's throat, cleanly severing the jugular.

The guard chokes and the torch falls to the ground, though its beam is still out of sight from the other guard. The spray of blood is terrific, painting the dark concrete wall before them. Sigrud holds the guard up, hugging the man's body so it won't fall and make noise. Warmth spreads throughout Sigrud's arms, then his thighs, a tremendous surge of blood soaking over him.

The guard struggles, his legs beating uselessly against Sigrud's knees. Then the blows taper off, weaker and weaker, and he goes still.

It takes less than twenty seconds. Sigrud is breathing a little too hard for his liking.

I'm out of shape, he thinks. *And slow . . .*

He gently lowers the guard's body to the floor. His entire front is wet with the man's blood. Then he creeps to the edge of the corner to peer out at the second guard.

In the darkness, his scarred, beaten face twists into a savage grin. *But one, alone – this should be easy.*

Khadse takes the silver knife, holds out his left arm, and makes a slight incision across the back webbing of his hand, grimacing as the blade cuts. At first he thinks he barely broke the skin, but then the blood comes welling up, bright red.

He squats over the perfect circle of darkness, stuffs his torch up under his armpit, and wipes his right thumb across the blood. Then he takes his thumb and reaches down to the circle of darkness . . .

I hate this part, he thinks.

His bloody thumb penetrates the dark circle as if it were just a hole, but then he feels a gauzy membrane, as if within the circle of darkness is a layer of spiderwebs, except he can't *see* them . . .

Something squirms up against his thumb, like a creature running its back under his hand, eager to be petted.

'*Eugh!*' cries Khadse. He pulls his hand away, shaking it as if it'd been burned. There's no pain, but the sensation is so disturbing, so *alien*, as if there were some blind, wet creature asleep in the bottom of that black pit, waiting for his touch.

Which might be the case. This being his third time here, he understands that the hole functions something like a safe, carefully guarding its package until someone can provide the right identification.

Though there's no visual change, he can't help but get the sensation that the circle of black is shifting, changing, flattening, and then . . .

Something rises up in the circle, like a fishing bob floating to the surface in a pond: a small square, made of black paper – an envelope.

Written on the front of the envelope, in spidery handwriting, is a word: KHADSE.

Khadse shivers. He bends down, picks up the envelope, and stores it away in his coat.

Well, he thinks as he turns around. *I'm fucking glad* that's *over*.

Even Khadse has his limits, though. After his first trip to the warehouse – the first night with the knife, the blood, and the gap of darkness – he was so disturbed he worked his own networks to find out a little bit more about his employer, trying to figure out who he was and how he had access to such . . . means.

What he found out was two things.

One was a name.

The other was a rumour that whoever said that name out loud, no matter who or where they were, tended to disappear.

He chose to drop his investigation there.

Remember your retirement. Remember the light at the end of this very long tunnel . . .

He walks out the office door. Zdenic looks at him, eyebrows raised. 'All good?'

Khadse is about to tell him it's all fine, thank you very much, now let's get a damned move on – but then they hear the gunshots and the screams from downstairs.

They stare at each other.

'What in the hells is *that*?' says Khadse.

It's all coming back to him now. Sigrud finishes up the second guard at the bay door pretty ably: he clocks him on the temple with the handle of his knife, rips the gun out of his grasp, and slashes his throat.

He takes the man's pistol. He has no intention of using it, as he wants to keep this as silent as possible: to fire a gun would give away his position, and could alert Khadse to the fact that he's just one man, not an army. He holsters the pistol, then runs to the ropes dangling from the side of the warehouse.

He tied these up two nights ago, a set of ropes dangling from the fourth floor all the way down to the very bottom, hidden up against one column.

Much of the coal warehouse is wet and crumbling, whole floors falling away after years of so many Ahanashtani rains. Using ropes to traverse the floors not only gives him the element of surprise, it also prevents him from taking one wrong step and tumbling to his death.

Though he *did* do some prep work on a few of the crumbling floors, just in case the fight spills off into some of the other portions of the warehouse. Always pays to be careful.

He grabs one rope, tugs on it to free it from its hiding place, and looks up. He's fairly sure it'll hold – he must have tied thousands of knots back in his sea days – but then, that was a very long time ago.

As if this, he says as he begins to climb the rope, *will be the stupidest thing I'm doing tonight* . . .

He climbs until he's just below the second-floor window, where he pauses, listening. No voices within, no movement. He continues up.

He pauses again below the third-floor window, listening carefully. He hears a voice, very faintly:

'. . . pretty sure I heard him shout just now.' A woman, Sigrud thinks.

'Something's up with this client,' says a second voice – a man. 'They've got Khadse doing some weird shit.'

'Weird enough to frighten Khadse?'

'Yes. That weird.'

'Quiet,' says a third voice, softly. Another man. 'We're on duty, remember.'

'As if anyone's coming out to this reeking shithole,' says the woman's voice.

Sigrud slowly, slowly inches up a few more lengths of rope, arms quivering under the strain, and peers into the third-floor window. He can see faint illumination down a hallway, the castoff of their torches, probably. They're close, in other words, but not too close.

Sigrud slips into the third-floor window, hunches down behind a row of moulding desks, and pulls out the shoulder-mounted, high-powered boltshot he hid there mere hours before.

Most war markers and operatives these days prefer pistols and riflings, since they shoot much farther and faster – but if you're operating in total silence, a bolt-shot is the weapon of choice, in Sigrud's opinion. This particular bolt-shot sacrifices convenience for power, though, firing only one bolt at a time. There are some models that have clips, reloading automatically, but the reloading mechanism is extremely loud and could give away his position. He's got a much smaller bolt-pistol hanging from his belt, which means he can get off at least two silent shots quickly.

Leaving the question, he thinks, *of what to do with the third guard*. He's caught a bolt in midair just twice in his long career, but he's not willing to try the same with a bullet.

He has one option: about twenty feet down the hallway is one soaking patch in the floor that he did some prep work on yesterday, using his knife to carve away at the beam below, his logging experience finally dovetailing with his operational work. He's not sure if it will do what he needs it to do – so many variables involved – but it's worth a shot.

He hops over the wet patch as he proceeds down the hallway, surveying his work. *If this doesn't work out*, he thinks, *there's a chance I catch a bullet in the back*.

He'll have to take that chance. He comes to the corner, darts his head around and back.

Three lights, three guards. All very much alert and ready.

Sigrud plots his move. *Three here. Then two more above. Then Khadse.*

He creeps around the corner and readies his high-powered bolt-shot and bolt-pistol. He aims the pistol first: its range is shorter and it's much less accurate, so it'll be harder to use under pressure.

He draws a bead on the nearest guard, a Continental woman.

He waits for her to look away, to expose her neck, waiting, waiting . . .

She sniffs and glances to her right.

Sigrud pulls the trigger.

The shot is sure and true, the bolt hurtling through the air to bury itself right in the left side of her throat, almost punching through her neck altogether. She gags, drops her pistol and her torch, and falls to her knees.

The guard immediately to her right – a man – jumps as he's sprayed with blood, and stares at her. 'What the fuck!' he cries. 'What the *fuck*!' He hesitates, torn between going to help her and determining where the attack came from.

Sigrud has already lifted the high-powered bolt-shot. He takes his time.

It feels like forever, but it's probably only four seconds or so, maybe less.

He aims carefully, then fires.

This bolt is slightly high: it hits the second guard right in the mouth, punching through his front teeth and his lower jaw, maybe lethally penetrating his throat. Sigrud doesn't stop to confirm the kill: he rises and runs back down the hallway.

The third guard cries, 'Hey! Hey!' and fires. The shots are wild and late – Sigrud's already rounded the corner, and the shots thump into the soaking walls behind him. He leaps over the wet patch on the floor, dodges through the moulding desks, and hunkers down, reloading his bolt-shots and listening carefully.

There's quiet for a long time – perhaps the guard's an experienced operative. Sigrud holds his breath.

Then there's a loud creaking, a tremendous *snap*, and a piercing, horrified shriek, which fades rapidly. Then, faintly, a crash from two floors below. Then silence.

Sigrud grins wickedly. *It is always so nice*, he thinks, *when things come together.*

He hops out the window, grabs the rope, and starts up to the fourth floor.

Khadse draws his pistol and motions to his two teammates to take up positions around the top of the stairs. There's someone down there, and from the crash and screams and the silence he's hearing, it sounds like the whole damn rest of his team is disabled.

He grimaces, thinking, *How many out there? Five? Ten? How did they follow us? How did they know?* He's not looking forward to the idea of battling his way out of here with just two of his crew left.

Zdenic looks to him. 'What's the move?'

Khadse holds a finger to his lips. They're likely trapped up here, if their attackers have brought a full team. The best option would be to find an alternate way out of the fourth floor – but Khadse's made damned sure there *isn't* another way. Which leaves one option.

'Hunker down,' whispers Khadse. 'Make them move first.'

'We're stuck up here like lobsters in a trap!' says Alzbeta, panicking.

'Keep your head!' snaps Khadse. 'We're *not* like lobsters in a trap, because we're armed, and they've got to come charging up those stairs! Take up defensive positions. *Now.*'

They begin moving some of the rotting office furniture around the top of the stairs, forming crude fortifications that might or might not stop a bullet. Then they hide, and wait.

And wait.

Khadse feels sweat running down his temples. He hasn't been forced into a situation like this in years. *My whole team taken apart in fifteen minutes . . . Why aren't they attacking? Why aren't they . . .*

Then there's a noise, one Khadse hasn't heard in over a decade or two: the sound of a bolt thudding into human flesh.

He jumps slightly as Zdenic slumps over, having seemingly sprouted a shaft of metal right where his skull meets his neck. He falls to the ground, shuddering and quaking.

'What!' cries Alzbeta. She wheels around, looking for the attacker.

But Khadse's already figured out the location of their shooter, and is diving away.

'They're behind us!' he snarls. 'How the hells did they get *behind* us?'

Another click, another *hiss* as the bolt flies through the air. Then Alzbeta jumps like she's just had an especially brilliant idea and crumples to the ground, a nine-inch bolt sticking out from just above her clavicle.

A good shot, thinks Khadse, terrified. *No, a great shot. But how the hells did they get up here?*

Khadse leaps up and darts across the hallway, popping off two rounds as covering fire. Then he sees a form sprinting down the hallway, away from him – a big form.

He chases them down the hallway, then turns the corner again to see his assailant sprint through a line of tables toward an open window.

And then they . . . jump.

Khadse is so surprised he nearly comes to a halt. 'What the *hells*,' he whispers.

But the figure appears to hang in midair, suspended in the night sky, before slipping down.

And Khadse immediately understands what all this is. He knows this, of *course* he knows this.

He comes to the window – where, as he expected, a set of ropes have been carefully tied up – and aims down just as the figure slips into the third-floor windows below. 'Fuckers!' snarls Khadse. 'You're Ministry, aren't you, you're *Ministry*!' He lifts up his pant leg, pulls out the knife he has holstered there, and slashes the ropes, letting them fall.

Cursing, Khadse holsters his knife and sprints back to the stairs. *I know that goddamn rope trick,* he thinks. *It's textbook!* Exactly what a Ministry operative does when badly outnumbered. Prep the environment against your opponents, then winnow them out, one by one.

He leaps over the barricade, rushes down the stairs, intending to intercept them, catch them before they can prepare any other tricks. *There's just one of them . . . One, or maybe two.*

He wheels around the corner. Then his hand holding the pistol – his right – lights up with pain.

Khadse cries out and tries to hold on to the pistol, but it falls to the floor. His right hand now feels curiously heavy, and it takes him a moment to realise there's a ten-inch knife lodged in its back, severing many of the tendons there.

He rips out the knife with his left hand, growling with pain. He finds the knife is familiar: the blade is black, the handle ornate, like some kind of royal heirloom.

He recognises it.

'*Harkvaldsson,*' he spits, furious.

A tall figure steps out of the shadows, dressed in black. They pull off their cloth mask, revealing a face Khadse hasn't seen in years – a dour, Dreyling face, one eye dim and dull.

'Well, you've certainly aged well,' spits Khadse, grasping his bleeding hand. 'I'd hoped the world had the good sense to shit your rotten Dreyling self into oblivion.' He leans closer to the pistol on the floor.

'No,' says Sigrud. He raises his right hand, which is holding a pistol. 'And drop the knife.'

Khadse, still growling with fury and pain, complies. 'Taking me alive? Taking me in for killing your filthy whore Komayd? Is that it?'

Sigrud's face is impassive, indifferent. Khadse had always hated that about him back during their Ministry days.

He tosses a pair of handcuffs at Khadse's feet. 'Put those on.'

'Fuck you.'

Sigrud sighs with an air of bored politeness, as if waiting for someone to make a play in a game of cards.

'Fine,' mutters Khadse. He crouches and, groaning as he does so, clips the handcuffs over his bleeding hands.

'Walk,' says Sigrud. 'Down the stairs. And I know you, Khadse. One move and I shoot.'

'Yes, but not to kill,' says Khadse, laughing savagely. 'If you wanted me dead, you would have done so.'

Sigrud says nothing.

'Your conversational skills,' says Khadse, turning to the stairs, 'have not improved.'

Khadse walks down the stairs, thinking rapidly. He watches over his shoulder as Sigrud pauses to pick up his knife, pistol still trained on Khadse's back.

'You're not here on real Ministry work, are you, Harkvaldsson?' asks Khadse.

Sigrud is silent.

'If you *were*,' says Khadse, 'you'd be here with a team. A whole army. But you're not, are you? You're all on your lonesome.'

Still silence.

'And you want to get me out of here,' says Khadse, 'to some secondary location, because you *know* the rest of my crew will come here to look for me.'

Still silence. Khadse surveys the terrain ahead, the shifting shadows, uneven stairs, the concrete pillars.

'Are your skills still top-notch, Harkvaldsson?' says Khadse. 'You've been out of circulation for what, ten years? My, my. How many traces did you leave behind? Someone will find me or you, surely . . .'

'If they have not found you,' says Sigrud, 'after killing Shara – then odds are they won't have networks wide enough to find me.'

'Are you so sure it's the networks?' asks Khadse softly. 'Are you so sure you aren't wading into the affairs of much, *much* bigger players than the Ministry?'

Khadse can feel it: the faintest flicker of uncertainty in Sigrud's bearing as he considers the implications of this.

In that one split second Khadse jumps forward, plants his feet on a concrete pillar, and shoves himself backward, hard.

He wasn't sure it'd be far enough – Sigrud was wise enough to keep his distance – but he just barely makes it, the top of his head crashing into Sigrud's belly. The pistol goes off just above Khadse's head, the harsh *snap* deafening him, but Khadse's already scrambling forward, pulling out his hidden knife from the sheath at his leg.

But Sigrud is faster: he raises the pistol, and fires.

Khadse cries out. He feels an immense warmth bloom in his right shoulder. He tries to gauge the damage done, grabbing awkwardly at his arm with his chained hands.

Yet there's no blood. Then he notices that – strangely – there's no pain, nor any shock. And as someone who's been shot before, Khadse knows he should be feeling these things.

Khadse and Sigrud both look at his right shoulder.

To their utter confusion, the bullet is hovering in the air about a half inch from the surface of Khadse's coat, just above where he's clutching his bicep. It's rotating very slightly, like a record in a phonograph, a slow, dreamy rotation.

Then, as if suddenly aware of their gaze, the bullet drops to the ground with a soft *clink*.

'What the *fuck*,' says Khadse, bewildered and elated.

Sigrud fires again. Khadse flinches.

Again, a heat in his chest. Again, the bullet hangs in the air just before the surface of his coat – this time right above Khadse's heart – before falling away.

Khadse and Sigrud stare at each other, unsure exactly how to handle this development.

So that's what this coat does, thinks Khadse. *Why didn't the bastard tell me that?*

He grins at Sigrud and springs, stabbing forward with the knife.

Sigrud leaps back and avoids the blade, but he's too slow: Khadse manages to catch the pistol with his handcuffs' chain and rip it out of his grasp. Then Khadse's on him, slashing in, down, up. Sigrud ducks one stab, then another, then he rolls away and pulls out his own knife. Khadse, cackling, feints to the left, then the right. Sigrud draws back, unsure what other miraculous items Khadse has on his person.

'Bit off more than you can chew, eh?' says Khadse, laughing.

The two men circle each other, trying to determine which one will give ground first. Khadse jukes forward, then springs wide and almost slices open Sigrud's shoulder. Sigrud ducks, thrusts his blade up and around – a clever move, one Khadse wasn't expecting – but the point of his black knife bounces harmlessly off the back of Khadse's coat, as if the fabric were made of thick rubber.

Khadse rolls forward, laughing, delighted with this turn of events. He presses his full advantage, slashing in, down, to the side.

Sigrud makes an unwise play, trying to strike Khadse's head – the only exposed area he can attack anymore – but Khadse ducks away and rakes his blade across Sigrud's arm, slashing it open. Sigrud roars in pain, falls back, and sprints down the hallway.

Khadse, laughing, follows. He had no idea he'd been so empowered with such protections. If he'd known this damned coat made him indestructible, he'd have killed Komayd's guards and gutted the woman with his bare hands.

Sigrud's faster than he expected, fast for a big man, running ahead into the warrens of the old warehouse. Sigrud turns down a set of narrow stairs, and Khadse speeds up, trying to keep pace, intent on putting his knife into the big Dreyling's neck one way or another.

As he crosses the last step he feels something strange at his ankle. A resistance, somewhat, as if he caught his pant leg on something . . .

His eyes widen. *A tripwire?*

Then a crash, a tremendous bang, and everything goes white.

The next thing Khadse knows he's lying on the stairs, groaning. There's a ringing in his ears, even louder than when the pistol went off next to his head. The world is white and bursting with black bubbles, and he can hardly think or move.

A flash-bang. That bastard led me right into it . . .

He can feel things, though, reverberations in the wooden stairs below him. He can feel a door open nearby, feel footsteps coming toward him. He tries to stab forward with the knife, but he's so stunned he merely stumbles forward.

Then there's pain. A lot of it. Pain in his hands, forcing him to let go of the knife. A *snap* as someone stomps on his ankle, making him howl, though he can barely hear his own voice. Then he feels big hands grasp him, undo his handcuffs, and rip his coat off him.

There's a voice in his ear, hot and full of rage: 'Like you said, I need you alive.'

Khadse is hauled to his feet, his broken ankle screaming. He feels himself being dangled above the ground, and is suddenly aware of how much larger Sigrud is than him, how much stronger. Khadse's vision begins to coalesce, the bursting white bubbles fading, and he can see now: he can see Sigrud's face just before his own, his weathered, scarred features twisted in pitiless glee.

'How happy I am,' says Sigrud, pulling a fist back, 'to finally get my hands on you.'

After he's done with him, Sigrud wipes sweat from his brow and leans up against the wall, still gasping for air. This was his first real combat in over a decade. He remembers it being a lot easier than this.

His gaze trails over Khadse's split lip and broken nose. Broken ankle and slashed-open hand.

This man killed Shara, he tells himself. *This man killed dozens of people just to kill Shara.*

And yet – why doesn't he feel better about what he's done? Why isn't he enjoying this more?

Remember what he took from you. Remember what you've lost.

An old survival tactic, for Sigrud: to forge a compass from your sorrow, and let it lead you ahead.

He kneels, groaning, picks up Khadse, and throws him over his shoulder. He staggers up the stairs, then winds down through the bowels of the warehouse, the air alight with the smell of coal and blood. At one point he steps through a spreading pool of blood from some corpse lying in the darkness, someone he can barely remember killing now. He makes sure to tread through a pile of coke dust to keep his footprints from being too bloody.

He exits the warehouse and carries Khadse's unconscious body to his stolen auto, a junky, rambling thing whose headlights keep flickering. He opens the boot and carelessly tosses Khadse in. The man moans when he falls on the tyre iron at the bottom.

Sigrud shuts the boot, then pauses as he climbs into the auto. He scans the wide concrete lot, listening, thinking. He's not sure why, but he can't help but feel someone's just been here.

He climbs in and starts the auto. The headlights strobe and flicker as he pulls away. He drives off in a different direction from where he came, just to be sure. As he does, the headlights slash over the reeds down by the canal.

Sigrud stomps on the brakes. The auto screeches to a halt.

He sits in the driver's seat, squinting through the windshield, before slowly climbing back out. He leaves the auto running, the flickering headlights shooting over his shoulder. He walks toward the canal. The concrete crumbles to an end, replaced by muddy grass that slopes down to the thick reeds by the water. Sigrud cocks his head, examining them.

A large patch of the reeds are bent. He looks down and sees footprints in the muddy grass. Recent ones, and quite small – though not small enough to be a child's. Perhaps an adolescent's.

Someone was watching me, he thinks.

He looks out at the canal. He suspects they're still there, crouched in the reeds. If they wanted to attack, now would be the time – he's winded and Khadse's out cold. It'd be easy to take a shot from the dark. But whoever they are, they don't make a move.

Sigrud grunts. When he walks back to his auto, he decides to stick with his original plan – getting Khadse to his safe house – only he'll make a few alterations to the site, just in case there are any surprises.

A very good thing, he thinks as he opens the door to the auto, *that I brought more explosives*.

4.
Don't You Know There's a War Going On

Change is a slow flower to bloom. Most of us will not see its full radiance.
We plant it not for ourselves, but for future generations.
But it is worth tending to. Oh, it is so terribly worth tending to.

— LETTER FROM FORMER PRIME MINISTER ASHARA KOMAYD
TO UPPER HOUSE MINORITY LEADER TURYIN MULAGHESH, 1732

Sigrud can tell when Khadse awakes. The man's breathing fluctuates, very slightly. A minute later he swallows, snorts.

Sigrud, sitting on the filthy floor, finishes stitching up the tremendous slash Khadse put in his arm. He sets the needle and thread back on the rickety wooden table, then grins at Khadse. 'Good morning,' he says.

Khadse moans. Sigrud can't blame him. He has the man stripped to the waist and hanging from a meat hook in the ceiling, and he beat Khadse so thoroughly that the man's face swelled up grotesquely, his cheeks and brow bulging, his lip split open, and his chin dark with blood.

Khadse snuffles for a bit. Then he does what Sigrud expected: he starts screaming. Loud. He howls and howls, screaming for help, screaming for someone to come and save him, that he's been locked up in here by a madman, and so on, and so on . . . Sigrud grimaces at the sound, wincing as Khadse sucks in breath to scream louder, until the screams finally subside.

Silence. Nothing.

Khadse glares at him, breathing hard. 'It was worth a shot.'

'I suppose,' says Sigrud. 'You knew I would put you somewhere far from prying eyes. And ears.'

'It was still worth a shot.'

'If you say so.'

Khadse glances around. They're in a long, thin room, almost as dark and decrepit as the coal warehouse. A track of hooks hangs from the ceiling, and the concrete walls and floor bear dark stains of old blood. Sigrud's hung oil lamps from a few of the hooks in the room, casting a dull orange light over everything.

'Slaughterhouse, eh?' Khadse snorts, coughs, and spits out a mouthful of blood. 'Cute. So I'm still on the waterfront. Probably in the same neighbourhood as the warehouse . . . Maybe someone could come calling.'

'Maybe,' says Sigrud. Though he's already prepared the site against any intruders. He holds up Khadse's coat. 'What is this?'

'A coat,' says Khadse.

Sigrud gives him a flat stare.

'How the hells should I know?' says Khadse. 'I didn't know it could stop *bullets*. If I had known that, I would've had a lot more fun.'

Sigrud rips the lining out of Khadse's coat. Inside is something remarkable. It looks like bands of black sewn into the fabric, and though the human mind and eyes insist this is impossible, they're different *shades* of black. Sigrud looks at it closely, and the longer he looks at it the more he believes that the bands of black are *writing*, tiny snarls of intricate designs.

'Huh,' says Khadse. 'I didn't know that was in there.'

'This is a *miracle*, Khadse,' says Sigrud. 'You have been *wearing* a miraculous item. Do you know how rare that is? There are almost none of these anymore, beyond Olvos's. Or there *should* be none anymore.'

Khadse doesn't react.

'But you knew that, didn't you,' says Sigrud. 'You knew it was miraculous.'

Nothing.

'You knew something. Where did you get this?'

Khadse's face goes strangely closed. Sigrud can tell he's trying to think of a way to bargain for his life. 'I'll tell you that,' says Khadse slowly. 'And then some. I have information you will find valuable.'

'I know. I found this on your person.' Sigrud holds up the black envelope. 'A list, it seems, on very curious paper. In code. Probably what this whole evening was about – yes?'

Khadse narrows his eyes. 'You have the message, maybe, sure. But I have the code.'

'Your life for the code?'

He nods.

'Not a bad trade. But you were out a very long time, Khadse, and I had time enough to work at it. I guessed it was the same code as you used in your telegrams – the Bulikovian partisan code – and found I was right.'

Khadse's jaw flexes, but he says nothing.

Sigrud opens the letter, and says aloud: 'Bodwina Vost, Andel Dusan, Georg Bedrich, Malwina Gogacz, Leos Rehor, and' – Sigrud glances at Khadse – 'Tatyana Komayd. Shara's daughter.'

Khadse's growing pale now. His brow is wet with sweat as he tries to think.

'Names. What is this, Khadse? Who are these people?'

'How should I know?' said Khadse. 'I only heard them just now. That's how information exchanges work – one usually hands off information the other guy doesn't know.'

'All Continental names. Are these your next targets? Are these the next people you were to hunt down?'

'I'll tell you everything,' says Khadse. '*If* you let me go.'

Sigrud lets the silence linger on for a long while.

'Why did you kill Shara?' he asks softly.

'You're not going to like the answer.'

A deadly stillness falls over Sigrud. 'Tell me. Now.'

Khadse snorts. 'Same damned reason most people do things. Because I got *paid* to. Paid a lot. More than I'd ever been paid in the whole of my life.'

'By who?'

Khadse is silent.

'I do not want to torture you, Khadse,' says Sigrud. 'Well. That is not *quite* true. I do. But I don't have time for such games. Yet I will make time if I must.'

'We were both trained to withstand torture,' growls Khadse.

'That's true. But I spent seven years in Slondheim. And there they taught me many things about pain, things the hoods in the Ministry could never dream of. If you will not tell me, why . . . I could teach you what I have learned.'

Khadse shudders. 'I always hated you,' he says. 'You and Komayd, dallying about on the Continent as if it were a fucking university trip. You never really served Saypur, never really valued honour, the job. You just did what you liked and played at being *historians*.'

'The name,' Sigrud says, standing. 'Now, Khadse.'

'I can't give what I don't have!' he snarls. 'The lunatic bastard went to extreme lengths *not* to meet me, and I him!'

'Lunatic?' asks Sigrud. 'A lunatic gave you a miraculous coat?'

'He's got to be,' says Khadse. 'He thinks the walls have eyes, thinks the world's out to get him, and he's willing to pay a damned fortune for my services! More than the Ministry ever thought them worth, anyways.'

'What were your services, Khadse, besides Shara?'

'The . . . The first time he hired me to find a boy. A Continental boy, living in the city. That's all. No murder, no tradecraft, no nothing. Just wanted me to hunt the little bastard down. Though it wasn't easy. All he gave me was a name. But old Khadse got the job done. I found him, and that was that. He must have liked how I worked, because he kept coming back to me.'

'Who was this boy?'

'Some damned Continental name or another. Gregorov, I think. Sulky teenager. Adopted, apparently. Nothing special about him, I thought.'

'What happened to him after you located him?'

'Oh, that . . . Well, that's trickier. I don't quite know. The boy vanished, apparently. But I know little Gregorov's parents met an untimely end. Just before his disappearance. Auto accident, it seems. Ploughed them over in the street. And then suddenly no one knew where little Gregorov had gotten to. It was about then, Harkvaldsson, that I decided that this new employer of mine was not one to fuck about with.'

'What then? What did he have you do next?'

'Many, many nasty things,' says Khadse. 'Which all came to an end when Komayd moved into the Golden. That put a scare in him. Or he acted like it did, I don't know.'

'Then he sent you out against Shara,' says Sigrud quietly.

'Yeah. Maybe he got tired of her. Or maybe he got something out of her, stole it from her operation. That list in your damn hand, perhaps.'

Sigrud glances at the piece of black paper. He remembers the line from the message to Shara: *This city has always been a trap. Now he has our lists of possible recruits. We have to act immediately.*

Khadse's controller steals a list of possible recruits from Shara, thinks Sigrud, *then tells Khadse to target all of them . . . But why is Tatyana on this list?*

He thinks for a long time. 'And your controller,' he says. 'That is who gave you this coat.'

'For the Komayd job, yeah. And the shoes.'

'The shoes?' Sigrud looks down at the pile of Khadse's clothing on the floor. He picks up one shoe, turns it over in his hands. There doesn't seem to be anything odd about it. Then he picks up his black knife, wedges it into the sole of the shoe, and pries off the heel. Underneath, nailed into the very sole, is a thin piece of tin, and engraved in the tin is a very curious glyph of some kind, complicated and . . . shifting, perhaps. It's a little hard for his eye to make sense of it.

'Huh,' says Khadse. 'I didn't know *that* was there either.'

Sigrud holds the piece of tin up to the light. 'I know this . . . I've seen this before, when we were tracking black marketers outside of Juko-shtan . . . This is one of Olvos's miracles. A blinding light in the snow, or something. It prevents people from following you, throws obstacles into their way, keeps them from seeing you properly.'

'Then how did you find me?'

'I didn't track you. I knew where you would be. You came to *me*. These things follow strict rules.' Sigrud thinks back, remembering the miracles at the doors of the Golden, on the streets outside . . . He knows from their fight tonight that Khadse's coat acts as protection. But what if Khadse's coat could protect against more than knives and bullets? What if Khadse's employer had given him the coat so that he could slip past all of Shara's wards and defences and place a bomb as close to her as possible?

But that's the least of his questions right now.

'Why is Komayd's own daughter on this list?' asks Sigrud. 'Why does your employer wish you to locate Tatyana Komayd?'

'That's above my pay grade,' says Khadse. 'Maybe you should ask Komayd's people. She was doing the same thing.'

'Same what?'

'Finding children. That damn charity she had, the orphanage thing or whatever?' He cackles. 'It was a load of shit. Had to be. She was finding recruits. Putting together networks. Training Continentals.'

'For what?'

'I don't know. Maybe a private army. And maybe little Tatyana was going to be her colonel. Who knows?'

'Except your employer wanted to get to these people first.'

'Again. Above my pay grade.'

Sigrud is silent for a long time. 'Have you ever met your controller, Khadse?'

'I told you, no.'

'Ever talk to him, perhaps on a telephone?'

'No.'

'Then how do you make contact?'

'I receive telegrams indicating where contact will be made. Then I go to that location, doing exactly what the controller says, and once I'm there I . . .' He shuts his eyes. 'I perform a ritual.'

Khadse then describes a miracle Sigrud's never heard of before: a hole of perfect darkness, awaiting Khadse's blood, and something sleeping at the bottom – something that releases a letter to him.

Sigrud looks at the letter in his hand. 'This letter . . . was belched up from a miracle?'

'Yes. Maybe. Whatever. You and Komayd always knew a sight more about the Divine than we ever did.'

'And you have no idea who put this . . . this darkness there, or placed the letter there for you to find.'

'No. I don't think it works like that. I think . . . All the times I've done it, it's like the hole connects to somewhere, someplace. Only it's like the place is under everything, or behind everything . . . I don't know how to say it. And I'm not fucking sure I want to know.'

'How odd it is,' Sigrud says softly, 'that you, a man who despises the

Continent so much, are willing to use Continental tricks to kill a Saypuri.'

Khadse shrugs. 'Like I said – he pays.' He spits out a mouthful of something bloody and reeking. 'Maybe my controller is a nutter, sure. Maybe he's some Continental hood who got his hands on a bunch of relics. But that's how it is. It's the game we've played since we were young pups, Harkvaldsson. The powers that be play their war games. And we pawns and grunts, we struggle among the trenches to stay alive. If things had gone but a bit differently, it could be you chained up here, and me with the knife.'

Sigrud considers that. He finds he agrees.

He turns and carefully stows the list of names away in his pack. Then he pries off the other tin plate from Khadse's shoe, takes them both and Khadse's coat, and stows them away as well.

'Robbing me, eh?' says Khadse. He spits again. Something *tinkles* to the floor, possibly a tooth. 'I don't blame you. But now we come to it, don't we? Now you decide how to end me. How to usher old Rahul Khadse off this mortal plane. You bastard.'

'Not yet.' Sigrud looks at him. 'You know more about your controller than you're saying, Khadse.'

'Oh, you want to go after him?' says Khadse.

Sigrud says nothing.

Khadse cackles. 'Oh, really. *Really*. Take your best shot! He'll grind you into pieces, big man!'

'What do you mean?'

'I mean he's not the sort to be trifled with. Me, I just have a name. Along with the rumour that whoever says this name . . . Well. They don't stick around.'

'Your employer kills them? Just for saying his name?'

'Hells if I know. No one knows what happens to them. But they don't come back from wherever they go.'

Sigrud cocks an eyebrow. 'What you are describing,' he says, 'sounds like a story created to scare children.'

'And I just put my bloodied hand in a hole in reality!' says Khadse, laughing. 'And you just shot me and saw the bullets fall to the ground! I don't know *what* to believe anymore, but I believe that it's wise to be careful.' He grins madly. 'I'll tell you the damned name if you want, Dreyling. I'll do it gladly. And it'll be the end of you.'

Sigrud shakes his head. 'I have never heard of any miracle or Divine creature that could hear its own name being spoken from across the world. Nothing short of a true Divinity could do that – and unless you're about to tell me Olvos is your controller, it means you are quite wrong.'

'I guess you'll find out.' Khadse's smile fades. 'And after I tell you the name,' he says, 'it's the end of old Khadse. Isn't it.'

'You would have done the same to me.'

'Yes. That's so.' He looks at Sigrud, his eyes burning. 'How are you going to do it?'

'If it were twenty years ago, I would have disembowelled you. Left you here with your intestines dangling out. It would have taken hours. For what you did to Shara.'

'But today?'

'Today . . . I am old,' says Sigrud, sighing. 'I know I do not quite look it. But we are both old men, Khadse, and this is a young person's game. I've no time for such things anymore.'

'True enough.' He laughs weakly. 'I thought I was going to get out. Retire. But these things don't let you run away quite so easy, do they.'

'No. They do not.'

'At least it's you. You and not one of these stupid young bastards. You didn't just get lucky. You earned it.' Khadse stares off into space for a moment. Then he looks at Sigrud and says, 'Nokov.'

'What?'

'His name,' says Khadse, breathing hard as if each syllable pains him, 'is *Nokov*.'

'Nokov? Just Nokov?'

'Yes. Just that.' He leans forward. 'You'll die, you know. Whatever he does will be a thousand times worse than anything you're about to do to me.'

Sigrud furrows his brow. *Never in my life*, he thinks, *have I heard of a Nokov – neither in the world of tradecraft or the Divine.*

Sigrud stands, unsheathes his knife, and gently lifts Khadse's chin, exposing the thread of white scar running across his throat. He places the blade of his black knife to the scar, as if following the cutting instructions on a child's piece of paper.

'And you'll deserve it,' says Khadse, staring into Sigrud's eyes. 'For all you've done. You deserve it too.'

'Yes,' says Sigrud. 'I know.' Then he whips the blade across Khadse's throat.

The splash of blood is huge and hot and wet. Sigrud steps back and watches as Khadse chokes, coughs, and gags, his chest and stomach flooded over with his own blood.

It doesn't take him long to die. No matter how many times he's seen it, Sigrud is always struck by how only a few seconds separate life from death.

How many seconds, he wonders, watching Khadse's body quake, *did it take for Shara to die?*

Khadse's head slumps forward.

Or Signe?

He stops moving.

The room is silent now except for the patter of blood. Sigrud, wiping his hands on a rag, sits down on the floor and pulls back out the list of Khadse's targets.

He stares at the last name on the list: Tatyana Komayd. A girl he's seen only once in his life, and perhaps the only piece of his friend that still persists in this world.

The pale Continental girl watches the slaughterhouse from the reeds by the canal. She slowly starts creeping up to the edge of the property, mindful of any movement in the windows. Thankfully the big man didn't take Khadse far, just a few miles downriver. As no one watches this stretch of the river, it was easy enough for her to follow, though she's now soaking up to her knees.

She doesn't know who this big man is, but she knows she doesn't like him much. It took months of work to track down Khadse's movements, months of work to tap into Khadse's communications, months of work to get this close to figuring everything out. It was especially hard since Khadse often had some kind of miracles on his person, something that made him hard to see, hard to follow – yet she'd figured out how to get around them.

And then this big, stupid man with his guns and his knife has to go in and ruin everything, swooping in at the last minute to haul Khadse off like he was a sack of damned potatoes.

She crept in after and saw the bodies. Saw what he'd done to them. Whoever he is, she doesn't want someone like that near her plans.

Dawn is slowly breaking, but it does nothing to lighten her mood. She looks around at the ruins of the slaughterhouse. She doesn't like this place. It's ugly and decrepit, sure, but mostly it's because she doesn't like its past.

And for her, the past is a thing she can see at any given moment.

She shudders. This was once a place of tremendous death. If she's not careful its past leaks through to her, and she glimpses giant herds of cattle or goats milling about in the fences, anxious and fretting, wondering what will happen to them. Sometimes she can hear them bleating and bellowing and screaming, smelling blood up ahead and knowing what's coming. She can hear them now, hear them shrieking in the slaughterhouse . . .

She shakes her head, banishes such sounds from her mind. She considers her options. The big man took Khadse somewhere deep within the slaughterhouse, and she's not willing to exercise her abilities to locate him, not yet. It could put her at risk. But she must get something out of this. She can't have watched Khadse for days and weeks for nothing.

Then the light begins to shift. She looks around, confused. The orange rays of dawning light filtering through the slaughterhouse yards stutter, flicker, and finally fade.

'Oh, no,' she whispers.

She looks up. The sky is darkening directly above, black hues bleeding through the pale blue, bringing cold, glittering stars in their wake. The patch of darkness intensifies and spreads, a curious, dark dawn in the centre of the sky.

How could he have found me? How could he be here?

Then she realises that the patch of night in the sky is not really above *her*: it's above the slaughterhouse, and presumably above the two men within.

She realises that, whoever the big man is and whatever he wants, he likely has no idea what's coming for him.

She debates what to do.

'Fucking hells,' she mutters. Then she stands.

Sigrud sits on the floor, thinking.

This isn't good. None of it's good, of course, but some parts are worse than others.

For starters: how did Khadse's employer get his hands on miraculous items? All the original Divinities – he frankly can't believe he's having to debate this *again* – are very dead, except for Olvos. But most of Olvos's miraculous items were lost when Saypur's secret warehouse of them burned down eighteen years ago. Sigrud knows that, because he was one of the people who burned it down. So even those should be incredibly rare.

Was there another secret storeroom of them? He scratches his chin. *Or – worse – has someone found a way to make more of them?* That shouldn't be possible without Olvos's help. At least, he *thinks* that's the case. He's well out of his league here.

He looks back at the list of names. He wishes there were more information, especially their locations, for one. *But if they had locations of these people,* he thinks, *odds are they would already be dead.*

He only really knows the location of one: Tatyana Komayd, whom he read had been living in Ghaladesh with Shara.

He folds up the list again and puts it in his pocket.

So what's the next move? There's one idea he's gravitating toward, though the concept frankly terrifies him.

He tries to think of any alternatives. Try to track down this Nokov? Ferret out any more contacts from Khadse's associates? Start pounding pavement and looking up these names?

He doesn't think any of these options will bear fruit. And none are more pressing than the task before him.

Someone is targeting Shara's adopted daughter. And odds are no one in the Ministry knows about it.

He needs to go to Ghaladesh. Ghaladesh, the capital of Saypur, the richest, most well-protected city in the world. The place with perhaps the most security in the civilised nations – and thus the place that he, a fugitive from Saypur's justice, is most likely to be caught, imprisoned, tortured, and possibly – or probably – executed.

He's not quite sure what he'd do if he was to find Tatyana, though. Warn her, get her somewhere safe, then get out. Yet Sigrud has seen what happens to people who fall within the shadow of his life. He has no desire to allow such a thing to happen to Tatyana.

But he must do *something*. It pains him to wake each day and know that he was not there when Shara needed him most. To imagine allowing the same thing to happen to her child . . . The idea is abominable to him.

Then Sigrud pauses. Listens.

There's silence, but something's . . . wrong.

He glances over his shoulder. The room stretches out behind him, the train of oil lamps dangling from the track of hooks. He cocks his head.

He's pretty sure he lit nine oil lamps when he first brought Khadse here. He found a giant cupboard of them in the south end of the slaughterhouse, so he figured he'd make use of them. Yet now there are only six lit, as if the three at the far end of the room have fizzled out. But there's no breeze in here.

Are they burning out? That's odd . . .

He watches as the farthest lamp dies. There's no noise, no hiss, no smoke. It's just . . . gone, with only five lamps remaining. And as the lamp dies, that whole end of the room fills with impenetrable darkness.

Then he hears footsteps. Someone is walking across the long, darkened room to him. He narrows his eye, peers carefully, but he can't see anything in the shadows. Whoever they are, they're not trying to be stealthy: they're walking with a quick, measured pace, like someone trying to make the next meeting.

Sigrud stands, grabs his pack, and pulls out a pistol. 'Who is there?' he says.

The steps don't slow.

The fifth lamp dies. The wall of shadow grows closer.

Sigrud throws his pack over his shoulder, raises the pistol, and points it down the long, thin room. 'I'll shoot,' he says.

The steps don't slow.

The fourth lamp dies. The darkness grows closer.

He gauges the position of the footsteps and pulls the trigger. The retort is incredibly loud in this confined space. The muzzle flash does nothing to illuminate the darkness. And though he's firing into a small space, the bullet doesn't seem to *hit* anything, or intimidate whoever's out there – because the steps just keep coming.

The third lamp dies. Just two left, hanging just above Sigrud. The wall of darkness is very close now, as are the footsteps.

Then he sees it.

Something penetrates the penumbra of darkness, only a dozen metres away now. But it's . . . impossible.

There at the edge of the light is a shadow, a shadow surely cast by two legs, walking toward him. But he cannot see anyone *casting* the shadow. There is the light from the lamp, and the shadow of a human figure walking toward him – but no actual human to project this shadow.

'What in all *hells*,' says Sigrud.

The footsteps stop. The shadow of the human figure stops advancing as well.

Silence.

Then a man's voice, high and cold and brittle. It doesn't seem to come from any one place – not from the shadow of the person before him, nor from the wall of darkness beyond – but rather it seems to be coming from *all* the shadows in the room, as if they were all vibrating at once, creating this . . . voice.

The voice says: 'He's dead.'

Sigrud glances over his shoulder at Khadse's corpse. He says, 'Uh.'

'I know this one,' says the voice. More footsteps. The second lamp dies, and the shadow advances across the floor, swirling as the invisible person – whoever or whatever he is – walks around the final remaining lamp. 'Khadse, wasn't it? He was a good one.' The footsteps stop, and the shadow hangs on the floor in a position suggesting that the invisible person is standing directly before Khadse's body. The voice says softly, 'He did as he was told. He didn't ask questions. I hate when they ask questions . . . I always feel obliged to answer them.'

A long silence. Sigrud wonders if he should attack, or dive away, or . . . what. But one thing he suddenly, fiercely believes is that he should *not* leave the light. He's not sure why, but he feels that if he crosses that border of shadow – which suddenly seems so firm, so very hard – then he's not coming back out.

'I had wished to do it myself,' says the voice with a faint tone of regret. 'Not wise to have a man walking around with so many secrets in him. But oh, well . . .'

More footsteps. The shadow of the human figure rotates as he circles around the lamp. The shadow falls across Khadse's corpse . . .

And then it's gone. It's as if the man's passing shadow wiped Khadse's being from existence, like a rag wiping away a spot on a windowpane.

Sigrud glances around at the tiny island of illumination at his feet, cast by the one remaining oil lamp. *Do not leave the light.*

The next thing he knows, the shadow of the figure is gone, blinking out.

Sigrud grasps the radio transmitter at his belt with his free hand – part of the preparations he'd put together in case someone tried to ambush him. *It wouldn't do any good here, so far from the entrance,* he thinks. He puts the idea aside, wondering what to do.

Then Sigrud feels it: a sudden attention, as if all the darkness in the room is turning to look at him and examine him.

There is a low, awful groaning in the darkness, like the sound of tall trees slowly shifting in the wind. His left hand suddenly aches, aches horribly, as if the scar there were made of molten lead.

From what sounds like a distant corner, the voice whispers, 'And who are *you?*'

Sigrud lowers the pistol. He's not quite sure what to do in such a situation – being addressed by a wall of shadow is not something he was trained for – but questions, well, those he knows how to handle.

He instinctively resorts to the cover story that corresponds with the Papers of Transportation in his pocket. 'Jenssen,' he says.

There's a silence.

The voice says, puzzled, 'Jenssen?'

'Yes.'

'And . . . what are you doing here, Mr. Jenssen?'

'Looking for work,' says Sigrud determinedly. 'In Ahanashtan.'

A much, much longer silence. Then a rhythmic tapping from his right, like the twitching of a snake's tail. And slowly, slowly, he thinks he can see light in the darkness . . . Tiny pinpricks of cold light, like terribly distant stars.

'I am not sure what this means,' says the voice softly. 'You are either stupid, or you are lying, which is still quite stupid.' Then, closer to him: 'But you *called* me. You did, or he did, or both of you did.'

Sigrud looks down. The circle of light is slowly contracting. Sigrud is reminded of a water rat being suffocated by a python.

The voice whispers, 'Are you working for them? Are you one of *theirs*? Tell me.'

Sigrud doesn't know whom the voice is referencing, but he says, 'No. I am alone.'

'Why did you kill Khadse?'

'Because . . . Because he killed a friend of mine.'

'Hmm . . . But it should have been quite hard, shouldn't it? I arrayed him in protections, in defences.' A brief, soft burst of cheeping, like crickets in a vast forest. Sigrud wonders – *Where am I? Am I still even in the warehouse?* Yet he sees the oil lamp still hangs above him.

The voice continues: 'You should not have been able to follow him, should not have been able to wound him. And yet I sense the protections I gave him are in your bag . . .'

The circle of light contracts a little more. Sigrud's one eye widens as he realises what the voice is saying. *Is this . . . this thing*, he thinks, *Khadse's employer? Could this thing be . . . Nokov?*

'And I smell about you,' says the voice in the darkness, 'my own writing, my own list, passed through my own channels. A letter. *My* letter.'

Sigrud swallows.

'You are lying to me,' says the voice. 'I don't believe you could have killed Khadse without some help. *Their* help.'

'I did it alone.'

'So you say. Yet I don't believe you.'

A long silence. Sigrud feels something shifting out there in the shadows, a dry rustling, a hushed shuddering.

'Do you know who I am?' whispers the voice. The border of shadow is just inches from Sigrud's toes now. He stands up very straight and tall, trying his hardest not to allow an elbow or knee to enter that veil of shadow. 'Do you know what I can do to you?' says the voice. 'You killed Khadse, certainly – but what I can do will make murder feel like a wondrous blessing.'

A sigh beside him. The scrape and scratch of something being dragged across the concrete floor. His hand hurts so much he can't stop making a fist.

'Wandering forever in darkest night,' whispers the voice, now on his other side. 'A vast, black plain, underneath distant stars . . . You'd walk and walk and walk, walking for *so long*, until you'd forget what your own face looked like, your own being. And only when this had happened – when you'd forgotten your own name, the very *idea* of yourself – would I breach your isolation, and ask you questions.'

Something hisses before him. A chuckling sound – certainly not a sound made by a human throat – comes from behind him.

'And you,' whispers the voice, 'sobbing, would tell me.'

The shadow inches closer. Sigrud feels like he's standing in a tiny tube of light.

A murmur in his ear, as if the thing in the darkness is just beside him. 'Do you wish me to do this to you?'

'No.'

'Then tell me if . . .'

The border of shadow trembles. Sigrud waits for the first blow to fall.

Then the voice makes a noise of peculiar discomfort: '*Unh.*'

Sigrud cocks an eyebrow. 'Unh?'

The circle of light at his feet expands, as if whoever – or whatever – is out there is losing their grasp on it. The voice says, 'Who is . . . Who is *doing* that?' It sounds as if the speaker is suffering a terrible migraine.

Sigrud glances around. 'Doing . . . what?'

The circle of light keeps expanding. And then he hears the cows.

The world shifts, changes, contorts.

Sigrud opens his eye all the way in total surprise.

He's not sure *when* things changed – last he knew, mere seconds ago he was in the darkness, being threatened by that . . . whatever it was. But he's sure they definitely *have* changed.

Because right now Sigrud is standing in a concrete hallway, staring at a giant herd of cows, all milling around and mooing in mild discontent. Bright white sunlight is pouring over his shoulder. He looks behind him and sees what appears to be a wooden gate to a livestock yard. Obviously at some point the gate will open, and the cattle will be herded out, but for now the cattle are all stuffed together in the hallway, and they vocally don't appreciate it.

Sigrud, personally, does not appreciate not understanding what in the hells is going on. It feels strange to say it, but the last time he felt at all sure of his reality was when he cut Khadse's throat. Now everything's gone . . . soft.

A woman's voice: '*Hey!*'

Sigrud turns back around. A young woman is dodging through the cattle to get to him. He finds he recognises her: short, pale, and Continental with a strangely upturned nose . . .

'You,' says Sigrud faintly. 'I know you . . .'

The young Continental woman dances her way past the last few cows. 'What in the *fuck* is wrong with you?' she demands.

Sigrud has no idea how to respond. He stares at this young woman, just five and a half feet tall, with a tremendous mane of black hair and a taut, pugnacious mouth, as if some acerbic comment is swilling around on her tongue.

Yet there's something off about her eyes: they're pale and queerly colourless, as if her eyes were the colour of miscoloured porcelain – not quite grey, not quite blue, not quite green. He feels like her eyes were created to see something . . . else.

'Did you say his name?' says the woman. 'Did you say it out *loud*? What is *wrong* with you? Did you want to get everyone killed?'

Sigrud raises a hand like a child trying to answer a question at school. 'I feel I must say here,' he says, glancing at the cattle before him, 'that I do not really understand what is going on.'

'I'll say you don't! Did you kill the assassin? Khadse?'

'Yes?'

'*Why?*'

'Because he killed Shara Komayd,' says Sigrud. 'And I could not abide that.'

The woman gives a long, slow sigh, as if this was the answer she expected but didn't want to hear. 'Well. Damn it.'

'Why?'

'Because that,' she says, 'was the same reason *I* was looking for him.'

'What's going on? Who are you? Where are we?'

'The same place. The slaughterhouse. Just in a slightly earlier time, before they added onto it, so there was daylight nearby. I can get you out of here – *maybe* – but w –'

'Wait a minute,' says Sigrud. 'Wait. Are you saying we're in the *past*?'

'Something very akin to it, yes,' says the girl. 'Far enough into it so that the past's daylight can filter through to the present. He's most powerful where shadows are, and though this makes him strong, it has its limitations as well. Where light is, he isn't.'

Sigrud tries to understand this. Then he pales, and asks a question he never expected to say in his life.

'Are you a Divinity?' he says quietly.

The woman laughs ruefully. 'Me? No. Him, well . . . He's trying his hardest. You don't know a damn thing, do you? Don't you know there's a war going on? Now we have to – *aagh*!'

She falls to her knees, her face twisted in pain. Sigrud looks up and sees a trembling at the walls of the slaughterhouse, and then the world seems to contract inward . . .

Darkness floods in, until finally it's like they're not in a slaughterhouse, but rather inside a tiny bubble of light floating in a sea of shadow. Inside this bubble is a *piece* of the slaughterhouse – Sigrud is reminded of looking at something through a telescope, allowing in only a tiny circle of an image but excluding everything else.

'What's happening?' asks Sigrud.

'I'm *losing*, is what's happening,' growls the woman. 'Part of us is still in the slaughterhouse, in the present, with *him*. He can beat on the walls of the little bubble of the past I've built. And he's breaking them open.' She blows a strand of hair out of her face and sets her jaw. 'Do you want to get out of here?'

'Yes.'

'Then follow me. *Closely*. You slip out of the bubble, you're gone.'

'To what?'

'To him. Into the night. Outside of this bubble is the *present*. Which is where he is. And you don't want to be out there with him.'

She begins to walk away, stepping through the cattle. As she does, the bubble moves with her, slipping through the darkness, as if she's projecting it around herself. Sigrud, startled, hops to it and stays close.

'I've been watching Khadse for days, even weeks,' says the girl, shaking her head. 'And then *you* come here and shoot up the place . . .'

'What do you know about Khadse and Shara?'

She glances at him. 'Oh, like I trust *you*. The one bellowing his name out loud.'

'Do you mean N –'

'*Don't!* Do you want to invite him *in*? In here, with *us*?'

Sigrud begins to understand. 'No.'

'Good! Keep your mouth shut before you cock up anything *else*.'

They turn the corner and see two stairways leading down. One is lit with gaslight, the other is dark. 'Let's hope this one leads us out,' she mutters as they approach the lit hallway.

A man in a bloodstained apron walks up out of the lit hallway and passes them without a word. Sigrud stares at him, bewildered. He saw these doorways not more than an hour ago, and both were almost collapsing. 'Are we . . . Are we really in the past?'

'Somewhat. Pieces of it, parts of it. They won't see us. The past doesn't change, it's hard and durable. Makes it easy to move across, walking from second to second like a frog jumping across lily pads. Do you notice?'

'Notice what?'

'The bridging between the seconds?'

'No?'

'Then I'm doing a good job. Let's just hope it holds long enough for us to get out . . .'

They begin down the stairs. Then the borders of the bubble tremble again, and the young woman cries out and stumbles like she's been stabbed.

Sigrud kneels to help her up. 'Again?'

'I . . . I can't keep this up,' she gasps. 'I thought I could, but he's stronger than me now. I put myself at risk, saving you. He's killed so many of us, and now he might have me . . .'

Sigrud doesn't understand much of what's going on, but he's starting to understand the crude dream logic of what the girl is suggesting. 'So . . . You mean to lead us down through a past version of the slaughterhouse . . . and then once we are outside, in the light, return us to the present?'

The girl cries out again in pain, fingers to her temples. 'Yes!' she cries. 'Are you slow?'

'But you won't make it that far,' says Sigrud.

She shakes her head, tears leaking out of her eyes. 'I don't think so.'

Sigrud looks down at the radio transmitter hanging from his belt. 'I *had* an exit strategy in place, in case the building was stormed . . . but it will do little good here.' He does some quick thinking.

What tools could possibly be of use against that thing? What tools do we even have?

Then he has an idea.

'Can you at least get us to the first floor?' he asks. 'Maybe close to the entrance?'

'Maybe. Possibly.'

'All right. Second question . . .' He rummages around in his pack and pulls out the pieces of engraved tin from Khadse's shoes. 'Do you know what these are?'

Her eyes widen. 'These . . . These are the miracles the assassin was wearing, weren't they? They kept me from seeing him properly, from following his movements. Sunlight on Mountain Snows . . .'

Sigrud snaps his fingers. '*That's* the name. I couldn't remember. Here. Put these into your shoes. Fast. Hurry.'

'Bu – '

'*Now*.'

She sits on the steps and does so, cringing and wincing as if hearing a painful noise in her ears.

'Good,' says Sigrud. 'Now. Third question. Whatever it is that, uh, you are – can you be harmed by an explosion?'

She stares at him. '*What?*'

'I will take that,' he says, 'as a yes.'

By the time they get to the bottom of the stairs it's become so bad the girl can barely walk. Sigrud has to nearly carry her. 'This is bad,' she says, woozy. 'I'm not sure if I'll even be able to run away.'

'You're going to have to,' says Sigrud. 'Just get us close to the door. Then we light the matches, and then you let the bubble fall – put us back in the present, I mean . . .'

'Yes, yes! I understand that!'

'Good. Then, after that, you move.'

They limp through the lower warrens of the slaughterhouse, some kind of packing and loading area, where trucks and carts once arrived and departed. The border of the bubble quivers and rattles, as if someone on the outside is beating on it, and each time the girl moans a little more.

'Who are you?' asks Sigrud. 'Are you a friend of Shara's? Of Komayd?'

The girl is silent.

'Are you . . . M? From Shara's letter?'

She laughs morosely. 'Aren't you a clever one. Listen, killer – you are a tiny fish in a very big pond. Odds are if you survive today – which I think unlikely, frankly – then you'll just be caught next week, or next month, or maybe tomorrow *night*. And when he catches you, he'll pull out every secret you've got hidden away in your guts. I don't intend for any of my own to be in there.'

'And if I do survive?'

'If you survive, and I see you again . . . Maybe I'll reconsider.' She eyes him suspiciously. 'Maybe.'

They're near the entrance to the slaughterhouse now. Sigrud gently sets her down. Their little bubble of the past is shaking quite hard now, like gates splintering before a battering ram. 'Hurry,' she whispers. 'Please hurry . . .'

Sigrud reaches into his pack and pulls out a box of matches and Khadse's coat. *Thank the seas*, he thinks, *that I still smoke*. He stuffs his arms into Khadse's coat, which barely fits, but that's the least of his problems. Then, moving carefully and smoothly, he lights one match. He hands it to the girl, then makes a bundle of half of the remaining matches and hands them to her as well. Then he strikes another match and picks up the other half of the remaining matches, so they're both holding a lit match in one hand and a bundle of unlit matches in the other.

He looks the young woman over: she's breathing hard, both in pain and in terror.

'Ready?' asks Sigrud.

'Yes,' she says.

'Then do it.'

She shuts her eyes. At the same time, they both hold their lit matches to the unlit bundles. The matches flare bright, sending shafts of light shooting into the darkness.

The bubble of past around them trembles. Shakes.

Dissolves.

Darkness comes spilling in, roaring and cheeping, the wild, strange sounds of the forest at night . . .

But it comes to a halt just around them, held at bay by the flickering matches in their hands. It's so dark it's difficult to tell that they're still in the slaughterhouse, but Sigrud can see the dawn light filtering through the cracks in one of the bay doors in the distance.

The girl nods at Sigrud and slowly begins to move toward the door, the flame flickering in her fingers.

Then the high, cold voice whispers in his ear, quivering with rage: 'Where is she? She's *here*, isn't she?'

Sigrud suppresses a smile. *So the miracles in Khadse's shoes are working*, he thinks. *He can't properly see her* . . .

'You *are* working with them,' says the voice. 'I knew it. I *knew* it. Your little light won't last long, you know. And then *I'll* have you.'

'I'll tell you everything,' says Sigrud. 'Right now.'

A pause. Sigrud can see the girl has almost made it to the door.

'Tell me *what*?' says the voice.

'About Komayd. The ones on her list. I know where they are.'

This is, of course, fabulous bullshit. But the voice in the shadows seems to be considering it.

The voice purrs, 'If you have something to say, say it.'

'I worked with Komayd,' says Sigrud. He makes sure to talk as slowly as possible. 'I worked with her for a long, long time. Even if she didn't know it, I worked for her and waited for her – right up until her death.'

A soft clinking and clanking as the girl slides the door open.

Then the voice speaks again, this time next to Sigrud's other ear. 'And?' it says, suspicious.

'And she was a careful person,' says Sigrud. He watches as the flame crawls down the matchsticks. 'But even the most careful person makes mistakes. As you know.'

Sigrud watches as the girl slips away to safety. She doesn't look back.

'Once we were in a safe house, doing an interrogation,' says Sigrud. 'But it was interrupted. Our enemies stormed in, you see, and almost took us prisoner. And from then on, I insisted on taking precautions in case it happened again. She hated it. But it was a very simple system.'

Sigrud takes a breath.

He picks up the radio transmitter, holds it up, and says, 'It looks like this.'

He drops the matches, pulls the coat up over his head with his left hand, and presses the button.

Then there's a bang.

Sigrud does not really hear it. He hears maybe the first .0001 second of the bang. Because then he's slammed to the ground so hard he briefly blacks out.

Light. Heat. Noise. And smoke.

He comes to, gasping and blinking, fire dancing all around him, and dimly realises he's not in any pain. The coat is still over his head, and his back and skull – which should have struck the floor at a lethal speed – have no pain at all. The coat must have stopped him from striking the floor, but, much like someone's head snapping around in a car accident, it didn't slow his brain down any.

He shakes himself, dazed, and sits up. The incendiary mines have done a good bit of damage: the shadows have been rent to shreds by a thousand little flames flickering all throughout the slaughterhouse. He looks for his assailant – this Nokov – but can't see anything.

Except . . .

In the far corner of the slaughterhouse bays is a form, a shadow cast on the wall, though there's no one to cast it. The shadow looks like the person, whoever they are, is bent over, hands on their knees, as if recovering from a stunning blow. Then the shadow shifts, and turns to look at him . . .

He sees eyes in the shadow, cold and glimmering like distant stars.

'Look what you did!' shouts the voice, outraged and bewildered. 'Look what you *did*!'

Sigrud stands and sprints for the doorway out, though he reels slightly like a drunk. As he runs he sees that his handiwork is not quite what it used to be: only two of the three incendiary mines he planted down here have gone off. He must have botched the third charge, which was the largest. Odds are that the receiver for the third charge was damaged in the explosion, but as he runs he covers as much of his body as he can with Khadse's coat and clicks the transmitter over and over again, hoping it could sputter to life.

He sees the shadows roiling, swarming, swirling behind him, thousands of little pools joining together to snatch him up before he can reach the daylight outside.

Sigrud is twenty feet from the door, then ten. He can see the Luzhkov River just beyond, rippling in the sunlight.

'No!' cries the high, cold voice behind him. 'No, no!'

Sigrud's thumb makes one last frantic beat on the transmitter button: *clickclickclickclickclick*.

Then there's a light on the walls, hot and orange, coming from somewhere behind him. A burst of searing heat washes over him.

The next thing he knows, Sigrud is shot through the doorway like a bullet from a gun.

Time seems to slow down. Sigrud slowly tilts ass over head over the surface of the Luzhkov, which allows him to see his handiwork: a bright ball of flame shooting out of the entrance of the slaughterhouse, licking at the waters like the tongue of a dragon.

Sigrud looks down – or, as he's upside down, up – at the water surface hurtling at him.

This, he thinks, *is not what I wanted*.

He tries to pull the coat around him, but then . . .

Impact.

The world goes dark and all his senses are reduced to a tinny *eeeeeeeeeeee* in his ears. When he comes to he's instantly aware that he's underwater, that bubbles are streaming from his nose and mouth and, actually, there's quite a bit of water in his throat.

Do not panic. Do not panic . . .

He begins thrashing, kicking, throwing himself up at the shimmering light above him, red and wicked orange. He bursts through the surface of the water, coughing and gasping, and is so relieved he nearly sinks back underneath again. He claws himself back up, his arms and legs working to tread water, and swims over to the far shore.

Finally he feels soft mud under his boots, and he hauls himself up the riverbank, gasping with exhaustion. There's a tremendous *crack* behind him, and he turns just in time to see the slaughterhouse begin to collapse.

He frowns. He had intended just to make a lot of flash and heat, not bring the whole building down. *I really do need to brush up on my explosives skills.*

He watches the building collapse. He wonders if that thing – Nokov – died in the fire, perhaps trapped in it. He doubts it. He saw a Divinity take a few dozen artillery shells to the face in Bulikov eighteen years ago, and it didn't even get a nosebleed.

But was it – he? – a Divinity? He sticks his pinky in his ear, trying to free a bubble of water. *And what was the woman? What exactly have I stumbled into?*

He remembers what the young Continental woman said: *Don't you know there's a war going on?*

He looks down at himself. Khadse's coat has been torn apart – not by any outside force, but apparently from Sigrud's very large arms pinwheeling and thrashing about in a coat about five sizes too small for him. Sighing, he pulls the shreds of it off him. He would have dearly liked to keep such a device, but he reflects that it's probably unwise to trust a miracle, especially one you've never seen before.

He stands and begins to limp away. Now to find his way back to his apartment and his cache of money and papers. And then to get the ever-living hells out of Ahanashtan.

And from there, on to Ghaladesh, he thinks, *to keep Tatyana out of the hands of whatever that thing was*.

Though he will need a local resource. But he has an excellent one in mind. One whose home address is a matter of public record.

Let's just hope, he thinks as he trudges over to the road, *she doesn't shoot me on sight*.

5.
All I Had Left

Sometimes people ask me about Vo. It's very forward of them to do so, I find, but the press gets more and more forward these days. Any more forward and they'll tip over onto their faces — or so I hope, perhaps.

I think the same thing I've always thought: that the status quo is lethally reflexive.

People don't change. Nations don't change. They get changed. Reluctantly. And not without a fight.

— LETTER FROM FORMER PRIME MINISTER ASHARA KOMAYD TO UPPER HOUSE MINORITY LEADER TURYIN MULAGHESH, 1732

Captain First Class Kavitha Mishra walks across the empty lots, hands in the pockets of her greatcoat. The wreckage of the slaughterhouse beyond is still steaming, ribbons of vapour unfurling from its depths. The Ahanashtani police have the area cordoned off, and she notes all the officers look very serious, frowning and shaking their heads, their cheeks and noses bright red under those tall, crested helmets. A couple of them have the glitter of gold about their shoulders — lieutenants, maybe, or perhaps a captain or two. A very serious affair, indeed.

The constable ahead holds up a black-gloved hand as she approaches. 'I'm sorry, miss, this is a crime scene, and I — '

Mishra pulls out her credentials and holds them up. 'Good morning,' she says.

He reads her credentials. Then his eyes widen and he takes a step back. 'I see, ma'am,' he says. 'Ah. Would you like me to get the lieutenant, ma'am?'

'If that's who's in charge — then yes, please.'

'Yes, ma'am.' He trots off. Mishra waits, casting an eye over the ruins of the slaughterhouse. She could walk into the scene if she wanted – no matter how much gold bedecks those uniforms, her position thoroughly trumps theirs – but she doesn't. She doesn't want to do anything especially memorable beyond appear and then depart.

The Ahanashtani lieutenant, his giant white moustache rippling with each indignant huff, strides across the pavement to her. 'Yes, yes?' he asks. 'How can I help you?'

She shows him her credentials. He, like the constable before him, is cowed, but he's a lot more resentful about it.

'I see,' he says. 'Well. How nice of you to join us, Captain Mishra. Ministry of Foreign Affairs, is it? What would this have to do with military intelligence? Unless . . . it has something to do with Komayd?'

The lieutenant looks uneasy at that, because the Ahanashtani authorities are under a lot of scrutiny right now. Allowing the former leader of the world's most powerful nation to get assassinated in your backyard has that effect.

'We're not sure yet,' says Mishra. 'We're still assessing the situation. Do *you* have any reason to believe it's connected?'

'No,' he says, surprised. 'Not yet, at least. Though I certainly hope not.'

'You said you had another series of deaths at another location, downriver?'

'A coal warehouse, yes. Professionally done. Very professionally done.' He looks her over. 'I do hope you're not about to tell me that Saypur had something to do with it, though. I thought the days of murderous conflict taking place at our back door without any warning were behind us.'

'There's little I can tell you now. But one thing I can tell you is that the Ministry of Foreign Affairs had absolutely nothing to do with this. Though it does worry us. Have you identified any of the bodies?'

'Not a one. It's early yet.'

'And . . .' She nods ahead at the burned-down slaughterhouse. 'No body found here?'

'Not yet. Though it's in a poor state. It'll take some time to search.'

'And nothing washed downriver?'

'No.' He gives her a hard look. 'Who exactly might I be looking for, Captain?'

'Someone tall,' says Mishra. 'Hair cut very short. A Dreyling. With a false eye.'

He shakes his head. 'We've found no body matching that description, ma'am. Can you give me any more?'

'If I knew more, Lieutenant, I would give it. Just an unsavoury character that has been identified at another recent incident.' She pulls out her card and hands it over. 'If you happen to learn of anything, can you notify me, please? We'd like to keep abreast of this situation.'

'I would be happy to, ma'am,' he says, though he smiles icily enough that it's obvious he means quite the opposite.

'Thank you, Lieutenant,' says Mishra. She nods to him, then turns and walks back to her auto.

She takes a short breath of relief. She expected someone from the Ministry of Foreign Affairs would have already paid him a visit – someone who would have had *official* orders to be there – and that could have been awkward. For while Mishra did have orders to check in on the scene, they didn't come from the Ministry.

She drives north, away from the industrial neighbourhoods, passing all the mills and the refineries and the plants belching up steam. She drives around until she comes to the traffic tunnels connecting east Ahanashtan to all the north–south thoroughfares – tiny, cramped arteries carved into the hillsides. She drives into one tunnel and pulls over about halfway through, guiding her auto onto the shoulder. Then she sits for a moment, watching the other autos. She looks in the rearview mirror, her amber-coloured eyes narrow and watchful. Once she's confirmed she wasn't followed, she pulls out the envelope.

The envelope is thick and very formal-looking, closed by a string tied around a brass button. Mishra checks her surroundings again, then opens the envelope and pulls out what appears to be a piece of black paper.

She's done this before, many times. But she still can't help shuddering every time she touches the paper. She knows it's not really paper, it's something *else*: its surface feels as soft as sable, yet if you push on it it's as hard as glass . . . Whatever it is, her skin recognises it as something alien.

And it is simply too black. Far too black.

She takes out a pencil and begins to write on the paper. She can't read what she's writing – grey on black is too tricky for her eyes, in any light – but she knows it won't matter to him. The controller, as he prefers to be called in casual conversation, can see in any darkness.

She writes:

BODIES NOT YET IDENTIFIED. NO CONNECTION TO KHADSE OR KOMAYD HAS BEEN MADE. I HAVE CONFIRMED THAT KHADSE'S OPER-ATIONAL HOUSE HAS BEEN THOROUGHLY CLEANED.

PROVIDED AHANASHTANI POLICE WITH THE DESCRIPTION YOU GAVE. NO SIGN OF THE SUSPECT YET. PLEASE ADVISE AS TO WHETHER OR NOT I SHOULD NOTIFY THE MINISTRY THROUGH OFFICIAL CHANNELS.

– KM

She folds up the paper and steps out of her car, wincing as a large, rattling truck goes cruising by, spewing exhaust. Though Mishra's a Saypuri, she's a country girl at heart, and much prefers a horse and cart over all these new autos.

She walks to a small service door on the side of the tunnel, checks her surroundings again, and opens it.

Inside is a small cement closet, just four bare walls and a floor. There's a broken broomstick standing in the corner, along with an old dusty glass bottle. Besides that, there's nothing.

She places the paper in the middle of the closet floor, then shuts the door, watching as the door's shadow falls across the paper.

Mishra checks her watch – *Five minutes to go* – leans up against the tunnel wall, and lights a cigarette.

She doesn't wonder if it will work. She knows it will work. All the bits of shadow paper find him quick enough, if placed in deep enough darkness. No matter where that darkness happens to be, for all darkness is one to him.

She watches the traffic, making note of the models of cars, the colours, the faces of the drivers. He's protected her, blessed her, given her defences – but after last night, who knows if they'll work. *What mad risks I take*, she thinks, *for a creature I can barely understand*.

But she knows that's wrong. She does understand him. And he understands her.

She remembers when he first came to her – 1729, she thinks it was, almost ten years ago. Four years after Voortyashtan. Four years after her brother Sanjay had died in combat there, stabbed by a shtani girl hardly older than fifteen. He'd been battling insurgents, trying to save the girl, but the girl didn't understand that – or perhaps she did, but didn't care. Who knows what these degenerates think?

And what did Saypur get for her brother's sacrifice? What was earned by his death? After Komayd left power, Mishra couldn't tell. The Ministry and the military were in tatters. Public trust in the national forces was at an all-time low. The merchants were spilling into government and treating generals and commanders as if they were simple bureaucratic officials, pencil pushers and seat-fillers. Mishra, like a lot of other loyalists, found herself disgusted with her nation.

She thought she kept her disgust a secret. But it soon became clear that she hadn't. Because one day, while she was stationed here in Ahanashtan, someone slipped a letter under her apartment door.

This disturbed her. Mishra's residential address was a carefully kept Ministry secret. Direct correspondence was strictly forbidden.

But another thing that disturbed her about this letter was the colour of its paper.

It was black. Not dyed black, like a shirt – but *black*, as if someone had taken the idea of blackness and cut a perfect square from it.

Mishra opened the letter. And though she couldn't understand how, she could see writing on it, letters in black, but it was in different *shades* of black.

. . . or perhaps the letter did something else. Perhaps when you looked at it, rather than seeing the words there, the paper wrote words upon your mind.

The letter said:

DO YOU FEEL THAT THE CONTINENT HAS FAILED?
DO YOU FEEL THAT SAYPUR HAS FAILED?
DO YOU WISH TO DO AWAY WITH BOTH?

DO YOU WISH TO START ALL OVER AGAIN?

IF YOU DO, I CAN HELP YOU. AND YOU CAN HELP ME.

SIMPLY SAY THIS WORD ALOUD:

And at the bottom of the letter was a name.

Mishra stared at the letter. Not just because all of this was so odd, but because the words spoke to a deep dread that had been metastasising within her, this idea that perhaps no state or nation could ever truly succeed in this world. The Continent had been an abomination, and now Saypur, the world's best chance at a fair, proud, and free democracy, was being ruined by mercantilism and vain, fruitless quests for peace. Ten years into her military career she'd found herself waking up and thinking: *We'll never get it right. We'll always find a way to cock it all up. Every time.* And as her comrades fought and suffered and died, she found herself doubting the point of it all.

To see these thoughts written down before her, no matter how strangely they arrived, was a powerful sensation for her. It felt, for the first time in many years, like she was not alone.

So she took a breath, and read the name aloud.

And then the boy came – he still looked like a young boy back then – and they talked for a long, long while.

Captain First Class Kavitha Mishra has done a lot of odd things for the controller in the years since. There are other members of the Ministry who work for him too – she knows this because she personally recruited some of them – but none of them work as closely with him as she does. He wouldn't have picked anyone else to send to Bulikov, for example, when they needed to trap that laughing boy, the one who could seemingly appear out of thin air. And though that was her oddest job yet, she suspects he'll have stranger ones for her in the future.

Especially after Komayd, and Khadse, and whatever in hells happened last night.

Standing in the tunnel, Mishra checks her watch. She takes a breath, then opens the door.

The piece of black paper is still on the floor of the closet. She picks it up and unfolds it.

There are new words on the letter. Just like that first time in her apartment, they seem to be written in black – or perhaps they write themselves on some deeper, hidden part of her mind:

DO NOT ALERT THE MINISTRY YET.

USE THE MIRRORS. WATCH THEIR ACTIONS. REPORT IMMEDIATELY IF ANY MENTION OR MOVEMENT IS SPOTTED, ESPECIALLY CONCERNING THE SUSPECT.

HE IS WITH THEM. HE IS DANGEROUS.

She sighs.

Then she takes a match, lights it on the wall of the closet, and holds the flame to the corner of the paper.

The flames slowly crawl across the black page, turning it into ash. She blows on it a little to help it spread, then stamps it out when it's finished. Then she climbs back into her auto and drives away.

'Shit,' she says. She *hates* mirror duty. But an order is an order.

In some ways the modern world now seems very new and advanced to Sigrud. In his day, autos were a rarity, telephones even rarer than that, and pistols and riflings were expensive exoticisms.

Yet in some ways, to his disbelief, it remains absolutely the same. For example, if you were to tell Sigrud that in this very modern, very advanced society, one could still use a forged labour visa – one of the stalwart fallbacks of the intelligence industry, when he was active – to cross the South Seas to Navashtra in Saypur, he would think you a fool. Surely the bureaucracies and authorities must have closed the various loopholes that made such forgeries possible? Surely this new generation, swimming in so much technology and innovation, must have found a way to eliminate this common deceit?

But it appears that the wheels of government move even slower than Sigrud imagined. For he, along with dozens of other scruffy Dreylings and Continentals, is able to painlessly book passage across the South Seas and sail to Navashtra without incident. The various Saypuri officials barely even glance at him. Perhaps Saypur is so hungry for skilled labour that it doesn't particularly care if a few of those labourers are malicious agents.

From Navashtra, it's a shockingly simple thing to make it down the coast to Ghaladesh. All forms of transportation, whether roads or boats or trains, inevitably curve toward Ghaladesh, second-largest city in the world, but the undisputed capital of civilisation. And though the checkpoints and security measures are higher in Ghaladesh than anywhere else, they're still not as high as what Sigrud had to go through in service to Saypur's Ministry of Foreign Affairs – so, to his surprise, they pose no threat to him.

Perhaps this is a world I could have never imagined, he thinks. *Perhaps this is a world that is, more or less, at peace.*

And then, suddenly, he's there. He's walking free and unthreatened in Ghaladesh, the city that, in many ways, has decided his life and the lives of countless others. Because the choices made here, whether about war or commerce, have surely had millions of consequences and casualties apiece.

Sigrud tries not to stare around himself as he walks through Ghaladesh. He is mostly struck by how *clean* the city is, how organised. Bulikov was a schizophrenic, crumbling mess, Voortyashtan was hardly more than a savage outpost, and Ahanashtan was built specifically to serve the shipping channel, creating a half-industrial, half-urbane hybrid of a city.

But Ghaladesh is different. Ghaladesh, unlike all the other cities he's ever seen, is *intentional*.

You can see it when you walk from block to block. From the graceful wooden posts that so many houses sit on to the drains in the street to the curves of the elevated train, you can see how this was not just done well but done just – *so*. Ghaladesh, he sees, is a city of engineers, a city of thinkers, a city of people who do not act rashly.

Or at least act rashly within their own territory. The rest of the world, well, that he knows is a different story.

He can't help but marvel at how it flows, how it breathes. How the old stone, commercial buildings downtown flow into the graceful residential sections, where all the houses sit on poles or posts in case of flooding – for Ghaladesh is a city built on the sea, and thus is at constant war with the waters. Perhaps that's why so much of the city feels planned and designed to a fault. Or perhaps Saypuris, who after all served as slaves to the Continent for centuries, are incredibly, *intensely* sensitive to the possibility of ever infringing on the life of another. After glancing at the papers, it seems that if someone ever proposes constructing a new building of apartments, Ghaladeshis immediately hold a giant debate about the ramifications and effects of such a building, and whether such effects are acceptable. It is a little too civilised for Sigrud, who was raised in a culture where the person who yelled the loudest was usually considered to be in the right.

He goes to work right away. In this highly organised metropolis, it takes no time at all to find the address. It's close to the heart of Ghaladesh, in one of the richest and most exclusive areas available. When he gets there he can't see the house behind the tall wooden walls, but he can tell he's come to the right place by the Saypuri guards out front – plainclothes, certainly, but he knows soldiers when he sees them.

Sigrud waits for evening, then skulks through the yards of the adjoining houses. No one sees him, no one raises an eyebrow. These are civilised people. They have no need to be watchful of their properties.

He waits on the other side of the walls, listening for a footfall or a sigh. He hears none. *They must only put security out front*, he thinks. *Which is . . . remarkably stupid*. He readies himself, then hops the fence.

He lands in a very austere garden in the back of the house. Mostly just grass and rock and the odd shrub, pruned within an inch of its life. There's a sliding glass door in the back, and he finds nothing remarkable about the lock on it. He picks it in less than a minute and a half, then slips inside.

He checks his pocket watch. It's late evening now. She should be getting home soon.

He pads through the house, finds a deep bit of shadow on the balcony above the foyer, and waits.

After about an hour, there's the clink of keys. The door opens. Then the old woman walks in.

She is slightly bent, her hair grey and white, her skin lined with years of sun and stress. She has a cane now, which she uses with a great air of reluctance, as if someone glued it to her hand and she's not sure how to get it off. He watches as she walks to the coat rack and sticks the cane in the bottom, muttering, 'Fucking thing,' as she does, and then she begins the long, slow, complicated process of removing her coat. Such a thing takes time, for not only are her joints clearly paining her, but her left arm is a prosthetic, shining metal from the elbow down.

Sigrud goes totally still at the sight of her, not even breathing. Not because he fears her, but because he never could have expected how *old* she's gotten. She is not at all the striding, powerful creature he once knew, the person who seemed like she could punch through the hull of a battleship if she but willed it. In thirteen years, she's become someone else.

He watches as she limps over to the kitchen, where she pours herself a glass of brandy. She stands there at the sink, sipping it. But he can tell something's different about the way she moves. It's too stiff, too careful . . .

She puts down the brandy. 'If that's not you, Sigrud,' she says, 'I'm going to turn around and start shooting.'

'It is,' he says, emerging from the shadows. 'How could you tell I was here?'

'Because you smell,' she says. 'Very bad. Smells like you've been stuck in the hold of some ship for weeks. Which you probably have. Turnabout's fair play, isn't it? You smelled me out in Voortyasht –'

General Turyin Mulaghesh trails off as she turns around and looks up at him. Her face goes slack with shock. 'By the seas, Sigrud,' she whispers. 'Look at you. Just look at you.'

Sigrud looks down at her from the balcony, unsure what to do.

'You haven't aged a day, Sigrud,' she says softly. 'Not a single, solitary day.'

Sigrud waits in the reading room, the spacious bay windows framing the rambling spill of downtown Ghaladesh beyond. He can't stop staring out the window at them.

'Ah,' says Mulaghesh, returning with a bottle of wine and two glasses. 'First time in Ghaladesh?'

He nods.

'Very nice city,' says Mulaghesh. 'If you can afford to live here. Most can't. This damn house they have here for me, I'd have to live my life ten fucking times over to be able to ever afford it.'

He smiles politely, not sure what to say.

'So has anyone told you yet,' says Mulaghesh casually, pulling the cork out of the bottle of wine with her teeth and spitting it out on the floor, 'how absolutely fucking stupid you are to come here?'

'Yes. Including myself.'

'But it didn't work.'

'No. Circumstances.'

'Those must have been some fucking circumstances. You're still a wanted man, Sigrud. Lots of military brass want to see your head on a platter for what you did.' She glances at him as she pours him a glass. 'And I'd be hard pressed to blame them.'

'Yes. I understand.'

'Where have you been for the past decade or so?' she asks, pouring her own.

'Nowhere good.'

She laughs sullenly. 'Doubt it was any better than where *I* was. Sitting in the Parliament chambers for over a decade, dealing with these little-minded fools . . .'

'It was probably better,' he says. 'You probably had a toilet.'

'Ah. Well, yes. That certainly puts things in perspective. Now how, exactly, did you get in here without alerting any of my security team?'

He shrugs. 'Quietly.'

She grunts and hands him a glass. 'Well. You were always one creepy spook, Sigrud. It's nice to see at least *one* thing hasn't changed. But I suspect I know why you're here.'

He picks up the glass and smells it. He won't drink tonight. He needs to be on his toes. 'Yes. Shara.'

'Yeah,' she says. 'Yeah.'

Mulaghesh eases herself into a chair beside him, groaning as she does. He watches her movements, watches her give her left hip a little more time to adjust than her right – arthritis, probably.

'Ah,' she says, seeing his face. 'Has time not been kind to me? Or is it kind to anyone, really?'

Sigrud isn't sure what to say. He'd imagined so much of how this would go, but now that he's here, words fail him.

'It certainly seems to have been kind to *you*,' she says, sipping her wine. 'You look exactly – *exactly* – as I remember you, Sigrud. And if you got in here without anyone noticing, you must be moving pretty good too.'

'My mother aged very well,' he says. 'Or so I am told.'

'If anyone ages as well as you have,' says Mulaghesh, 'It'd be a medical fucking miracle.'

The mention of the word 'miracle' makes him cringe. His left hand throbs. To be so close to the woman who was there when his daughter died . . . It all comes rushing back to him, too much, too fast.

'How are you doing, Turyin?' he asks, wishing to think about anything else.

'Good, or so I'm told. Now that Shara's policies have really kicked in during the past, what, five or six years, I'm hearing a lot less "no" and a lot more "how may we assist you, Minister." Quite an about-face. Turns out people *like* opening up borders, if it makes them money. Maybe they'll thank Shara, now that she's dead. If it doesn't put their seat at risk, that is. That's politicians for you.'

'You are . . . the minority leader?'

'Mm,' she says, sipping her wine. 'Of the Upper House of Parliament. But next year, they say, I'll be the majority leader. Won't *that* be fun? I expect I'll have to talk to a lot more foreign delegates then.' She glances at him. 'Speaking of which . . . Do you want to know how Hild is doing?'

Sigrud blinks, startled at the mention of his wife. 'You've been in contact with her?'

'She was the trade chancellor for the United Dreyling States. I couldn't *avoid* talking to her.'

'I . . . suppose.'

'She just stepped down, actually. They're doing quite well up there, so they don't need her on the watch anymore, or so she said.' She glances at him. 'She's remarried. I suppose you should know that.'

'I see. I had wondered.' He rubs his mouth, his face slightly puzzled. *How odd it is to hear of the lives of your loved ones in a briefing.* 'Is she . . . I don't know. Happy?'

'I think so. There are more grandbabies now.'

Sigrud swallows. 'Carin's?'

'I would assume so. You only had her and . . . and Signe, right?'

He nods, feeling strangely alien, as if someone else is wearing his body.

'Carin has had five now,' says Mulaghesh. 'Four girls and one boy.'

He lets out a breath. 'That's . . . that's quite a brood.'

'Yes. It would be.' She pauses, then asks kindly, 'Would you like to see if I could get their pictures for you?'

He thinks about it for a long time. Then he shakes his head.

'No?'

'No. It would make what I am about to do much harder.'

'What do you mean?'

'Saypur will not let me go back,' he said. 'So there is no need for me to know of such things. Because I will never have them.'

There's an awkward silence. Mulaghesh sips her wine. She says, 'Did she ever contact you, Sigrud?'

'Who? Hild?'

'No. Shara, of course.'

'No,' he says. 'I only learned she was dead secondhand.'

Mulaghesh nods slowly. 'So . . . You don't know what she was doing on the Continent.'

'No.' He sits up. 'Why? Do you?'

She smiles mirthlessly. 'No. Not a whit. Wish I did. And I did ask. She wouldn't tell me. Seemed to think it'd put my life in jeopardy. Which, considering what happened to her, might have been true. The only thing she told me was that it was . . . how did she put it . . . Ah, yes. She said it was, quote, "increasingly likely that Sigrud will visit you one day." '

Sigrud blinks, surprised. 'She told you I would come to you?'

'Correct. I didn't understand it. You were a gods damned criminal. But she said that, if you were to come to me, I was to give you a message – but I assume you have no knowledge of this message, do you, Sigrud?'

He shakes his head, stunned. He hadn't anticipated this at all.

Mulaghesh stares into space, thinking. 'She must have known,' she says. 'Must have known there was a chance she'd be killed. Must have known you'd find out. And that you'd come to me. Eventually.' She laughs hollowly. 'Clever little woman. She finds such delightful ways to make us all do her dirty work for her, even beyond the grave.'

'What is the message?'

'It was very simple,' says Mulaghesh, 'and very confusing. She said that if you ever came to me, I was to tell you to protect her daughter. At all costs.'

Sigrud is still for a moment. Then he shakes his head, exasperated. 'But . . . But that's what I'm *already* here to do,' he says. 'I came to you to find out where Tatyana Komayd is!'

'You didn't let me finish,' snaps Mulaghesh. 'Because *no one* knows where Tatyana Komayd is. And apparently no one has for months.'

'What?'

'Yes. After the assassination, finding Tatyana was a national priority – and yet the Komayd estate was utterly empty. Apparently Shara had been circulating the idea that her daughter was staying behind at the Komayd estate . . . yet that was far from the truth. But now is where it gets confusing,' says Mulaghesh, sitting forward with a pained grunt. 'Fucking arthritis . . . It's just bullshit, how your body rebels against you. Anyways. Shara told me to tell you to protect her daughter – but she *also* told me that her daughter could be found with the·only woman who ever shared her love.'

Sigrud stares at her, bug-eyed. '*What?*'

'That's what I thought too,' says Mulaghesh. 'I never really thought she was, you know, that kind of a person. I try not to assume anything, since *lots* of people have assumed things about *me* over the years, none of which I've exactly *appreciated*, and I – '

Sigrud holds up a hand. 'No. I don't think this is right.'

'Well, hells, Sigrud. What right do you have t – '

'*No*. I mean, that sort of message, Turyin. I think it is intended to be confusing, to anyone but me. Perhaps she is referring to someone both she and I knew, once.' He sighs and grips the sides of his skull. 'But . . . I don't know who that could be.'

'Why wouldn't she just *tell* me who it was?' asks Mulaghesh. 'Wouldn't that be easier?'

He remembers the pale Continental girl saying that Nokov would pull every secret out of his guts. 'Your address is publicly listed,' he says. 'And your security is not very good, as I have proven. I think she believed she could take no chances. Even with you, Turyin. But wait . . . When she told you this, did you not do anything? Did this not alarm you?'

'It alarmed me plenty,' says Mulaghesh. 'But by then I was already pretty alarmed.'

'By what? What had Shara done?'

Mulaghesh sighs, sits back down, and drinks the rest of her wine in one giant gulp. 'Now, *that* is a very interesting question.'

'It was early 1733,' says Mulaghesh. 'I hadn't seen hide nor hair of Shara in, what, two years? She left office in 1726, and though we'd stayed in touch it'd been a damned while, I'll say that. But then one day my assistant lets me know that a woman left a message for me, and this woman was quite insistent – said she was a friend of Captain Nesrhev, from Bulikov.'

Sigrud smiles. 'The police captain you were involved with.'

'Right. But it was only a *few* times,' says Mulaghesh defensively. 'At least, by *my* standards it was only a few. Anyways. So I'm damned curious to find out who this woman is, and I show up at the restaurant mentioned in the message, and who is it but Shara. I was surprised. I mean, the former prime minister can get a meeting with anyone she wants, right? But she wanted to keep all of it a secret. She couldn't be seen meeting with me, couldn't be seen asking me what she was about to ask.'

'Which was what?'

'It was about an intelligence compartment, an operation. One she didn't have access to, had *never* had access to throughout her career in the Ministry, even when she was prime gods damned minister. One called Operation Rebirth. You know it?'

'I have been forced to do a lot of remembering in the past few days, Turyin, but this I do not know.'

'I'd never heard of it either. She asked me to look into it. She looked shaken too. Paranoid. It was odd – she'd been living on the outskirts of Ghaladesh with her daughter, just . . . keeping quiet. But then there she was, coming out of nowhere with this. Said it'd be a pretty old operation – back when Vinya was running the show, maybe during the 1710s, while you and she were just young pups and barely knew how to slit a throat.'

Sigrud was actually very much aware of how to slit a throat by 1710, but refrains from correcting her.

'So I did some checking. Reached out to some trusted sources in the Ministry, in the archives. And all they came back with was a file with one piece of paper in it. Just one. A report on a Saypuri dreadnought, the SS *Salim*. Know it?'

Sigrud shakes his head.

'Me neither. It was lost in a typhoon in 1716. That was all I had to give her. But it seemed to excite her plenty. She suggested she'd discovered something ratty, and it smelled pretty ratty to me too. "I see Vinya's finger-prints all over this," I told her, and she . . . *suggested* that was right but said she wouldn't tell me more. Again, for my own safety.'

'What happened then?'

'After I gave her that file she stopped living so quietly. Threw herself into her charity work, started visiting the Continent more and more, arranging shelter and foster homes for orphans. Seemed like the usual charity shit. But I wondered – was it *really* a charity? It couldn't have been a coincidence that I'd told her about this operation and then suddenly she starts practically living on the Continent. And then, three months ago, she makes a surprise visit to me, tells me the bit about you and Tatyana – and then . . .' She trails off. 'I had to identify the body, you know.'

Sigrud sits up and looks at her, alarmed.

'They found parts of it,' she says. 'Of . . . *her*, I suppose. And it was odd to ask me to see her. She was the fucking prime minister, everyone knew what she looked like. But I guess you have to be formal in such situations. I thought maybe she'd faked it all, up until that moment. But maybe that's just what one does in reaction to such things. The unreality of death. Hoping it was a dream. You know?'

Sigrud shuts his eyes. He sees Signe standing on a pier, staring out to sea, watching all her astonishing contraptions going to work, forging a new age.

'Yes,' he says softly. 'I know.'

'Did you come straight here once you heard about her?'

'No,' he says. 'And I am here to tell you that you were right, Turyin. Shara was not just involved in some charity. I think when she went to the Continent, she was going to war.'

*

Mulaghesh listens as he tells her about the past month of his life. When he tells her what happened in Ahanashtan, she drops all pretence of polite attention and instead grabs the bottle of wine.

By the time he finishes talking the bottle of wine is almost gone. Mulaghesh, rolling her eyes in dismay and sighing heavily, keeps pouring glass after glass of it, tossing each one down her throat with a weary resignation. The one piece of information he withholds is Nokov's name: he's not willing to take the chance that she could repeat it and bring that creature down on her head.

When he's done, Mulaghesh takes a deep breath and says, 'Okay, first off – *you* are the stupid asshole who left *seven bodies* in a coal warehouse in Ahanashtan last week?'

'Oh. You heard about that?'

'Gods damn it, Sigrud, a former prime minister got assassinated in Ahanashtan a month ago! If so much as *one* body hits the ground in the whole of that province, I get briefed about it, let alone *seven!*'

'Well. If it is any consolation, things mostly went to plan . . .'

'Except for the part where it sure sounds like a gods damned Divinity showed up and nearly killed you!' says Mulaghesh, furious. 'Not to mention you telling me that the streets of Ahanashtan are apparently riddled with what sounds like some damned Divine booby traps. And *fuck knows* if I can understand what that's all about!'

'You will need to keep your voice down,' says Sigrud. 'Your guards have ears.'

Mulaghesh rolls her eyes again and tosses herself back in her chair.

'I do not think,' he says, 'that the things I met were Divinities.'

'Oh? And what makes you say that?'

'In . . . In Voortyashtan . . . When you held the Sword of Voortya. What did it feel like?'

'What are you digging up *that* awful memory for . . .?'

'Turyin. Please.'

She stares out the window, her eyes wide and haunted. 'Like I could have . . . could have done anything. Anything. Cut the world in two if I wanted to.'

'Yes. Even a shred of a true Divinity's power is incomprehensible to the human mind. They can warp reality without even thinking. But the two beings I encountered . . . They struggled. They had limitations. The world was filled with boundaries and limits for them.'

'So, what are they? Divine creatures? Living miracles?'

'I've no idea,' says Sigrud. 'But I think Shara knew. They both knew Shara, I suspect. Though one fought against her, and the other with her. And it sounds as if all of what she did on the Continent was started by the file you found . . .'

'Operation Rebirth.'

'Right.' Sigrud breathes deep. 'So. This is . . . a lot to take in.'

'You're telling me, asshole. What I can't figure is, if Shara was tangling with these things that sure as hells acted like Divinities, why not use her black lead on them, just as she did Kolkan? Why not use the *one* thing she knew could kill them?'

'I don't know,' says Sigrud. 'I assume she still had it. She did not even trust it with the Ministry, after Bulikov. Such weapons, she said to me, should not be trusted with governments.'

'As someone who's been trying to lead one for a while, I can understand that.'

'I think she trusted nothing and no one,' says Sigrud darkly. 'The Shara I knew would have at least written a message for me. Something encoded, something secret. But a spoken word, passed along verbally . . . Such methods speak of desperation.'

'I don't like the idea of Shara desperate.'

'Nor I,' he says. 'Especially when her enemy, whoever he is, seems to be after her daughter.'

'I don't understand that at all. She's just a kid.'

'Khadse said his employer was targeting Continental youths,' says Sigrud, thinking. 'Children. Adolescents. First their parents were killed, then the children vanished.'

Mulaghesh's face grows grave. 'Then you . . . You think Tatyana might already be . . .'

'I don't know. It sounded as if Shara's enemy had just got that list of Continentals. So there might still be time.' He pokes at his false eye, trying to get it into a better position.

'Can you please not do that?' says Mulaghesh. 'It's creepy.'

'Sorry. Tell me. I only saw her the one time. What do you know of Tatyana?'

'Not much,' says Mulaghesh. 'Shara zealously guarded their privacy after she left office. I suppose she put her Ministry skills to good use there. People barely even knew she'd adopted a daughter, let alone a Continental. I met her only once. She was young. And she was obsessed with the stock markets.'

'The . . . the what? The stock markets?'

'Yeah. She was a weird kid, I'll be honest. Read a lot of economics books. But being around Shara probably makes anyone weird.'

Sigrud sits back in his chair, thinking. 'Where did Shara live? Before she died, I mean.'

'Her ancestral estate. Eastern Ghaladesh.' She gives him the specific address. 'It's a huge place, belonged to her aunt. Why?'

'Because I think, yet again, that there is something I need to remember,' he says, 'and I need something to jog my memory.'

Mulaghesh frowns at him. Then her mouth falls open. 'Whoa. Wait. Are you saying you're thinking of breaking into Shara's estate? Just to jog your *memory*?'

Sigrud shrugs. 'That is where I was going originally. I don't know where to go otherwise. Shara was trying to make me think of someone, but we knew so many people . . . If I can see her records, see what she was doing, it would help me understand.'

'Are you mad? Sigrud, that place is part of an international investigation! A *Ministry* investigation! It'll be watched!'

'Then I will have to be careful.'

'Shara's house won't be like *mine*,' says Mulaghesh. 'She was beloved, hated, and now she's *dead*. They're taking this fucking seriously, Harkvaldsson! It's not something for you to go gallivanting into. They'll have soldiers and guards!'

'I will not do any gallivanting,' says Sigrud. 'I will be very good.'

'Are you even listening to me?' says Mulaghesh. 'I don't want you killing any more *innocent people*, people who are just trying to do their *jobs*!'

There's a long, awkward silence.

'You know,' Sigrud says quietly, 'that I did not mean to do any of that.'

'I know those soldiers in Voortyashtan are dead. I know that people who tangle with you tend to wind up that way. And I don't like the idea of pointing you toward any other dumb kids who happen to be in the wrong place at the wrong time.'

'It was thirteen years ago,' says Sigrud. His voice shakes with a cold fury. 'And my daughter had just died.'

'Does that justify it? Some other parents are still mourning their kids, because of you. You're a hard operator, Sigrud, that's the truth. Are you willing to play hard for *this* operation? Are you willing to react lethally if you need, to get what you want?'

Sigrud doesn't meet her eyes.

'That's what I thought,' says Mulaghesh. 'We trained you to do one thing, Sigrud. And you're good at it. But I think maybe it's all you know how to do anymore. Looking at you now, it's downright disturbing – because you don't seem worried about this at all.'

'I am worried,' says Sigrud, confused.

'Yes, but not about *yourself*,' snaps Mulaghesh. 'When most people talk about going up against what sure sounds like a Divinity, they at least mention that they're anxious. But I've heard not a peep of that from you, Sigrud je Harkvaldsson. You don't seem to care about whether that thing can kill you.'

Sigrud sits in silence for a moment. 'She was all I had left,' he says suddenly.

'What?' says Mulaghesh.

'She was all I had left. Shara was. For thirteen years, for thirteen miserable years, I waited for her, Turyin. I waited for word from her, waited for her to tell me that . . . that things were going to go back to normal. But it never came, and now it never will. It has been thirteen years and I am still here, still alive, my hand still hurts, and I . . . I am still *exactly* that wretched fool that Shara dug out of prison so many years ago. Nothing has changed. Nothing has changed. Except now I have no hope that things could ever change.'

Mulaghesh glances at his left hand. 'Your hand still hurts?'

'Yes.' He opens it up, shows her the grisly scar there. The sigil of Kolkan: two hands, waiting to weigh and judge. 'Every day. Sometimes more than others. I thought it would stop, after Shara killed Kolkan. But it never did.' He laughs weakly. 'It is the one thing I still have. Everything else has been taken from me. Everyone else. This is all I am now. I am scrabbling for memories and pieces of the people I have lost. Trying to save the fragments that are left. If I can keep Shara's daughter alive, keep a bit of her burning in this world with me, then maybe . . . Maybe I can . . .'

He trails off, and bows his head.

'Sigrud . . . Sigrud, listen to me. Signe . . .' She grabs his shoulder and squeezes it. 'Signe's death was not your fault. You know that. You know that, don't you?'

'Even if I believed that,' says Sigrud, 'it would not make me any more whole, Turyin. So much has been taken from us. I must do something about that.'

They sit in quiet for a long time. The scar on his left palm aches and throbs. Mulaghesh shifts in her chair, her metal prosthetic clicking softly.

Sigrud softly asks, 'Can I see your hand?'

'My hand?'

'Yes. Your prosthetic.'

'I . . . Sure, I guess.'

She holds it out to him. Sigrud gently takes it, holding it as if it were some holy relic, and adjusts its fingers, feeling the movements of its thumb, touching every dent and scrape and scar in its metal surface.

'Still holds up,' he whispers.

'Signe did a good job making it,' says Mulaghesh. 'She did a good job on everything she made.'

Sigrud holds the index and middle fingers of the prosthetic a little longer, perhaps imagining the grasp of the young woman who once created it.

'It's not the only thing left of her in this world, Sigrud,' says Mulaghesh.

He looks at her, brow creased.

'She changed Voortyashtan,' says Mulaghesh. 'She changed Bulikov. She changed your country. Those things are all still here. And all those things are worth saving. As are you.'

He shuts his eyes and lets her fingers go. 'Thank you for your help,' he whispers. 'I'll leave now.'

They walk back downstairs to the sliding glass door. 'It was good to see you again, Turyin,' he says.

'It was good to see you too,' says Mulaghesh. 'Listen . . . I suspect you don't have too many friends in this world now, Sigrud. But if you need anything – *anything* – you tell me. I owe you that much. Send a telegram to this address with a telephone number on it.' She writes a note and hands it to him. 'I'll call the number you give me from a secure line.'

'But what if I'm very far away?'

She smiles gently. 'Oh, Sigrud. How long have you been in the wilderness? Telephones can call very distant places now.'

'Oh.' He looks at her. 'There is one thing you can do.'

'What?'

'Find the SS *Salim*.'

Mulaghesh sighs. 'I was wondering when it'd come to that. I didn't find much the first time, you know.'

'There's more. There has to be more. Hidden in nasty places.'

'You're asking me to turn over a bunch of very classified stones, Sigrud.'

'Shara must have found it, or something about it. If you find that, it can help me understand what her war was about. I would not ask if I did not think you could do it.'

'I'll try. I promise nothing. But I'll try.' She looks into his face, exploring its scars, its bruises, its wrinkles. 'Be safe, Sigrud.'

'I promise nothing,' he says. 'But I'll try.'

He slips out the door. When he reaches the wall, he readies himself to jump it, but looks back. He thought she'd still be there, watching him, but she isn't. Instead, Turyin Mulaghesh has sunk to the ground and now sits, one hand still absently resting on the handle of the sliding door, her eyes staring into space, as if she's just heard the news about the death of a very dear friend.

He watches her for a moment longer. Then he leaps over the fence and slinks into the night.

6.
Older Grounds

*You and I have confirmed that Olvos's Frost of Bolshoni — the miracle that
allows us to converse through panes of glass — was originally intended to operate
within frozen lakes. It was not intended to work in glass, nor was it intended to
work in mirrored surfaces, as we have both seen that it can do, with the right
guidance.*

*In addition, Pangyui's recent work on Jukov suggests that the miracle called
Sadom's Breath was originally created to turn tree sap into wine, and was oper-
able only during certain phases of the moon so that Jukov's followers could turn
a pine tree into a fount of wine for their wild rites. However, during the latter
stages of the Divine Empire we have records of shepherds using Sadom's Breath
to turn tree sap not into wine but into water, and it could be used at any time of
the month. They used this miracle to survive in the wilderness, leading their
flocks across ranges that were previously impassable. But there are no records of
Jukov or Olvos directly altering any one of these miracles.*

*There are more instances. The conclusion I draw is not, as you suggested,
that miracles fade as their existence goes on, causing fluctuations in their function. Rather, I believe that miracles changed and mutated just as any organism
might: the Divine Empire was a teeming ecosystem of miracles and Divine enti-
ties, all with varying levels of agency and purpose, all shifting and altering as the
years went by. Though many have gone, those changes still shaped this land.*

*The Divine was not absolute, as we might prefer to think. And though it is
gone, these mutations echo on. We must prepare for what happens if one miracle
should change and shift enough that, improbably, it could adapt, and survive.*

— LETTER FROM FORMER PRIME MINISTER ASHARA KOMAYD
TO MINISTER OF FOREIGN AFFAIRS VINYA KOMAYD, 1714

After the soft rains comes the fog, swelling up from the countless rivers and tributaries winding through Ghaladesh. It fills the yards and county lanes of the eastern portion of the city. Sigrud can tell that this is the astronomically wealthy portion of Ghaladesh, the neighbourhoods inhabited by the scions of industry: the actual houses become more and more elusive, hidden far back from the road behind walls and hedges and fences and gates, the barest hint of lit windows in the distant hills. Whereas Mulaghesh lives downtown, close to where all the action is, the people here are so powerful that they force the action to come to them, and can refuse entry to those they disdain.

Sigrud wipes moisture from his brow as he steers the puttering little auto along the lanes. He tries to tell himself it's just the warmth and the damp. He tries to tell himself he's not sweating because he just stole an auto, along with a pistol and ammunition, and is now about to bring both of these stolen goods right under the nose of Ministry officers.

Sigrud stops the auto at the top of the hill and surveys his surroundings. He glances at a nearby mailbox and confirms he's close to Shara's estate.

He pulls over. Turns out the lights. Then he slips out of the auto.

Sigrud received sparse training on wilderness tactics when he trained for the Ministry, but he's had a lot, *lot* more in the past ten years, having spent so much time in the forests north of Bulikov. Those wintry, piney places are about as different from the steamy hills of Ghaladesh as one can imagine – but trees and grasses are still trees and grasses.

He pulls a grey-green cap down low over his head, steps into the brush, takes out his spyglass, and stays low.

For the next three hours he surveys the area. The Komayd estate isn't the biggest one, but it's pretty damned big, situated on a seven- or eight-acre lot, with high wooden walls and the main house clinging to a stream that runs across the grounds. His eyes widen when he actually sees the house. He thought it would be big – he recalls Shara acidly saying, *Auntie's sitting on quite the nest egg, I'm told her neighbour's a steel baron* – but not *this* big. The house is more of a mansion, with dark stone walls on the lower floor and a dark plaster second floor – a common style in Saypur.

Despite its size, the estate is well guarded. Sigrud doesn't get close, but he manages to count one car at the front gate, one guard on foot at the side gate, and a third guard in a blind set up just behind the estate in the woods. There's also a roving car that makes runs up and down the country lanes, taking up vantage points to check the area.

It'll be hard to get in. The walls are watched from all angles. The grounds themselves, though, seem relatively deserted, at least from what he can see.

So how to get in?

He stands on one small hill below a towering teak tree and eyes the stream that runs across the Komayd grounds. It looks deep, maybe six or seven feet.

'Hm,' he says.

He creeps to the south of the estate, listening closely. Brightly coloured birds and even the odd monkey stare down at him. The trees are nothing short of tremendous. He's heard before that Saypur boasts the most impressive foliage in all the world, due to its wet climate, and he can't disagree. The trees are tall, thick, and, he hopes, concealing.

He cocks his head, listening, and then he hears it: the quiet trickle of water.

He finds the stream and sees that it is deep, or at least deep enough. He wonders how far the stream will take him, how far he'll have to go. *One mile? More? And I'll have to avoid detection throughout . . .*

He looks up at the sky. Evening will be here soon. He takes off his grey-green coat, then pulls out his pistol. He contemplates bringing it, but he's had bad luck with wet ammunition before: supposedly some Saypuri-made rounds can fire underwater, but Sigrud's always found their performance to be spotty. Maybe they've made advances since he was in the service, but if so he hasn't heard of them.

Tsking, he hides the pistol in his coat, then shoves the bundle underneath some ferns. *Better to come back to it later, when I know it will work.* He checks to make sure his knife is still strapped to his thigh and the waterproof electric torch is strapped to his belt. Then he takes a deep breath, dives in, and begins to swim upriver.

It's full dark by the time Sigrud emerges onto the Komayd grounds, just beyond the southern wall. He moved upriver agonisingly slowly, swimming and sometimes creeping through the waters. He's fairly confident he passed under the walls undetected, swimming through the deep shadows of the stream. Now he's more worried about who could be on the grounds.

Dripping wet, he crawls up to one towering garden hedge and peers at the giant home beyond. He crouches there for a full twenty minutes, watching carefully. The windows of the home are dark and empty. There's no one he can see. There must not be enough ready personnel to waste time inside the home of a dead politician.

He takes stock of the house. The stream runs across the east grounds of the estate, and a big teak tree stands just beside one of the second-floor windows. He considers shimmying up it and jumping in – but if there's no one guarding the interior grounds, why not just go in through the back door?

Sigrud slowly stalks up to the Komayd mansion, listening for the errant snap of branches or rustling of leaves. Then he dashes across the back patio, hunches by the back glass doors, and listens.

Nothing. Silence.

He pulls out his lockpicks and goes to work. It's a weak lock, and in seconds he's inside, gently closing the doors behind him.

Sigrud turns to get his bearings. Then he stares, perplexed.

The entrance hall is huge and grandiose enough to be startling – but what's even more startling is that it's completely and utterly empty. Not a stick of furniture in sight and nothing on the walls, except for the drapes on the far windows and a small round mirror hanging from one of the columns.

Did they move out all her belongings?

Listening for any footfalls, he creeps toward the main hallway. The floor is pink marble and the walls are wood, painted a soft green with crimson crown moulding and bright gold gas sconces. The room must have played host to countless paintings, some of enormous size – he can see where the hooks once hung – but they're gone too.

I am going to feel very stupid indeed, he thinks, *if I risked my neck to break into an empty house.* He sucks his teeth. *But if it is empty . . . then why guard it at all?*

He silently stalks down the main hallway and looks in the first few rooms, parlour rooms and games rooms and libraries and such – or at least that's what he *assumes* they are, because they're all empty as well.

It's confusing on two levels for him: not only is it odd to find the house empty, with no signs of furniture being here recently, but it's odd to imagine Shara living here. She always had a deep dislike of large, wide spaces. She never said it, but he suspected it was her training: in a big room, lots of people can see you from far away, where you might not be able to see them.

Odder still – where are her books? Shara loved books more than nearly anything else in the world. As someone who occasionally had to move her belongings, Sigrud – and especially his lower back – can attest to that.

Then he gets an idea. He walks back where he came from, headed toward the dining area. *Not in any of the big, wide rooms . . . But perhaps she lived in –*

He freezes as he crosses the entrance hall.

He sinks low and looks over his shoulder. Waits. Watches. But there's nothing.

He could have sworn he saw movement before the columns by the door. Maybe even a face. But the only things in the room besides him are the sconces, drapes, and the mirror, which is still hanging from one of the entry columns.

He peers at the mirror. *Perhaps I glimpsed myself moving in the reflection*, he thinks.

That's possible, he supposes. Though the angles are not at all the right ones for him to have seen himself in the mirror . . .

'Hm,' says Sigrud softly.

He tries to focus on the task at hand. But as impossible as it might be, part of him insists he glimpsed someone in the mirror for one second, someone who was *not* him: a Saypuri woman, with hard, dark features and amber-gold eyes.

He walks forward and looks closely at the little mirror. All it shows is the empty entrance hall and his own scarred face. Frowning, he retreats to the dining area.

This area is quite empty, but not totally empty: there's a small table in this room, along with four small chairs. He can see a bit of food stuck to the side of the table, perhaps a smudge of jam. It must have been used within the past few months, possibly.

He goes to the servants' stairwells and creeps down.

This portion of the house, below the mansion, is shorn of all grandiose displays of wealth and power. It's white wood, scuffed stairs, and creaky wooden doors. He knows it's intended to house the servants, so its spaces will be much smaller, much more cramped, and much more hidden.

In other words, he thinks, *much more to Shara's liking.*

He comes to the bottom step and pulls out his waterproof torch. He flicks it on, keeping its light trained on the floor. He opens the door to the servants' quarters and shines the light in.

Inside is a long hallway, but unlike all the others, this one is not empty: it's lined with bookshelves, tall and towering, each piled high with thick, ancient tomes. He walks down the hallway, shining his light about, and sees that each of the servants' rooms – small, with a single door – is also filled with bookcases, not to mention countless overstuffed chairs and small side tables, each covered in old tea doilies.

He walks over to one table and picks up the doily sitting there. It's old, limp, stained, something that really should have been washed and changed, but the person who lived here clearly never had the time.

He holds it to his face, and smells it. The powerful scents of tea fill his nose, sirlang and pochot and jasmine.

Tears well up in his eyes. 'Hello, Shara,' he whispers.

Just a little under five hundred miles north, across the South Seas in the dark basement of a small but well-guarded house in Ahanashtan, Captain First Class Kavitha Mishra drums her fingers and grimaces.

Hm, she thinks. *This is bad.*

She looks at the mirrors before her. There are sixty-one in total, all of varying sizes and widths, all hanging from the mouldering brick walls here in the basement. It's quite dark in the basement, with one tiny candle burning; yet despite this lack of light, sixty of the mirrors are reflecting things that they really should not be reflecting.

Most of the mirrors show nothing but darkness. Others show meeting rooms, doorways, hallways, bedrooms, garages, and one reflects the eye of a telescope, which appears to be pointed at an apartment balcony across a city street. The mirror sits so close to the telescope that she can look right through it and see the magnified windows beyond.

None of this should be possible, of course. There is no conceivable, logical explanation as to why, for example, one mirror appears to be reflecting a forest lane, when there is no forest lane anywhere close to the mirror's face. What it *should* be reflecting is Kavitha Mishra, sitting before a small burning candle at the desk, frowning and wondering what to do. But it doesn't.

She knows how these particular mirrors work. It's a miracle, of course, one she herself has performed dozens of times.

But she's never had this happen before.

Did he see me? she thinks. *Did I turn it off fast enough? Does he know?*

Mishra sighs softly and sits back. It took the better part of three years for her to get the mirrors situated in the right places throughout the Continent and Saypur: by, say, placing a small, tiny mirror in the desk drawer in a meeting room in Parliament, for example, or hanging a small mirror on the trunk of a tree outside a military barracks, or slipping a narrow mirror behind a painting on the wall of a major financial trading firm. Mishra doesn't have a lot of close allies alongside her in the Ministry, but she had enough for this. And knowing what everyone of importance is doing or thinking at any given moment can make a handful of people far more effective than an entire army.

Though they had to be very careful with where they put the mirrors, since, after all, it's a two-way connection: just as she can see and hear the things happening on the distant mirrors, the people on the other end could see and hear her in the basement. As such, many of the mirrors act solely as listening devices, hidden away in dark places near important action.

She remembers what the controller said when he first tasked her with this duty: *Vinya Komayd used this miracle all the time, when she was in the Ministry. They all did, they were all hypocrites, preaching fear of the Divine while also using it. But this particular one, the Frost of Bolshoni, allowed her to gain control of all of the Ministry, and much of the Saypuri government, peering out of windowpanes and mirrors far away, watching and listening . . . And her niece, of course, almost certainly did the same . . .*

The thought troubled her deeply at the time. Though she knows the controller is now far more powerful than Vinya or Shara Komayd ever were.

Mishra waits a moment longer. Then she grimaces. *No more fretting about it. I've got to tell him.*

She stands and walks into one of the three broom closets at the far end of the basement. Usually she or whichever other contractor is on duty will use these rooms as a fallback: if one mirror displays a lot of activity – a loud meeting, a fight, people enthusiastically making love – they'll take the mirror off the wall and sit with it in one of the dark, soundproof closets, so the noises it's making won't filter through to any of the other sixty mirrors. But she won't be using it for such, not today.

She opens the door, steps inside. Total darkness embraces her.

Then she takes a breath, and says one word.

'Nokov.'

There's a pause, and then from somewhere in the closet there's the sound of a soft shuffling, like something creeping through nearby weeds.

A high, cold voice wafts through the darkness: 'Mishra.'

He chooses not to physically manifest before her. This is increasingly normal now: she senses that, as he grows in power, he also becomes more and more abstract, and harder to comprehend. But understanding it doesn't make it any less uncanny.

She clears her throat and tries to focus. She definitely tries to ignore the low groans coming from somewhere out in the darkness, like trees weighed down with ice. 'I have a report for you, sir.'

'Ah.' The voice is right beside her now. 'Excellent. Thank you.'

'I've observed an . . . unwelcome visitor to the Komayd household in Ghaladesh. His appearance matches the man you encountered here in Ahanashtan, at the slaughterhouse.'

A long pause.

'Does it.'

'Yes. Tall. Dreyling. He appears to have infiltrated without the awareness of the Ministry officers stationed there. He was, ah, wet – which makes me think he approached through the stream running by the house.'

A long, long silence. There is a strange, curious rumbling in the darkness, like the sound of a wild boar growling in the undergrowth.

She shivers. Whenever she talks to him like this she can't help but get the feeling like she's alone in a deep, ancient forest on a moonless night . . .

'What . . . what orders would you have, sir?' asks Mishra.

'Do you have assets in Ghaladesh?' asks the voice, cold and fierce.

'Yes. I can reach out to them with the Frost of Bolshoni. I've become somewhat adept at it.' *Being as I have to do it about thirty to sixty times a day*, thinks Mishra, *to maintain the mirrors*.

'Can they respond quickly?'

'Quite quickly, sir.'

'How many? Ten? Twenty?'

'I think I have twelve ready contacts, sir.'

'Good. mobilise all of them.'

'Um. All of them?'

'Yes. And do they have access to the trunk full of soil?' says the voice. 'The one we sent along?'

'Yes, sir, they do, but . . . Are you saying you wish to *personally* approach this man?'

'Yes, if I can,' says the voice. 'I have questions for him – if he survives that long. He's in Saypur, which makes it difficult for me . . . Even though I have grown since my last encounter with him, I still cannot extend my influence far beyond the Continent. But he knew Komayd. And one of the *others* interrupted my time with him. He is valuable, I'm sure of it. We must treat him with the utmost precaution. Tell them to use the trunk to prepare all entrances and exits to the Komayd estate.'

'Certainly, sir. Shall I keep watch on him through the mirror?'

'Yes. And if he tries to leave, stall him if you can.'

'Yes, sir.' As Nokov seems so interested, she opts not to tell him that she might have been seen in the mirror. *We'll just cross that bridge if we come to it.* 'And . . . for the assets and contractors you wish to mobilise . . .'

'Yes?'

'They will expect payment, sir.'

'Oh. Right. Yes.' The voice pauses, as if he'd forgotten about this inconvenience. 'How much? And to which bank accounts or locations?'

She gives him the amounts and the accounts.

'One moment,' says the voice.

There's a pause. The flicker of faint, white stars up above, pinpricks of luminescence that somehow fail to illuminate anything.

Then the voice is back. 'It is done,' he says. 'As you said. I have also provided you with a sum, in case you need to deal with any . . . irregularities.'

'Thank you, sir. I'll proceed shortly. And, ah, one last thing?'

'Yes?'

'The Ministry officers there at the Komayd estate?'

'Yes?'

'What should we do with them?'

'Oh.' A pause. 'Well. I don't see another option but to kill them.'

Mishra winces. 'I see. Yes, sir.'

'I mean, do you? Do you see another option?'

'I . . . No. I don't think so, sir. Not if this man is that valuable.'

'Yes.' A pause. 'Mishra . . .'

'Yes, sir?'

'Do you still believe our actions are for the good? That what we are
accomplishing here is necessary?'

From his tone, she understands he is not interrogating her: this is a genuine question, as if he'd like to hear her thoughts. 'I believe I do, sir.'

'The Divinities failed,' he says. 'Now Saypur has failed. You know that.
It is just a long, grand cycle of suffering. Someone must end it. I shall take
up that task, if no one else will. I never thought it'd be easy. It will test me.
And it will test you. Do you see?'

'I see. I think I see, sir.'

'Good. That is good.'

Then silence. It's difficult to tell, as it always is with him, when he's
really gone.

She opens the door to leave. Light floods in. She's alone in the tiny room.
Except now there are three items on the floor at her feet, items that definitely weren't there before.

One item is a large burlap sack full of silver drekels – probably a thousand of them or so. The other two items are solid gold bars, about ten
pounds each, at least.

She sighs. She appreciates the payments he gives her, being as it's a fortune every single time – she just wishes he paid her in ways that were easier
to hand in at the bank.

*

Sigrud is very accustomed to moving through the homes and spaces of other people. He's operated beyond the normal boundaries of law and property for so long that the idea of ownership has faded and blurred for him. If he can grab anything, or break into anywhere, then it's difficult for him to imagine a real reason not to do so.

Yet he feels a powerful violation here, here in the living quarters of his friend.

Her books, worn but cared-for. A half-finished painting she'd made of a pair of hands – Tatyana's? – peeling an apple with a knife. Stacks of letters to friends and confidants, none in code, not that they needed it: these are all innocent inquiries and missives, letters of 'how are you' and 'doing fine, thanks' and 'oh my goodness she's gotten so big.'

And then there are the pictures. Sigrud leans close to one, staring at the woman – and the child – trapped behind the glass, arms thrown about each other as they laugh, unable to bear the ridiculousness of posing for a picture . . .

By the seas, he thinks, *is that old woman really you, Shara?*

He stares at her lined skin, her greying hair – prematurely white, surely. The effects of office. Her eyes are still the same, though, large and dark, magnified behind her bulky spectacles. He imagines that, though he hadn't seen her in a decade and a half, she still looked at the world the same way.

But he looks closer at the girl next to her.

It's a very curious thing. Tatyana, maybe six in this photo, is obviously adopted: the pale white skin and brown hair, cut in a short, modern bob, make that very clear. Her nose is a little sharp and pointed in a way he finds strangely familiar, yet he can't place it. But the way she stands, the dresses she wears – all of it is so much like Shara that it's disorienting to him. It's as if this little girl wished so much to be like her adopted mother that she took on all of her physical mannerisms.

And the love in their eyes . . . That is very real. He doesn't think he's ever seen Shara make such a face in his life.

I should not have come here, he thinks, ashamed. *This place is theirs . . . I should have let it sleep.*

He keeps walking, moving silently from room to room.

A half-empty bottle of plum wine. A handful of rings soaking in a cup of cleaner. A bundle of yarn and crochet needles, unused – a hobby picked up but never pursued. Fragments of a life interrupted.

He pauses at Shara's room. It feels deeply dishonest to do so, but he steps inside. He looks at the books on the desk, and notes one in particular, very worn and stained: *Collected Essays Upon the Divine*, by Dr. Efrem Pangyui.

Sigrud thinks, then picks up the book and holds it. Then, operating off of a hunch, he holds the book above the table, spine facing down, and lets it fall.

The spine of the book clunks into the table, and the covers fall open. For a moment the pages hang in the air, unsure where to fall, but then they part . . .

And the book falls open to a well-annotated page, one that Shara must have looked at a lot, slowly breaking the bindings. Sigrud smirks, pleased to see this trick actually work – he wasn't at all convinced it would – and reads:

> . . . *perhaps dozens of Divine offspring, if not hundreds, or thousands. And each offspring was naturally granted with a domain of reality that was affected by the domains of their Divine parents. For example, Lisha, the daughter of Olvos and Jukov, was a spirit of all fruiting trees, thus making her a creature of hope, like her mother – for who has more hope and anticipation than a farmer awaiting a crop? – and a creature of wildness and excess, like her father, as fruit ferments into wine.*
>
> *There was one Divine offspring, however, whose domain is unclear, and was particularly dreaded and feared in the Continental texts, so much so that the Divinities defaulted to a common tactic of theirs: they edited history and memory, preventing all mention of this offspring from persisting to this day. We do not even know the being's name or its parentage.*
>
> *But we do know some things. One is that the offspring's domain was apparently so vast that it somehow threatened the original six Divinities themselves. There have been numerous ideas about exactly what this offspring's domain could have been – the sun, death, perhaps motion itself – but we have no real way of confirming this.*
>
> *Regardless, the original six Divinities, fearing disruption, took an unusual action: they mutilated the child horribly, crippling it. Exactly what they did is*

also unclear — vivisection and amputation are both mentioned — but as with all things Divine, one cannot be sure if this is metaphorical or literal. But this mutilation, whatever it was, weakened the offspring terribly, and prevented it from threatening reality ever again.

As with many of the Divine children, we are forced to conclude that the Kaj either successfully slaughtered this being during the Continental holocaust, or perhaps the being perished during the Blink. But I note that we are forced to conclude this solely because we have not witnessed any evidence of its existence as of today. We know little about the original Divinities, but we know even less of their children, who were often too unimportant to record, except perhaps for this one child, who was too important to put to paper.

Sigrud stands in Shara's room, thunderstruck.

It all begins to make a terrible sense to him.

'Holy hells,' he whispers. He slowly sits down on the bed.

The two beings he encountered in the slaughterhouse must not have been true Divinities, but *children* of Divinities. This would be why the Continental girl had such queer control over the past, and the other, the thing in the shadows, had such control over darkness: they each had their specific domains, which would naturally come with boundaries and strictures.

But how could they have *survived*? He supposes that, since they are very much like a Divinity, then the only way to kill them would be with the Kaj's black lead — the last piece of which was held by Shara. Yet what she's done with it he has no idea.

He scratches the stubble on his chin as he thinks. *So this Divine child, this Nokov, was fighting a war. Perhaps one against Shara, or one Shara had waded into. But a war over what? And why target Continental adolescents? Why send Khadse out to track down children and teenagers?*

He slowly leans forward, elbows on his knees.

Unless, of course — the Continental children he targeted were not really just children.

He remembers the girl from the slaughterhouse, desperately gasping: *He's killed so many of us, and now he might have me . . .*

The gods are dead, thinks Sigrud. *And when a ruler dies, what happens? The children fight over the kingdom, eliminating competition*. It's all so startlingly clear now. Perhaps some of these Divine children hid themselves away, pretending to be average, to be normal, to be mortal. But if you wish to rule your parents' territory, you must be thorough. Every scrap of your family must be eradicated except for you.

He glances back at the page and reads one line that's been repeatedly underlined: *There was one Divine offspring, however, whose domain is unclear, and was particularly dreaded and feared in the Continental texts . . .*

He remembers the scraping and shifting sounds in the shadows, the cold voice whispering in his ear: *What I can do will make murder feel like a wondrous blessing . . .*

He shudders. *I must find Tatyana*, he thinks.

Though now he worries about her too. If some of these children were just pretending to be normal, then . . .

No, he thinks. *It could not be. I saw her as a child, as a little girl. She was hardly more than a toddler. Surely she has aged and grown like any other mortal?*

He walks down to Tatyana's end of the quarters. He expected something strange, something curious, but he finds it is . . . very average. A bed. Some books, all more or less intended for children or young people. Lots of books and papers about economics, which is a little odd – but not *that* odd, he supposes. It does not look like the bedroom of a child of the Divinities, in other words.

He shakes his head. *You're going mad with paranoia. Focus on finding her before worrying about such foolishness.*

He walks farther down the hallway and comes to the kitchen. It has a gas oven – a rare luxury – and a small, modest table. A drying rack, still full of dishes. Bottles of plum and very potent apple liquor. He peers into the rubbish bin by the far wall. Not much inside: a few napkins, a cracked jar.

Sitting on the counter above the bin is a folded-up newspaper. He glances at it, and sees it's old – very old, nearly two years.

Which means Shara kept it . . . but why?

He picks it up. The paper's folded back so that whoever was holding it was reading one page, the financial section, and it looks as if they were paying attention to one article in particular. He reads it carefully, wondering if it could have mattered to Shara.

Then his eye falls across one name that sounds familiar, something about land purchases outside the walls of Bulikov:

. . . however, the deal has been consistently blocked by Ivanya Restroyka, the largest shareholder of the trust company, who refuses to break up any of the parcels for sale, though she has refused to comment on exactly why. Despite having the reputation of being a recluse, Restroyka has consistently been an active and forceful figure in Bulikovian real estate – regardless of whether that real estate lies inside or outside the city's walls.

Sigrud cocks his head, thinking.

Restroyka . . . He knows that name. Doesn't he? He massages his forehead as he thinks. The Ministry trained him for this, trained him to learn how to compartmentalise and then access his memories when needed . . .

And then it comes to him.

Smoke, wine, a fire. A party. Years ago, in Bulikov, before the Battle. Shara had been there, as had Mulaghesh – the first time he'd ever met her. And the man who had been throwing the party . . .

'Vohannes Votrov,' Sigrud says quietly.

Speaking the name aloud summons up his face: a handsome Continental man, with curly, brown-red hair and a closely cropped red beard. His jaw is strong, his smile bright, and his blue eyes have an equal measure of confidence and wildness to them.

Sigrud takes a breath as the memories come flooding back to him. Votrov had been Shara's ex-lover, a Continental construction magnate who'd died during the Battle of Bulikov. Sigrud had not been there to see him die, but Shara had, and the trauma had been terrible for her. The man had given everything for his city, for his nation, for the future he wished to build. Sigrud knows that sacrifice wore off on Shara, catalysing her to return to Ghaladesh and try to genuinely change things.

Which she had. Though they killed her for it. Much as the Divinities had Votrov.

But Votrov had been engaged before the Battle, to a woman. A girl, really, barely in her twenties. A pretty young Continental thing who wore entirely too much make-up. He remembers meeting her at the party, how she laughed in delight at the sight of him, thinking him – a crude, glowering Dreyling – to be a tremendous amusement.

'Ivanya Restroyka,' he says quietly.

He keeps reading the article. To his surprise, he finds that Restroyka is now one of the richest people in the world. *If she inherited all of Votrov's money*, thinks Sigrud, *then she is probably the richest Continental alive by leaps and bounds*.

Why would Shara keep a two-year-old article about Restroyka?

He remembers Shara's message: *She is with the one woman who has ever shared my love.*

The sight of Vohannes's face swims up in his memories again.

You were Shara's only love, he thinks, *at least as far as I know. And what other woman shared you* . . .

'Could Tatyana Komayd,' he says aloud, 'be hiding with your ex-fiancée?'

Sigrud paces back down the hallway, checking each room. He finds nothing more, no sign of a struggle or hidden secrets. Just two women living their lives, hidden from society.

He thinks about Restroyka as he paces from room to room. She's surely not a girl anymore; she must be in her forties or fifties by now. The more he considers it, the more he's sure he's right: if Shara was so intent on building up the Continent's economy during her time in office, who else would she speak to but the Continent's foremost millionaire? One with whom she had a personal connection, to boot? *And perhaps they became allies*, thinks Sigrud, walking toward the stairs. *Allies close enough that, if Shara needed to hide her daughter, she felt she could reach out, and ask* . . .

It's all still theoretical. But it's also all he has.

'Time to get the hells out of here,' he says, starting up the stairs and switching off his torch.

He comes to the dining area, trots down the hall, and heads toward the glass doors leading to the back patio, and the stream beyond.

He places a hand on the doorknob. Then he hears a voice behind him: 'You're not leaving so soon, are you?'

He leaps to the side, whirls, and pulls out his knife, readying himself for an attack . . . though now that he looks, there's no one in the entry hall with him.

A burst of laughter. A voice says: 'My, my, you're quite high-strung, aren't you? You know what you need? A vacation.'

Sigrud cocks his head. Then he stands and stalks over to the mirror hanging on the wall.

As he approaches, a face comes into view: a middle-aged Saypuri woman with curiously amber eyes. She smiles at him, an expression that's a mixture of pity and mockery.

He looks at the mirror. *The Frost of Bolshoni*, he thinks. *The very miracle Shara and Vinya used so often . . .*

'You know what this is, don't you?' says the woman. Her Saypuri accent is guttural, unrefined, from some rural area like Tohmay. She wears a thick coat and scarf. 'You've seen this before.'

He steps forward, putting his face right up to the mirror, peering in at her room.

'Are you so taken with me?' she says, smirking. 'If so, you're terribly forward, sir.'

He ignores her, craning his head up and looking inside the reflection, taking in the desk beneath the mirror . . . and the walls on either side, which are also covered in mirrors. His eye widens: the mirrors are all depicting things happening throughout Saypur and the Continent, places like the prime minister's mansion and the Bulikovian Chamber for the City Fathers.

They've been performing the Frost on a level I've never seen before, he thinks. *A window in every important room in Saypur, or the Continent . . .*

The woman is startled by this – she obviously didn't expect him to take advantage of the two-way connection – and pulls the mirror off the wall. 'Now, now,' she says. 'Let's not get nosy.' He watches, feeling slightly nauseous, as the view pivots wildly. She walks with the mirror to a darkened room.

He can glimpse the ceiling as she does so – he notes the oak, the limestone, the blooming patches of mould.

'I know you, don't I?' says the woman. 'Yes . . . I saw you in Voortyashtan, ages ago. You're the *dauvkind*, aren't you? You're the gutless

Dreyling son of a bitch who killed those soldiers.' She laughs again, but there's a touch of anger to it. 'I usually enjoy my work, but I'll enjoy seeing you dead a little more than usua –'

'Ahanashtan,' he says.

'Mm? What's that?'

'You're in Ahanashtan,' he says.

'Oh? And what makes you so sure?'

'The limestone,' says Sigrud. 'And the red oak. Both common there. And your scarf. Still quite warm in Saypur. And you're not Ministry, are you.'

She smirks. 'What makes you say that?'

'Because if you were,' says Sigrud, 'you'd have signalled to your operators working outside, and I would be dead.'

'Oh, that's a good point. But you're still dead.'

Sigrud looks at the windows. No movement. He gives the woman a cocked eyebrow.

'You can't run from him,' she says. 'He's everywhere. He's in everything. Wherever there's darkness, wherever light doesn't reach . . . That's where he is.'

'Then why isn't he here?' asks Sigrud. 'The shadows are thick. Where is your master's whisper?'

Then he hears it: the distant, throaty *boom* of what he's sure is a scatter-gun.

Sigrud looks toward the front door, concerned.

The woman laughs. 'There,' she says. 'That's where it is!'

Sigrud thinks rapidly. *Ministry operators don't use scatter-guns.* There's another deep *boom.* It's from the north, he thinks, toward the estate gates. *So whoever's out there isn't Ministry . . . So who are they shooting at?*

The woman grins at him. 'See?' she says. 'I told you you were dead.'

Sigrud smashes the mirror with one fist. Then he runs back to the glass doors before the patio. He crouches, peering out, and then he hears it: the harsh *pop-pop* of small-arms fire, south of the estate.

'They're all around me, aren't they?' he says. 'She was stalling me.'

He rubs his chin, wondering what in the hells to do. She must have seen him enter the mansion, then alerted a team to his location. *How many,* he says, *I don't know . . . But enough to take on four or five Ministry operatives placed all around the estate walls.* And all he has is a waterproof torch and a knife.

He looks around the room, which is totally empty, trying to think of ways he could use the windows, the doors, the drapes, the lamps . . .

He stares at one gold sconce. *The gas lamps.*

He thinks about it. It's an idea, certainly, but . . .

Just once, he thinks, *I would like to think of a solution that does not involve me nearly blowing myself up.*

He runs downstairs. Not much time now. The estate is big, so it'll take time for his assailants to cross to the main house, but he probably has only a handful of minutes.

He sprints down the servants' quarters to Shara's kitchen. He grabs the bottles of plum and apple liquor, about ten of them, and tosses them into the oven. Then he shuts the oven and turns the dial up to high. He hears the little gas jets inside flick on and hiss.

This is a stupid idea, he thinks. But he doesn't stop.

He sprints through the servants' quarters, turning all the gas lamps up as high as they go but not lighting them. Instead they just keep hissing, filling the hallway with a reeking stench, the air trembling as the fumes keep pouring in.

They'll have the doors watched, he thinks. *And the windows. So how to get outside?*

He runs upstairs and turns on all the gas lamps in the entry hall. Then, remembering the layout of the estate – *It's got a second floor*, he remembers, *with wooden walls* – he runs down the main hallway, finds a grand, twisting staircase, and runs upstairs.

He runs east, away from the servants' quarters, sprinting past grand bedrooms and salons, all empty. He pauses at one room and creeps over to the window. He braces himself, then peeks out.

He can see the long gravel driveway stretching north to the gates. There are figures walking down the lawn toward the house in a broad formation, sweeping the grounds.

He narrows his eye, trying to see how they're armed, when there's a sudden *crack!* noise.

The glass just above his head explodes. Something cracks into the wooden wall behind him. Sigrud, startled, jumps away, then covers his head as more bullets come cracking through the window, chewing up the frame and the far wall.

Sigrud crawls toward the door, then rolls into the hallway, breathing hard. *Okay*, he thinks. *So. They are pretty good.*

But that should draw them into the house. They'll think he's cornered upstairs now.

He keeps running east down the hall, though now he makes sure to stay clear of the windows. He slaps his head, trying to remember how close the stream came to the house. When he comes to the far bedroom he drops to all fours and crawls across the floor until he's clear of the window.

He stands when he gets to the bedroom wall, tapping it as he walks its length, listening. *There was a tree out there*, he thinks. *Out there somewhere close . . . At least, I'm pretty sure there was a tree, and the stream beside it.* If he's wrong, then this will go quite spectacularly bad.

Finally he knocks on the wall and hears a hollow *thump*. He nods – sweat pours off his nose with the motion – and he pulls out his knife. Then he begins stabbing at the wood and plaster in a messy line, a drunken, perforated seam. He almost laughs with relief when he sees moonlight shining through the holes.

A crash from downstairs. The chatter of gunfire. *Clearing the room*, he thinks. *Just in case I was hiding behind the door.*

Once he's stabbed a wide, messy circle in the wall, he sheathes his knife, steps back, takes a deep breath, and runs at it.

He lowers his shoulder, pushes forward, and . . .

Crunch.

The wall falls away like a trapdoor. The next thing he knows he's tumbling through the night air, then through leaves. Then he's stopped sharply by a tree branch, which crashes into his left side very, very painfully. He almost cries out, but he keeps his senses. He's dangling in the air, exposed to everyone, and he needs to get to the stream below.

They must have heard the sound, he thinks. *They had to have. Hurry. Hurry . . .*

Groaning with pain, Sigrud drops from branch to branch, trying to descend in a controlled plummet. His side complains each time – probably a cracked rib, but there's no time for that. He can hear someone shouting on the west side of the grounds, and then gunfire, and something hot and angry parts the air above him . . .

He hits the ground and rolls.

Run. Run.

He sprints for the stream and dives into it. As he dives he sees there was someone guarding it – *They must have known I came from the stream*, he thinks as he falls – and watches out of the side of his eye as they raise a rifling . . .

He plunges deep down into the stream, trying to hug the walls. Soft pops from above. Bullets zip through the moonlit waters, leaving tiny, delicate chains of bubbles.

Sigrud curls into a ball and tries to stuff himself up under a tree root. His side is screaming and his lungs are bursting, as he didn't take nearly as deep a breath as he should have.

More bullets zip through the waters, curving down in strangely graceful motions. Sigrud waits.

Did my trap work? he thinks. *Did it fizzle out or will i –*

Then the world above goes bright.

Everything seems to shake. The tree above groans, twists, sags, and Sigrud suddenly wonders if it was wise to take shelter under the root of a tree directly beside a building he was intending to blow up.

He shoves himself out, swimming away. The water fills with silt and soil. The explosion, impossibly, keeps going on, a never-ending roar and a bright orange light filtering through the cloudy water. The surface above sizzles as flaming detritus patters across the stream.

I need air, he thinks, growing faint. *Only I hope there is air up there for me to breathe . . .*

He waits. And waits. And waits.

Finally the roar seems to subside, and he swims up to the surface and hauls himself to the shore.

The world is bright and broiling. He draws a deep, gasping breath, and his ribs painfully creak with the inhalation. His breath catches and he starts coughing, which only hurts him worse.

He blinks and looks behind him. The house is a raging inferno. Steam is suddenly pouring off of his arms and legs as the heat boils the moisture out of his clothing.

Sigrud glances around with watering eyes and sees a smoking human form lying about fifteen feet from the stream. He staggers over to it – it's a woman, very dead – and pulls the rifling from her hands. He hopes it's still in working condition.

He looks around at the wreckage but can't see anyone. *Better to find out now*, he thinks, *rather than later*. He confirms the rifling's loaded, figures that the sound of the fire is loud enough to muffle any gunshot, and points the rifling at the water and pulls the trigger.

The rifling jumps in his hands and discharges neatly and cleanly. He reloads, sinks low, and looks back down the river, toward the wall. Most of the gardens are on fire and some of the smaller trees have collapsed into the water, so he doubts if he can go out the way he came in. He hugs the estate wall and makes his way north toward the front gates, where he knows the mercenaries likely wiped out the Ministry operatives – hopefully leaving the way clear.

Once he's a little north of the house he stoops beside a hedge – which is flaming like a torch – and surveys his work. If it were any other structure, any other place, he'd take a professional pleasure in its utter destruction; but this was Shara's ancestral home, the place where she raised her child.

He watches as the western roof collapses with a *crunch*. 'I am sorry, Shara,' he whispers.

He approaches the gate, one half of which hangs open. He can see the Ministry auto beyond, riddled with bullet holes, three human forms slumped over in the seats. The ground around the gate is curiously dark – it's like someone laid mulch while the mercenaries approached – but besides that he can't see anyone.

He stoops down beside a large stone and sets the rifling's sights on the gate. Then he lets out a loud groan and calls out, using a rough approximation of a Saypuri accent: 'Are you there? We're hurt! He's dead, but we're hurt!'

Nothing.

Sigrud cries, 'Please! *Please!*'

Still nothing for a bit.

Then a man's head pokes around the corner.

Sigrud puts his finger on the trigger and fires. There's a spray of blood and the man falls to the ground.

He waits for a good five minutes, not moving a muscle. There's silence except for the roaring fire behind him. Then he stands, sweeps to the left, crossing before the half-open gate and scanning the drive out front for any movement.

He knows he'll be vulnerable as he exits, if there's anyone left out there – which he doubts, but you can never be sure. *Slip through the gate*, he thinks, *take cover next to the guard's corpse, and watch for any other assailants.*

He creeps up, walking along the wall toward the open gate. He keeps his rifling trained on the husk of an auto, which is where he'd be hunkered down if it were him out there.

He creeps forward, taking one step, then another, then another . . . Then finally he wheels out, rifling ready – only to find the driveway empty, the scene totally still. Just corpses in the auto, and nothing else.

But then he realises something. The intense blaze from the burning home has been so consistent he's almost stopped noticing it for the past ten minutes. Yet now as he crosses the gate, the heat fades behind him, the stupefying, broiling warmth abruptly dwindling as if a giant had come along and blown out the fire much as one would a candle flame.

Sigrud pauses. He stays close to the gate. Then he looks behind him.

The fire is gone. No, more than that – the *house* is gone. The landscape of the estate has faded into darkness behind him, like a cloud passed before the moon and darkened out all light above.

No, it's even more than that: the world simply stops thirty feet south of where he stands.

Sigrud whirls around, wondering what in hells is going on now, and tries to seek shelter against the wall – but the wall isn't there. There's nothing around him but darkness – except for the gates, bizarrely enough. The gates appear to hang on nothing, big rib cages of iron dangling in the air, one half in an open position, the other half closed. There's nothing beyond them. Just a wall of black.

Then the closed half of the gate opens, its hinges whining softly, as if pushed from behind.

Sigrud whips the rifling up. He keeps it trained on the entryway, unsure what to look for.

Then he sees them. Eyes in the darkness. Eyes like those of a cat, just barely caught by the light. Or perhaps they're like tiny, distant white stars . . .

He fires. He fires the rifling at the eyes once, twice, three times, four, five . . . Then he stops, conscious of his ammunition.

He waits.

The eyes blink, very slowly. Then they begin to advance, one step at a time.

And as they approach they seem to pass some kind of barrier, and a face appears around the eyes: a young man's face, pale and starved, with ink-black hair and a skinny neck. At first it seems like the young man's head is hanging in the air just as the iron gates are, but then Sigrud sees that he's wearing what appear to be black robes, which ripple despite the lack of any wind. And as the young man approaches, Sigrud begins hearing many strange things . . .

Chirrups and distant rustlings and a curious, arrhythmic tap-tapping. Small stones falling down a slope; the shiver of leaves; the groan of trees; the slow drip of water. Sigrud suppresses a shiver as he hears them: they make him feel like he's alone in the woods at night, listening to countless invisible watchers circling him.

A thought strikes him as he realises this.

Circling me . . .

He looks down. The gates are not quite the only thing persisting in this vast darkness: there's a wide patch of earth at his feet, the mulch he saw earlier.

'Continental soil,' says the young man, and his high, cold voice is instantly familiar to Sigrud. 'It helps me assert myself across the South Seas, you see.'

Sigrud looks at him. 'Nokov.'

The young man smiles slightly and nods. 'Few would dare to say that word aloud. Were I not here already with you . . .'

Sigrud smiles back. Then he starts shooting again.

*

There are only two rounds left in the rifling. They don't seem to do anything to Nokov: it's like Sigrud's firing blanks, or like the bullets vanish the instant they leave the barrel.

Sigrud looks at the empty rifling, grimaces, and hurls it at Nokov. The rifling passes right through him like he's made of smoke.

Nokov blinks, slightly perturbed. 'That was not really necessary.'

Sigrud ignores him, pulls out his knife with his right hand, and lunges at Nokov, slashing and stabbing at the boy. Nokov frowns – again, an expression of the slightest inconvenience – and seems to flicker away each time, evaporating before the blade even comes close to him.

Despite this, Sigrud doesn't give up. He's killed Divine creatures with this blade before, so he's determined to at least try again. Panting and wincing as his ribs creak, he dives at Nokov over and over again.

Finally Nokov sighs. 'Enough,' he says.

A frail, white hand flicks out. His knuckles graze Sigrud's cheek . . .

It's like he's been hit by a stack of bricks plummeting out of the sky. Sigrud crashes to the muddy soil below him, his damaged side shrieking in pain. His knife falls from his grasp and all the air is driven from his body. He tries to roll over but he doesn't even have the strength for it.

'This is my place,' says Nokov calmly. 'You can't harm me here. You can't escape from me here. I can do whatever I'd like to you.'

Nokov stoops and grasps Sigrud under his jaw. Though Nokov appears to be a young man just barely out of adolescence, he lifts all two hundred and seventy pounds of Sigrud like he's no more than a child's stuffed animal. He slaps at Nokov's wrist with his right hand, but his fingers pass right through as if the boy's limb isn't even there. His ribs on his left side yammer and yowl as he's lifted up, and he's forced to keep his left arm awkwardly pinned to his torso, which twists him and makes him gag in Nokov's grasp.

Nokov stares into Sigrud's reddening face. His eyes are hooded in shadow, as if no matter where he stood they'd be lost in darkness. Yet Sigrud can see two very distant specks of light glimmering from somewhere deep within his skull . . .

'Where are the others?' asks Nokov softly. 'Where are they hiding?'

Sigrud has no idea what he's talking about, but he taps his throat, signaling he cannot talk.

Nokov frowns and removes his hand. Sigrud, however, keeps dangling in the air, as if he's hung on invisible strings.

Sigrud stares down at himself, hanging several feet above the ground. *Are you so sure*, he thinks, *that he is not a Divinity? He certainly seems capable of changing reality at his will* . . .

'Tell me,' says Nokov.

'Tell you what?' gasps Sigrud.

'You work with the others. That is clear. So where are they? Where are they hiding from me?'

'W-What?'

'What function do they use? Which wrinkle in reality do they hide behind?'

Sigrud wonders what to say. He only got into this because of Shara's death. But he suspects Nokov might be looking for these other Divine children. Including Tatyana Komayd, whom Nokov likely believes to be one of them – and he'll be damned if he gives Nokov her location.

Keep him talking.

Sigrud wheezes and says, 'You . . . You killed Shara, didn't you? You paid Khadse to.'

Nokov just watches Sigrud, his face queerly clean of emotion.

'Why?' says Sigrud. 'What threat could she have posed to you?'

'Threat?' Nokov's tone is politely puzzled. 'I hated her, certainly. Just as I hated her aunt. But she was no threat to me.'

'Then why kill her?'

'She was . . . a requirement. A step in a process, I should say.' The distant stars in his eyes seem to flare, just ever so slightly. 'It is, after all, a terribly complicated thing, to kill a god.'

'Was it for Tatyana?' asks Sigrud. 'Is that why you did it? First you kill the parents, then you target the child?'

'Why pretend to be so foolish?' asks Nokov. 'You work with them, you worked with her. You know what it is I hunger for.' He leans closer. 'I will find them. And I will devour them. You know this. It is inevitable.'

'Tatyana Komayd,' says Sigrud, 'is not Divine.'

Nokov laughs. 'I almost believe you when you say it.'

'I do believe that.'

'Perhaps so. But have you *seen* her?'

'What do y —'

'Enough of this,' snaps Nokov. 'Tell me. Tell me where the others are.'

Sigrud tries to think. His left side throbs, yet his left hand aches even more. It's an old pain, a familiar one, but it's at an intensity he hasn't felt in a long time: his hand hasn't hurt this bad since the days when it was first maimed in prison . . . or, he realises, when he was this close to a Divinity.

'I'll find them eventually,' says Nokov. The boy steps closer. 'They can't hide forever. Each one I find, I grow stronger and stronger.' He leans forward, his queer dark eyes like deep chasms in his face. 'They *will* dwell within me eventually. It's just a matter of time. And once they do, I will right all the countless wrongs that have been done in this world. I will right them, one by one. A just world. A *moral* world. That is what I will make.'

Sigrud remembers what the pale Continental girl told him: *When he catches you, he'll pull out every secret you've got hidden away in your guts*.

Sigrud realises that, though he's been captured before, he's never been captured by a Divinity.

I'm going to die here, aren't I?

'I can dash you against all the stones of this world,' whispers Nokov fiercely, 'and make it so that you stay alive, feeling each burst of pain, each crack of rock. And when I have broken every bone in your body, I will find some forgotten shadow deep within the world, and I will leave you there, forever. Do you hear me? I will visit every pain and every torture upon your head that was visited upon *mine*. Do you understand me?'

Sigrud hears him. *If I am to die*, he thinks, *I should at least die without telling him a thing*.

He shuts his eyes.

He thinks of the ocean. Of the waves, alternately harsh and gentle, spreading themselves out across smooth white sands. And the smell of salt on the air . . .

He opens his eyes. 'Jukov.'

Nokov blinks. 'What?'

'Jukov,' says Sigrud. His voice is hoarse and raspy. 'He was your father, wasn't he? You are a child of Divinities, aren't you?'

Nokov's face darkens.

'Jukov could bear a grudge,' says Sigrud. 'And like you he was a wild, dark thing . . . I know. Because I saw him. I was there when the last shred of him died.' He grins. 'I was the one who piloted a ship full of explosives right into his face. Did you know that?'

Nokov's lip curls. 'Enough,' he says. 'Tell me. Tell me everything you know!'

'I destroyed his army,' says Sigrud. 'It was me. He and Kolkan made their army, but I dashed it all to pieces with but a single broadside.'

'Shut up,' says Nokov.

'They were mad,' says Sigrud. 'But even mad gods couldn't hold a candle to the modern world . . .'

'Shut up!' cries Nokov. He snatches Sigrud out of the air and slams him to the ground, both hands around his throat. The impact is like being run over by a train. 'You shut your mouth!'

Do it, thinks Sigrud. *Kill me. Kill me before you torture me into telling you a thing.*

He can barely speak, but he manages to laugh and gasp, 'He was barely Jukov anymore by then . . . He made such a mistake, you see. Imprisoning himself with Kolkan, he was crushed into him, the two smashed together over decades . . .'

'Shut up!' says Nokov. He picks Sigrud up by the throat and slams him down again.

Sigrud coughs and says. 'Your father was barely recognisable . . . It was almost all Kolkan, at the end . . .'

'*You shut up!*' cries Nokov. His face twisted in adolescent fury, he raises his right hand to bring it down on Sigrud's skull with a devastating blow.

Sigrud thinks of the ocean.

He thinks of Signe's face, bathed in the dawning sun, the day when he and she swore to rebuild Voortyashtan. How proud he was of her, and she of him.

Do it, he thinks. *Just do it.*

Yet as Nokov's hand comes hurtling down at him, Sigrud can't resist his training: even though it's sure to do nothing, he reaches out with his left hand, his side screaming in pain, and tries to block the boy's blow.

Nokov's hand flies down at him with all the speed of a lightning bolt.

Sigrud's left hand rises . . .

And catches the boy's fist.

Nokov blinks, startled, and stares at his hand, which is now held in Sigrud's grasp.

Sigrud frowns, confused. Previously when Nokov touched him it was either like being struck by a falling tree or trying to grab smoke. But now Sigrud's left hand holds Nokov's right fist, and it definitely feels . . .

Well, *human*. It feels like the fist of a very young man. And, he notes, it didn't feel like some superhuman punch when he grabbed Nokov's fist: rather, it felt like a teenager's awkward, ungainly swing.

Nokov looks positively alarmed. 'What . . . How did you do that?' He tugs at his hand. Sigrud's grip holds fast. 'How . . . What's going on?'

Sigrud doesn't know. But he knows that it feels like he's holding a flesh-and-blood hand in his.

So he squeezes it. Hard.

Nokov gags, shocked, and releases his hold on Sigrud's neck, trying to use his free hand to pull away.

But Sigrud holds fast. He keeps squeezing, his big, hard fingers crushing Nokov's skinny, frail fist.

Nokov cries out in pain. He falls to his knees. 'Stop!' he pleads. The cry is so plaintive, so pathetic, Sigrud is almost taken aback by it.

Hold on to your rage, thinks Sigrud. *Remember what he did to you.*

'*Stop!*'

Shara, thinks Sigrud. A black rage begins to fill him, a familiar one. *You killed Shara, boy* . . .

He feels his teeth grinding in fury, feels blood beginning to flood out of his nose. He thinks of Shara's house aflame, of Mulaghesh old and stooped and tired, of Khadse's neck, slashed open and pouring blood . . .

'Let me go!' screams Nokov. 'Let me go, let me go!'

Sigrud squeezes harder.

Something crackles unpleasantly in Nokov's right hand. The boy screams in agony. The shadows begin trembling all around them.

Nokov, howling, brings his free hand down on the ground.

The shadows break apart.

It's as if Sigrud were standing on top of a black glass surface and it just shattered underneath him. He lets go of Nokov and the boy seems to vanish, sinking back into an errant shard of shadow.

Sigrud falls.

That's what he *thinks* is happening, at least. It's hard to tell if you're falling when there are no air molecules hitting you. He realises he's falling through some kind of shadowy sub-space, probably not the reality he knows but the reality Nokov occupies and moves through. He knows this because he heard Shara talk about such things during his time with her – but though she described these facets of reality, she neglected to mention how to get *out* of them.

And he feels terribly cold. Terribly, terribly cold.

I am not supposed to be here, he thinks. *Mortals were never supposed to be in such a place . . .*

He looks down. Shards of broken shadow spin around him, different shades of black flittering across a deep darkness.

He shifts and twists, and tries to dive toward one big shard, as if he's aiming for a deep pool of water to break his fall.

He shuts his eyes, and . . .

He starts shooting up.

The temperature changes around him: it's no longer that queer, frigid void, but a chilly, clammy night. And Sigrud can tell he's flying up because the second he passes through that shard of darkness, gravity violently reasserts itself. He starts spinning around, catching glimpses of his surroundings – dark trees, leafy undergrowth, the moon above – before he starts falling *down* again, finally crashing to the cold, wet earth.

Sigrud lies on the ground, groaning. His left side feels like it is made of barbed wire. Then something shoots up out of a shadow beside him.

He can see it spinning and twirling in the air, moonlight gleaming on its black blade. He recognises it right away.

His eyes widen as his black knife rises high, and then starts falling back *down* – specifically, back down at him. He tries to move, but he's too weak.

The knife *thumps* into the soil about three feet to the left of Sigrud's head. He slowly turns his head to stare at it, and lets out a huge sigh.

Groaning and whimpering, Sigrud forces himself to sit up and look around.

He appears to be in a dark forest — and if he understands everything that just happened to him, it seems he got here by being ejected out of the shadow of a tall tree cast on the forest floor.

He remembers what the woman in the mirror said: *He's everywhere. He's in everything. Wherever there's darkness, wherever light doesn't reach . . . That's where he is.*

He rubs his aching face. His understanding of all this is rudimentary at best: but he suspects that Nokov resides in some shadowy sub-reality, one connected to all shadows everywhere. That would explain how he could hear his name being mentioned across the Continent, and how he could arrive instantaneously. It would also explain how Sigrud and his knife were just spat out of a shadow on the ground like a farmer spitting out pumpkin seeds.

He crawls over on all fours to pick up his knife. *At least this isn't the strangest thing that happened to me today.*

He shivers as he sheathes his knife. He feels cold and weak, as if his heart has dropped a few degrees while the rest of his body has stayed the same temperature. He tries to tell himself it's just shock, or perhaps a side effect of the injury done to his left side, where he is now certain that he's broken a rib or two.

It will pass, he thinks, shivering again. He flexes his fingers, listening to the knuckles crackle. *And it's a cold night. It will pass.*

He fashions a walking stick out of a sapling and uses it to stagger out of the forest. He can see he's on the Continent somewhere by the way his breath is frosting, but there's no telling exactly where on the Continent.

The forest ends and he comes to a stretch of farmland. Bales of hay glow silver and spectral under the moon. He looks at the sky, still shivering a little. He's heading west, if he's reading his stars right.

Before he starts off across the pasture, he pauses, pulls off the glove on his left hand, and looks at his palm.

The scar there shines in the moonlight. He can still remember that day in prison as if it was yesterday: the guards, cackling wickedly, goading the starving inmates to pick up what they claimed was just a little pebble, saying that whoever could hold it would be rewarded with food. Neither Sigrud nor the other prisoners knew it was the Divine tool of punishment known as the Finger of Kolkan, causing unbearable pain when touched to flesh. None of them knew how horribly it could harm them.

And yet he had done it. He'd succeeded. Sigrud had held the pebble, blood streaming through his fingers, for three minutes. It had scarred him forever, and its damage has never truly faded: though the pain has sometimes receded, it's never wholly gone.

He thinks about how it was his left hand that was able to grab Nokov and hurt him, not his right. And this isn't the first time his injury aided him: before the Battle of Bulikov, the touch of the Finger of Kolkan helped him carve his way out of the belly of a Divine monstrosity named Urav.

He stares at his palm. *What else was done to you in that prison? What else changed?*

He thinks on it, troubled. Then he pulls back on the glove and starts across the pasture. He shivers again and rubs his arms, trying to beat back the cold. Eventually he comes to a wooden fence and beyond it a road, running north–south. He walks south, since that's often where civilisation lies on the Continent. It's not too long before he sees a city in the distance, an orange halo of artificial light brightening the horizon.

He comes to a tiny intersection, finds a rickety wooden road sign, and reads the sign pointing south: AHANASHTAN.

He groans. *I did not want to come back here*, he thinks, limping in its direction. *I did not like approaching this town with money in my pocket and a pistol in my belt. I like it even less now that I'm injured, penniless, and almost completely unarmed.*

He glances back at the forest and thinks of the queer, dark, sub-reality of Nokov.

But it's better than the alternative.

He limps ahead. With each step, Nokov's words echo in his mind: *Where are the others? Where are they hiding?*

He trembles again. It's as if he has snowmelt in his veins. *Shara*, he thinks, *what were you doing here?*

7.
A Social Acquaintance

It is a fool who lives his life believing the waves upon which he sails shall remember him. The seas know nothing.
This makes them beautiful. And this makes them terrible.

— DREYLING PROVERB, ORIGIN UNKNOWN

It takes him most of the next day to hike back to Ahanashtan. He can't stop shivering, and by this point, he knows it's more than just the cold and his injury. Sigrud's swum through freezing water before and was raised within spitting distance of glaciers. He remembers having to crack through the ice at the top of his washing basin every morning as a child.

Cold he knows. And this isn't cold.

I really do not think, he says to himself as he limps onto a trolley bus, *that I was supposed to go to Nokov's . . . place. If it can even be called a place.*

He gets off at a telegram office. There he sends a message to Mulaghesh, using the instructions she provided, and awaits her call in a nearby phone booth.

He almost falls asleep as he waits. Then the phone blares to life, ringing so loudly that Sigrud nearly reaches for his knife. He takes the earpiece off the hook, then waits a moment, unsure what to do.

'Sigrud?' says Mulaghesh's voice. 'Are you there? Answer me, damn it!'

'I am here,' says Sigrud into the mouthpiece. 'Turyin, I –'

' "Am a fucking *idiot*"? Is that what you're going to say? I tell you Shara's address, and the next day you trot out there and detonate her house like it was a damn firewo –'

'Ivanya Restroyka,' says Sigrud. The words are little more than a gasp. He can't stop shaking, and suddenly it's very hard to talk.

'What?' says Mulaghesh. 'Huh? What in hells are you talking about?'

'The only woman to share Shara's love.' He swallows. 'That love being Vohannes Votrov.'

'You . . . Wait. You think Tatyana is with *Restroyka*? The richest damn woman *alive*?'

'If you were to hide your child with someone,' says Sigrud, 'wouldn't it be with a person of means?'

'Yeah, but, Sigrud . . . You sound like shit.'

'I know.' He swallows again. His teeth chatter a little. 'I saw him there. He surprised me. Attacked me.'

'He? He who?'

'Shara's enemy.'

'Wait. *Wait*. So you fought a *god*?'

'Yes. No. Sort of. I don't know.' He tries to explain what he put together about the Divine children, hiding away among the population of the Continent, as well as the woman with the golden eyes in the mirror.

'That doesn't make a damn bit of sense!' says Mulaghesh. 'How could they have survived? I thought the Kaj killed anything and everything Divine, children or not!'

'I don't know,' says Sigrud. 'But I think Shara's enemy, this person of darkness . . . I think he's wiping out his siblings one by one. He said something about devouring them, about hungering, making them reside inside him . . .'

'He sounds loony as fuck-all.'

'Well. Yes. But I think he . . . eats them, in a way. Absorbs them. And gets more powerful each time.'

'And the mirrors you mentioned . . .'

'Yes. Turyin . . . You *cannot* trust the Ministry. There are eyes and ears everywhere. Who knows who is on their side? Who knows what they've heard?' He stops. 'Wait. Where are you calling from now?'

'A secure line,' says Mulaghesh. 'And by that I mean the phone booth behind my favourite bar in the wrong part of town. If Ghaladesh even has a wrong part of town. I don't really think they would have put a mirror up here.'

'Assume nothing,' says Sigrud. 'Be as cautious as possible in everything you do. In searching for the *Salim* . . . or in helping me find where Restroyka is right now.'

'Ah, *shit*,' says Mulaghesh. She grumbles for a moment, then sighs. 'Well. You may be in luck. Restroyka throws around a lot of money, enough that people notice.'

'Such people including yourself?'

'Yeah. She donated to a few parliamentary campaigns a couple of years ago. Caused a minor scandal, what with her being, you know, not actually a resident or a Saypuri or anything, which then brought up the whole "sovereignty of the Continental states" subject, which is just a giant ongoing clusterfuck, as you are well aware.'

'Yes.'

'Anyways, I had to handle it. Had to do a bit of research on Miss Restroyka, not to mention send her a couple of trees' worth of correspondence. She's got some kind of sheep ranch in a little town just west of Ahanashtan – last I heard, that's where she operates out of. Apparently she's a total recluse. Never leaves the town, barely leaves the ranch. Sends a shitload of letters, though. Now – if I give you the name of the town, are you going to blow up her damn house too?'

'I guarantee nothing.'

'You know, you don't exactly inspire confidence, Sigrud.'

'I am just being honest. But I will try.'

Mulaghesh sighs again. 'Dhorenave. The name of the town is Dhorenave. Population of about two hundred. You'll stick out like a red turnip there, so be careful.'

'Thank you,' says Sigrud. He touches his brow and sees his fingertips are glistening with sweat. 'Thank you, Turyin.'

'You need to get some help, Sigrud,' says Mulaghesh. 'You sound terrible. Find a doctor. You talked about forgettable ends – seems like falling over dead in a phone booth would be mighty forgettable.'

Sigrud thanks her again and hangs up.

Stealing automobiles is second nature to Sigrud. So many operations required improvised or untraceable transportation that it became standard practice for Ministry officers to steal an auto, do their part of the operation, and then promptly drive the automobile into the nearest river. Sigrud suspects that he alone is probably the cause of hundreds of thousands of drekels of lost property.

Enough damage, he thinks as he cracks open the door of an old jalopy, *that one more won't make a difference.*

He climbs in, starts it, and pilots the coughing old wreck northwest, out of the city. Driving proves to be surprisingly difficult. His hands shake and tremble enough that he has to grasp the wheel hard, so hard his wrists ache. More than once he thinks he's going to drive the auto off the road.

He glances at himself in the mirror. He's pale, and his eye sockets are blue. He looks like a man who's just been hauled out of an icy stream. Which is also what he feels like.

He focuses. *Just a little farther. Just half a day's drive to Dhorenave, and from there to Restroyka.*

The trip feels impossibly long. He uses every ounce of energy to stay focused on the road. He realises he needs to eat, yet he doesn't feel hungry. He needs to drink, yet he doesn't feel thirsty.

What happened to me when I fell into Nokov's realm? He pulls over once, to rest and to check his body for puncture wounds, certain that Nokov or someone poisoned him somehow. He finds nothing, though his left side is an ugly, mottled blue-black. *That cold infected me, worked its way into me.* He starts the auto again. *Will it pass? Or is this how I am to be from now on?*

Finally he makes it to Dhorenave, part of the rural southern coasts of the Continent that share the moisture of Saypur's climate but not the heat. But while the climate of the Continent continues to go through massive shifts as the weather sorts itself out following the death of the Divinities, people have been forced to figure out how to survive.

Which, for a lot of the southern coasts outside of Ahanashtan, means sheep. And a lot of them.

Sigrud peers out the window at the muddy green hills, dotted with muddy, off-white sheep. The housing he sees is rudimentary, mostly stone, with no heating that he can see. *So when Mulaghesh said 'ranch',* he thinks, *she really meant ranch.*

He's worried he'll have to get out and ask one of the locals where he can find Restroyka, which he knows won't go well: a big, ill-looking Dreyling wandering around town asking where the wealthiest resident lives would certainly raise eyebrows. But there is just the one main road, and he drives a little farther than he should – and to his surprise, he gets rewarded for it: he spots a pair of huge, elaborate, white stone gates set in the hills to the west of the town.

He pulls over and stares at the gates. They're at least two or three storeys tall.

'That's it,' he says, wiping sweat from his brow. 'That's got to be her.'

Sigrud climbs out of the automobile and nearly falls over. *I hope Shara told Restroyka I'd come*, he thinks. *And I hope I can make it up the hill.*

He does, though it's not easy. He slows as he approaches. The gates are huge and intimidating. A single name is carved at their top: VOTROV.

Inherited, then, he thinks. *And she hasn't even taken time to change the name.*

He looks closer. The old Worldly Regulations from twenty years back must have missed this place, because the gates are covered in Divine references, most of them Kolkashtani. Sigrud identifies the bent, veiled, dour-looking figure in the centre of most of the bas-reliefs as Kolkan himself, and each carving of him is paired with his sigil: the hands of Kolkan, forming a scale, ready to weigh and to judge.

Sigrud flexes his left hand. It doesn't hurt today. But perhaps that's just because he feels so cold.

He walks through the gates. For the next forty minutes he limps along the muddy road – the only path or road of any kind that he can spot – and sees only hills and streams and shrunken little shrubs, and lots and lots of sheep.

Finally he crests a hill and sees the ranch house ahead, sitting atop a small ridge. It's big, but nothing like Shara's mansion. It's a low, rambling, stone structure that has obviously aged and not aged well. What really attracts his attention, though, is the extensive steel fence running around the perimeter of the house, topped with barbed wire.

'Gates within gates,' says Sigrud with a sigh. *In some ways, the Continent never changes.*

He staggers down the muddy road to the fence. It has a big set of steel gates that stand locked, though the lock doesn't look too complex to Sigrud. He looks for some kind of way to signal to the house that he's here, but there is none. He certainly doesn't have the voice to shout right now. He considers cutting through the barbed wire atop the fence, but he doesn't trust himself to be able to scale the fence in his state.

He kneels before the lock and takes out his lockpicks. *I'll knock on the front door*, he thinks, *and just apologise later.*

The lock clicks open after twenty minutes of work – unusually long for him, but then his hands are shaking like mad now. He pulls the gate open, the hinges whining slightly, then shuts it behind him and continues up the road.

He wonders what to say. He hasn't seen this woman in twenty years, and they met only briefly. He hopes that 'Shara sent me' will suffice.

And he hopes she has a fire. It feels as if his very bones are freezing over.

Then he hears the gunshot.

He immediately identifies it as a rifling, very high-powered. Then the muddy road six feet in front of him suddenly pops, spattering him with wet earth.

Sigrud instinctively leaps away. He lands on his left side and nearly screams in pain as his broken ribs creak and crackle. He manages to stifle the sound, then lies in the ditch facedown, not moving.

What in hells, he thinks. *What in the hells was that?*

He waits. There's nothing, no other shot, no shout to stand up. He begins to crawl away, back to the gates.

Another shot, this one striking the earth about four feet to his right. Then a second one, three feet to his left.

Warning shots, he thinks. *I'd be dead if they wanted me to be dead.* Though he isn't sure if this counts as a comfort.

Sigrud stays still, facedown, right hand on his head – his left, of course, he can't lift. He can't stop shaking now.

He hears footsteps on the hills above. He considers lifting his head, but decides not to bother. This proves to be the wise decision when a woman's voice barks, 'Don't move! Don't you *think* about moving!'

He waits, listening as they approach. He wonders how he got himself into this, then realises: *Electric alarm system in the gates. They must have known I broke through. Stupid. Stupid and sloppy.*

'Are you armed?' the woman's voice asks.

'Yes,' says Sigrud.

'Take it out and throw it away, please.'

Sigrud complies, throwing away his knife – though he does wonder what sort of person says 'please' when giving orders from behind a gun.

'Good. Stand up, please. Slowly.'

Sigrud, groaning and whimpering as his left side screams in pain, clambers to his feet.

There's a woman standing up the hill from him. He wipes mud from his eyes and peers at her.

She doesn't *look* like a millionaire. She's dressed in appropriately rural clothing, wearing a sheepskin vest and leather boots, and the high-powered rifling – one that even has a telescopic sight – is an uncommon accessory for the wealthy.

Yet the face that looks down the rifling at him . . . It's clearly Ivanya Restroyka, clearly the girl he met all those years ago, laughing in delight as he lit his pipe with a coal from the fire. But she's aged in the time since, and toughened. She is not at all the glittering socialite he remembers from Bulikov, but a thin, weathered, stone-faced creature with her long black hair pinned back behind her head.

'And who,' she says, 'might you be?'

'Sigrud je Harkvaldsson,' Sigrud says. He tries not to tremble as he speaks, but it's a lost cause. 'Sh . . . Shara . . . She –'

Restroyka laughs. It's a cold, brittle sound. 'Sigrud je Harkvaldsson! The fearsome Dreyling from Bulikov! So here's the top man Shara said she'd send to us!' She looks him over. 'You'll pardon my saying so . . . but I'm not quite sure how much help you can offer.'

Sigrud tries to say that he's not sure what he can do either, but then he shivers again. And this time it doesn't stop. He keeps trembling, keeps shaking, keeps shivering until his sight fails, until he can't see or speak or even breathe.

The next thing he knows, the muddy road is rising up to him. He hits the ground and he's conscious enough for it to hurt. But not for long.

The last thing he hears is Restroyka sighing and saying, 'Oh, for the love of –'

Then things go dark.

*

Kavitha Mishra awakens in the night.

She's not disturbed by how dark it is. Though that is disturbing, certainly – she left a candle burning by her bedside when she fell asleep, so it *shouldn't* be dark, or not impenetrably dark, like it is now – what's most disturbing is that her apartments are filled with the sounds of cheeping and rustling and creaking, as if she's not sleeping in her bed but in some giant, vast, ancient forest, a forest so thick no moonlight could ever penetrate it.

Then a voice: 'Mishra.'

Ah, she thinks. She asks aloud, 'Yes, sir?'

'He hurt me, Mishra. The man *hurt* me.'

She sits up. 'Nokov? Sir? How did you . . . How did you find me? I didn't say your name.'

'I remembered where you once called me,' says his voice. 'I remembered. I remembered where it was. I'm getting stronger, Mishra. I can go to places uninvited, if I've been there before. But still, he . . . Still, despite this, he *hurt* me, Mishra.'

'Who do you mean, sir? The *dauvkind*?' She knew that the operation in Ghaladesh had gone wildly south. The decimation of Komayd's house was all over the news. She'd received one message from Nokov – a letter, made of black paper, which mysteriously manifested itself in her dresser drawer the morning after – saying to distribute a sketch of the *dauvkind* to all Ministry sources, which she'd done. But she hadn't seen Nokov himself – and she certainly didn't know he'd been hurt.

Or even been capable of being hurt, really. That's disturbing.

There's a grunt to her right. Then something in the shadows . . . shifts.

And she sees him. Or, perhaps, he allows her to see him.

When she first saw him that day nine years ago, when he left her the letter asking if she would join him, he looked like an ordinary Continental boy – though his eyes had been a little dark, as if difficult to see, and he'd been able to slip in and out of shadows unusually well. Yet as time went by and their mission progressed, he changed.

Nokov stares down at her. He's still a young man, certainly, appearing to be not yet twenty, but his bearing and his eyes have changed, faint stars flickering in endless darkness, capable of seeing . . . more.

He's stronger now. A prince arrayed in his vestments of power.

Yet then he holds up his hand, and she sees his fingers are bruised and swollen.

'He *hurt* me,' says Nokov. 'How is this possible? How could he have done this? Do you know?'

'I . . . No. I didn't know that you could be hurt.'

'I can't! I'm stronger than any of my siblings now!' His voice comes from all around her, as if all the shadows are vibrating at once. 'I know that, you and I *both* know that. If I could just *find* them I'd . . . I'd . . .' He struggles for a moment, and then says, 'It's not fair, damn it. It's not *fair*! I shouldn't . . . I shouldn't be able to be hurt anymore. Not anymore.' He looks at her, troubled. 'How strong do I have to be to stop them from hurting me?'

Her mouth opens. Though she finds it hard to believe, she suspects he's looking to her for comfort. But what's odder still is that there's an unspoken *again* in that comment, as if he's suffered once and has since been running from it.

'Are you all right, sir?' she asks him.

He lowers his hand. His face hardens. 'No. I am not. A *mortal man*, who can physically hurt *me*? That makes it much harder for me to personally intervene! Because wherever I approach, *he* could be there. And now he knows what he can do to me. As do my siblings, I have no doubt.' He shakes his head. 'This is bad, Mishra, this is very bad.'

'How did he escape, sir?' asks Mishra.

'He . . . Well. I accidentally pulled him into my domain.'

'I don't understand, sir.'

'It is . . . quite difficult to put this in simple terms,' says Nokov. 'There is a place where I am purely me. In that place, I touch every shadow, every bit of darkness. I pulled him into this place, and he . . . I think he slipped through another shadow. Entered and promptly exited.' Nokov narrows his eyes. 'I think. Which might have killed him.'

'Why would it kill him, sir?'

'Because that place was made for me,' says Nokov. 'It is where I am *I*. Mortals were not meant to be there, even for one second. But this mortal is . . . concerning. He might have survived. He *might* have.'

'Where would the shadow have exited, sir?'

Nokov makes a face as if trying to balance a complicated budget in his head. 'I suspect it would be . . . to here. To Ahanashtan. The place I visit the most. They are like doors . . . And I've left more doors open around Ahanashtan than any other place.'

Mishra slowly exhales. 'Ahanashtan is where we have the most resources. But there are also lots of exits. We'll watch the train station, and the docks — as much as we can. Which might not be enough, sir.'

Nokov is silent for a long while.

'But . . . But what do we do besides that, sir?' asks Mishra.

Nokov says, 'Did you know, Mishra, that you were my first?'

'The first what, sir?'

'The first mortal that . . . that I showed myself to. That I approached and spoke to. I'd been watching you before then, I thought you might help me. But I wasn't sure. Yet I chose to show myself to you anyway.'

'I didn't know, sir.'

'I have never asked you this — you have always done what I asked, and you have every right to refuse to answer — but . . . why did you join with me? Why did you say yes that first time, so many years ago?'

'I . . . I'm not sure, sir.' She thinks about it. 'I suppose that when I first said your name, it was to see if what you were offering could possibly be real. And you came, and it was real. And we talked, but . . . But when I saw you, you . . . reminded me of someone.'

'I did?' he says, surprised.

'Yes.' She bows her head. 'My brother, Sanjay. He was killed in Voortyashtan.'

'Oh.'

'I know you're not the same age, sir, but you both *look* sort of the same age, and . . . Well. You both . . .' She struggles to search for the term. 'You both believed. In something. Anything. Which, at the time, I couldn't.'

'I see,' says Nokov quietly.

'Might I ask, ah, why you asked, sir?'

'It's complicated. Have you ever heard of a seneschal, Mishra?'

'I'm sorry, sir?'

'A seneschal. It was something the old Divinities used to do. A mortal who bears the miracles and blessings of a Divinity, and speaks and acts for them. A representative or a champion, in a way. It was considered a tremendous honour among the old Continentals. But it comes at a price. A seneschal bears the miracles of a Divinity – but a miracle is a *piece* of that Divinity. To be a seneschal is to consume and be merged with a god – and that is no small thing.'

'What are you saying, sir?'

He looks at her, his eyes glimmering. 'I am saying,' he says, 'that if you were to become my seneschal, Mishra, you might not be *you* anymore. You would be something new. And I am not *quite* a Divinity yet. I am close to it. With each victory we have, I grow closer. But I know that I am not yet there. So I do not know how this exchange could go.'

'I . . . I see, sir.'

He thinks for a while, then sighs. 'I will not ask this of you, not yet. But we face hard choices ahead, Mishra.' He stands. 'Notify me the moment you know anything.'

'Yes, sir. We will listen carefully for any whisper of the *dauvkind*.'

'Good.' He steps farther back into the shadows. 'Sleep well, Mishra.' He flickers, as if a nearby candle flame is being buffeted by a breeze. Then he's gone. The darkness disappears with him, soft moonlight returns, and Mishra stares around at her empty apartments.

In the dark, Sigrud dreams.

He dreams of a memory, of things as they once were.

His father, small and weary, waiting in a dark hallway as Sigrud walks out of a door. Torchlight quakes on the stone walls. The air is moist and cold.

His father smiles at him, looking at something in his arms. Sigrud looks down. He holds an infant girl in his arms: Signe, mere minutes old.

'Look at you,' says his father to the child. Then, to Sigrud: 'And look at *you*.'

Sigrud frowns at the look in his father's eyes. 'You don't look happy.'

His father smiles. 'I am happy. But I am also not happy.'

'Why? Why are you sad?'

'I'm not sad, Sigrud. You will learn many beautiful things about life now. But also many sad ones.'

'Like what?'

'Well, to start with . . .' He looks down at his granddaughter, still sleeping, still beautiful. 'Now that she is in this world, your life will never truly be your own.'

Sigrud looks down at Signe, this tiny, perfect, frowning thing.

The infant opens her mouth. A scream comes out, loud and pained, an adult scream of genuine terror.

The scream continues, but the scene changes. He's in Voortyashtan, in Fort Thinadeshi, screaming madly, one hand around the throat of a Saypuri soldier, the other thrusting his knife up into her belly again and again and again, slashing her open until her intestines begin spilling out . . .

Her eyes are wide as they stare up into his. Her face, though blood-spattered and pale, is smooth and soft – the face of a girl hardly older than eighteen.

She was a child, he thinks. *She was just a child*.

Sigrud opens his eyes, terrified. The dream is gone, and he thinks he's awake – but he's not sure. He's wrapped in blankets and lying on something wooden. There's a fire beside him and the moon in the distance, huge and bright. And standing over him is . . .

Someone familiar. Someone small, skinny, with slumping shoulders, their thick glasses flickering in the firelight.

'Shara?' Sigrud whispers. 'Are you there?'

He sleeps.

He feels air moving out of his open mouth. His tongue is dry, his head aching, and his back feels scored for some reason he can't fathom. But he's alive.

He cracks open his eye. He appears to be lying on the porch of Restroyka's ranch house. It's night now, and he's wrapped in a pile of woollen blankets, and there's a fire in some kind of stone chimney next to him, built up to a roaring height. He can feel the heat, but just barely.

The fragments of his dream are still flittering through his head. He tries to look around. There's someone in a chair beside him, looking out at the stark hills, a rifling in her hand. She hears him move and turns to look at him. It's Restroyka.

'Awake,' she says. 'Are you thirsty?'

Sigrud nods. It feels like he hasn't had a drink in years.

Restroyka rises and goes inside, rifling slung over her shoulder. She brings back a wooden cup, brimming with ice-cold water. He slurps it down greedily, but chokes on it, which makes him cough violently.

Restroyka watches him closely, her thin, hard face still and inscrutable. 'What happened to you?'

Sigrud considers telling her that he was injured and poisoned after struggling with a near-Divinity, but decides such a claim would not be the best way to start off their relationship.

'What do you know?' he asks, though his voice can't rise above a whisper.

'I know you broke onto my property, unannounced,' says Restroyka. 'And I know you look like you're dying. Though I haven't dug the grave quite yet. I apologise if your back hurts. You were too heavy for me to carry, so I had Nina drag you up to the porch.'

'N-Nina?'

'My mule. Getting you into the house was impossible. So we improvised,' she says, waving to the fire. She looks at him, and he sees a hardness to her gaze he didn't expect. 'I remember you, you know.'

'What?'

'From the party. In Bulikov.' She sits back down. 'I don't forget a social acquaintance. There was you, with your big red coat and your hat and your pipe. And then there was her. Little Shara. And the second Vo saw her, I . . .' A bitter smile. 'I felt the world falling apart. Even before the Battle of Bulikov.' She looks back at him, her eyes flicking over his face. 'You – you've held up marvellously well, haven't you? You look almost exactly as I recall you. Except not quite as alive, of course. That can't be right, can it? I must be misremembering how you looked . . .'

Sigrud watches her as she talks. She keeps one hand on her rifling at all times. There's an easy familiarity to how she holds it that suggests this weapon might be her constant companion out here – if not her only companion.

He tries to take a breath to ask about Tatyana, but his side hurts too much. 'Don't bother talking,' says Restroyka. 'You've slept all day, and it looks like you needed it. Someone has worked you over like a cheap piece of mutton, and you still seem terribly sick. But you won't find any more harm coming from me. Shara told me to check the eye, and the hand. She said you might come. And you are who she said you'd be.' She taps her left eye. 'I like the false eye, though. It's very pretty.'

She and Sigrud look at each other for a moment, his breath shallow and ragged.

'Did anyone follow you?' she asks quietly.

He shakes his head.

'Are we in danger?'

He nods.

'But is our location known?'

Sigrud tries to shrug, but he's not sure if she can see it.

'I told her it wouldn't last,' says Restroyka to herself. 'I *told* her these things always fall apart . . .'

There's a *clunk* from down the porch. Sigrud can't lift his head to see, but Restroyka sits up, alarmed. 'Dear, I thought I told you to go back in and stay in the house!'

'You also told me to fetch another cord of wood,' says a voice, low and sullen. 'Those are two contradictory orders, Auntie.'

Sigrud frowns. *Auntie?*

'I don't like you being out of the house,' says Restroyka. 'If someone skulking around in the trees out there took some potshot at you and got lucky, I'd never forgive myself!'

'Unless the sheep have rebelled and taken up sharpshooting, I suspect we're quite safe here.'

Someone steps into view, though they're still in the shadows. Someone small and thin, their glasses glinting in the firelight, someone familiar.

Sigrud blinks in shock. 'Sh-Shara?'

His vision focuses more. He sees he was wrong: though this new girl carries herself like Shara, dresses like Shara, and even talks a bit like her, she's clearly a Continental, short and pale with curly, inky black hair.

'No,' she says quietly. 'Not Shara.' She looks at Restroyka. 'Why does he keep saying that?'

Then the girl draws closer, toward the light, and he sees her fully. He sees her wide, pale face, her upturned nose, her small, thin-lipped mouth.

It's a face he recognises instantly. Not from the photograph he saw in Shara's house, though, not the laughing six-year-old girl he saw there.

It's the girl from the slaughterhouse, he thinks, astonished. *The one who saved me. She looks exactly like her! But . . . that's impossible . . .*

'I suppose I should ask you to introduce yourself, Tatyana,' says Restroyka, rising to stand beside her. 'But then, I never properly introduced myself to our guest either.'

'We've met,' says Tatyana, her eyes a little wide with awe.

'You have?' says Restroyka, surprised.

'Yes. Once. I thought I dreamed it.' She stares into Sigrud's face. 'I was a little girl, and I walked into Mother's room, and she was talking to a man in a mirror. The man was on a ship, and he was weeping. He was so sad, that man. And I never learned why.' She cocks her head. 'She said it was a dream. But it was real. It was you. Wasn't it?'

Sigrud is still so surprised that he's hardly listening to her. He can't stop looking at her face, watching her every movement. He can't believe that Tatyana Komayd, Shara's adopted daughter, could possibly look so much like the girl from the slaughterhouse.

He remembers Nokov, laughing at him in the dark: *But have you seen her?*

Sigrud swallows. 'How are you . . . How are you . . .'

'How am I what?' Tatyana asks.

His strength fails. He lets his head fall back, and he blinks once, twice, then a third time. He can't keep awake any longer. Consciousness slips out of his grasp, and he sleeps.

He awakens to the smell of something cooking, something thick and starchy. It's not something he would ordinarily find appetising, yet his stomach feels so totally empty that it growls at the merest whiff of it. He realises he hasn't felt hungry in hours, if not days – which means he must be getting better.

He opens his eye. It's morning, and he's still on the porch. There's an awful taste in his mouth, and everything feels moist. He realises he's been sweating pints and gallons all night.

And sweat means . . . that I feel warm.

And he does feel warm, he finds. He feels very, very warm. He needs to get these blankets off him, and now.

He shoves them off, which releases a cloud of saline stench that's almost overpowering. His left side is still in terrible pain, but his skin delights in the feel of the cold morning air.

Slowly, slowly, he stands. His sweat-drenched clothes steam slightly in the cold air, as if his pockets were full of candles. He limps to the front door of the ranch house.

He looks inside. Everything is quite rudimentary, all candles and torches and spindly wooden chairs, not at all the trappings of a millionaire. He can smell a wood fire somewhere, and the creamy, starchy smell is stronger. He limps down the hallway.

The hallway ends in the kitchen. There's a small kitchen stove in the corner with a little wood fire flickering below an iron cauldron. A thread of steam unscrolls from the edge of the cauldron, where something white and lumpy has calcified.

'It's porridge,' says a voice.

He turns and sees Tatyana Komayd sitting in the corner, reading a tremendous book whose spine says: THE RISE AND FALL OF THE CONTINENTAL COPPER INDUSTRY. She peers over the top with an expression of measured disdain, as if remembering some personal slight he did to her.

'Oh,' says Sigrud. He scratches his arm, feeling awkward. 'Is it.'

'Yes. It is. It's all Auntie Ivanya eats. That and mutton, and carrots, and potatoes.'

For a moment they just look at each other. Sigrud can't stop looking at her arms, her legs, her feet, as if to verify that every visible piece of her is human and normal – which they all seem to be.

She is just a girl. Just a teenage girl, watching him with an air of resentment. It's so surreal to think that this is who he risked his life to save, who he fretted over in the dark, the person who vexed and concerned him as he sailed across the South Seas to Ghaladesh.

And yet to look at her . . .

'Something on my face?' asks Tatyana.

Sigrud stares at her for a second more. *She has no idea. No idea who she looks like. Or what she might be.*

He coughs awkwardly. 'Restroyka is . . . your aunt?'

'She's a family friend.' A frosty smile. 'Bowls are on the top-right shelf. Spoons in the drawer below.'

Sigrud opens the cabinet and sees there are indeed bowls on the middle shelf, but on the bottom shelf sits something far more alarming: a big, black, revolving pistol.

'She also left *that*,' says Tatyana from the corner. 'I think she left it for me . . . but you might have more use for it.'

Sigrud stares at it for a moment longer before filling his bowl with porridge. 'Why would she leave you a gun?'

'In case anyone leapt in here and threatened my life, I suppose. I sort of think I'd welcome it. Nothing else has happened since Mother brought me here.'

'Your mother brought you here?' asks Sigrud.

'Who else?'

He looks around. 'Where is Restroyka?'

'Feeding the sheep and the pigs. I think. I can't confirm it, because I'm not allowed out of the house. I'm a person of some importance, you see.'

Sigrud sits at the table. He's about to take a giant bite of porridge when Tatyana rises and sits opposite him. She fixes him with a steely look, as if he were some bizarre animal and she's not quite sure how to categorise him.

'So,' she says. 'You knew my mother.'

'Uh,' says Sigrud. 'Yes.'

'Do you know how to use a pistol?'

He glances at the cupboard. 'I do.'

She nods. 'And were you a spy as well?'

Sigrud pauses. It's naturally a hard rule of espionage that one should avoid running around confessing one is a spy. But you don't get to be a decent operative without being able to read people – and he senses that Tatyana Komayd already knows the truth, and expects it from him.

'Something like that,' he says.

She nods again. 'I see,' she says, just a little too pertly. Then she stands, grabs her book, and marches out of the room.

Sigrud stares at her as she goes, wondering what just happened. Then the back door opens and Restroyka strides in, wearing a thick leather coat and muddy boots, the scoped rifling slung over her back.

'You're up, I see,' she says. 'And eating. Perhaps you'll live yet.' She frowns when she hears a door slam from far back in the house. 'What's going on?'

Sigrud gestures helplessly at the empty chair across from him. 'Tatyana was here, and . . .'

'And?'

'And she asked if I knew her mother.'

Restroyka narrows her eyes. 'And what did you tell her?'

'I told her I did. Then she asked if I was a spy.'

'And *then* what did you tell her?'

'I told her . . . Well. Yes? Though that is a poor word for it. Then she just walked away.'

Restroyka sighs and blows a stray thread of hair away from her face. 'Oh, dear. Well. That's how it's been out here. Can you walk?'

'I would prefer not to,' says Sigrud, thinking of his injured side.

'And I would prefer not to play babysitter to a pissed-off girl and a half-dead Dreyling, but here we are. When you're done with your breakfast, come outside. I wish for you to see something, please.'

'Will Tatyana be all right?'

'Taty? Hells, certainly not! Not only is she still grieving, but worse . . . Well. Apparently Shara didn't tell her the truth. About anything.'

'The . . . truth?'

Restroyka smiles acidly. 'I liked Shara, believe it or not. She was something of a friend of mine in later years. But I do question some of her parenting decisions. Especially hiding from your only child that you were one of the most accomplished espionage agents in Saypuri history, and that you personally killed two gods.'

Sigrud's mouth falls open. 'She . . . She never *told* her?'

'Not a word of it. Apparently Taty grew up thinking her mother's tenure as prime minister was little more than another stage in the career of a milquetoast high-level bureaucrat. How Shara managed that, I've no idea. And now that she's dead, all the truths have come out. I couldn't keep the news from her when her mother's life is *international* news. So trust me, after all the crying and screaming and weeping that I've put up with in the past month, Mr. Sigrud, a bedridden man who can barely talk is an absolute vacation.'

Sigrud follows Restroyka as she strides toward a small barn in the corner of her lot. He glances back at the ranch house as they leave it. He sees that though it's in need of repairs, security has been a priority: the windows have bars on them, and a few of them have been covered up with plates of iron.

'So,' says Ivanya. 'You're to be our bodyguard. Yes?'

'I believe that was the general idea,' says Sigrud. He glances at her rifling. 'But you seem to be doing a very good job. You call her . . . Taty?'

'Yes. She is Taty, and I am Ivanya. None of this Miss Restroyka nonsense, all right? You're not my damn errand boy. I had one, but I fired him. Didn't trust him. Also he seemed to be somewhat fearful of the sheep. Bad fit all around. Tell me – how did you know to come here?'

'Shara told me, in a way.' He tells her about his journey here, though he doesn't yet tell her about Nokov and the Divine.

Ivanya laughs lowly. 'Old Mother Mulaghesh . . . How she hated me. Didn't like me interfering with Saypuri politics. Ironic, isn't it, since Saypur has had its hand in every Continental ballot box since the Kaj's day. Though Shara tried to fix some of that.'

'How did you come to know Shara?'

She stops and looks at him, her gaze bright. 'How did *you* come to know her, Sigrud je Harkvaldsson?'

He shrugs. 'She got me out of prison.'

'Hm. How I'd wish for such a simple story.' She continues walking. 'She started sending me letters about, what, five years ago or so? Said she wanted to know if I was interested in starting a charity. Some kind of thing about providing shelter for Continental orphans. I ignored her at first, but she was persistent. Eventually I let her come to Dhorenave and pitch me in person. And she struck a chord with me. Still a lot of kids displaced from all the disasters we've had. These things . . . They linger. They linger for generations.'

Sigrud listens carefully. 'So . . . You were involved in her charity on the Continent?'

'I don't know about *involved*. I paid for a damned lot of it. Consulted on her board via correspondence. And sometimes I let her daughter come and stay with me, when Shara's life got too busy, and I had more of a staff here. Little Taty thought it was fun, riding the ponies and whatnot. I got rid of all the staff when Shara died. Didn't trust them anymore.'

'It was Shara who brought Taty here, though – correct?'

'Yes,' says Ivanya. 'You don't know any of this?'

He shakes his head. 'I only became involved after she died. I knew nothing.'

'After she died, eh? Are you her self-anointed avenging angel? How very masculine of you.'

'When did she bring Taty here?' asks Sigrud.

'A little over three months ago,' says Ivanya, 'after she moved into Ahanashtan. And then . . .'

'She was murdered.'

'Yes.'

'And she sent no other communications to you during this time?'

'No. But that's not abnormal. I do everything at a distance these days. I try not to involve too many people in my life, or what I do here.'

'Which is what, exactly?'

'I manage my assets,' she says, walking up to the little barn. 'I raise the sheep. And then there's this.' She unlocks the padlocked door and throws it open.

Sigrud stares. Inside is an armoury of weaponry and munitions that would give even the most veteran operative pause. Dozens of pistols and riflings – both of the semiautomatic and fully automatic variety – as well as cleaning kits, ammunition belts, and boxes and boxes of bullets. There are also tins of food at the back, and boxes of things like rice and flour, all of them very carefully sealed to make them last as long as possible.

Ivanya carefully gauges his reaction. 'I've trained,' she says. 'As much as I can, at least. But I suspect you know a lot more about such weaponry.

You said you were told to come here and protect Tatyana. I wanted you to know where these were. In case anything happened.'

'And . . . do you expect anything will happen?'

'I've expected something will happen for a very long time now, Sigrud je Harkvaldsson,' says Ivanya, staring off into the hills. 'Disasters, on the Continent, are more common than rain. And I want to be ready, and for you to be ready too. Come on. Let me show you the roads.'

Ivanya Restroyka spends a good part of the next two hours showing him the territory. She starts with the one road that leads through the sheep pastures – the one he came in on – but she also shows him the two or three dozen various footpaths through the hills that are accessible from the town.

Or from the river. Or from the forest. Or from the lowlands. Or from the neighbouring sheep ranches.

Sigrud listens as Ivanya points out all the various routes and methods someone could use to attack them. He watches as her hand never leaves her rifling – always a very tight grip on it. He nods thoughtfully as she tells him how the fences are alarmed. And he understands immediately that Ivanya Restroyka has not been preparing an attack just in the month or so since Shara died – she's been preparing for an attack for years. Maybe even a decade. Or more.

'. . . could float up the river,' says Ivanya, pointing. 'If they brought inflatables of some kind. Rafts, perhaps. That's another possibility.' She glances at him, then stops. 'Why are you looking at me like that?'

Sigrud thinks for a moment. 'I remember you too, you know. From the party.'

'Do you.'

'Yes. You were very young.'

'Younger than young, it feels. I was twenty-one.'

'Yes. But you were also very . . . unconcerned. Very social. Very talkative. You talked to everyone.'

'So?'

'So . . . I am trying to reconcile that memory with the person before me. Someone who has no company on her property except sheep and quite a lot of guns.'

She laughs bitterly. 'You want to know how I got to be here?'

'I would be curious why a millionaire does not appear to enjoy any creature comforts, yes.'

She shrugs. 'What happened to you? What happened to Shara? What happened to any of us? I lived through the Battle of Bulikov, Mr. Sigrud, just as you did. I saw the world fall apart around me, just as you did. I saw death on a scale I could never have imagined. And I lost the one thing that felt real to me. I lost Vo. Or perhaps he was taken from me.' She looks off into the barren wilderness. 'I tried to get better afterwards. We all did. But then Voortyashtan happened. And I stopped looking at cities and civilisation as refuges. I started looking at them as *liabilities*.'

'So you came here?'

'Here was better than anywhere else. It used to be a horse ranch for Vo's family, but sheep are a lot more valuable now. What was I supposed to do, go to cocktail parties? Wear a slinky dress and gossip? None of that meant anything anymore. Some new Divine horror could come along and blow away all of those quaint notions of safety and security as if they were but the seeds of a dandelion. People think me a madwoman, but I know I'm not wrong. Even the humans can't be trusted these days, as we've learned. I just hope the bastards who killed Shara get tracked down fast. Then maybe we can get Taty home soon, and you can be on your way, Mr. Sigrud.'

Sigrud glances sideways at her. 'So . . . What did you think Shara did for your charity?'

'Huh? What do you mean, think? You mean besides run it?'

'Yes.'

'Well. Whatever was needed? I was sent all of her minutes, all of her meeting reports, her finances, all of her –'

'Were any of the orphans she located,' asks Sigrud, 'considered special?'

'What do you mean, "special"?'

'I mean things Shara would handle personally.'

'We had escalated cases,' says Ivanya. 'Cases of danger or extreme circumstances.'

'Which were escalated to Shara.'

'Of course. She was the head of the charity.'

Sigrud nods absently as he stares into the fog-laden hills.

'Why?' she asks. 'Why all these questions about the charity? Surely the charity had nothing to do with Shara's death.'

Sigrud takes a deep breath in, then quickly regrets it, as it pains his side. 'You were right, Ivanya. You are not a madwoman.'

'What does that have to do with anything?'

'Shara did not die due to some mortal plot,' says Sigrud. 'She was murdered by agents of the Divine.'

Ivanya stares at him. 'What are you talking about?'

'I will tell you,' says Sigrud. He grunts a little as he shifts his shoulders, trying to find a more comfortable position. 'But I am going to need a chair. And I suggest we have this conversation . . . *away* from Taty.'

'Could this upset her?'

'Something like that.'

Sigrud talks. He talks for a long time, more than three hours, seated crookedly on an old, cobwebbed chair in Ivanya's armoury, with her standing in the corner opposite him. When he finishes, Ivanya is silent for a long while.

'You're . . . You're mad,' she says.

Sigrud nods, for this is the natural response. He stands and walks among Ivanya's armaments, lightly touching a pistol or rifling or knife, leaning this way and that to confirm the make or model or the integrity of the weapon.

'You're mad,' says Ivanya again. 'You're absolutely mad!'

He nods again, then picks up a carousel pistol. He smiles a little, remembering Turyin running around Voortyashtan with one of these monstrosities on her hip.

'Quit nodding!' snaps Ivanya. 'It's patronising!'

'Your reaction is completely reasonable,' says Sigrud. He puts down the carousel and picks up a revolving pistol. He flicks open the cylinder and examines the chambers. 'What I am telling you is mad. But also true. On the Continent, as you know, things can be both.' He shuts the revolving pistol with a *snap*.

'You are telling me that Shara Komayd was using her damned charity to . . . to locate Divine *children*?'

'Yes. From what I have gathered.'

'Because there's some Divine child tyrant out there trying to gobble them up?'

'Yes.'

'And . . . And you think Tatyana might be one of them?'

'I think her name is on a list I have,' says Sigrud. 'And she looks almost *exactly* like the girl who saved me from the slaughterhouse. There is too much similarity for any doubt, to me.' He pauses and looks over the many barrels of riflings at Ivanya. 'Has she done anything odd?'

'Her mother was assassinated!' says Ivanya, exasperated. 'And now she's stuck out here in the hills, with me, and I know *I'm* no storybook ladies' maid! All she's done is cry!'

Sigrud sucks his teeth. 'That doesn't make sense.'

'Oh, *that's* the part that doesn't make sense! All the rest of the shit you just told me, yes, *that's* perfectly logical.'

'She must do something strange. Be something more than what she is.'

'Or you're dead wrong, and Shara's murder was just some, I don't know, Continental separatist plot!'

'Are you not curious,' says Sigrud, walking over to the fully automatic section of weaponry, 'as to why Ministry agents haven't been pounding on your door, asking where Taty is?'

'I do a good job controlling my connections to the world out there! We don't even have a telephone here.'

'But nobody's *that* good,' he says, 'unless Shara did such a good job slipping Tatyana out of Saypur that they still don't even know she left the country. The Ministry is not here, Ivanya Restroyka, because Shara did not trust the Ministry. She knew it had been compromised. That was why she chose to do all this herself.'

'If what you're saying is true,' says Ivanya, 'then why isn't her Divine enemy knocking on our door either? Why haven't Taty and I been murdered in our beds?'

Sigrud pauses to think, for this has troubled him too. Nokov seems capable, competent, and preternaturally dangerous. How could they have survived on the Continent for three months without his notice?

Then he gets an idea.

'Do you have a jar?' he asks.

'A what?' says Ivanya.

'A jar. And . . . When livestock dies. Where do you bury it? Or their ashes, if you burn them.'

'What are you –'

'And if there are any star lilies that grow near here,' he says, 'I would appreciate if you would point them out to me.'

An hour later, Sigrud stands next to the armoury barn and tries to ignore Ivanya's bug-eyed stare as he smears the bottom of the muddy little glass jar with grave dirt. *I hope it counts as grave dirt*, he thinks, *if it's sheep that occupy the grave*. He also hopes that onion lilies – apparently the most predominant wildflower around here – count as lilies, for he has a handful of them at his feet. It could really go either way: they smell like onions, but look like lilies.

'So this is a miracle,' says Ivanya flatly.

'Not yet.' He picks up the lilies, shreds their petals, puts them into the jar, and gives it a good shake. '*Now* it's a miracle,' he says, dumping them out and scraping off the grave dirt.

'Oh, obviously. *Obviously*. I didn't check your temperature, Mr. Sigrud, but I'm increasingly worried you boiled your brain.'

Sigrud smiles politely and looks around. It's late afternoon now, so the hills are dappled with the gold-yellow light of sunset. It'd be prettier if it weren't for the hot ball of dread churning in his stomach.

Sigrud lifts the jar to his eye. And, as he expected, the hills light up.

It's like they've been drawn on with some kind of glowing paint, forming giant rings of phosphorescence surrounding the ranch house, rings and rings and rings. The muddy road back to Dhorenave has received the most attention, it seems: the path looks like a huge, glowing stripe cutting through the hills, and it shines so bright it hurts his eye.

'Well?' says Ivanya.

He hands it to her without a word. She looks at it suspiciously, then back up at him. Then she makes a face, lifts the jar to her eye, and peers through.

She gasps. She stares into the jar, leaning forward as if the Divine designs were right in front of her, and then slowly, slowly turns about. 'What in the world . . .? It's a trick, isn't it? You're fooling me, aren't you?'

He shakes his head. 'This is what I saw outside the Golden Hotel in Aha-nashtan. I think someone did this to protect you. Just as they did for Shara.'

Ivanya takes the jar away, blinks at the hills, then puts it back to her eye again. 'But . . . Who . . .'

'Shara's helpers,' he says. He peers at the sun-dappled landscape. 'Perhaps other children she saved. I don't quite know. I have no doubt that she would ensure her daughter had as much protection as she had – if not more.'

She goes pale. 'You're . . . You're saying that Divine children came here, crept through the forest, and built invisible, miraculous walls around my *house*?'

'It would explain why you haven't been found yet. Shara did her work. I don't know what these protections do. Perhaps they ward away people or agents who mean well. Wipe the memories of those looking for Taty. Or perhaps these wards just kill trespassers outright.'

'I'm fine with any of those results.'

'Yes. But Shara's enemies found a way past the barriers at the Golden. And worse, it means more people – if they can be called people – know where Taty is than we realised. If Shara's enemy gets a hold of whichever children made these protections – and it sounds like he would dearly love to do that – then he will know where we are as well.'

Ivanya slowly puts down the jar. She turns to look at Sigrud, her face wan with horror. 'You mean that . . . You mean Taty could really be . . .'

'What's going on?' says a voice.

Sigrud and Ivanya turn to look, and see Taty standing on the back porch of the house, watching them. 'What . . . what are you doing with that jar?' she calls. 'Are you playing some kind of game or somethi –'

Ivanya turns and hurls the jar away, smashing it against the wall of the barn, which makes both Sigrud and Taty jump. She whirls back around and stabs out a finger. '*Get back in the house!*' she snaps.

Taty gapes at her, shocked. 'Auntie, I –'

'Now! Back inside! *Now!*' Her face is bright red, her mouth tight with fury.

Taty watches her a second more. Then she glares at Ivanya and Sigrud, walks back in the house, and slams the door behind her.

Ivanya stands there without saying anything, just breathing hard.

'That,' says Sigrud, 'was probably an overreaction.'

'Oh, was it?' snarls Ivanya. 'You've just told me that not only am I probably targeted for Divine assassination, but so is the girl entrusted to my care, *and* you've shown me that my property has been infiltrated by Divine agents! Agents working for Shara, perhaps, but still people who took away the . . . the *one* thing I had out here. The chance to be *lost*, to be *forgotten*, to keep all that *away* from me.' She looks at the back porch. 'But now here it is, right next door to me . . . In my home. In my *home*.'

Sigrud watches her as she tries to regain control of herself. He's not sure if Ivanya's going to have a panic attack or burst into tears. But to his surprise, she does neither: she shuts her eyes, clenches her jaw, turns to him, and growls, 'What do we do?'

'I am not sure yet,' he says.

'We can't stay here.'

'Not forever, no.'

She laughs miserably. 'Can we even stay here tonight?'

'I think so,' says Sigrud. 'We can risk a few more days. I injured our enemy. Maybe for the first time ever. He will avoid being where I am, for a time. But I need rest as well.'

'And we're supposed to just go back into the house with' – she looks toward the porch – 'with her? A girl you think might be Divine?'

'I . . . Yes. I think so.'

'She's just a girl, Sigrud,' says Ivanya softly. 'Just a hurt, scared girl. You can't be right. You can't be.'

'I know.'

'You don't. You just met her. She's hardly older than I was when . . .' Ivanya shuts her eyes, swallows, and shakes her head. 'It's not fair, damn it. Not to me. Or to her.'

'Yes,' says Sigrud. 'But "fair" is but a word.'

Ivanya sighs. 'What are we going to do?'

'Do you have a telegraph office here?'

'Yes. There's one in town.'

'I need you to send a telegram,' says Sigrud. He finds a scrap of paper in the armoury and writes down the information. 'For Mulaghesh. So she knows where to contact me.'

'I'm sending telegrams to ministers now? What can she know?'

'She's doing me a favour,' says Sigrud, 'looking for the location of a ship.'

'And what's so special about this ship?'

'I think it can tell me what our enemy really is – how he thinks, how he works – and perhaps where the Divine children came from. All of these will be crucial to staying alive.'

Ivanya takes the scrap of paper and, grimacing, shoves it in her pocket. 'Do you want a weapon or not?'

Sigrud raises his eyebrows and nods.

'Go on, then.' She gestures at the armoury. 'I don't want to be out here past dark, not after what you told me.'

Sigrud selects a nice handheld revolving pistol with decent stopping power, and a semiautomatic Kamal rifling – a reliable, efficient service weapon he's had some experience with.

'I thought you'd go for one of those giant machine guns,' says Ivanya.

'If I were running from house to house in street warfare, maybe,' says Sigrud. 'But out here, in the wilderness . . . When I shoot at someone, I want to hit them.'

Ivanya shuts the armoury and locks it. Then she leans against the door and sighs again.

Sigrud looks her over as she tries to struggle through this. 'Thank you,' he says.

'For what?'

'For saving my life.'

'You're welcome,' she says. She starts off back to the house. 'I hope you can return the favour, and soon.'

8.
Target Practice

Youths are such a danger, I find. You must watch them carefully: if unemployment or the poverty rate ticks up too high among a nation's youths, that's when the trouble starts.

Young people congregate too much, feel too much, and know so little of life, so they don't know what they have to lose. It's wisest to distract them, keep them engaged with something else, until they grow old and lose that wild fire in their hearts.

Or use them, if you can. The young are eager to find a cause, and nobly die for it — it's just a matter of finding the cause that works in your favour.

And before you point it out: yes, this is something I have personally learned within my own family.

— MINISTER OF FOREIGN AFFAIRS VINYA KOMAYD,
LETTER TO PRIME MINISTER ANTA DOONIJESH, 1708

Sigrud spends over a week staying with Ivanya and Taty. He spends almost all of his time indoors, since that's where Taty stays. It's time he desperately needs to heal and rest, but it's also nice to simply not move for a while. He knows they will need to move soon.

Yet Taty avoids him like the plague. The girl is a ghost to him, finding ways to evade him in a ranch house that should feel at least somewhat confined. It troubles him.

'She doesn't like me,' he says to Ivanya one evening.

'Should she?' says Ivanya.

'Well. Yes? I risked my life to come here for her.'

'You're a spectre out of her mother's past,' she says. 'You remind her of her mother *and* you remind her she didn't really know her mother. Of course she hates you. You knew Shara better than she ever did. Or ever will, now.'

The revelation is striking and dispiriting for Sigrud. To lose someone you loved is one thing. To lose someone you loved but never truly knew is another.

'I'll be going into town tomorrow to buy more damned books for Taty,' says Ivanya. 'I swear, the girl goes through door-stopper tomes in a day . . . I'll check the telegraph office again, of course. Do you know when we should hear back from Mother Mulaghesh?'

'No. I do not.'

Ivanya feeds another log into the fire in the kitchen. 'Have you given any thought to where we're going next?'

'I've given thought, yes,' says Sigrud.

'But?'

'But I've had few ideas.'

After Ivanya leaves for town in the morning, Sigrud is not sure exactly what to do, so he sits on the back porch and disassembles and cleans the Kamal rifling he chose. It's a meditative practice for Sigrud: to disassemble and clean one's weapon is like disassembling and cleaning and reassembling one's mind by proxy. He does it again and again and again, listening to the cries of the sheep and the wind in the hills and the click of each rifling assembly slotting into place.

'I think it's clean by now,' says a voice.

He turns and sees Taty watching him through a window. He nods to her, then resumes what he was doing.

She opens the door, walks out without a word, and sits in one of the wooden chairs on the porch. She watches him in silence for nearly ten minutes.

'Why are you doing that?' she asks.

He snaps the clip latch pin back into place. ' "There is no such thing as a bad situation," ' he recites. ' "Only bad gear." I must know this weapon, every piece and every part, better than I know myself, if I am to use it wisely.'

'Did my mother teach you that?' she asks.

Sigrud pauses. Then he shakes his head. 'No. Your mother was not an eager hand at firearms.'

'No?'

'No,' he says firmly.

Taty turns the chair a little to face him more. 'What was she an eager hand at, then?'

He slides the firing pin back into the bolt housing. He thinks for a moment, then says, 'Papers.'

'Papers?'

'Yes.'

'What do you mean, "papers"?'

'Everything Shara read,' says Sigrud, 'she remembered. Or so it seemed.' He fits the extractor spring and plunger into the bolt. 'Papers about history. Papers about people. Papers about papers. They were all in her brain, whenever she needed them. Perhaps she only ever learned the basics of firearms because she had too much paper in her head.'

For a while she says nothing. Sigrud works in contented quiet. He's not sure what has made her come and talk to him now, but he chooses to speak only when spoken to. It's like she's a nervous deer, and he must make no sudden movements.

'What did you both do?' she asks eventually.

'What we were told to do,' he says. 'Mostly.'

'That's it?'

He slots in the ejector spring. 'That's it.'

'From what the newspapers said,' says Taty, 'I would have thought that it was . . . grander. More adventurous.'

'Nothing is more romanticised than war,' says Sigrud. 'But war is mostly waiting. Waiting for orders, waiting for movement, waiting for information.' He sits back, thinking. 'I could measure my life by sleepless nights spent in empty rooms, staring out of windows.'

He goes back to work. After a while he says, 'You seem to be very good at reading.'

Taty tucks her knees up against her chest and stares at the rifling components on the porch. 'Yes. Economics.' She sighs. 'It's what I'm good at.'

'You don't seem to be very happy about what you're good at.'

'It's been . . . It *was*, I guess, a disagreement I had with Mother. She said I have a talent for it. Hired a lot of tutors. More than the ones I had already, that is. I had plenty to begin with. It's just forecasting, really. Trying to paint pictures of what things might look like.' She plays with a piece of loose binding on the corner of the chair. 'The tiniest tremble of an interest rate or a commodity price – what does that change? That's all it is.'

'Do you miss your friends?'

'Some. There was really only Miss Goshal's girls, Sumitra and Lakshi. She was our housekeeper, she lived on the property for a while. I see them in the summers or on holidays. Or I did.' She gives Sigrud a hard stare. 'They go to the regular school. I didn't. Mother has tutors for me. Had, I guess. How weird it is, to talk in past tense about someone you still think is there.'

Sigrud slides the ejector assembly into the hole on the bolt face. He can suddenly imagine a lot of Taty's life: a child raised by adults, with adult friends, and only the barest concept of childhood. He can tell by the way she talks, using mature phrasing and words, but it's as if she's trying to do a dance based solely on instructions she saw in a booklet.

'Did you like her?' Taty asks suddenly. 'My mother, I mean.'

Sigrud pauses and slowly looks up at her, staring into her large, dark eyes. 'She was the best person I ever knew,' he says.

Taty blinks, surprised. 'Oh.'

He thinks for a moment, staring off into the dour forests. 'I am jealous of you,' he says.

'What?' says Taty, even more surprised.

'You got to know her during peacetime,' he says. 'When she wasn't scared, or worried, or following orders. A time when she could just be herself. I did not see this Shara. And I am sad to have missed it.' He looks back at her. 'I'm sorry about your mother.'

'Thank you.' Taty swallows. She's breathing rapidly. 'Are you going to kill the people who killed her?'

Sigrud looks at her for a second. Then he returns to his work, fitting the extractor back into the bolt. 'I have already done that.'

'You . . . You what?'

Sigrud says nothing, placing the rear of the bolt on the soft wood of the porch as he orientates the ejector.

'You killed someone?' asks Taty, aghast.

'Yes,' he says.

'Did you really?'

'Yes.'

She stares at him as he completes the Kamal's bolt, which takes some time.

'Do you feel bad about it?' she asks.

'I . . . do not know.' He places the bolt aside, then looks at her. 'Somewhat.'

She meets his gaze, then looks down at the wood of the porch, breathing harder and harder. 'I hope it hurt. What you did to them.'

Sigrud frowns and looks away.

'What?' says Taty. 'Is it wrong to want that?'

'Perhaps not. If I were you, I might want the same.'

'Then what?'

He remembers Shara once saying to him: *Violence is a part of our trade, yes. It is one tool of many. But violence is a tool that, if you use it but once, it begs you to use it again and again. And soon you will find yourself using it against someone undeserving of it.*

In a flash, he remembers her: the soldier from Fort Thinadeshi, not much older than Taty is now. He remembers her wide, terrified eyes, and how he, blind with fury, slashed at her belly . . .

He returns to the rifling. 'One should not seek ugliness in this world. There is no lack of it. You will find it soon enough, or it will find you.'

Taty is quiet for a while. Then she says, 'But wait . . . If you killed them . . . If you've already killed the man who killed Mother . . .' She sits forward. 'Then can I go home now? Is this all over?'

'If it was over,' says Sigrud, 'don't you think I would have told you all so?'

'But who else is there? Who else could there b –'

'I killed the killer,' he says. 'But he was not alone. We must be cautious.'

'For how long?'

'Until there is no need to be cautious.'

'Gods,' says Taty, sighing. 'Don't you understand how *frustrating* that is? It's so . . . so damned *galling* to have you and Mother and Auntie leading me around like a damned mule!' She looks at him every time she swears – he can tell she's not sure if he'll let her get away with it. 'First Mother dumps me off here, where there isn't even a flushing toilet, then she dies and Auntie stops letting me leave the house! It feels like purgatory, but I'm not even sure what we're all waiting for, because nobody ever tells me!'

Sigrud finishes up with the Kamal. 'Have you ever fired a gun?'

'What?'

'A gun. Have you ever fired one?'

'Well . . . No?'

He checks the bolt, making sure it all slides properly. 'Would you like to?'

She stares at him. 'What? Fire *that*?'

'It is a good gun,' says Sigrud. He places it across his knees. 'I should know.'

'I don't think Mother or Auntie would have appro –'

'Neither of them are here,' he says. 'But I am.'

She looks at the Kamal for a long time. He can tell she's anxious. 'I've never done anything like that before,' she says.

'Then come,' says Sigrud, standing, 'and I will help you.'

He makes her dry-fire it for ten minutes first. She's shocked at how heavy it is, which makes him doubt his choice of firearm, but when she sees his face flicker she insists she can do it.

He has her aim it at a line of tin cans he's stuck up on the fence, telling her to feel the weight of the thing, feel how to distribute the weight across her arms and her shoulders. 'Keep it snug against your shoulder,' he says. 'It will kick. It will likely kick hard.'

He watches her, this pale, skinny thing, holding on to the rifling and blinking nervously as she stares down its sights. She pulls the trigger, wincing each time at the *click*.

'It is not a magic stick,' says Sigrud. 'It is a machine. It is like a little factory, with all the parts clicking along to chamber the round, fire the round, expel the round. You must listen as the factory works, understand its beat, work within its cadence. All right?'

She dry-fires again, pulling the trigger, imagining its kick. 'All right,' she says softly.

He takes it back, double-checks the safety. Then he shows her how to lock the bolt all the way to the rear to avoid it snapping her thumb. He explains how she's going to load it – and *she* is the one who will load it, he says, he won't help her do this – how she's going to take the clip, the brass of the bullets bright and eager, and insert it into the rifle, feeling it give her resistance, until she feels the click. Then he explains how she's going to let go quickly, the bolt sliding to the front and automatically chambering the top round.

'That's it?' she says.

'That's it.'

'I thought it would be harder.'

'Wars are won by efficiency,' says Sigrud. 'The easier a weapon is to operate, the easier it is to train many soldiers at once. When the safety is off, it will be ready to fire. Eight shots. When the weapon is empty, it will eject the clip.'

She hesitates, holding the clip in her hand. 'Should I be nervous?'

'Yes. It is a firearm, after all. It is a tool designed to do one thing. Just as one might fear a mechanised saw, it is reasonable to fear a firearm. But you cannot let your fear of the thing keep you from operating it, or operating it well.'

Taty licks her lips, then inserts the clip. She pushes, but not hard enough.

'Push hard,' he says. 'It is a machine. Like you are opening a can of soup.'

She pushes down harder. The clip slides into the rifling with a loud *click*. She keeps it pressed down for a moment, then quickly draws her hand away. The bolt smoothly slides into place, chambering the top round. She gasps, half in astonishment, half in delight that she did it.

'Good,' he says. 'Now it is loaded. Keep the safety on. Always point it at the ground. Do not take the safety off unless your field of vision is clear and you are ready to take aim. Do not put your finger on the trigger unless you are ready to fire. All right?'

'All right,' she says. She's breathing quite hard.

'I will stay behind you. Then we will shoot at the cans. From there.' He points. 'Fifty yards.'

'That seems like a long way.'

He says nothing. He does not say that she will likely never get much closer than that in combat. He does not want her to think about combat – even if this is what he is preparing her for, however peripherally.

He walks her out to the spot, then stands behind her. 'Take your time,' he says, his tone carefully neutral. 'This is not a test. I simply want you to understand this machine.'

'All right,' she says, nervous.

She takes a lot of time, as he suspected she would. Tatyana Komayd is every bit her mother's child: raised indoors, to read vast truths hidden in papers and numbers. This is not at all what she was bred for.

Yet she must learn it, he thinks. *If we are to move again*.

She raises the rifling. She stares down the sights. He can tell she waits too long – her arms begin to tire. Then she fires.

The shot is loud, powerfully loud. It's also a wild miss, and it startles her so much she falls back and almost drops the rifling. 'It *hurts!*' she says, astonished and outraged. 'It kicks so *hard!*'

'Keep it snug,' he says.

'I did keep it snug!'

'Then keep it more snug.'

She glares at him for a while, scanning him for any judgement, any condescension. He gives her none. Frowning, she raises the rifling and fires again, this time too soon.

'Argh,' she says, rotating her shoulder. 'It hurts . . . And I missed again. Why am I missing?'

'If you had hit one of those cans on your second or first shot, I would have been amazed,' says Sigrud. 'We are not here to learn to sharpshoot, Taty. That would be like expecting a person behind the wheel of an automobile for the first time to be able to win a motor race. I want you to learn how the machine works. How it feels and what it does. Nothing more.'

She thinks about this, then nods. Over the next few minutes, she fires the clip empty. All are misses. But each time she fires, she does so with a little more confidence.

She fires three more clips, and in the middle of the fourth she finally hits a can.

'I did it!' she says, amazed. 'I hit it!'

'You did,' he says. It was likely not the one she was aiming at, but Sigrud doesn't take this victory away from her.

'Ugh, my shoulder *hurts*. Will I ever get used to that?'

'You will,' says Sigrud. 'Or you won't. It's up to you. Do you want to keep trying?'

She thinks about it. 'Yes.'

He nods at the cans. 'I want you to hit all of them at least once.'

She gapes at him. '*All* of them?'

'Yes.'

'I thought you said we weren't going to practice sharpshooting!'

'One must have a goal if one wishes to practice. You can get a little closer, if you would like.'

'But . . . Won't we run out of ammunition?'

'Uh, Auntie Ivanya has rather a lot of ammunition. That is not a concern of mine. I want you to know what it is like to hit all the targets.'

'But my arms are tired.'

'Then they will need to get stronger.'

She scowls at him for a moment.

'Or did you have something else you wanted to do today?' Sigrud asks.

Growling, Taty spends the next two hours shooting the Kamal. She complains that it's painful, that it's exhausting, that it's frustrating. Sigrud does not disagree – it is certainly all of those things. But each time she complains, he says nothing. He waits, and watches. Each time, she picks up the rifling and tries again.

She gets both better and worse. She learns how the rifling works, but by now her upper body is fatigued. *Yet she must learn that too*, he thinks. *How to shoot when exhausted*.

Finally she strikes the last remaining can. When she does she cries out, a raw, ragged shout of exhausted victory. Sigrud smiles. 'You did it,' he says.

'Finally,' she says. 'Gods damned *finally*.'

He raises his eyebrows, allowing this excessive dalliance into adult language to pass. He waits for her to put the safety on, then he takes the rifling and shows her how to eject the clip. 'Let's get something to eat.'

*

They sit in the afternoon light and eat black bread and bright yellow cheese. 'Mother never let me do anything like this,' Taty says around a mouthful. 'She never let me do anything dangerous, or . . . I don't know. Fun. You'd think she would have taught me this first.'

Sigrud shakes his head. 'Shara's life was not easy. It was not normal. And it was not *fun*. I think she wanted yours to be different.'

Taty sighs, a purely adolescent movement. 'Again. I feel like an animal in a cage being fed by my owners.'

Sigrud tears off another hunk of cheese. Once more he is reminded that this actually might be exactly what this girl is: perhaps Shara, fearing her daughter's true nature, penned her in like a wolf in a trap. He has trouble imagining Shara doing anything like that – but people can change over thirteen years. And Shara might have known more than he does.

'Why were you crying when you first came here?' asks Taty.

'What?' says Sigrud, startled.

'When you first came, and Auntie built the fire on the porch for you. I went out to see you, and you were crying.'

'I . . .' He puts his plate down. 'I was not sure if that really happened.'

'If what really happened?'

'I . . . was having a dream. About my daughter. She . . . She died some time ago.'

'Oh,' says Taty. 'I'm sorry.'

Sigrud nods.

'What was she like?'

'Young. Smart. Brilliant, even. She read a lot of books. You would have liked her, maybe. At least, I think she was these things. My time with her was very short, and difficult.' He's quiet for a while. 'I did not know her as well as I would have wished.'

'What puzzles the dead are,' says Taty. She looks away into the wilderness. 'They take so much of themselves with them, you're not even sure who you're mourning. It's mad, but I still . . . I still can't believe she's dead. There's this little bead of belief stuck in my heart that just won't get crushed up, and it says it's all fake. Like it's all theatre. Gaudy drama. She must still be alive in this world, only backstage, away from the theatrics. I read the papers, I know what you and Auntie say. And yet there's this piece of me that *knows*, or *thinks* it knows, that she's still here somehow. It's not fair. I feel like I can't really mourn her until that's gone. Yet it refuses to go.'

'I'm sorry,' says Sigrud. He smiles a little. 'You did well today. When I was young I was trained on bolt-shots and the like, for that was all we had. They were a bit easier on the body than firearms.'

Taty perks up. 'Why don't you show me how you shoot? I expect you must be amazing.'

He shakes his head. 'I am injured. It wouldn't be wise.'

'Oh, please.'

'No.'

'*Please.*'

'No, Taty.'

'Just once?'

Sigrud is silent.

'What if I toss a can up in the air,' says Taty, shoving the rifling over to him, 'and you ca –'

Sigrud slaps down on the rifling's stock, stopping it. 'No!'

Taty recoils a little, surprised. 'Why not?'

'Taty . . . This is not a toy,' he says. 'Do you think this is a game? Why do you think I am showing you how to shoot?'

'What do you mean?'

'Your mother was *murdered*, Taty. The people who killed her are still looking for you. This I know. I must keep you safe. And part of that means you must know how a weapon works.'

She stares at him, incensed. 'So this was all . . . This was all . . .'

'This was all *survival*,' says Sigrud. 'I nearly *died* making my way here to you. If the circumstances call for it, I am willing to die to keep you alive. Those are my orders. But you must understand your reality.'

Taty looks at Sigrud, a mix of emotions pouring into her face: anger, terror, total disbelief. He can tell she's about to leave, or shout, perhaps. It's all too much for a grieving seventeen-year-old girl who previously just worried about depreciation and commodities.

He cuts it off before it can grow. He points to Ivanya's armoury and says, 'In that barn are over fifty different types of firearms. During the time we have together, I want you to shoot all of them at least once. You are your mother's daughter. I know you can face down dangers just as well as she could. But you must learn. You *must* learn. Your mother did not want this life for you, Taty, but it has found you. And together we must get ready.'

Taty blinks for a moment, taking this in. Then she bursts into tears, burying her face in her hands. He supposes this reaction is not that surprising – she's exhausted, and shocked.

He hesitates before laying his right hand on her back. 'You did well today,' he says. 'And tomorrow, you will do even bette –'

Then, to Sigrud's total shock, she flings her arms around him and holds him tight. The hug causes almost intolerable pain for him, but he grimaces and manages to not let a sound out.

They sit there for a moment. Then the back door opens and Ivanya walks out. She looks at Taty, holding Sigrud and weeping, then the Kamal on the porch next to them, then the pile of brass casings littering the yard.

'What . . . What in *hells* is this?' she asks.

'Progress,' says Sigrud.

Despite everything, sleep comes slowly to Sigrud that night.

He can still feel it: still feel her arms around him, still feel her tears on his shoulder. A small, frightened girl who badly needs his help.

He remembers Signe, and Shara, and all the other comrades and operatives he's lost. He knows beyond a doubt that the same could happen to Taty, to Ivanya, to Mulaghesh. It feels as if sorrow follows him like a fog.

He thinks of Nokov, laughing in the dark as Sigrud swore Taty couldn't be Divine: *I almost believe you when you say it.*

He remembers Taty, scowling and saying: *They go to the regular school. I didn't. Mother has tutors for me. Had, I guess.*

Sigrud sits on the edge of the bed, rubbing his face.

Little Tatyana Komayd, raised in captivity, far from her natural environment, kept isolated and quarantined from public life.

Shara must have known, he thinks. *She must have known what Taty is.* A dreadful idea begins to calcify in his thoughts: *Perhaps Shara wasn't keeping Taty close to her. Perhaps she was keeping Taty close to her black lead – the one thing that could kill a Divinity . . .*

He shakes himself. That can't be right, it just can't be. The girl today felt terrifically human: scared and young, yet strong. Ashara Komayd would not be willing to kill such a creature, not her own adopted daughter.

He remembers Shara again, twenty years ago, outside of Jukoshtan: *Our work asks us to make terrible choices. But make them we shall.*

Sigrud shuts his eyes. He does his best to quiet the many doubts now clamouring in his mind. He tries to crawl back into his sorrow, into his cold wrath, to veil himself with the emotions that have guided him through so much of his life, and seemed to give him licence to do so many things he did not wish to do.

I must find the Salim. *I must find out what they are and how they work. I must find out, and soon.*

Another day, then another. Each day Sigrud practises with Taty in the wilderness, focusing on pistols now. Sometimes Ivanya helps – 'He is training you to shoot like a three-hundred-pound man,' she sniffs once, 'so *please* let me show you how a smaller person would do it before you dislocate something' – but she frequently goes into town to check the telegrams, so it is mostly him and Taty, alone.

He can feel her growing close to him, desiring his approval, his care, his attention. He gives her only what she needs, just enough to get through the day.

He realises he is falling back on his training, acting as a handler would when working a flighty source. He hates himself for it.

He knows it is the right choice. But he also recognises that he fears growing close to someone, and losing them again. He can't crawl out from under the feeling that he is a man cursed to carry death in his wake across this world, death that seems to fall far more on the innocent than the wicked. Though perhaps this is abject self-pity.

Am I being a professional, he thinks, watching as Taty cleans a revolving pistol, *or a coward?*

When Ivanya returns from town that day, she jumps out and doesn't even take off her driving goggles. She points at Sigrud, and barks, 'You. Inside. Now.'

Sigrud stands, giving Taty the slightest shake of the head to indicate that things are all right. Then he follows Ivanya into the house.

'I finally heard back from old Mother Mulaghesh,' says Ivanya with a trace of scorn. She reaches into the pocket of her jacket, pulls out a telegram, and tosses it to him. 'Though what this means, I don't know.'

Sigrud opens it up. It's extremely short, reading simply:

SQ QG6596 STOP

LAST KNOWN ACTIVE SQUARE STOP

LISTED AS ACTIVE IN 1718 STOP

Sigrud sits back, scratching his head, and thinks.

'Well?' says Ivanya. 'Does that help you any?'

'It does,' he says. He sighs deeply. 'I will need a map, though. A world map.'

'But . . . wait. How could that actually help? It looks like . . . nothing.'

'The Saypuri Navy doesn't use latitude and longitude. It has its own classified compressing system, these large tiles that make up the ocean. Squares within squares.' He taps the first portion of the telegram. 'This code is for one specific square – from the first two letters of the code I can tell it is the Sartoshan Sea, south of the Mashev Mountains. Basically, along the border in the ranges dividing Jukoshtan and Saypur. If I had a map I could get more specific.'

'So that's where your boat – the *Salim* – was last reported active?'

'If what Mulaghesh says is true, yes – in 1718, two years *after* it supposedly sank in 1716.'

'So the sinking bit – that was, what, a cover-up?'

'I assume so. The ship must have been doing something out there, serving some covert purpose, but I've no idea what.'

Ivanya takes a file out of a small satchel, then sits opposite him. 'So now you're sailing out there to go see?'

'How can I sail if I don't have a boat?'

She shrugs. 'I have a boat.'

'You do?'

'Certainly. I have *lots* of boats. I own a small shipping service that operates out of Ahanashtan. Or, specifically, I own a company that owns a company that owns a company . . . you get the idea. I can get you a boat . . . if you think it's really wise to go.'

He sighs again, deeper. 'I . . . I think I do.'

She glances at him. 'You were told to protect Taty.'

'How can I protect her if I don't know what she is? Where I can take her that is safe if I do not truly understand our enemies? I don't know his limits, his behaviour, his desires. This ship, the *Salim* . . . It was the genesis for everything. For Shara's war, for all these Divine defences – it set off all of it.'

'So now you're off to travel the world?' asks Ivanya. She snorts. 'It's absurd we're even discussing it . . . How long will it take to get out there? And what kind of boat will you need?'

'From Ahanashtan to the northern tip of the Sartoshan Sea . . . That's no quick jaunt. Over eight hundred miles, certainly. A week or more to get there, at least. And since I would prefer it to just be me on this particular trip, it would need to be a ship that I can pilot by myself. Maybe a forty- or fifty-foot ketch with a mizzen staysail set.'

'I won't pretend to understand any of that,' says Ivanya, 'which is why I pay Dmitri to understand boats for me. If you're really sure of this – if you're sure this is the way forward – write down your specifications, and I'll ask him to see if we own something similar. If not, I'm sure he can find one for you.' She takes out a tin of cigarettes and a long, ivory cigarette holder – one of the few aristocratic affectations she allows. 'Two more weeks here. Is that really safe?'

'No,' says Sigrud. 'But I see no other choice. And I am unwilling to take you with me. It could all be a trap.'

'Terrific,' says Ivanya flatly. 'Well, while you've been thinking about our enemies, I've been thinking about your supposed allies. You mentioned escalated cases with the charity, and I remembered something . . . Does the name Malwina Gogacz mean anything to you?'

Sigrud cocks his head. 'That was one of the names on the list our enemy had.'

'I see. Well. Your theory is proving correct.' She flips open the file on the table. 'Gogacz was one of Shara's first escalated cases, but Shara never *quite* got a hold of her. She tried over and over again. Gogacz would come to an orphanage. We'd find out about her placement within the shelter systems. Shara would go to see her. But before she got there, the girl would be gone.'

'She figured out you were after her? And fled each time?'

'I'm not sure. Shara mentioned to me that each time she walked into a shelter to meet with Miss Gogacz, she would get the *strangest* sense that she'd been there before. Just minutes before, really, as if she'd walked in earlier that day and then walked out, and then forgot all about it. It was most peculiar. It frustrated her to pieces. And then she'd find Gogacz was gone. It went like this over and over again, at least four times. Then she tried to find this Gogacz one last time, in Bulikov. And she never told me what happened after that.'

'Shara got to her, you think?'

'Yes,' says Ivanya. 'I do think our Shara finally caught up with Miss Gogacz. They met. But what happened next, I'm not sure of. I found a photograph of her in the file.'

She pulls out a small photo, and holds it up.

Sigrud's eye widens. There, rendered in the grey hues of a cheap camera, is the face of the young girl who saved him at the slaughterhouse: the same strangely upturned nose, the same mass of curly black hair, and the same defiant, unrelenting look in her eye.

'That's her, isn't it?' asks Ivanya.

'Yes,' he says. 'Without a doubt.'

'Of course it is,' says Ivanya softly. 'The first one she pursued, and the one she chased the most . . . This photo was taken when the girl first entered the Bulikovian orphanage system in 1732. So it was nearly six years ago. Has she aged much in that time, by your estimation?'

Sigrud, grimacing, shakes his head. He finds he does not enjoy having anything in common with the Divine.

'And . . . she does bear a striking resemblance to Taty,' says Ivanya in a small voice. She puts the photo down and stuffs it behind some papers in the file, like she doesn't wish to see it.

'It's even more striking when you see it in person,' says Sigrud darkly.

'You think this Gogacz was avoiding Shara through Divine means, somehow?'

He nods.

'And then once Shara caught up with her – then they started collaborating in this war?'

He nods again.

'But we've no idea if Taty can do anything like what this girl does?'

'If she can, I haven't seen it.'

Ivanya sighs. 'Well. Are you going to tell her you're leaving?' she asks, her words blooming smoke. 'Or shall I?'

Sigrud sighs and closes his eyes, wondering what to do. He was never really a case officer, but he remembers Vinya telling him once: *Always tell a source you'll come back to them. Tell them they're safe. Tell them whatever they want to hear. Anything. A desperate source will believe the wildest lies.*

How I hate myself, he thinks, *for falling back on Vinya's advice at such a time.*

Taty blinks slowly, her knees against her chest on the back porch. Sigrud sits beside her, huge and slumping next to this short, frail girl, her hands filthy with oil and grease.

'Two weeks, then,' she says.

'Yes. Maybe more. But not very long, really.'

'But you might not come back.'

'I . . . I will come back,' he says. 'I will.'

She says nothing.

'I've asked Ivanya to continue your lessons.' He tries to smile at her. 'I said I wanted you to try all the weapons. I meant it.'

Still she says nothing.

'I *will* be back,' he says. 'As soon as I can.'

'Did you know,' says Taty, 'that I dreamed about you last night?'

'Did you?'

'Yes. I dreamed you'd go away. But I dreamed you'd come back far sooner than we expected. Than *you* expected, even. It would be as if you hadn't even left.'

He smiles. 'Perhaps we'll be lucky.'

'Luck has nothing to do with it,' she says, and her voice is missing all the affected wisdom he's used to hearing. These are the dry, firm tones of a confident woman. 'What will be will be.'

9.
Too Much Night, Not Enough Moon

What troubles you, then? What ails you?
A drink of water, surely? Then summon you a water sprite, a child Divine
To sprinkle sweet drops upon your tongue.
Speak her name forcefully enough, speak it with power,
And she shall be forced to listen, and come.
So speak! Speak! Speak, and see!

— MENDING THE MUSE'S MEDDLE (V.III.315–21),
AUTHOR OF PLAY UNKNOWN

Alone. Again.

All his old sea training comes back to him as Sigrud pilots the little ketch east along the Continental shore. For hours at a time it is only him, the ache in his side, the wind, and the beastly squalls on the horizon, battlements of dark, curling storms, dragging behind a hazy veil of thick rain. He says not a word for these travels, not to himself. He lost much use for words over the years alone in the wilderness. As civilisation fades on the horizon behind him, that deep, thoughtless silence returns to him.

His side hurts, but not as much as he expected. Ivanya provided him with some painkillers, but not the opiate sort, so he can still do his duties while sailing. It's not easy, but he manages.

He drops anchor only twice, first in the tiny Shuri Islands. Some nomadic Saypuri tribe has set up on the eastern rim of the largest one, and since they cannot build on the land they build on the sea, little huts and piers set on stilts. He pays them a small fee for fresh water and some salted fish. They pore over the handful of drekels as if it were a fortune.

The next time, he drops anchor at the edge of the Sartoshan. He has his nautical maps now, so he's able to use the code Mulaghesh gave him to target a much more specific area.

A tiny lagoon, right at the top of the Sartoshan. International waters, almost – that subject, like so many things relating to territory and sovereignty, is always dreadfully tricky on the Continent. But if he were going to hide anything, it'd be in a place like that.

He folds up the map and stares out at the horizon. He hopes there's something there. He hopes he didn't endanger Taty and Ivanya over nothing. He hopes that, come a few days, he will no longer be moving in blind desperation.

It's at times like this that he misses her the most. She always knew what to do. Where to go. Who to see.

Shara, he thinks, *am I a fool to try this? Would you do this? Or is this what got you killed?*

Two days later Sigrud sails along the Jukoshtan coast, watching as the cliffs climb and climb north of him, climbing until they become the Mashevs, the tallest mountains in the known world, much taller than the Tarsils. This tiny isthmus of land, hardly five hundred miles wide, is all that connects the Continent to Saypur, yet with the Mashevs in the way it might as well be an ocean in between the two.

The Mashev River (if Sigrud recalls what Shara once said, all of this region is named after some Jukoshtani saint who died out here after a particularly wild party) is a narrow thread of water that must become a raging torrent in spring, when the snowpack melts. He finds the first of the long, thin islands that cluster around its delta and steers around them, mindful of the lagoon's shallow waters.

Then he sees it.

It looks like a building in the distance, perhaps a long, low, slumping bunker built atop the fattest of the isles. Then he gets closer, and closer.

It's a massive ship, over a thousand feet long. Sigrud never had much to do with the Saypuri Navy – his maritime experiences as a Dreyling in the

North Sea were with far more primitive vessels – so even he's a bit taken aback by the size of the wrecked dreadnought. Its wreckage is obscene, tangles of metal and debris lodged in the delicate white sands of the lagoon. The beaches glitter with metal, yet most of the debris is rusted over, devoured by the sea spray and the elements.

He pilots his ketch over to an appealing side of the island, then drops anchor. Ivanya's man provided him with a canvas inflatable raft – a new innovation he's not sure he can bring himself to trust – but he manages to inflate it, set it in the waves, and climb aboard, rowing to shore with the two measly little oars.

He drags the raft up onto the beach and tries to find something to tie it to, as the winds here are fierce. There's a beaten, bitter-looking tree sprouting from the soil a bit beyond the beach. He lashes the raft up, taking care to avoid the jagged, rusted shards of metal on the ground, then steps back to review his work.

On the second step back, something crunches unpleasantly under his bootheel. He looks down. A sliver of something grey-white has surfaced from the sands.

He steps aside, kneels, and pushes the sand away. He recognises what's below almost immediately. He's dug things like this up before, after all.

Vertebrae, scattered through the sand. Neck vertebrae, from their width. And just next to them, a skull with two iron teeth.

He digs more. Though the corpse is old, he finds fragments of their clothing. Buttons and medals and pins. He holds one button up and blows the sand off it. He's seen such buttons before, many times, running down the pert, handsome blue uniforms of the Saypuri Navy.

He drops the button and sits back on his haunches, staring in the direction of the wrecked dreadnought. Its hull is split and torn, forming something like ribs, grey light slanting through the gaps. He stands and squints and shields his eyes, looking at the beach leading up to the ruined ship.

He spies lumps in the sand. Calcified forms that he now suspects are certainly not seashells.

Sigrud grabs a torch, his lockpicks, a pistol, and his knife. Then he walks toward the wreck of the SS *Salim*, stepping around the bones lying in the sand, the jumbled, skeletal remains of the several hundred souls who surely once served aboard that behemoth.

Some of the skulls have been crushed. And though he can't be certain, one such skull has been crushed in a manner that's highly reminiscent of fingers, as if it was destroyed by human hands.

He approaches the bow of the ship, which has mostly held together. The *Salim* is about four or five storeys tall, a massive construction, though it's tipped very slightly toward the west, so it's hard for him to get perspective on its size.

He comes to the starboard side of the bow and looks up along its hull. The ship has bowed slightly as it's laid for however many years on the curving surface of the island, causing its sides to split and separate like someone bending a piece of soft cheese. The hull is ragged and gaping at the seams, with rivets sticking out as though a drunk tried to put the thing together. Though Sigrud's a skilled climber, even this gives him pause.

Still, he thinks. *Nothing else to do.*

Grimacing, he pulls on a pair of thick leather gloves and approaches one seam that runs all the way up the hull. He should be able to hold on to either side of the seam, wedge himself inside to bridge the gap, and slowly climb up using his hands and feet on either side.

Provided everything holds together, of course. Which is by no means a guarantee.

He starts up. The hull is incredibly thick, especially along the armoured belt – the portion of the ship's sides that would be just above the waterline, where a shell could strike it – so it's quite sturdy. He could even crawl through the bulkhead to the inner decks, but he's unwilling to try this. To enter where the ship is terribly damaged would be suicidal.

But he can tell something's different about the *Salim*, from the sliver of the interior he can see as he climbs. Most dreadnoughts would have what's called a citadel, a heavily armoured 'box' beneath the four main gun turrets, protecting their ammunition and the ship's coal bunkers from being penetrated by an enemy shell. He's trafficked in naval intelligence, so he's aware of such an engineering feat – yet what he glimpses through the cracks of the ship's hull is . . . unusual.

He pauses about midway up, makes sure his feet are tightly wedged into the seam, pulls out the torch, and flicks it on.

The two fore ammunition stores have been heavily altered. He can see no feeds running up to the two fore gun turrets above, meaning the guns wouldn't have been battle-ready. The ammunition chambers are still there, but they've been merged into *one* chamber, and it's been closed off, and has been heavily, heavily armoured, to the point where the chamber is nearly as armoured as the belt running along the sides of the ship.

Which makes him wonder – what could they have been keeping in there, if not ammunition?

He grunts, puts the torch away, and continues up.

Finally he comes to the main deck. The gap in the hull is getting wider and wider as he goes up, until he realises he won't be able to bridge the gap anymore. Sighing, he swivels so he's clinging to one side of the seam, pinching it between his feet and palms, and slowly, slowly hauls himself up.

The main deck of the ship is tilting, so while he very badly wishes to roll on to the top and catch his breath, he's aware that this would send him rolling down the deck until he tumbled off the port side. So instead he crawls over and holds on to the railing, breathing hard and wishing he'd brought kneepads with him, as some of the torn plates snagged his legs.

Then he sits up and freezes. 'What in the hells . . .?'

The deck of the *Salim* has been . . . decorated. Specifically, they appear to have removed the two fore gun turrets and, in their place, they have used some kind of welding torch to melt a sigil or glyph of some kind into the deck – a mark referring to one of the Continental Divinities.

Sigrud stares at this, unable to comprehend it. The idea of a piece of equipment belonging to the Saypuri Military essentially being blessed by one of the Continental Divinities is unthinkable. He stands, wobbling a little on the slanted surface, and tries to get a better view of it.

The sigil is familiar, he finds: the jagged top, sloping swoop below, and curling sash . . . He remembers Shara making something like that once in Taalvashtan, burning the symbol into a big wooden board with a match, and then they both had to hold the piece of wood above their heads as they walked over ground that had been cursed.

What was it she said? It comes swimming up to him, slowly: *Kolkan's Sanctuary*, she told him. *It dampens the effects of any Divine activity occurring below or above it – except Kolkan's, of course. Story has it Kolkan created it specifically because Jukov and his followers kept trying to break into Kolkan's monasteries to debauch his virginal followers, and he got quite sick of it. He burned this symbol into the entrances and exits of his monasteries so no one could miraculously penetrate the grounds . . .*

Sigrud cocks his head, looking at it. He gauges that the refurbished ammunition chamber he saw through the split hull is directly below the sigil.

He considers where to begin. Whatever was happening on the SS *Salim*, it seems it was approved by the Saypuri government in some form or fashion: one doesn't do massive internal refurbishments to the interior of a dreadnought without considerable resources and skilled labour.

So start with the officers, he thinks, *and command*. He looks back at the ship's bridge, then down at the main deck between it and where he currently stands. The deck is split in many places, like a roadway that's just been through an earthquake. Some of the armour plating has collapsed entirely. One wrong step and he'll tumble into a ragged chasm of torn metal.

He sighs and stretches his quadriceps. *Let's hope I haven't gained too much weight.*

He has to jump only twice to cross the splintering deck. Both times he hangs above a dark, rusty gorge for one instant, the torn decks yawning below him, before his boots slam down on the plating on the other side. Both times he's convinced the ruined metal won't hold him, and it will bend and buckle beneath his heels, sending him spilling down to be shredded to death. Both times he's wrong.

Lucky, he thinks. *Very lucky.*

He approaches the bridge ladder and finds a ruined door lying at the bottom. It's the door that would normally lead into the bridge, and from the look of its pulverised deadbolts it was locked when it was ripped out of its doorway. He touches the metal, noting how it's been nearly ripped in two. He touches one rent, and can't help but feel that they match human digits, as if someone had grabbed the metal in one hand like a piece of wet clay and given it a mighty tug.

He climbs the bridge ladder and looks in. The controls have been destroyed, and the floor is littered with bones and refuse and bird droppings. Whatever took place here happened long ago, as the only smells he can catch are salt and rust.

He looks to the aft of the ship. The main deck there is rent and ravaged in a very strange fashion. The force of the damage seems to have come from below, as if someone fired a shell up *through* the ship.

Or perhaps something else. Maybe something clawed its way through the various decks and burst out like a bird of prey breaking through a forest canopy.

He hops back down the ladder and rounds the platform until he finds the entrance to the captain's stateroom.

The door is locked, but it's in some state of decay, so with a few stout kicks Sigrud's able to cave it in. He switches on his torch and climbs in. Like most staterooms, this one is or at least once was quite fancy, considering the environs, with a leather sofa, several paintings, and – most important – a private head. The room must have flooded at one point, though, based on the water marks on the walls.

Sigrud walks over to the desk and pulls out the drawers, which scream and squawk. The bottom one has a bunch of mouldering files in it, stained beyond legibility. The second one has a revolving pistol and a box of ammunition, though he doubts if the bullets are any good after the flood. The top drawer is locked.

Sigrud looks around and finds a piece of iron plating that has fallen off the wall. He picks it up, shoves it into the gap above the drawer, and gives it a kick.

The drawer pops open with a crunch. Inside is a leather-bound journal. It seems to have escaped most of the water.

He pulls it out and flips through the pages. Some have sustained water damage, causing the ink to run, but a few at the middle are readable. He holds it up to the light and reads:

> . . . *n and blast if I cannot wait for this to be over. Today is the worst day in recent memory. I had to cut down a member of the crew this morning. Kudal,*

his name was, Petty Officer 3rd Class. He hung himself in the lower decks last night. And though no one said so I know very few could blame him for it.

As cowardly and unpatriotic as it might seem, this is one duty I desperately wish to end. It is a waste of our time, a waste of our resources, and though we are not in any physical danger, I sincerely believe that this duty is causing psychological harm to my crew. I hope we have no more like Kudal. But I doubt we shall be so lucky.

Worst of all, I cannot personally imagine how that thing belowdecks could help military intelligence in any way. I want to tell her to just be done with it and slaughter the thing — but to be honest I am not sure if such a thing can be slain.

I will distribute ear guards to the crew tonight. The pounding and the screaming could be heard even up in the depths of the fo'c's'le, and none can sleep. I can even hear it myself on the nights when the thing gets ornery. And it does tend to get angrier at night, or at least louder.

I do not like the nights out here. They taste wrong to me. There is too much night, and not enough moon, if that makes any sense.

— LIEUTENANT COMMANDER BABURAO VERMA,
17TH OF THE MONTH OF THE SNAKE, 1717

Another visit from Ghaladesh today. She comes boating in on that damned yacht looking like an industry heiress — which I suppose she is. If politics could be an industry, Vinya Komayd would most certainly be its most lauded scion.

Once again the crew and I stayed above deck while she and her toadies interviewed it. I much prefer it when the other toadies do the interviewing, as they are not half so severe about dictating our duties to us.

I could tell they hit the thing with the lights again because it howled and howled like the most monstrous of squalls. I am sure you could have heard its howling up in the Mashevs. Some of the men grew sick and I had to find a place for them to be seen to as I could not send them to their quarters or to the medical bay, for that of course was belowdecks. We eventually simply treated them on the bridge. It is not like we shall ever sail this ship anywhere, anyway. We are a floating prison, not a proud vessel of our nation.

They recorded the transcripts again and made us leave the bridge while they encrypted them. This is, of course, not protocol. Perhaps they do not wish to have any element of what they are doing here discovered. Such behaviour could cause a less devoted sailor than I to wonder precisely how official this all is.

I do not know what we are intended to Rebirth, but I do not wish to see it be reborn.

— LIEUTENANT COMMANDER BABURAO VERMA,

21ST OF THE MONTH OF THE DOLPHIN, 1717

I went down to see it tonight. I know I shouldn't have. It's against my orders. But I did it anyway, to ask it to stop crying. It was too much, too loud.

The glass was thick and I could not see it in the darkness, so I spoke to it through the microphones they set up. Again, I know this is a breach of my orders. But I asked it to quiet. I asked it to please stop its weeping.

It would not listen. I have gathered from what she's said that it is in pain. They put the lights on it so often.

I did not turn on the lights. I left the chamber dark, as I am told it prefers it. But it did not answer me.

I wish it did not cry like a child. I wish it did not cry with the voice of a young boy.

I am a commander in the Saypuri Navy, and I am proud of my duty and my service and my country. But I did not sign up to become a jailer. Especially not a jailer of children, even if the children are quite strange.

I have neve . . .

The words begin bleeding again there. The rest of the pages are legible only in spots.

Sigrud stands there, thinking. Then he tosses the book aside and walks back out.

This is all Vinya's doing, he thinks. *All of it, all of it. Before Bulikov, before Voortyashtan, before everything.*

He finds the ladder belowdecks and starts down.

This was her project, her plot, off the books and far out in disputed waters.

Belowdecks is a reeking warren, dark corners flooded with sediment and teeming with sea creatures.

What did she trap here?

Sometimes a splinter of bone with gleam in the dark mud, or a button or piece of brass will shine bright in the light of his torch.

What did she torture and question?

Yet he thinks he knows what. Or, more likely, whom.

He feels as if he's in the innards of a great sleeping creature, the dark surfaces dripping or creaking, the wind whipping through the rents in the hull.

Down, down. Down, down, down.

And as he climbs down, Sigrud remembers.

He remembers Slondheim, the prison he was held in for more than seven years. A monstrous fortification built into a gash in the tall cliffsides, a black crack swirling with sea. The dark walls of rock, riddled with cell-blocks and chambers, the lapping waters below. The jail boats trundling from side to side, lanterns swinging, their iron cages filled with screaming, filthy people.

He remembers his first journey in such a cage. The creaking, ancient boat. The cliffs stretching above him, echoing with howls, glimmering with torchlight. And how he bellowed for freedom.

Sigrud slips down another deck, flexing his knuckles. *Passionate is the love*, he thinks, *that a nation has for its prisons*.

Finally he comes to it, the massive chamber he glimpsed as he scaled the hull. From this angle there is no doubt at all that its primary purpose was a prison.

The tremendous metal door, covered in locks. The thick glass portholes, like staring eyes. And mounted in the sides, huge electric lights, lights bright enough to illuminate a city square.

The port side of the chamber sports a magnificent hole, a tangled, blooming flower of torn metal, petals of steel unfolding out like some strange sculpture. Sigrud walks over to it and shines the light inside the chamber.

Bare metal interior. Almost airtight. But every surface of the metal is riddled with dents in the same pattern, over and over and over again, four small divots, all in a line.

The knuckles of a hand, a small one. A boy's hand.

How long did they keep you here? How long did they keep you down here in the dark?

He shines his torch on the tangled metal around the hole in the chamber's side. Like the door to the bridge above, like the skulls he found on the beach, there are finger marks in the metal, as if someone unfathomably strong took it and warped it as though it were no more than soft sand.

And how did you break out?

He steps back from the chamber and looks up. He can see it from this angle: he can see the tunnel carved upward through the layers of steel, a passage made as whatever was held in that chamber clawed its way to freedom.

Do we ever truly escape? Am I still battering against the walls of Slondheim, somewhere in my mind?

For a moment, he feels a glimmer of sympathy for the creature that was once bound here. He does his best to smother it.

Do not pity him. Remember what he took from you. Remember Shara. Remember what you've lost.

Down in the dark, Sigrud je Harkvaldsson tries to rekindle his many grievances, hoping they will keep him warm enough to keep moving – a mental exercise he is deeply familiar with.

He sighs. The ship creaks around him with the wind.

But one creak seems to last . . . a little too long. Longer than the breeze lasted, surely. As if something besides the wind was pushing at the metal.

Sigrud pauses. Listens.

Another creak.

He whirls and snaps the beam of the torch up into the tattered decks behind him.

He sees her only briefly, half-hidden behind a girder: the pale face, the upturned nose, the mouth twisted in distrust.

The girl from the slaughterhouse. Malwina Gogacz.

His jaw drops. 'What?'

She makes a gesture with one hand. And then things . . . blur.

The wind beats against him. Sigrud bends low, trudges up across the sand, and lashes the inflatable raft to the little tree, taking care to avoid the jagged, rusted shards of metal on the ground. He's surprised the little raft survived so well, he's never tried an inflatable vessel before. Then he steps back to review his work.

On the second step back, something crunches unpleasantly under his bootheel. He looks down. A sliver of something grey-white has surfaced from the sands.

It looks like bones. The bones of a person, buried here on the beach.

He bends low to dig in the sand at his feet, but then stops as he realises . . .

'Wait a minute,' he says aloud. 'I've done this before.'

He looks around. He's back on the beach outside the *Salim*. He looks down, bewildered. He examines his knee and sees it isn't cut – though didn't he snag his right knee on the jagged hull? And his boots aren't covered with the black mud he waded through to get to the prison chamber.

He remembers her. Malwina Gogacz, watching him from the decks above.

He scratches his head. 'What is going on?'

He walks back to the hull of the *Salim*. He has no desire to try to scale it again. Instead he sticks his face into one of the gaps and bellows, '*Malwina Gogacz!*'

Silence. Nothing but the wind.

He tries again. '*Malwina Gogacz! Are you in there? Can you hear me?*'

More silence.

He takes another breath and shouts: '*You saved my life in the slaughterhouse! If we were to meet again, you said you'd tell me more!*'

Silence. At least, for a bit.

Then a voice from above, speaking with a mixture of astonishment and outrage, 'How the *fuck* do you remember me?'

Sigrud looks up. He can see her just barely through the crack in the hull, but she's there, standing on the second platform above the hold.

'Remember you?' he says.

'I reset time!' she says. 'You shouldn't remember me! *Everything* should have been reset.'

'I . . . don't really know what you mean,' he says. 'But why don't you come down so we can talk about it more?'

*

She refuses to come all the way out to him, and instead speaks to him through the crack in the hull, like an old woman reluctant to open her door for a salesman.

'You survived,' she says.

'I did.'

'You look terrible.'

'Thank you.'

'How did you find me?'

'I wasn't looking for you,' he says. 'I was looking for this ship.'

'Why?'

'Because Shara Komayd was looking for it, once.'

Malwina's mouth twists, as if she's struggling not to say more.

'You knew her, didn't you?' asks Sigrud. 'Worked with her? She caught up to you at an orphanage on the Continent and recruited you. Was she the one who told you about this ship, that it was here?'

'Yes,' she says reluctantly.

'And this ship started everything, didn't it? Once she found it, it started her efforts to locate some very . . . *special* Continental orphans. But what happened here started more than that, didn't it?'

'You're a damned clever creature, aren't you.'

'Sometimes. If I recall, you said you would tell me more if we met again. So why don't you come outside to me?'

'It's safer in here.'

'Why?'

'You've seen what's chasing me,' says Malwina. 'You've seen what's out there, how powerful he is. I've survived because I've learned not to trust people unless I have the advantage over them. And right now, sir, you seem to have a lot of advantages over me.'

'Yet one would think,' says Sigrud, 'that the past would be more powerful than an old Dreyling.'

Malwina's eyes grow wide. 'How . . . How did you . . .?'

'Am I right?' he asks. 'That's your – what is the word – your *domain*, isn't it? That's where you are, or were?'

She draws back a little from the crack in the hull.

'You are a Divine child, are you not?' he says. 'Your domain is the past, the world of things that were. That is how you were able to project a bubble of the past around yourself back in the slaughterhouse. And that's how you just . . . sent me back through time? Is that what you did?'

'I reset things,' says Malwina.

'You . . . reset things?'

'Yes. Just a bit. You can't change the past – or at least, you *shouldn't* be able to – but you can reset things before the present *becomes* the past. I make the past replay itself all over again, but the present of that instance – the present at which I reset the past – is different. Got me?'

'No,' says Sigrud with total honesty.

'Whatever. The past *should* have played out again as it did. You *should* have gone back inside the ship, dug through the files, gone to see the prison. Only this time I wouldn't let you see me. I'd have stayed hidden. It would have been a redo.' She looks him over. 'But it didn't. How did you remember? Your memory should have been reset too.'

'I don't know.' He makes a fist with his left hand, his fingertips feeling the scar there. 'But . . . I have some ideas.'

'This is all a tremendous violation, you know. Right now, what's happening *right now*. This is a problem for me, and a fucking big one. You shouldn't be able to change the past. You're running amok in my personal, Divine domain! How the hells did you do that?'

Sigrud frowns and looks away. *She is not the first Divine thing whose power you've defied*, he thinks. *That cannot be accidental.* 'Never mind that,' he says. 'What was here? What happened here? What did Vinya Komayd trap inside this ship?'

'Don't you know?' she asks.

He remembers the boy in the dark outside of Shara's estate: *I will visit every pain and every torture upon your head that was visited upon* mine . . .

'I suspect,' he says. 'But I want you to tell me.'

'The night,' she whispers. 'They held the night itself here for years and years . . . That's why I chose to hide here, after all. This is one place he'll never, ever want to return to. It's the one place I can be safe.'

They sit on the beach, staring out at the grey skies hanging low over the dark ocean.

'He is . . . the night?' asks Sigrud.

'Yes,' she says. 'The night itself. The purest idea of it, the first night.'

'What do you mean?'

'The first night humanity experienced. Before light, before civilisation, before your kind named the stars. That's what he *is*, that's how he works. He is darkness, he is shadows, he is the primeval manifestation of what's outside your windows, what's beyond the fence gate, what lives under the light of the cold, distant moon . . . All darknesses are one to him. All shadows are one to him. That was his function, as a child of the Divine.'

'How . . . How are you all alive?' asks Sigrud. 'How did you *survive*?'

'Most of us didn't,' says Malwina. 'Most of us the Kaj got to. He executed them as if they were no more than sickly livestock. But not all of us. What would you do if your lands were being invaded, and people were specifically seeking out your heirs to kill?'

'I'd send them away.'

'Let's say you can't. You can't leave your home, and neither can your kids. They're bound to it. So what do you do?'

Sigrud nods. 'I hide them.'

'Right. And which Divinity was the trickiest, cleverest one of them all?'

He lets out a slow sigh. 'Jukov.'

'Correct.'

'By the seas . . . How many plots and plans did he put in place before he hid himself away?'

'I don't know. But it's not unreasonable. He'd have been a real shit to have saved himself but not his children.' She grows solemn. 'Though what he did to us . . . I'm not sure if it counts as saving.'

'Why? How did it work?'

She appears to struggle with it for a moment. 'You didn't . . . You didn't even really know it was *happening*,' she says. 'That's what it's like, living with a Divinity. They point a finger, and reality changes.' She looks away. 'He came to you. And suddenly your memories started . . . shifting. They grew hazy. Suddenly, you didn't even think you were Divine. You thought you were mortal. Just a little mortal child, a little lost orphan. And then . . . Then you *were* that thing. And maybe, if you were lucky, you got adopted by a common mortal family, and they loved you, and they cared for you, and you lived with them. Grew up with them. And maybe, for a while, you were happy. Ignorant, sure, but happy.'

She swallows. 'But then . . . Then one day people started getting suspicious. You got older for a while, but then you just . . . stopped. They started wondering, when was this child going to grow up? When was this child going to become an adult? Why does this child stay adolescent? Why was this child still here? And when people started asking these questions and getting suspicious, then Jukov's miracle took care of you.

'It hid you away again. Made you a child again. It bent reality around you, ever so slowly, ever so slightly. And without ever being aware that you were doing so, you left that family, just walked away from it, and went back to being alone again. It reset *everything*. You forgot all about them, and they forgot too. It was as if you'd never come to live with the family. And to them, it was as if they'd never adopted that sweet little girl. Both of you totally forgot one another. Because you have to be kept safe, free from suspicion. And for you, a blessed child of the Divine, this happened over and over and over again. And over and over and over again. A sleepwalking child, repeating your youth over and over again, drifting from family to family. Without even leaving a memory behind.'

Malwina shuts her eyes, as if trying to forget something. She picks up a handful of sand, works at it, lets the grains filter through her fingers. 'Later, after you awoke from the spell, you'd wonder – would you and your old family sometimes see each other on the streets? The mother and father that took you in for months, maybe years, maybe longer? And you wouldn't have even *recognised* each other. You'd have forgotten all about it. The miracle would have wiped your mind, returned you to your sleepwalking state. Except maybe a little bit. Maybe just a ghost of love would stir in your heart. Like feeling an amputated limb that isn't there anymore. But you wouldn't have known. You wouldn't have known why your heart ached to see these strangers.' She shakes her head. 'The . . . The awful choices we make to survive.' She laughs. 'Is it even worth it?'

'Why?' asks Sigrud. 'What end goal did Jukov have in mind? Why put you through this?'

'He thought he'd survive, and come back, and wake us all up,' says Malwina. 'I think. He wasn't a big explainer. He did as he pleased.' She smiles bitterly. 'One day, we'd all be together again, one big family again – and then, perhaps, we'd start our war, and retake the Continent.'

'But you woke up before then?' says Sigrud.

'Yes,' says Malwina. 'Bad luck. It happened to some. You'd be living with your adopted family, and something would happen. An accident. A fire. Something. And you'd lose them. And when that happened, that memory you had trapped in yourself of your Divine family dying, of Taalhavras and Voortya and all the rest dying, that came shooting back up in your mind. One trauma releases another. That intense, emotional experience would break open the dams inside you. And then you remembered . . . *everything*. Who you were, and what you could do. Some things even a miracle can't suppress, I guess. Sometimes I wonder if we're little more than walking patchworks of traumas, all stitched together.'

They sit in silence for a moment, watching the waves churn and roil under the overcast skies.

'He got the worst of it,' says Malwina. 'Our . . . enemy. I don't like him. I hate him. But he had worse luck than we did.'

'What happened to him?'

'At first, the same thing that happened to all of us who are awake now,' she says. 'An accident. A family, tragically lost. A child awoken. But then he . . . did something unwise. When he was in yet another orphanage, he did . . . shadow tricks. Someone noticed. And word got through to the Ministry. And then on to old Vinya Komayd.'

'How did she trap him?'

She shrugs. 'She was a brilliant old bitch. She must have duped him somehow. She came to him, maybe threatened to do to him what the Kaj had done to everyone else. He was still traumatised, having just lost his adopted parents. He probably didn't know which way was up. She put him on a boat, drove him far out here where he's away from the land that powers him, from those that believe in him, shape and influence him – and that made him weak.'

'Then she put Kolkan's sigil atop him,' says Sigrud. 'And that made him still weaker.'

'Yes. And then she interrogated and tortured him. Day and night. Hit him with lights. He hates those, being what he is.'

'And when Shara killed Kolkan, and Jukov . . . That's when this happened, isn't it?' He waves at the *Salim*. 'That's when what was trapped here escaped. Because the protections faded.'

'Yes. Kolkan's sigil, which had suppressed the power of the night for so long . . . When Kolkan died, the sigil lost all meaning, all influence, just like everything else Kolkan had made. And the boy trapped here was free to go. Though he is not a boy any longer.'

'Why?' asks Sigrud. 'Why do this to him? Why meddle in such things?'

Malwina looks at him, smirking. 'Ah, sir. What is the one thing Saypur fears more than anything?'

'The Divine, of course.'

'Yes. Against which the Saypuris have no defence. Back then the Kaj's black lead was still lost, remember. And what's the only thing anyone had any historical record of that could stop a god?'

'I don't know. Nothing, I thought. Except . . . another god?' He looks at her, astonished. 'Wait. You are saying Vinya Komayd wanted to make her *own god*?'

'Rules of warfare,' says Malwina grimly. 'Always escalate. If your opponent has a weapon or technology beyond you, do everything you can to develop one of your own.'

'But . . . But how could that have *worked*?'

'Well, she wasn't sure, but she was game to try. She had a child Divinity on her hands. Maybe she wanted to torture him, break his mind, reprogramme him. And she was willing to break a lot of rules to do more research. Anything that might give her a clue as to how to remake him.' Malwina glances sideways at Sigrud. 'And she'd look *anywhere* for ideas. Open up any door, any crypt, any warehouse, no matter how old or cursed or *unmentionable* it was . . .'

Sigrud sits in silence for a while. Then his mouth opens. 'Wait . . . Are you trying to tell me that . . . that *that* was the true reason Vinya Komayd sent Efrem Pangyui to Bulikov so many years ago? To try to find a way to take that child and make him into *a god of Saypur*?'

'I think so, yes,' says Malwina. 'Wouldn't you? She wanted to find out more about the origins of the Divinities. She told the world it was a mission of understanding, a way for these two nations to bridge the gap. Then she told the Ministry and those in power that Pangyui's mission was a secret, preventative measure, meant to keep another god from developing. But she really just wanted to know how the Divinities worked. Like a science student trying to open up a monkey. Maybe Pangyui would find some musty old tome that would tell her how to take that boy apart.' Malwina grins cruelly. 'But then Efrem discovers the wrong secret. He finds out something nasty about Vinya Komayd's family. She has him murdered to keep his mouth shut. This makes little Shara Komayd go to Bulikov and start sniffing around . . . And you know the rest.'

'Shara discovers that Jukov and Kolkan are still alive,' says Sigrud. 'She kills them in the Battle of Bulikov. She learns a secret that can depose Vinya. And by killing Kolkan, she accidentally frees the boy trapped here.'

'You ever wonder why Vinya Komayd gave up power so easily?' asks Malwina. 'Maybe Shara did a good job of threatening her, sure. Or maybe Vinya got a report that the SS *Salim* had been torn apart from the inside out, and whatever was being held there had not only killed a couple of hundred soldiers with his bare hands, but he's now free to walk the world. Maybe Vinya knew that something extremely powerful now had a damned good reason to kill her very nastily. And maybe she didn't want to stay so public anymore. Maybe *that's* why she went into hiding. And then, in 1722 . . . he catches up to her.'

He sits up. 'Are you really telling me that N – '

She whirls on him, terrified.

Sigrud freezes, slaps himself in the face, and holds his hands up. 'Sorry, sorry. I was not thinking.'

Malwina lets out a sigh. 'Okay . . . Just . . . Just watch it, all right?'

'All right. You are saying that *this boy* killed Vinya Komayd?'

'I am.'

'How? She died in Saypur! Naturally too. I thought the boy had no power on foreign soil. He had to have someone spread Continental soil on the ground in Ghaladesh in order to manifest and attack me.'

She looks at him quizzically. 'Wait. What? When did *this* happen?'

'I will tell you later. Just . . . Vinya. How did he do it?'

'Well . . . He is night, you know? All shadows are one to him. In his mind, they all interconnect.' She draws a line in the sand with her finger, then makes three other lines, forming a box. 'And where do people like to keep their wealth? Why, in cupboards. In closets. In drawers. Big, thick ones. In the dark, in other words. Places where he can access it.'

'So . . . he just paid people? He stole money and contracted out the work?'

'He has the entire Continent's fortunes at his disposal. *All* of them. You were in the intelligence game. Sometimes that's all it takes, right?'

'Everyone has their price, I suppose . . .'

'After decades of war, the Continent is awash with old spies,' says Malwina. 'Old murderers, old contractors, old crooks. Like you. Pay a dozen of them a boatload of someone else's money and tell them you want Vinya Komayd dead, just make it look all natural-like so no one gets suspicious. One of them is bound to succeed, given the odds. I'm surprised it took as long as it did.'

'Then years later, Shara catches wind of Operation Rebirth and finds out about this ship. She goes hunting for the Divine children, then found you and recruited you. Is that right? You and she worked against the night, in this war?'

'War?' says Malwina. 'You think Shara was leading us in the *war*? No. No, no. She was *protecting* us. She just wanted to keep us safe, not send us to war against him.' She bows her head. 'She was our mother, in a way. Our last mother. But now she's gone. And *now* there's a war.'

'How many of you are there?'

She hugs her knees to her chest and rests her chin on their tops. Then she says in a very small voice, 'Far less than there used to be.'

'Where are the survivors?'

She shakes her head, as if she cannot or will not speak of such things, and stands and walks back along the beach.

They trudge back toward the *Salim*. It's getting late, and fog is creeping up the island's banks. Malwina walks with her hands stuffed in her pockets and her chin pulled low in the green scarf around her neck. Sigrud is reminded of an old man reviewing all his grudges and failures on a long evening walk.

'The Continent has seen decades of death,' Sigrud says. 'Decades of warfare and slaughter. It's getting rarer, sure, but . . . Bulikov, and Voortyashtan . . . Thousands of people died.'

'Yes.'

'So dozens are awake,' he says. 'Dozens of Divine children remember, after violence robbed them of their parents, making them re-experience this trauma.'

She turns on him, eyes blazing with fury. 'Maybe. However many there were, there are a lot less now. He's killing us, you see. Brutally. Horribly. He eats us up, like a shark swimming in the depths of the sea. He has to make us remember that we're Divine first, otherwise he gains nothing, but that's not hard for him to do. Kill a family, wait for the child to remember, then pounce. He devours us, takes us into the depths of the night, into *himself*, where we can't ever escape. And then we're gone. Forever. The only thing that can kill the Divine is the Divine, Sigrud. And he's gotten very good at it. Each time he gets a little stronger and a little better. Whatever power we have over reality, he takes it and adds it to his own.'

'That's why he does this? Just to grow stronger?'

'What's better than being a Divinity?' says Malwina. 'Being the *only* Divinity. Without a check against your power, you could do . . . anything. Anything at all. Bend the world around your finger, or make it disappear with but a thought. He began as the first night – but gods change. If he succeeds, and grows strong enough, then he will be the *last* night. And all of reality will be a plaything to him.'

'That . . .' Sigrud pauses. 'Actually, that makes sense. The second time I saw him he said that he wished to kill a god. That all that he did was but a means to that one end.'

'Like, a *true* Divinity?' she says. 'So, since there's only one left . . . He must mean Olvos.'

'That was my conclusion as well.'

'How the hells could he do *that*? None of the rest of us could even find Olvos, and we tried damned hard to do it! She's walled herself off from the world. She could crush him if she wanted to!'

'I'm not sure why. But I read something in Shara's home . . .' He walks ahead, stopping her, so she has to face him. 'There was once a Divine child that even the Divinities themselves feared, for its domain was too large and too vast. Big enough to challenge even them. So they mutilated this child, crippled it. I think the boy was this child. And this might be why he hates Olvos especially. She must have been one of the ones that did this to him.'

Malwina shakes her head. 'I've never heard that story. It sounds like bullshit to me.'

'Shara never mentioned it?'

'Never. And I've been awake enough that I remember a lot of the old days. I don't remember that story from them either.'

'You remember the Divine days?'

She nods, eyes hard and thin.

'What were they like?'

She smiles humourlessly. 'Better than this.'

'Who from those old days have survived so far?'

'Very few.' She spits into the dune grasses. 'Listen, Mr. Sigrud, there are some things I can't talk to you about. Not because I won't, but because I *can't*. I am miraculously prevented from doing so. I can't say those certain things unless I'm in a certain place – and we are not in that place now. It's a safety protocol, you see. It's the only way to be sure, with him out there.'

'Would Shara's operations be one such thing?'

Malwina is silent.

'The number of Divine children, as well?'

Still silence.

'And the place where you are hiding all these children away – that too?'

She looks away, off into the seas.

'One last thing,' says Sigrud. 'Do you know of Tatyana Komayd?'

'What, Shara's daughter? Yeah, I know about her. Who doesn't? Why?'

'Do you think that . . . that she could be one such Divine child?'

She stares at Sigrud, bug-eyed. 'What! No! Shara and I worked our asses off to track down the others; she would have told me if she had one right under her nose!'

'Have you ever *seen* Tatyana Komayd?' he asks.

'No. Why?'

'I was just with her. You and she . . . Well. I find you look very alike.'

Malwina laughs. 'You're out of your depth,' she says. 'I *know* my siblings. I know who they are, what they are, what they look like. She isn't one of them.'

'You're sure?'

'I'm positive,' she says. 'Besides, if she was a Divine child, wouldn't she have awoken and remembered who she was after her mother died?'

'I suppose,' says Sigrud. 'But that might have been why Rahul Khadse chose to kill Shara in such a public fashion. Rather than cutting her throat, he did something splashy, something that would be noticed.'

'So?'

'So, since the boy thought Tatyana was Divine, such a public murder would have been a good way to make sure the news got to her, and that it would be as devastating and traumatic as possible. Enough to break the miracle holding back her memories.'

'What makes you think the boy thought Tatyana was Divine?' asks Malwina.

'Well, he told me so.'

She gapes at him. 'W-*What*! When? Do you just have chats with him over tea?'

Sigrud relates what happened to him at Shara's estate. As he talks, Malwina's mouth opens in horror.

'So, wait,' she says. She holds up her hands. 'You . . . You fell into his *domain*?'

'I suppose so. He didn't exactly give me a tour.'

'But . . . Even *I* can't go there. That's the place where he *is*, a place that *is* him. Do you understand?'

'Not at all.'

She looks him over, her face twisted in suspicion and no small amount of revulsion. 'How did you *survive*? How did you *live*?'

'I almost didn't,' says Sigrud. 'I very nearly died. It was like a fever . . .'

'Like a fever!' she says, incredulous. 'You should have died *instantaneously*, not gotten the sniffles! You are a damned odd bird, sir. I don't like it. You resist what I do to the past, you manage to injure our enemy, and *then* you survive a trip through his damned domain. Have you done anything else strange?'

Sigrud remembers Urav, coiling and whipping through the dark waters of the Solda – how the beast swallowed him, yet could not consume him, not truly. He thinks of his own face – queerly unaged after all these years.

'Yes,' he says quietly.

'Anything I need to be worried about?'

He thinks for a long time. 'I don't know.'

She looks at him hard. 'I want you to know – I'll kill you if I have to. I know you were close to Komayd, but if you threaten what we're doing here, I – '

'I understand,' says Sigrud. 'And I hope it will not be so.'

Malwina rubs her lips with one knuckle, a nervous tic. 'You said you have Komayd's daughter?'

'Yes. In Dhorenave, with Ivanya Restroyka.'

She gasps. 'She's still *there*? I thought you would have had the mind to move her by now! Our enemy can bypass all of our defences, it's unbelievable he hasn't gotten to her already!'

'Move her where?' asks Sigrud. 'I knew nothing about what was going on. Where is a safe place for us?'

'Bulikov,' says Malwina instantly. 'Get her to Bulikov. As quickly as you can. If you think our enemy's looking for her, that's where you need to take her. That's where we're strongest. I wish you'd come here a few days ago; we could have taken care of you quickly then . . . But you didn't. So you have to get there within a week. Do you hear me?'

'Why a week?'

'Our movements are carefully controlled. It's like a high-security bank vault: it doesn't open when you want it to, it opens on a schedule. That way no one can manipulate it.'

'What is this *it*?'

She shakes her head. 'I can't tell you that. I can't tell you what it is unless I'm *in* it. And the only way you can get in *it* is if you're there at the right time.'

'But . . . it will take me a week alone to sail back,' says Sigrud.

'Shit,' she says. 'You're sure?'

'At least that, if the weather is forgiving.'

'Damn it all. Then you can't get there in time. How in the hells are we going to get around this?' She grunts. 'Here. Let me think real quick.'

She steps back and looks away. Her eyes appear to grow faintly silver, as if a dense fog is rubbing itself along their backsides, inside her skull. It's an incredibly disturbing sight. 'When did you leave Dhorenave?' she asks.

'Nine days ago.' He cringes. 'What are you . . . doing?'

'Looking at the past. So that would be . . . Ah. Huh. All right.' She blinks and the fog drains from her eyes. She takes a deep breath with the air of someone about to try to jump over a wide gorge. 'Okay. I am about to try something, ah – how should I put this? – completely crazy.'

'All . . . right?'

'You survived me sending you back, what, two or three hours?' she says. 'You kept all your memories. That should be wildly impossible. I mean, it's an offence to me, *personally*, that you can do that.'

'I apologise.'

'Shut up,' says Malwina. 'But . . . I mean, if you can do it with a two-hour jump, then . . . why not a nine-day one?'

Sigrud frowns for a moment, then stares at her when he realises what she's intending. 'You mean to . . . to send me back through *time*?'

'Yeah,' she says. 'Basically.'

'To before I ever left to come here?'

'Yes.'

'But then . . . will what just happened now . . . will that have happened?'

She seesaws a hand in the air. 'Ehh. Kind of. It gets squishy. We're basically manipulating a loophole in the rules here, one that only affects *your* time. *I* can see how it all adds up, and I'll retain these memories, but explaining it to you . . . I mean, it's not like you've understood anything else I've said when I've talked about this, right? The main thing here is that there's a previous instance where we can receive you in Bulikov – but it'll be four days ago, meaning five days from when I send you *back*. Five days to get to Bulikov – do you hear me?'

'But . . . could this go wrong?'

'Oh, absolutely,' says Malwina. 'It's a violation of the universal order to rewrite the past, even slightly. *I* can't do it. No one can, theoretically. It's bad enough that we just did a couple of hours – so nine days could, perhaps, have some giant universal ramifications.' She shrugs. 'But then, if we're talking about our enemy killing the last living Divinity, we're already kind of dealing with giant universal ramifications – aren't we?'

'Could I die?' asks Sigrud.

'Normally I'd say you'd *certainly* die,' she says. She looks him over again like she's not at all pleased with what she's seeing. 'But you seem preternaturally talented at survival, Mr. Sigrud. You've survived our enemy not once, but twice. You entered his domain and walked away with but a fever. And you've resisted all the manipulations I've done. I think you'll survive. And if you do survive, meet me on the Solda Bridge five evenings from when I send you back. I'll have more to say to you there.' She steps toward him. 'Are you ready?'

He steps back, wary. 'You're going to do it now?'

'Do you have a better idea?'

'Do . . . Do I need to get anything from my boat?' he asks.

'No, because you won't have ever *had* your boat when I send you back. Do I need to write this all down for you?'

'Wait – why not just send me back to a time when I could . . . I don't know, kill our enemy, or save Shara?'

'What, send you back weeks, months, or years? Listen, I'm already screwing with the fundamentals of reality enough with this little trick. I'll have to package all these aborted moments into a sort of temporal side loop that can . . . Well. Suffice to say, I'm unwilling to push it that far, okay?'

Sigrud scowls. 'Fine. Just do it already, whatever it is you're going to do!'

'All right. I've never done this before, so you might . . . see some things, or re-experience them.'

'What kind of things?'

'Things that have already happened. It shouldn't be a problem. It's likely they'll be from a past so long ago even you can't alter them. Now . . .' – her eyes turn fogged and silvery again – 'hold on.'

She reaches out and touches his brow, and then . . .

Things . . .

Blur.

Sigrud was in an automobile wreck once, long ago, during his operational days. A Continental hood ferreted him out and ploughed a truck into Sigrud's auto, sending it rolling down a riverbank with Sigrud inside. This particular hood had intended to kill Sigrud, but succeeded only in dislocating his shoulder – an injury Sigrud would later pay back, and then some.

But what Sigrud remembers of that moment – the world spinning around him, gravity losing all meaning, the lights and structure of the world churning outside the shattered windows – is a lot like what he experiences now, as Malwina Gogacz warps his past for him, pushing him out of the present and into a handful of seconds nine days ago . . .

Sigrud sees images flashing – but like the outside world during the auto wreck, they're muddy and swirling.

He sees himself as a child, himself as a young man, himself sobbing in Slondheim. Snow and ice and the ruins of Bulikov. They're all there, floating in the murky past, distant but unchanging. He can't access them. They are beyond him. He knows, in some deep, wordless fashion, that they have already happened.

We float upon a sea of moments, he thinks. *And never are we truly free of them.*

Then one moment seems to stretch. Then blur. Then it . . .

Water. Mist. A woman walking across a pier.

Sigrud recognises this moment instantly.

No, no, he thinks. *No, I don't wish to see this.*

The woman is walking over to a man, who sits fishing on the pier.

Not this. Not this . . .

He tries to shut his eyes, but he cannot.

Eighteen years ago. After Bulikov, but before Voortyashtan. During the days when he'd first returned home and met his family in the Dreyling Republics. The first time he'd seen them in more than twenty years.

Sitting on the little pier, holding a thin, reedy fishing pole, his line drifting in the water. There was bait on the hook, a single sardine, but he didn't need it, really. Sigrud hadn't actually come there to fish, but rather to be alone. He hadn't even brought a bucket for his catches.

She walked up the pier behind him. He didn't turn to look, but he smelled the oil in her hair, and the scent of the horse she rode down the hill. She did not smell as he remembered her, so many years ago, and for some reason that wounded him.

'Sigrud,' said Hild quietly. 'How long have you been out here?'

He looked over his shoulder at his wife. He'd seen her since he returned, of course, but each time they met it had been stifling and muted. They'd slept in different beds, and had not even mentioned the idea of sharing one again. But she was still beautiful. Somewhat plumper, and older, and more care-worn, but still the woman he first met in the marshes that day many years ago, her blue eyes crinkled with concentration, muddy fingers gripping the frog-spear in her hand with all the artistry of a conductor holding a baton. Frog hunting was an art, and Hild had always been a virtuoso at it.

'A while,' he told her. He turned back to look at the waters. 'No catches yet.'

She walked to stand behind him, looking down on him. 'This is the fourth day you've spent fishing. And yet you've caught very little.'

'Perhaps my skills have faded.'

'If so, you're not making much progress in relearning them.'

Sigrud pulled his line back in, looked at the sardine, and tossed it back out into the waters.

'Carin has been asking about you,' Hild said. 'She saw you only the one time. She wants to see you again. She doesn't say so, but I can tell. Will you please come up to the house?'

Sigrud said nothing.

'It's her right, Sigrud. It's her right to see her father.'

'Is it?' he said. 'Could I be said to be her father?'

'What do you mean?'

He was silent.

'Please,' she said. 'Please, say something.'

'I . . . I feel that when she looks at me, she is seeing something that I am not,' said Sigrud. 'Something I perhaps cannot be anymore.'

'That's not true. You've changed, of course you've changed, but you're still you.'

Sigrud glowered into the water, watching his line rise and fall.

'Signe will be coming back from Ghaladesh in three days,' said Hild. 'She remembers you even more than Carin does. And she has had a hard time of it. Will you be there to greet her, at least? Will you be there for her?'

'I . . . will try,' he said reluctantly.

Hild was quiet. Then she walked around to his side, and she crouched and leaned forward so he could not avoid looking at her. He warily met her gaze, feeling as if she were reading in his scars all the secret doubts he'd had since his return.

'Do you remember how we met, my husband?' Hild demanded. 'Do you remember what I said to you, that first thing I ever said to you?'

Sigrud looked into her face for a moment. Then he dropped his eyes and started pulling the line back in.

'No,' he said.

Hild sat next to him for a few seconds longer. Then she stood and walked away, and she was gone.

It was a lie, of course. Of course he remembered what she'd said to him when they'd first met – he barging into the marshes to ask her what she was doing, and she barking at him, 'You're going to scare all the fucking frogs away, you damned fool!' And he, of course, having still been something of a prince in those days, had never been spoken to like that, and was awestruck by this muddy, fierce creature with the long, slender spear.

Why had he lied? Why had he told her he'd forgotten? It had been a mystery at the time – but as the past whirls about him, Sigrud thinks he knows.

It's the same as the reason why he did not go to meet Signe when she first came to see him, why he let her wait for him in the house for hours and hours while he hunted for elk outside, why he evaded her and the rest of his family with furtive desperation.

Because he was afraid. He was afraid to try to be decent, because he felt sure that he would fail.

The moment falls away from him. The world turns, more and more.

And then . . .

Air strikes him. Hard.

Sigrud gasps. He feels like he's plummeting down, but he's not – he's walking along the side of a road, the ground sloping away to his left, and he's wearing a very heavy pack on his back. He tries to reorient himself, tries to deal with this sudden change in . . . well, everything. But he can't, and he topples sideways into the brush, branches scratching at his face and hands before he crashes to the ground.

He lies there for a moment, looking up at the pale morning sky. He takes a breath in – apparently he forgot to breathe at some point during the whole ordeal – and then he slowly sits up.

He looks around himself. He's back in the southern Continent, he can tell that just by glancing around. But the abruptness of the change is so powerful, so impossibly strange, that it makes him nauseous.

All the world could be rewritten in a moment, he thinks. *All of it. All of. . .*

He turns sideways and vomits into the brush. It's porridge, mostly, and the convulsions make his ribs hurt – his side isn't nearly as healed up as when he met Malwina. From these two things, he can guess where he is – and when he is.

He stands, staggers back down the road, and sees the white gate to Ivanya's ranch just ahead.

I am where I was when I went to get the auto, he thinks. *I was going to get the auto and drive it to Ahanashtan, where I would meet Ivanya's man . . . But I remember the sea, and the ship, and Malwina.*

He rubs his eyes, presses the heels of his palms to his forehead. 'Did it really happen?' he asks, his voice hoarse. 'Did it really ever happen?'

It feels like it was real. It feels realer than real, if that could even make sense. He can remember the crunch of bones under his feet, the drip of water in the *Salim*, and Malwina's fogged, silvery eyes . . .

Sigrud walks toward the white gates. *How will I explain this to Ivanya and Taty? I'm not even sure if I can explain it to myself.*

As he walks through the gates, that moment of the past he saw burns in his mind. The woman and the girl, alone in the house, waiting for him. A queer shame floods his belly as he walks back toward Ivanya's ranch house, where another woman and another girl await him.

Will I fail you as well?

Somewhere in the dark – in the darkness behind all things, under all things – the boy feels things shift.

The world flexes, stretches, and snaps back into place, just for an instant. Someone has just moved things, bent things, and now is trying to quickly put it all back in order.

When he is in his purest state, Nokov has no face, and certainly no mouth – but if he did, he would be frowning with his right now.

What was that?

He probes at the edges of the world, feeling the distortions.

Dilations. Contractions. Dangling tumefactions drifting through reality. Distended veins running through space and time. He closes in on the disturbance . . .

The east, in the physical realm. Far to the east. *Very* far, in fact. There's been movement there. No, not just movement – a tremendous, *tremendous* violation: the past has been reset, and a gap hangs in the air – as if a mortal was ripped out of reality and stuffed into somewhere else.

But why would one of his siblings go there? To wander so far from the Continent that birthed them would diminish their influence, make them close to mortal. And there's nothing out there except . . .

Nokov freezes.

No.

No, no, no, no . . .

Panicking, he searches for any unexpected apparition, the abrupt manifestation of a mortal mind or body. He finds these are much easier to track than the movements of his siblings, as they, being just as Divine as he is, can slip through the walls and crawlspaces in reality with hardly a ripple. But mortals and other things of the physical realm . . . Well, that's like trying to stuff a mango down the sink.

It's easy to locate the destination in his mind. Another rippling in Ahanashtan, of course – right under his nose. Right where the Dreyling almost certainly went when he slipped out of Nokov's own domain.

He's moving.

He focuses, speaks to the darkness, forces it to calcify into windows and avenues and channels, cutting it up like a cheesemonger does curds, until the vast blackness has coalesced into tiny little windows into reality.

He finds her shadow rapidly. He's been there so often, to her rooms in Ahanashtan. Sometimes to watch her sleep, though she doesn't know it – at least, he thinks she doesn't.

Kavitha Mishra. The one mortal who's ever helped him willingly.

He stares down at her, watching her quietly breathe in her slumber.

He wonders, sometimes – if she had been his sister, his Divine sibling, would she have sought him out? Would she have saved him? Perhaps not if she'd been his sister – his siblings, he knows, were as weak and ignorant as he was – but what if she'd been some other part of his family?

What if she'd been his mother? Would she have come to his rescue? Would she have saved him, as no one else did?

He watches her as she sleeps. He's acted as her commander for so long that it's become harder and harder to maintain his detachment from her. She is, after all, the only other person he really has in this world.

And he does not wish to do what he knows he's about to do. He does not wish to ask her to do this.

Then a sudden, stabbing memory.

Trapped in that ship, trapped for years in that tiny box. And in the window, a face: Vinya Komayd, smiling wickedly.

You will come to love me, child, she said. *You will have to, eventually. For I will be the only thing you know. For years and years.*

He shudders. *It's not the same. I don't just care for Mishra because she's the only person I have. I don't.*

He doesn't want to say that he's alone. To acknowledge that you are alone is to be truly alone. And he's stronger than that now. He's evolved beyond those miserable, terrified days of his childhood, abandoned and forgotten.

We must all become stronger. He swallows, lifts his hand, and plunges it into his dark chest. He shuts his eyes, feeling for it. *We must all become more than we are. I must . . .* He feels it, and pulls it out. *And she must as well.*

In his hand is a black pearl, a tiny, perfect piece of himself. A piece that, if ingested by a mortal, will make them something . . . more.

They will be a piece of him. His seneschal.

He takes a breath and says, 'Mishra.'

10.
A Road in the Air

In the Divine days it was the purpose of the gods to shape the reality of the world's citizens.

The gods are gone. But this need remains.

Now it is the task of governments to tell their citizens what reality is, to define it for them. For citizens are, by and large, wholly incapable of doing this for themselves.

— MINISTER OF FOREIGN AFFAIRS VINYA KOMAYD,
LETTER TO PRIME MINISTER ANTA DOONIJESH, 1713

Ivanya Restroyka cocks an eyebrow as she takes an enormous drag from her cigarette. 'So,' she says slowly. 'You've . . . already been there, you say.'

'I know it sounds mad,' Sigrud says.

Taty and Ivanya say nothing. They just watch him. His rickety wooden chair creaks as he leans forward, rubbing his face. He's done this many times before — returning to tell a case officer a wild story about what happened on the front lines — but it seems peculiarly difficult to pull it off right now. Probably because this story is particularly wild.

And particularly dangerous. It was impossible to explain his almost immediate return without referencing the Divine — which meant discussing Malwina, which then meant revealing Shara's involvement with the Divine to Taty. He didn't tell the girl everything, of course — he certainly didn't tell her that Nokov was targeting Continental orphans who were secretly Divine, or the girl's own extreme similarity to Malwina — but he had to tell her *something*.

He'd expected the girl to react violently, yet she sat there, blinking slowly, absorbing it all but not saying a word. She still hasn't said a word since he started talking. For some reason her stillness feels worse than any amount of rage.

'It doesn't *just* sound mad,' says Ivanya. 'It sounds madder than mad. All of it does.'

'I know,' says Sigrud. 'I know it feels like I walked out the door just an hour ag – '

'But it doesn't *feel* like that,' says Ivanya. 'That's what happened.'

'I knew when I came to you both,' he says forcefully, 'that we were playing with forces that were greater than ourselves. But now I am starting to get some idea of *how* great.'

'Yes, great enough to . . . I don't know, stitch two moments together like pieces of cloth . . .' Ivanya laughs dully. The sound is animated in the air by the smoke from her lips. 'I'm so *happy* to have the Divine as an ally.'

'An ally . . .' says Taty softly.

The two of them glance at her uncertainly. Those are the first words she's spoken in a good while.

'Yes,' says Sigrud reluctantly. 'An ally.'

'I see,' says Taty. She sits up a little. 'And . . . and *when*, exactly, were you going to tell me about that? It's one thing to find out your mother used to be some kind of intelligence agent, quite another to find out she was assassinated by a *god*!'

'A god who's also after us,' says Ivanya.

'Yes,' says Sigrud, trying to change the subject. 'We cannot stay here any longer.'

'And your Divine little friend – she says we need to get to Bulikov to escape him?' asks Ivanya.

'In five days,' he says. 'Yes.'

'That's not much time,' says Ivanya. 'That's *no* time, really. The only thing I'd trust to get us there is the express train.'

'How long does that take?' asks Sigrud.

'Four days, if the weather is decent. Which, it being the Continent in autumn, it likely won't be.'

'Then we shall have to hope for five, and that will have to do.'

'Are you *hearing* yourselves?' says Taty, horrified. 'Discussing train time-tables like you're planning for a holiday? You're insane. You're all *insane*! If any of this is true, then you've . . .' She shakes her head as she struggles with it. He can tell she doesn't want to believe it, but he can also tell that she does. 'You've been hiding things from me all along! The whole damned *world's* been hiding things from me all along!'

'Taty,' says Sigrud. 'I know it is a lot, but –'

'A lot?' says Taty. 'A *lot*? You . . . You knew who'd killed my mother and didn't tell me! You knew who was out to kill *me*, and you didn't even tell me that! What kind of a person *are* you?'

'What good would it have done?' says Sigrud. 'What could you do, besides sit up sleepless and anxious every night and every day? You will know what you need to kn –'

'I'm not your damned secret agent!' says Taty. She stands and sticks her finger out at him. 'You don't feed me only the information that I need! I didn't opt into this, I didn't ask for it, and you've no right to treat me like I did! There's still more that you aren't telling me, I can *feel* it. Both of you. The way you look at each other, the way you say things . . .'

Ivanya does a good job of not glancing at Sigrud, though she is trying very hard to smoke a cigarette that's now mostly ash.

'Taty . . .' says Sigrud.

'The way I see it,' says Taty, stepping closer to Sigrud, 'you need to get me on that express train very quick indeed. But what if I don't go? What if I refuse to leave? What *then*, eh?'

'I was ordered to protect you,' he says, bristling. 'Not to keep you comfortable. I can throw you in a trunk and drag you along if I need to.'

'And what gives you the right?' says Taty. 'Why should you get to tell us what to do?'

'Because I've *survived*!' says Sigrud. 'I'm still around to be here for you! You may not like what I do, and I might not like it either, but it works!'

'Does it?' says Taty. 'It didn't work for Mother! Who else has it failed? Who else has it let down?'

'That is why I've been training you!' says Sigrud, shouting so loud his side hurts. 'That's why I've been showing you how to defend yourself!'

'What do you mean?' says Taty.

'I . . . I am showing you so when the time comes, you will know what to do, and you won't wind up like . . .'

Sigrud stops, startled, and trails off.

The silence stretches on. Ivanya and Taty watch him, tense.

'Like who?' says Taty.

Sigrud slowly sits back in his chair.

'Like who, Sigrud?' says Taty, now genuinely puzzled.

He blinks and looks down at his hands. They're trembling. Little white half-moons are fading on his palms – indentations from where his finger-nails were digging into his flesh.

Sigrud swallows. He stares into the table for a long, long time. Neither of the women move.

He quietly says, 'You . . . You are right.'

The two women look at each other. 'Who is?' says Ivanya.

'Taty.' His voice is strained and hoarse. 'I should not play games, or keep secrets. I should not . . . hide from you.' He looks at her balefully. 'The Divine children have been hiding for many years among Continental orphans. Many of them did not even know they were Divine. Our enemy has been killing them one by one. And he thinks you are one such child.'

Taty stares at him. She looks back at Ivanya, who walks to the kitchen, takes out a teacup, and promptly fills it to the brim with potato wine.

'He does?' asks Taty, bewildered.

Sigrud nods.

'So . . . he thinks that I'm . . . I'm Divine?'

He nods again.

Ivanya downs the potato wine in a single gulp.

Taty laughs – a single, short sound of scornful disbelief. 'You're joking.'

He shakes his head.

'What, he thinks I have magic powers? He thinks I can fly, or . . . or walk through walls?'

'I do not know what he thinks you can do,' says Sigrud. 'Only what he thinks you are.'

'And why does he think that?'

'Because . . . Because you bear a very strong resemblance to the girl I met at the shipwreck.'

'What, this Malwina girl?'

He nods.

'Oh, so because I look like a girl, I must be like her?' she says. 'Is that it?'

'She denied it too,' says Sigrud. 'But her opinion does not matter. Nor does mine, or yours. Only his, and what he plans to do about it.'

'Which is . . . what? Eat me up? Like a creature from an old story?'

'Something like that.'

She laughs again and slowly sits back down. 'Unbelievable. It's all so stupid. All so bloody *stupid*.'

'Do you see why I did not wish to tell you?' asks Sigrud. 'Did you see that I didn't want to scare you, to – '

'Scared?' says Taty, her cheeks colouring. '*Scared?* I'm not scared, Sigrud!'

'Then . . . what?' says Ivanya.

'I'm . . . I'm *angry*!' says Taty. 'I'm angry that . . . that all this happened over such a stupid idea! Such a stupid, ridiculous, nonsense idea! The idea that I could . . . That I could *do* more, that I could *be* more, or that I could ever want to be more! Do you know what I want? Do you know what I really want right now?'

'No,' says Sigrud.

'I want to go *home*,' says Taty. Her eyes fill with tears, but her words are firm. 'I want to go home, and sit at the breakfast table with my mother, and read the newspaper with her. Right now, there is nothing in the world I can think of, no magic power or fantastical afterlife, that could ever be any better than that. I want my life to be normal again. I *liked* being normal. And if I had any Divine powers, I would . . . I would put all of them toward getting that back.' She sits in silence. 'But it's not coming back, is it.'

'No,' says Sigrud.

'And now we have to run again?'

'Yes.'

Another miserable laugh. 'Do you know what it's like, to lose everything in an instant?' Taty asks. 'To lose normal overnight?'

'Yes,' says Sigrud.

'Yes,' says Ivanya.

Taty blinks tears away and looks at them both. 'You . . . You do?'

Ivanya walks over, sits opposite her, and sighs deeply. 'Yes, dear. Us and many, many others.'

'But . . . How do you do it?' asks Taty, sniffling. 'How did you just . . . just keep going?'

'We can try to show you,' says Sigrud. He stands and walks over to her. 'But first, Taty, we need to move. Quickly.'

He holds his hand out to her. She looks at it for a moment, then reaches out and takes it.

Ivanya opens the trunk, showing him where the clothes hangers can hook on, the little drawers where the shoes can be stored. 'Looks normal, yes?' she says.

'Yes?' says Sigrud.

'But . . .' She reaches into the back, undoes some clasp, and the entire back of the trunk opens up, revealing a hidden compartment that is obviously meant to store firearms. 'See? There we go. It's got capacity for two long riflings, broken down, maybe a scatter-gun, and probably three to four pistols. We need to secure them with these ties here, so they don't rattle . . .'

Sigrud nods, impressed. 'Sometimes you give me pause, Ivanya Restroyka. It's like you were preparing for an invasion.'

'Oh, and what happened in Voortyashtan wasn't an invasion? When all those Divine soldiers almost rowed ashore and started slaughtering everyone?'

'Fair point.' He points at two smaller clasps in the back of the trunk. 'What are those for? Blades? Rapiers?'

'Yes,' says Ivanya with a sniff. 'Do you know, I'm actually much better with a sword than I am with a firearm? Fencing is a time-honoured ladies' sport in Bulikov. Mother drilled me quite mercilessly in the art. But, like everything Bulikovian, it's hopelessly out of date. Only a fool goes to battle with a sword these days.'

She walks around her bed to her chest of drawers. Ivanya Restroyka's bedroom, much like Ivanya herself, is bare, stark, and economical, only possessing enough to do what is necessary. He regularly forgets he's in the room with the richest woman on the Continent. 'I'd take a damned cannon to Bulikov if I could,' she says, opening up her drawers and pulling out clothes. 'I have a house there, but I never use it. Used to be Vo's, just like a quarter of the damned city. I can't stand to be within those walls anymore. But I suppose I'll have to try.'

'I have heard the city has changed.'

'Oh, it's changed. Just like everything else, Bulikov's changed as well. But . . . Ah.' She reaches into one drawer and takes out a slender, sparkling black dress. She unfolds it and holds it up to the light. It's old and lined, but still beautiful, a relic of some past era of her life. She smiles at it, a sad, wistful expression, then holds it up to herself, pressing it against her wiry frame. 'Think it still fits?'

Sigrud looks at Ivanya Restroyka. He takes in her lean, hard face, her neck long and smooth, her eyes bright and brittle like flint. 'I do, actually,' he says.

'Shows a lot of shoulder. Shoulders that probably aren't much to look at after a few years spent out here.' She sighs, perhaps remembering better days, then slowly places it back in the drawer. 'Bulikov might have changed, Sigrud, but like so many things, it can't forget what's happened to it. It is still what it was. And that can't change. So I shall step lightly.'

'I see,' says Sigrud quietly.

'Do you have any clothes?'

'Not beyond what I packed for the sea voyage,' says Sigrud. 'And that will have to do.'

Taty walks to the door with a suitcase at her side. She's dressed absurdly, like a schoolgirl dressed for a trip to the mountains during holiday, but Sigrud refrains from commenting on this. 'It feels mad to be going to Bulikov on a whim like this,' she says. 'The oldest city in the world . . . And we have to get there in *five days*?'

'Yes,' says Sigrud.

She scratches her chin. 'Well, I've been thinking about that . . . Why not take the aero-tram?'

He frowns. 'The . . . The what?'

Ivanya scoffs as she packs her trunk. 'I said the express was the only thing I *trusted*. And I do not trust that . . . contraption.'

'It's not a contraption,' says Taty. 'I read all the financing papers on it.

It's an engineering marvel! Why not take that? It can get us there in three days in any weather at all!'

'Because it's madness!' says Ivanya.

Taty sighs heavily. 'Auntie Ivanya simply doesn't trust progress. I keep telling her that Bulikov's different – and she ought to know, since she's financing a lot of what's new!'

'I can hope a thing has changed,' snaps Ivanya, 'while still not believing it has!'

Sigrud holds up a hand. 'What is this? This . . . aero-tram?'

'You don't know?' says Ivanya. 'It's the biggest thing to happen to the Continent this decade, for better or worse.' She slams a drawer shut. 'In my opinion, the latter.'

Taty waves a dismissive hand at Ivanya. 'Have you ever been mountain skiing, Sigrud? You know the lifts they use to get people up the mountain? Well, it's like that, but done on a *massive* scale, going straight to Bulikov over the mountains. And it departs from the very same station that all the major trains use.'

He scratches his head. 'They have . . . a big ski lift that carries people to Bulikov?'

'Basically, yes,' says Ivanya. 'I've heard the toilets are a nightmare.'

'It's a lot easier to mount towers on mountains than it is to blast a tunnel through them for trains,' says Taty. 'And though we had rails *around* the hard part of the Tarsils, connecting Ahanashtan to Bulikov, no one had a direct route in between. That's when someone proposed the aero-tram. It's like the railroad but hundreds of feet above the ground, with cars holding twenty, thirty people running along huge cables!'

'It's very popular,' says Ivanya in a tone that suggests she feels quite the opposite.

'It is,' says Taty. 'It'd get us there in three days flat. It was partially designed by SDC, so it's about as reliable as anything.'

Sigrud is quiet for a while. 'SDC? The Southern Dreyling Company?'

'What else?' asks Taty.

He thinks for a moment. He remembers going to his daughter's work-room in Voortyashtan, the giant loft filled with blueprints of all the things she'd ever designed, most of them unbuilt.

Could this have been among them? Is this strange machine Ivanya and Tatyana are describing something Signe dreamed up when she was alive?

He shakes himself, returning to the subject. 'So we would be dangling from a little train car,' he says, 'hundreds of feet above the ground. For three days.'

'Yes,' says Taty.

A pause.

'Ah,' says Sigrud. 'No.'

'No to what?' says Taty.

'To all of it. To everything you just said.'

Her shoulders slump. 'But it'd be so much faster . . .'

'No. The train we know. We will take the express.'

'If we can even get into the train station,' says Ivanya, snapping up the trunk. 'If this enemy of ours is as clever as you say, Sigrud – surely he'll be wise enough to watch the station?'

Sigrud frowns, for this has been something that's concerned him since he met Malwina. 'How many firearms fit in that trunk?'

'Six total.'

'Good. Choose carefully. Because we may need them.'

They arrive at the train station at 0500 the next day, before dawn. Ivanya and Tatyana are yawning and rubbing sleep from their eyes. There's barely any light to see by. Sigrud slouches low in the auto, looking at the gates, the doors, the glass roof of the giant train station. It's a madhouse even at this hour as Ahanashtanis come pouring in, caps clapped to their heads, valises and briefcases and packs clutched tight. He grimaces as he watches their silhouettes sprint through the turnstiles. *Any one of them could be one of Nokov's*, he thinks.

But does Nokov have an army? Sigrud strongly suspects he doesn't. The Saypuri Military, and the intelligence industry that's grown up around it, are quite a lot of things, but Continental collaborators and saboteurs . . . that's a stretch. It seems more likely that Nokov has but a handful of active agents operating from within the Ministry. Not enough to watch every road and train station on the Continent – so perhaps the madhouse ahead will be safe.

He looks north, to where the . . . thing begins. He's never seen such a machine before in his life. He has no real word for what he's seeing, though he supposes 'aero-tram' will have to do. He remembers he saw it from the train when he first came to Ahanashtan – when was that? It must have been mere days ago but it now feels like years – and at the time he thought it was some kind of electric utility pole, only far, far too tall.

But now he hears the engines whirring and grinding, and he watches as the thick cables haul a bronzed, egg-shaped capsule into the air, the windows glowing with cheerful yellow light. The capsule shrinks as it climbs until the windows are indistinguishable from the stars still visible in the sky, except that these little pinpricks of light begin slowly crawling north.

Sigrud starts to think up a backup plan, just in case. It's a very bad backup plan. But it's better to have a bad one than not have one at all.

'You're sure we have the tickets for the express train?' he asks.

'Yes,' says Ivanya. 'There are some benefits to being rich. We've got the whole cabin to ourselves. It departs at 0730, as always.'

'We'll be going in during rush hour,' says Sigrud. 'We want to be as difficult to spot as possible. So we have a bit to wait. Be on the lookout for a Saypuri woman of about forty, with yellow eyes.'

'Is she . . . Divine?' asks Taty.

'No. I get the impression that she is our enemy's lieutenant. And I am almost positive she is stationed here in Ahanashtan. If anyone is here, it will be her.'

Two hours later they pull into the train station garage and step out of the car. Sigrud is dressed in his usual peacoat and knit cap: the civilised world has grown accustomed to the sight of Dreylings in sea labourers' wear, though he keeps black gloves on, to hide his scar. Ivanya, however, is dressed like a Continental businesswoman, with a stern black skirt and a high grey jacket, and a sharp-brimmed hat perfectly perched atop her pinned-back hair. It's a terrific change of pace from her usual attire, which is about as fancy as a bandsaw. Taty is dressed in similarly formal wear, though she's been given a clipboard and a large leather bag – clearly the harried young assistant to this reputable businesswoman.

'The station has two floors,' says Ivanya as she arranges herself, 'and the concourse is usually very well trafficked, with big crowds. Or, at least it used to be. I haven't been here in years.'

Sigrud eyes the doors. 'You both walk ahead of me. I'll stay behind surveying the area. If something goes wrong – anything – wipe your nose and drop a handkerchief. All right?'

'All right,' say Taty and Ivanya at the same time.

Together they walk toward the station. Sigrud drops back, hauling the weapon-filled steamer trunk, and watches as the two women enter the door. He waits ninety seconds, then follows, entering the station.

Heat and smoke and noise. The Ahanashtani train station is a long, thin, busy structure, with two floors: restaurants and shops up top, and train platforms below. The tunnels are dim with smoke, and the concourse at first appears to be just a sea of hats, dark hats and white hats and grey hats, surging back and forth like schools of fish. He spies Taty and Ivanya in the crowd and lumbers ahead to keep up with them.

As they move, Sigrud keeps his eye open. He sees many people, all nondescript, and a few Ahanashtani police officers – these he is especially mindful of – yet he sees no one looking, no one watching, no one quietly surveying the concourse. He wonders if his skills have faded, but he doesn't think so: he cannot help but feel that they are alone, safe, and unwatched.

That's not right, thinks Sigrud. *Could it be this easy?*

They continue on. A conductor whistles loudly, and a crowd of passengers streams toward one open train door and slowly congeals into a messy line. The express platform is somewhere up ahead, but he can't see it yet. It feels like the journey through the station is taking an eternity. He keeps watching for hostile movement, yet none comes.

Perhaps we're not important, thinks Sigrud. *Perhaps we don't matter. Perhaps Nokov has better things to attend t –*

Taty and Ivanya have stopped on the concourse. Sigrud watches as Taty bows her head, wipes her nose, and a small, flittering handkerchief falls to the floor.

Something's wrong.

Sigrud rolls the giant trunk over to a small wooden bench beside them, where he sits and pretends to examine his shoelaces. 'What's wrong?' he says quietly.

Taty's eyes are terrified, while Ivanya's are simply confused. Then Taty, still smiling, says in a quavering voice, 'If we get on that train right now, we are all going to die.'

Sigrud pauses, bewildered. He glances at Ivanya, who gives the tiniest of shrugs. '*What?*' he says.

Taty gives a nervous laugh and says, 'If we get on the express train to Bulikov, we will die. All of us.'

'What do you mean? I haven't seen a tail yet.'

'Because we've already been spotted,' says Taty.

'You think we a —'

'Look across the concourse, northwest. Then look up. Up above the shops on the second floor. As if there's a *third* floor, a hidden floor. Look. Look for the mirror.'

Sigrud casts a quick glance northwest . . .

And sees it. It's a small mirror, smaller than your average window, mounted in the brick wall about eight feet above the shops.

'A two-way mirror?' says Ivanya.

'It must be,' says Sigrud. 'A security office, perhaps.'

'And that's where *she* is,' says Taty. 'The woman with the yellow eyes.'

'Are . . . Are you sure, dear?' says Ivanya. 'How can you know this?'

'I just know,' says Taty. Panic leaks into her voice. 'I just know!'

'How will she kill us?' says Sigrud.

'She'll get on the train car behind us,' says Taty. 'Then she'll wait two days to do it because there's a snowstorm. On the third day she'll use some kind of device . . . Something that throws explosives. She'll shoot at our car and stick explosives to us, then detach us from the rest of the train and blow it off the tracks. Us and everyone caught with us.' Her voice shivers. 'It takes you longer to die, Sigrud. The car smashes into the mountain slope and most of us die on impact. But you die with the snow around you turning bright red from your blood . . . Cherry red.' She shuts her eyes. 'And your last thoughts are of the sea.'

'How do you *know* this?' asks Ivanya. She's starting to sound terrified.

'I don't know,' says Taty. 'It was like I could smell it in the air . . . And then I just knew.'

The three of them fidget in silence for a moment, trying halfheartedly to maintain their various charades.

'What do we do?' asks Ivanya. 'Do you believe her?'

'It . . . It seems impossible,' says Sigrud.

'I know,' says Taty. She sounds like she's on the verge of tears. 'But it's true. I *swear* it's true. I don't know how, but it is.'

'Do you believe her, though?' asks Ivanya.

Sigrud remembers Taty sitting on the porch, knees clutched to her chest. *I dreamed you'd come back far sooner than we expected. Than you expected, even. It would be as if you hadn't even left . . .*

And she'd been right. He hadn't thought of it until now, but somehow, impossibly, Taty had known what would happen.

'I . . . I believe she believes it,' says Sigrud. 'And I think that something is wrong. I think this is a feint, a trap. There is no one looking for us.' He glances up at the mirror in the wall. 'Because we've already been found.'

'So now what?' says Ivanya. 'We don't exactly have a backup plan for getting to Bulikov in five days.'

'I . . . think we do.' He sighs deeply and looks at Taty. 'I suppose all those finance papers you read wouldn't have told us if the aero-tram has any tighter security, would it?'

'The *aero*-tram?' says Ivanya, aghast. 'You really want to try *that*?'

'It's almost impossible for someone to just swoop in and nab a ticket for that!' says Taty.

'I suspected so,' says Sigrud. 'A very good thing, then, that we happen to have a millionaire in our midst.'

Kavitha Mishra narrows her eyes as she watches from behind the mirror. Something's definitely wrong. Restroyka, the Komayd girl, and the *dauv-kind* have all stopped on the concourse and are conferring with one another. Which shouldn't be happening.

She looks back at her four officers. They're all waiting in the back hall-way of the security office, ready for her orders. One raises an eyebrow, as if wondering if they need to move.

'What in the hells,' she mutters, turning back to the concourse. 'What in the hells . . .'

'Problem, ma'am?' says the train station security chief behind her. He's a Continental, and is far too interested for his own good.

'Yes,' she snaps. 'But not one of your concern!'

'Oh, ah . . . Sorry.' He turns away, and she's glad of it: she's been allowed to commandeer the office here solely through her Ministry credentials, but she doesn't need any more attention than this. She definitely doesn't want the train station security officers trying to stage an arrest: knowing the *dauvkind*, that would get messy fast, and messiness attracts eyes. If someone finds out that Ministry officers or even station security officers were trying to arrest Ivanya Restroyka and the daughter of Komayd, it'd be sure to cause a stir.

It was pure luck that they caught it. Mishra had told all of her sources to watch every communication going into or out of the Ahanashtani train station – and one just happened to come through late last night, purchasing an entire train car. Mishra had reached out to a few of her Ministry contacts, who assumed she was working a case, and traced it back to the tiny, sheep shit-spattered town of Dhorenave. Which had one very famous yet reclusive resident.

Mishra frowns as she watches Restroyka listen to the *dauvkind*. Her contacts had long suspected that Restroyka was somehow connected to Komayd's 'charity' networks, but they'd never been able to prove anything. Because Komayd had been good. Surprisingly good.

But all this is quite bad for Mishra. She doesn't like the *dauvkind* having a damned real-estate tycoon on his side. It's a lot easier to hunt desperate people, and that much wealth can keep desperation at bay for a long, long time.

She watches the three of them talk. *They're spooked.*

Without thinking about it, Kavitha Mishra pats her right pocket. The small silver box is still there, and inside that, she knows, is a little, tiny black pearl . . .

Only use it if it's an emergency, he told her. *Only if everything is at risk.*

And things aren't at risk yet, but she's worried.

Suddenly there's movement: Restroyka and the Komayd girl turn and go north. Fast. The *dauvkind*, however, stays behind, standing next to the big steamer trunk. He turns and looks up, staring directly at the mirror with a grim, implacable look on his face.

Mishra looks at the two departing women, then back at the *dauvkind*. He's still looking up, looking right at her.

Does he know I'm here? Does he . . . Does he see me?

She hesitates. Restroyka and the Komayd girl aren't going for the train platforms, she sees, but going north, far north, to the . . .

'Shit,' says Mishra. 'They're going toward the fucking aero-tram!'

'What's that, ma'am?' asks Nashal, one of her officers.

'Let me think,' she snaps.

This wasn't at all what she expected – they bought out a damn train car, not an aero-tram ticket! The aero-tram is, unfortunately, pretty damned exclusive. She could *maybe* commandeer one of the cars, but doing so would raise a lot of questions back in Ghaladesh, and piss off a couple dozen very wealthy Continentals.

It'd ruin me to do that, thinks Mishra. *I'd be blown. Ghaladesh would know right away something was amiss.*

She debates going downstairs and stopping Restroyka and Komayd. Yet the *dauvkind* is still staring up at her with that grim expression on his face.

His meaning is painfully clear to her: *Come downstairs, and things will get violent.*

Which is not what Mishra needs right now.

'How the fuck did he know,' she whispers.

Then, finally, the *dauvkind* turns and strides away – but he's stayed long enough to give Restroyka and Komayd a good lead.

'Hurry!' Mishra says to her team. 'Downstairs, to the aero-tram platform! Now!'

'The *aero-tram* platform?' asks Nashal, bewildered.

'They've changed something up! They know they've been made! Hurry!'

'How in the hells are we going to get on *that*?' he asks.

'I'm going to have to pull rank,' says Mishra through gritted teeth.

The team turns and starts off downstairs. 'That's a lot of rank to pull,' Nashal says.

'We don't have a choice!' says Mishra.

As she follows them out the door, she grabs the big, heavy briefcase in the corner. Inside this is a relatively new Ministry creation, a device that hurls an adhesive mine several hundred yards. Of course, the Ministry can't publicly avow that it has created and is deploying such a device in the field – it is, obviously, a weapon system used specifically for sabotage, and the public feels very negatively about such things – but it should do well in this situation, with all these trams and trains and whatnot, all very big with such delicate connection points.

Make it look like an accident, he told Mishra. *The girl will survive. I know she will, she just will. And when she does, capture her. And bring her to me.*

Mishra, grunting with the weight of the briefcase, runs downstairs.

'I will have you know,' says Ivanya indignantly as she rejoins them in line for the aero-tram, 'that I have never bribed anyone in my *life*.' She hands them their tickets.

'There is a first time for everything,' says Sigrud.

'How much did you have to give them?' asks Taty, looking at hers.

Ivanya says a number.

'*Wow*,' says Taty.

'Wow,' says Sigrud, who has never thought of money in such sums before.

'Yes, so it had better be a damn pleasant ride!' says Ivanya. 'It was some commercial banker and his family who thought the tram would make a fun jaunt across the Tarsils. The rich, it turns out, are very, very expensive to pay off. Apparently we'll be in the Jade Cabin – so we'll be alone for the journey.'

'Hopefully *very* alone,' says Sigrud, looking backward through the crowd. The golden-eyed woman is nowhere to be seen. Hopefully their last-minute gambit paid off.

The line's moving again. The three of them shuffle forward, Sigrud hauling the big trunk up the ramp to the aero-tram platform. The cold morning air slaps his cheeks, and he finally gets to see the vessel they'll be spending the next three days on.

The aero-tram car is like a giant, long, bronzed egg, with a fat glass bubble or dome in the top, some kind of viewing room for passengers or perhaps the crew to see forward and backward. Above this dome is a large frame, sprouting up to cling to a thick cable running above the car. Within the frame, Sigrud sees, are a dozen or so wheels, which currently aren't rotating. A second frame is below the tram car, clinging to a bottom cable. The whole thing is about seventy-five feet long and twelve feet wide at its thickest point, about the size of a small ship.

But how will it perform in the air? Sigrud knows he has an unusually specific experience in this: he has piloted a watercraft through the air before, in Bulikov – but that one was buoyed by miracles. What is in front of him is very loud, very heavy, yet also very fragile – and not at all miraculous.

'It's amazing, isn't it?' says Taty, her voice hushed with awe. 'It's amazing . . .'

'It's something, all right,' says Ivanya. She stares at the tram car as if it were a large, threatening dog.

Sigrud watches as two mechanics open up a large hatch at the back of the tram car using a wrench, which they then store away in a bag of tools. One of the mechanics climbs into the hatch and hooks a hose up to a spigot. They then begin to pump something out of the tram car – human waste, he suspects. After all, the passengers probably can't just void their bladders out the windows.

The conductor smiles at them and says, 'Tickets, please.'

The three of them hand over their astronomically expensive tickets. The conductor takes them, then does a little bow. 'Much appreciated! Please take your seats quickly, if you would. We depart in five minutes. No exceptions, I'm afraid – there's a big storm coming.'

'Will that be an issue for the tram?' asks Ivanya.

'Oh, no, ma'am. The tram's as steady as a mountain. But it can make getting up on the line a bit longer.'

The three of them thank the conductor, then turn and board the aerotram car. No one on the platform notices as Sigrud grabs the bag of tools from beside the mechanics as he boards.

The door and interior are, as Sigrud expected, incredibly tiny. The trunk barely fits: people grouse and grumble at him as he hauls it down the tiny aisles, glaring as he mutters 'excuse me' and 'pardon me'. Finally the three of them stagger through to the private quarters at the very back – the Jade Cabin that Ivanya purchased.

The Jade Cabin is small but relatively opulent, considering the lack of space aboard the tram car. Four berths, wooden walls, bronzed fixtures, electric lighting, and – perhaps most important – a private toilet, which he examines carefully, thinking.

'Is that it?' asks Taty. 'Are we safe?'

Sigrud shuts the door, sets down the stolen bag of tools, and walks over to a porthole on the aft wall of the quarters. Through it he can see the tram platform and the tremendous rotating gears of the massive machine. At first there's nothing. But then . . .

The Saypuri woman's face surfaces in the crowd.

'Shit,' he says.

'What? What is it?' asks Ivanya.

The Saypuri woman doesn't move. She just looks at the tram car with a furious expression on her face. Sigrud knows beyond a shadow of a doubt that, at the very least, he's thoroughly ruined her morning.

'Is that . . . Is that her?' asks Ivanya.

'Yes,' says Sigrud.

'And she knows we're on board?'

'Yes.'

'Why isn't she . . . Why isn't she doing anything?'

'She's waiting for us to depart,' says Sigrud grimly. 'So that way she knows we're trapped on here.'

Someone blows a whistle. There's a knock at the door, and one of the service crew sticks his head in. 'All comfy?' asks the man. 'We're about to start up the line.'

'Very comfy,' says Sigrud.

The crewmember looks at Taty and Ivanya, who are pale with horror. 'Ah – are you sure?'

'Yes,' says Sigrud angrily.

'Oh. Uh. All right. Well, you'll want to take your seat, ladies and gentlemen. It could be a bit bumpy at the start.'

'Thank you,' says Sigrud.

The man leaves, but none of them sit. They keep looking out the window, watching the Saypuri woman. Then there's a whistle, then a clacking, and the car slowly begins moving forward.

The tram car apparently rides along a belt of some kind before gliding onto the main transport cables. Sigrud can't see it, but he can feel it when this happens, the entire car shuddering with a heavy *clunk*. Some people in the passenger areas ahead squeal or laugh. Sigrud stays focused on the Saypuri woman, who, as if on cue, strides forward, pulls out some kind of badge, and begins to talk to the conductor.

'She's commandeering the tram car behind us,' says Sigrud.

'*What?*' says Ivanya. 'She can *do* that?'

'Apparently.' He glances sideways at Taty. 'They must want us very bad. Because what she is doing now will quickly get back to Ghaladesh, and that woman's career in the Ministry will almost certainly be over.'

He watches as the Saypuri woman argues with the conductor, but it's clear she's going to be the victor. Sigrud waits to see if Taty plans to make any other predictions – perhaps they'll meet the same fate on the aero-tram as they would have on the express – but she just trembles, pale and terrified, as any young girl would.

'So,' says Ivanya. 'Now what?'

Sigrud looks out the aft-facing porthole in their quarters. It's a terrifically odd view to him: the hills of the southern Tarsils curdle and coil about four hundred feet below him, the rich green growing brown as they enter the steppes. The whole view is vivisected by the huge cables running both above and below them. About every half-mile or so they come to another cable support tower, and the car jumps and jostles a little as it goes up the cables, through the towers, and then back down the next section of cable, which seems to arc from tower to tower like drapes of bunting on a mantelpiece. There's another set of cables and towers about a hundred feet to the east, and sometimes he sees another tram car crawling along them heading south to Ahanashtan. Farther to the southeast he can see dark storm clouds churning, heading their way.

Ivanya is pacing back and forth while Taty sits on her bunk, pale and anxious. 'Of all the things that could happen,' says Ivanya. 'I never thought . . .' She stops and looks down. 'Wait. Where did you get this bag of tools?'

Sigrud ignores her, squinting as he peers down the cables. He can see the next car a way behind them, though it's getting a bit misty and difficult to see. 'They have controls in the cars,' he says. 'Don't they?'

'I don't know,' says Ivanya. 'Taty?'

Taty blinks, distracted. 'What?'

'How do these damn cars work?' Ivanya asks. 'Do they have controls?'

'What? Well, of course,' says Taty. She sounds dazed. 'It's not automatic. If . . . If a car in front breaks down, the one behind has to slow to a stop.'

'And the cars can speed up as well?' asks Sigrud.

'Well . . . certainly?'

'Then that's what she plans to do,' he says. 'She's commandeered her own tram car. Then she will speed up, plant her bomb on our car, slow down so she's no longer in danger, and detonate it.'

Ivanya's mouth opens in terror. 'Are you . . . Are you *serious*?'

'Very.' He kneels in front of Taty and looks into her face. 'But she hasn't done it yet. Nor will she do it soon. And you know why, don't you Taty?'

Taty cocks an eyebrow. 'I . . . I do?'

'You said we'd be killed on the train,' he says. 'But you said she had to wait two days, because of a storm. Very soon we will be in that same storm of which you spoke. Won't we?'

Taty looks away, disturbed. 'How should I know?'

'Didn't you know what would happen if we took the train?' he asks.

'Well . . . I . . .'

'So is this any different? Or were you wrong?'

'I don't *know*!' she says. She stands and walks to the window. 'I don't . . . I don't understand anything about it! It was like . . . You know the shell games you see people playing, on the street? Where you have to guess which cup has the ball? It was like watching that, and realising at the end that you tracked it all along and knew where it would be. But you hadn't *known* you were watching.'

Sigrud and Ivanya exchange a glance. None of this metaphor, of course, explains how she knew a woman she had never met was watching them from behind a mirror three floors above them.

'Let's get back to our possibly imminent deaths,' says Ivanya. 'So you think we have two days? Before she blows us and everyone on this tram car to smithereens?'

'I think so,' says Sigrud. He joins Taty at the window. 'Those storm clouds will hit us before evening, or I never sailed a day in my life. I think she will wait.'

'So what's your plan?' she asks. 'Exactly how do you plan on preventing our deaths?'

Sigrud watches the cable below as the tram car clanks and cranks up one section of cable to the next cable support tower. The support towers themselves are tall, thin metal frames with a box at the top. Running around the interior of the box is a very small ledge, and on one side is a small platform with a spiral staircase leading down. A place to stop in an emergency and disembark, it seems.

Sigrud thinks.

Within an hour the storm's upon them. They've moved high enough into the mountains that the precipitation is snow rather than rain, the fat white flakes striking the windows and walls, wet, crunchy *smacks* echoing through the vessel. The visibility outside the tram car grows limited, though Sigrud can see the faint halo of lights behind them as their pursuers trundle down the cables.

'It will get worse tomorrow,' he says, listening to the wind.

'How do you know?' asks Ivanya.

'I just know.'

He listens as they trundle along and pass through each cable support tower. He pulls out his pocket watch and starts timing them. They come to a tower about every twenty minutes, it seems, though it's a little variable.

Their lunch is sandwiches, served on silver trays. 'Very few soups get served,' remarks Ivanya, 'in a craft that sways with the wind.'

Taty is grave and silent as she eats. She barely eats. After ten minutes of nibbling, she says, 'They're Saypuris.'

'What, dear?' says Ivanya.

'The people after us. They're Saypuris. From the Ministry.' She looks at Sigrud. 'Isn't that what you said?'

'It is,' says Sigrud.

'So . . . correct me if I'm wrong, but . . . These people are *against* Mother? Or were against her, I suppose.'

Sigrud finishes his sandwich half, then brushes off his fingers. 'Yes.'

'But . . . why?' asks Taty, perplexed. 'I mean, they're from the same country. Right? She was their prime minister.'

'People often don't love their rulers, dear,' says Ivanya, sniffing.

'And they loved Shara even less than most,' says Sigrud. He says it thoughtlessly, speaking the plain truth, but he pauses when he sees Taty's face.

'What do you mean?' she asks, hurt.

'Your mother . . . Your mother tried to change a *lot* of things when she was in office,' explains Ivanya. 'She thought Saypur was doing many things it shouldn't, and not doing many things it should. She tried to change that. But this made her the enemy of those in power.'

'But . . . But couldn't she just have thrown them out?' asks Taty. 'Exiled them? Jailed them? I mean, she was the prime minister!'

'She could have,' admits Sigrud. 'Probably. But I think in her early days, Shara thought she could convince people to come to her side. She had just defeated two Divinities, and unseated Vinya Komayd. It looked like things were different. And I think she wanted her government to be different. Vinya was all too happy to persecute those who disagreed with her. Shara did not wish to go down that road. She hoped things would change with her.'

'But change is slow,' says Ivanya. 'And painful. And incremental.'

'And those people in the tram car behind us,' says Taty slowly. 'The yellow-eyed woman, and her friends, and the man who killed Mother . . . They didn't change at all. Did they?'

'No,' says Sigrud. 'They did not.'

Taty slowly sets her sandwich down. 'If she had been more . . . more like Vinya . . . If she had been willing to jail or exile the people who opposed her – would my mother still be alive?'

'Who can say, dear?' asks Ivanya sadly. 'What's done is done.'

'But it isn't done!' says Taty. 'It's still happening! Those people are still trying to undo everything Mother did!'

'That is so,' says Sigrud. 'But if your mother had been the sort of person who would have persecuted and oppressed those who opposed her – if she had been the sort of prime minister to root out the very people who pursue us right now, and ruin them – then I very much doubt if she would have also been the sort of person to adopt you, Taty.'

Taty bows her head. 'What are you saying?'

'I am saying, I think,' says Sigrud slowly, 'that what happened to Shara happened not because she was weak, or lenient. I think it happened because she was *Shara*. And it could not have gone another way.'

She looks at him, her dark eyes burning. 'But you won't be lenient with them – will you?'

'No,' he says. 'I will not.'

'Good,' she says darkly. 'They don't deserve it. If I could, I would . . . I would . . .'

There's a moment of silence. Sigrud watches out of the side of his eye as Taty picks at her sandwich. *The girl is grieving*, he thinks. *Such sentiments are not unusual.*

'Before I forget to say this,' says Sigrud. 'Eat well, but please do not use the head.'

'I'm sorry – what? The head?' asks Ivanya.

He nods, chewing. 'Use the communal one,' he says. 'Out in the main cabin. If you have to, that is.'

'Am I allowed to ask why you can dictate which latrine we utilise?' asks Ivanya.

He takes another huge bite. 'Do you ever notice where roaches and rats get into your house?'

Taty wrinkles her nose. 'I think Mother had people for that . . .'

'Doors,' says Sigrud. 'Windows. But also *plumbing*. You've got to make a lot of room for all the pipes, all the repairs, and so on, and so on. It is a strange thing, pumping pressurised water into a structure. It takes room, which lets lots of unexpected things in or out.'

'So what?' asks Ivanya. 'What will be going in or out of our toilet that shouldn't?'

Another bite. 'Me.'

Taty stares at him. 'You're going to flush yourself down our commode.'

'No. I am going to *remove* the toilet. Then I will open up the hatch they use to vent or pump out the waste tank. Then I will get out of this tram car, onto one of the cable towers, wait, and jump on' – he points southward, in the direction of their pursuers – 'that.'

Taty's mouth is hanging open, agog. 'And then you'll do what?'

He finishes his sandwich and pulls out his pipe. 'What I do best.'

Ivanya sets her sandwich down. 'You're going to take out our toilet, climb through the hole onto a tower – however many hundreds of feet above the ground – and just wait for the tram car full of assassins to come your way?'

He lights a match and puffs at his pipe. 'Yes.' Then he thinks about it. 'I would *prefer* the toilet go unused, but it is not totally necessary.'

'Could . . . Could that possibly work?' asks Taty.

'The snowstorm will be intense tomorrow,' he says. 'They will not be able to see me there. Nor will they expect someone to try it.'

'Well, I must say that I certainly fucking wouldn't!' Ivanya says. 'Why not just, I don't know, tell the crew that we're being pursued by assailants?'

'They'd likely stop at the next available platform tower and pull us off to investigate,' says Sigrud, 'and then see that the car behind us is full of Ministry agents – who would then override them, arrest us, and take us somewhere bad, where they would do very bad things to us.'

'How will you get back on?' asks Taty.

He frowns, considering it. 'That is not the priority right now. The priority is us and everyone else on this car not dying.'

Ivanya rubs her eyes. 'And what are we to do while you're off in the snowstorm, boarding enemy vessels like some kind of ridiculous aerial pirate?'

'Taty, I would wish to have her hide somewhere safe. For you, Ivanya, well . . .' He glances at the trunk.

'Well, what?' asks Ivanya.

'What Taty said . . . She said that the Saypuri woman has a device used to throw bombs.'

'So?' Ivanya says.

'I think I know what kind she's talking about. I think it throws sticky bombs, adhesive grenades. We used them once to sink ships. You'd float by on a rowing craft and throw the bombs onto the weak parts of the hull, and they'd stick on. They used timers back then, but now they probably use radio transmitters. I expect it's a device that shoots them forward several hundred feet. Very nasty, very convenient, and very quiet – up until the detonation, of course.'

'Again – so?' asks Ivanya.

'So . . . You said you had practiced with long riflings.' He puffs at his pipe. 'But have you ever practiced clay shooting? Or duck hunting?'

Ivanya pales. 'Oh, dear.'

The next day, they get ready.

The snow persists. Great white chunks of it go tumbling off the top of the tram car like lumps of icing. It's impossible to see it fall very far, though: the flakes are so fat and come so fast that neither of them can see much farther than forty or fifty feet below.

Sigrud spends a lot of his time examining and preparing the head. Using the stolen tools, he unscrews the plates around the base of the toilet and studies the piping underneath. 'Should be easy to turn the water off,' he says. 'And then disconnect the toilet, and remove it. But the way out through the hull is the hard part . . .'

'I feel like we're breaking out of prison,' says Ivanya.

'No,' says Sigrud. 'This is easier.' Then he pauses, remembering the altitude. 'I think.'

He puts everything back as the crewman brings their lunch – this time, some kind of flat, cheesy bread he likes not at all. Once the man's gone they shut the door, lock it, and move the trunk in front of it, along with one of the few chairs in the private quarters.

'Ready?' says Sigrud.

'I . . . suppose so,' says Ivanya.

'Then prep the weapons,' says Sigrud, 'while I tend to the toilet.'

It takes less than an hour to completely remove the commode, placing it in the middle of their quarters, but figuring out how to get to the hatch is harder. He lowers himself down into the guts of the tram car, deep in the dark with all the pipes and wiring and clanking machinery. If he turns the wrong screw too much or sits on the wrong plate in the hull, there's a very good chance he could get dumped out and go tumbling through the air until he smashes into the hills below. He makes an improvised harness out of one of Ivanya's belts, and lashes himself to one of the sturdier pipes, but that's no sure thing either.

He feels it first: one back panel of the tram car is burningly cold, as if exposed to the air. He finds the latch for it and realises it will only open if pulled from the exterior. Grimacing, he pulls out his knife and tears the latch off.

The entire back panel lifts up. Flurries of snowflakes come swirling in at him, and he smells exhaust and the cold sting of winter air. It's big enough for him to fit through, but only just.

'Success?' shouts Ivanya from above.

He cranes his head down and sees the thick cable streaming along not more than five feet below the hatch. This close, the cable looks about as thick as a tree trunk. The metal appears to have crushed sugar stuck to it, and he realises it's actually ice: the cable must be covered in a quarter-inch of ice, which gets pulverised and crushed by the wheels of the tram car – but likely not so much that it's no longer slick and slippery.

He groans. *Excellent*.

'I said – any success?' shouts Ivanya again.

He looks up through the shaft. 'Somewhat.' Then he pats the space next to him. 'Here is where you'll be sitting.'

Her face drops. 'Oh, no.'

Sigrud clambers up and out of the shaft where the toilet once was. 'I'll take the pistols,' he said. 'And I'll leave the riflings and the scatter-gun to you. Hopefully you won't need to use either.'

She looks down into the shaft. 'I did not really train on shooting from such confined spaces . . .'

'Well, if it helps any, just remember that your aim will determine if every man, woman, and child on this tram car lives or dies.'

'It . . . It certainly doesn't!' says Ivanya, horrified.

'I'd also suggest putting on some trousers,' says Sigrud. 'I do not think you want to wear your evening apparel down there.'

Sigrud goes into the gutted washroom and puts on a number of holsters

— two for the pistols, one for his knife — as well as thick leather gloves. Usually he prefers to do any climbing with his bare hands, but then he's usually handling rock or wood, not ice-slick steel.

Once he steps out of the washroom, Ivanya glances out the window at the cabling. 'Would it be rude to say that I am now losing faith in this plan?'

'Yes.'

'All right. Well then, I will reconcile myself with just thinking it very loudly.'

'If this is actually happening right now,' asks Taty, sitting in the corner, 'should I go?'

'Yes,' says Sigrud. 'Get as close to the other end of the car as possible. Do whatever it takes to stay there. Pretend to sleep, if that helps.'

Taty hesitates, fingers gripping the doorknob behind her.

'Taty?' asks Sigrud.

She says nothing.

'What are you waiting for?' asks Sigrud.

She lowers her eyes. Then she clenches her jaw and says quietly, 'You taught me how to shoot.'

'I what?' he says.

'You taught me how to shoot. How to do this, how t –'

'How to do *this*?' says Sigrud. 'No. I do not recall that. What are you asking me, Taty?'

'I can help you,' she says, defiant. 'You know I can. I can give you support, just like Auntie.'

Ivanya cringes. 'Taty, dear . . .'

'You *know* I can!' she says.

'I taught you to shoot, yes,' says Sigrud. 'Some. But I also taught you *when* to shoot. Knowing when to avoid a fight is just as important as knowing how to fight.'

'But I can help you!' says Taty desperately. She walks close and looks up into his face. 'Please. Please!'

He looks down, impassive. 'No, Taty.'

'But it's not fair!'

'Not fair? Not fair that you will not be risking life and limb in this ordeal?'

'These . . . These people took Mother away!' she says, furious. 'I am . . . I am *owed* the chance!'

'Owed?' Sigrud asks quietly. 'You are saying it would be just to spill their blood? It would be equitable? As if being repaid a debt?'

Taty stares about the room as she tries to find the words. 'I . . . I . . .'

'I have heard many of Shara's words come tumbling from your lips, Tatyana Komayd,' says Sigrud. 'But those are not hers. Shara Komayd would neither say nor think such a thing.'

Taty, fuming, falls silent. Then she takes a breath, swallows, and says, 'They deserve it. They do. I wish Mother had jailed them . . . or executed them! Imagine all the heartache she could have saved with but the deaths of a few.' She shakes her head. 'Perhaps the only way to truly clean a slate,' she says furiously, 'is with *blood*.' Then she turns and walks out the cabin door, slamming it behind her.

Sigrud walks over to the toilet shaft, examining his pocket watch. 'It's been sixteen minutes since the last cable tower. Four more to go, thereabouts.'

Ivanya takes a shuddering breath. 'Oh my gods. Oh my gods . . .'

Sigrud puts his watch away. He doesn't wish to say so, but Taty's words rattled him. To hear such raw fury pouring out of the girl is disturbing to him. 'Let me go first. Then you get situated. You have one advantage: any explosives that come your way will be coming straight along the cable from the car behind us. Nothing from the sides. Keep the scatter-gun trained down the cable, and shoot *anything* you see coming. If I fall . . .' He grimaces, knowing this plan is far less likely to work. 'If I fall, tell the crew you saw an explosion or something in the tram car behind us. They'll stop this one and investigate – hopefully.'

'And if I can't convince them to stop . . .?'

'Then our enemies will bomb the tram. And you and everyone else will die.'

She pales. 'Don't fall. Yes, because I want you to be safe, but – please, *don't* fall.'

He straddles the shaft. 'I will keep that in mind.' He looks at her. 'Whatever happens, someone must get to the Solda Bridge. You must be there to meet Malwina. She can help you, help Taty, help everyone. But someone must be there. Understand?'

'I understand.'

'Good.' He drops down into the dark.

Sigrud crouches before the open hatch. It's hard to tell how fast the car is going: the snow erases any sense of perspective, and the cable runs by so quickly it's like staring into the surface of a streaming river.

He checks his pocket watch. The next tower should be coming up in a handful of minutes. He crouches in the open hatch, knees bent, arms open.

The tram car shudders, quakes. They're climbing up now, he can feel it.

He wonders how long he'll have. How quickly will the cable tower go by? Ten seconds? Less?

He can feel the tram car ascending farther. The tower should be coming soon. Very soon, he thinks, very, very soon . . .

Then he sees it. The massive frame of steel slides by underneath him, with an extremely, extremely narrow platform running around its edge.

Sigrud hesitates. Then he jumps out.

The second he does, he realises he hesitated too long.

The tower's already gone. Slipped by far faster than he ever expected. There's nothing but the cable below.

He falls. Time stretches on for those five feet down to the cable, each second a millennium.

The cable.

His right arm flies out and loops around the cable, like he's putting the massive metal cord in a headlock. He hits it hard and twists around awkwardly, straining his right shoulder, and he growls with pain. The cable is shaking furiously as the tram car churns away behind him, and he feels his right arm slipping, sliding out from on top of the cable, threatening to send him tumbling down. Sigrud struggles, then manages to link his left hand to his right, locking himself to the frozen cable, which vibrates and thrums wildly as the tram car departs.

The tram car disappears into the snow behind him, its bone-shaking rattle slowly fading. His legs swing freely below, dangling above a swirling white sea of snow. There's nothing but the wind and the ice now. He grits his teeth, holding tight, but then the cable begins to vibrate again.

Because the next car is now coming, he thinks, *and it will very gladly crush you.*

Sigrud sets his jaw, then twists around until his body's underneath the frozen cable. Then he crunches his stomach, lifting his waist up so that he can put his legs around the cable as well, like someone sliding down a pole – only this pole is horizontal, covered in ice, and hanging several hundred feet above the snowy Tarsils. It's also sloping down, away from the tower, which doesn't make going up it any easier.

He begins to inch his way back toward the tower, which now seems very far away. His gloves and clothing keep sticking to the ice, so he has to rip them away each time.

The thrumming in the cable grows harder. Soon he can hear the tram car just beyond.

He looks up along the cable, seeing the world upside down. The tower is just ten feet away. The next section of cabling is sloping away from it, but through the swirling snowflakes he can see faint lights climbing its thin, dark form: the lights of the Saypuri woman's car.

Hurry. Hurry.

He inches up the cable. The tower's now almost within reach. It's much skinnier than it looked from the tram car, some kind of engineering feat he would have never imagined. No wonder it seemed to come and go in an instant.

He climbs up to the very edge of the tower. Then he twists himself around until he's sitting on top of the cable. He sits up, riding it like one would a horse – he wobbles a bit, which makes his heart skip a beat – and gauges how to get on to the ledge and then on to the staircase on the western side without losing his grip or getting smashed by the oncoming tram car.

The lights are brighter now. The tram car is very close.

Just do it.

He falls forward. His fingers find the front rim of the ledge and his grip holds, leaving him dangling off the side of the tower. He knows he can't go up this side of the platform, as he'd be crushed by the oncoming tram. He'll need to inch around, to the platform on the western side of the tower. Which won't be easy, as the tower is just as icy as the cable.

He looks down. There are crisscrossing supports about ten feet below him, but they don't look like anything he could stand on. He grimaces, reaches out with his left hand, and begins slowly making his way along the edge of the tower to the corner, one handspan at a time.

He comes to the corner and grabs the corner strut. The staircase is only ten feet away now. He hauls himself up until he can lift his feet up to the side edge.

Finally, he thinks, relieved to be able to stand on something. Especially because the tram is less than a hundred feet away by now, and approaching fast.

He tries to push up with his legs, but finds he gravely underestimated how icy the ledge is: the soles of his boots slip and his feet go flying out from underneath him, sending him shooting back down the tower.

He shouts and hugs the corner strut of the tower platform as he falls. The steel edge of the strut bites into his left bicep, and his feet fruitlessly try to find purchase on the slippery metal. Once again, he's suspended over a precipitous drop, clinging to an icy piece of metal; but this time the tram car is much, much closer.

His eye widens as the car climbs up the cables toward him. He knows he won't be able to get onto the platform in time. He's out of the car's way, so he won't be crushed, but it will fly by him, leaving him alone up here on the tower, and be free to move closer to Ivanya and the other passengers.

The tram car slows just a bit as it mounts the last few feet of cabling to the tower. The whole tower is vibrating like the string of a vasha as the giant machine draws closer. He can see its wheels churning, see exhaust pouring out of its undercarriage . . .

And there, on the underside of the machine, the rungs of a metal ladder – one probably used by service crews to scale the hull.

A huge *clank* as the tram car finishes mounting the tower. It's close enough that he can see ice clinging to the metal rungs.

This time, he thinks, *do not hesitate*.

With another huge *clank*, the tram car shoots forward, and begins to climb down the next segment of cabling.

Sigrud lifts himself up and shoves off the tower, hand outstretched.

His right fingers catch the rung of the ladder, and he's jerked forward like a fish caught on a hook.

The next thing he knows, Sigrud is hurtling through the snow, feet swinging wildly below him. His right armpit and shoulder are bright with pain – it feels like the damn thing nearly tore his arm out of its socket. But he holds fast, clinging one-handed to the metal rung on the bottom of the tram car.

Another tram car flies through the snow on the other set of cables, going south to Ahanashtan. He sees children staring out the glass viewing dome at the top. They spot him, this strange man dangling from the bottom of the moving car. One of the boys points, and Sigrud can see him say: *Wow!*

This, he thinks, *is not what I wanted.*

Growling, he fights gravity and the wind and the cold, and lifts his left hand up until he can grasp the next rung. He grabs it, his grip holds, and he hauls himself up. When he's four rungs up he can finally use his feet – which he applies very carefully to the ladder, mindful of what just happened on the tower.

He doesn't slip. He takes a breath, shuts his eyes, and revels in the solid feel of the tram car, something hard and durable to hold on to.

Alive, he thinks to himself. *You're alive.*

He scales the hull of the tram car. At the top there's the large apparatus with the car's upper wheel set on it, which runs along the upper cable. Below that is a glass viewing dome, which sits on the top of the car – and beside that, a very small hatch. He thinks the hatch is far enough away from the cockpit – where the assailants will likely be stationed, he imagines – that if he opens the hatch, perhaps they won't notice the sound, or the change in pressure, or the sudden influx of cold air.

Which he knows is a stretch. So he readies one of his pistols.

He manoeuvres himself up to the hatch, lying flat against the hull of the tram car. The glass dome is beside him, its blue glass warped with layers of ice. He can see the viewing area below. It seems empty, which comforts him. He wasn't sure if the Saypuri woman had commandeered her own tram car or just boarded a full one, but it seems now like it was the former, which means no innocents would be caught in the crossfire: anything moving in there will be an enemy.

He rubs snow out of his eye, blinks, and examines the lock on the hatch. It's complicated – very complicated. If he's lucky, he'll be able to –

He stops. There's motion out of the corner of his eye.

He looks down through the glass dome on top of the tram car.

A young Saypuri man in a dark coat is strolling through the viewing area, smoking, a rifling in his hands.

There's nowhere to hide on the side of the car, so Sigrud flattens himself to the hull of the tram car and tries to crawl back down the ladder.

It's too late. The Saypuri guard – Ministry, certainly – sees him through the glass. The guard's mouth drops open; his cigarette, still smoking, clings to his lip for one second, then falls. Sigrud can faintly hear the man saying, 'What the *fuck*?'

Then the guard raises his rifling and the glass dome explodes.

Sigrud shuts his eye and turns his head away as the glass goes whirling around him. He feels something hot and hard strike his chest, and thinks, *That's it. I'm done for.* But though there's pain, there's not much of it, which is curious.

Sigrud hears shouts, gunshots, and the clanging of metal. He opens his eye just in time to see the hull right in front of his face suddenly poke outward, as if it were a sheet of rubber and someone on the other side just jabbed it with their finger.

He sits back from the hull and looks down. The hull is riddled with such dents, and right where his chest was pressed are two of them, pointing outward: places where the bullets almost punched through the hull, but not quite. They must have jabbed his sternum, but it's far better than being shot.

Lucky, thinks Sigrud. *Damned lucky.*

The guard is still firing, shredding the frame around the viewing dome. Sigrud raises his pistol, listening as the guard says, 'Bastard! Bastard!'

Sigrud waits. Two more shots. Three. Then a pause.

Reloading.

Sigrud pops up over the frame of the dome, raises his pistol, and points it at the guard kneeling in the viewing area, fumbling with his gun.

The guard looks up.

Sigrud fires once, a sharp *pop*.

A small, neat hole appears over the guard's left eye, and he slumps over.

Sigrud cocks his head, listening to see if there are any other opponents directly below the shattered glass dome. He hears someone shouting a question from inside the tram car – '*Chandra? What's going on?*' – but it's not close. Grunting, he lifts himself up and slips through the broken dome, landing quietly on the seat of a leather chair.

He looks around. The viewing area is on the upper level of the tram car, a small rest area with chairs and tables and a tiny bar. There are two short stairways to his immediate left and right that lead down to the next level.

He hears footsteps sprinting down the level below. Two sets, one on either side of the car. Then they stop – taking up defensive positions, surely. If he were to so much as stick his head around the corner at the bottom of either set of stairs, they'd shred him.

He's lost the element of surprise – which is bad. He looks around himself, wondering what to do. His eye falls on the dead young man at his feet.

Sigrud pulls off his gloves, as it's much easier to work firearms with bare hands. He crouches, tugs the man's coat off, then takes off his own knit cap and pulls it down over the dead man's face.

He frowns at his work. *Just different enough to be alarming. I hope.*

He lifts the corpse over his shoulder, then pauses, listening – no movement, not yet, unless they've moving very carefully.

He turns, shifts the corpse in his grasp, and hurls the dead young man down the stairs on his right. It lands on the floor with a loud *thump*.

The instant the body crosses the threshold at the bottom of the stairs, someone down the aisle from it opens fire. The corpse's chest bursts open, then its arms and legs.

Sigrud doesn't stay to watch further: he stalks down the stairs on his left and ducks his head around the corner.

Compartments and berths line the left wall of the tram car. The doors are open. Crouched in one door, just ten feet down the aisle, is a Saypuri man in black clothing, pistol in his hand, brow furrowed as he peeks across the middle aisle to try to see what his comrade on the right side of the car is firing at. He's not, however, looking down the aisle at the left-hand stairway.

Sigrud pulls out his knife. *I do hope*, he thinks, *that the tram doesn't sway . . .*

He pivots out around the corner and, in one smooth motion, flicks the knife forward. He's in luck: the blade hurtles toward the Saypuri man and finds a home on the right side of his neck, just below his jaw. The man chokes and tumbles backward, firing one wild shot into the ceiling as he falls.

A voice from the right side of the car, a man's: 'Azad?'

Sigrud crouches low and creeps into the aisle. There are leather chairs in rows in the centre of the tram car, and through them he can see a form huddled in the door of the middle compartment. He could get a better angle if he went farther down the aisle, but it'd draw attention.

He looks at the leather chairs separating them. *Built for comfort*, he thinks. *But not for combat.*

He points the pistol through the leather chairs and opens fire, five quick shots. The bullets punch through the leather and thin wood easily, raining on the doorway of the compartment. The huddled form collapses, but Sigrud doesn't pause to look: he dashes forward, still staying low, and takes cover in the first compartment.

There's no movement, no sound. He creeps out and across the tram car to the body lying in the doorway. Another young Saypuri man, gunshot wounds in his face and belly.

Sigrud reloads, glancing around for any sign of movement. Then he stalks back across the aisle to the compartment with the other dead Saypuri man, the one with Sigrud's knife still lodged in his throat. The carpet is soaked in blood. It squishes wetly under the soles of his boots.

He kneels, pulls the knife out. A weak burst of blood flows forth from the wound. Not the way a living person bleeds, he knows.

As he wipes off the knife, the tram car jerks underneath him. He blinks as he regains his balance. Then he realises what's going on.

They're speeding up, he thinks. *They're going to try and bomb the car.*

He leaps out of the berth and runs down the aisle to the crew quarters. The door is closed. He peers through the glass window in the door. It's dark inside but he can see the faint outline of the cockpit door on the other side of the quarters. He's got to get to the cockpit, got to stop them from mining the aero car ahead, got to at least slow them down or –

There's movement in the window. Someone shifting, rising up from a crouch. Sigrud sees the gleam of a gun in their hands.

He throws himself to the floor among the seats. Then the world fills up with gunfire.

Bullets chew through the doorway like it's made of straw. The wood is shredded, pulped, pulverised into toothpicks. As he covers his head he identifies the sound as a high-calibre, fully automatic weapon, which means it's very rare, very expensive, and very, very dangerous.

A pause in the gunfire. A woman's voice shouts, '*Nashal! Do it now! Fucking do it now!*'

He's got to do something, got to stop it somehow. He sits up, but then the gunfire resumes, sawing through the wall just above him, and he drops again.

She's got him pinned down. There's nothing he can do.

Crouched in the greasy, reeking, clanging guts of the tram car, Ivanya Restroyka stares down the cables in terror.

There's not much she can hear over the sounds of the tram car's engine, but she can hear *that*: it's gunfire. And lots of it.

She stares down the cable, scatter-gun in her hands, its stock pressed to her shoulder. She raises it, not sure what she's going to aim at or, gods forbid, what she's going to shoot at.

Am I about to shoot a gun? Am I really? At a bomb? It's all too preposterous to believe.

Then she sees it, crawling down the cable at them at a very fast rate: the second tram car. It's far too close to be safe.

Something's wrong.

She points her scatter-gun at the advancing car, feeling ridiculous and impotent.

It's quite close now. Close enough for her to see that the front window is open, just above the tram car's nose.

There's a man in the window, a Saypuri man with a beard and a grey cap. He's pointing something at her. It looks like a big piece of plumbing, made of green metal and with a big, gaping mouth. The man hunches low, pressing his cheek to its side, and shuts one eye.

He's aiming it at her. He's about to . . .

Something dark flies from the thing's mouth.

Ivanya's instincts take over. She squeezes the trigger, and . . .

The world lights up.

The explosion is loud enough that at first Sigrud thinks the tram car's been knocked off its cables. It's a bone-rattling, punctuated blast, not the dull roar of an incendiary mine but something high-impact. And from the smoke that's now pouring through the bullet-riddled door to the crew's quarters, it detonated very, very close.

The tram car slows to a stop. He expects it to fall – but it doesn't.

Sigrud's still reeling from the blast, but he manages to think: *Ivanya. She shot it, didn't she? And it went off right in their faces . . .*

He stands. The chatter of gunfire seems to have ceased. The stream of smoke from the crew's quarters is thickening.

It's a miracle we weren't blown off the cables, he thinks.

He bursts through the pulverised door, which comes apart easily under his bulk. He crouches low, struggling to see through the smoke. The cockpit door is speckled with holes, some big, some small. Shrapnel – which means whoever's in the cockpit is probably in no laughing mood. He narrows his eye and spies a woman lying in the corner, a massive, fully automatic rifling beside her. A bun of black hair has unravelled on top of her head. *The gold-eyed woman I saw in the mirror*, he thinks.

She's not the priority right now, he knows. He needs to make sure whoever has that mine-throwing device isn't going to use it again.

He walks through the smoke, kicks open the cockpit door, and is slapped in the face by the cool winter air. The front windows and the nose of the tram car are a blackened mess. The top front of the outer hull has been blown in, peppering the cockpit with shrapnel. Lying beside the door is a Saypuri man, still clutching the battered mine-throwing weapon. Something has shaved off a lot of his scalp, or perhaps it's been blown off – regardless, his face is a mottled mass of blood. Sigrud thinks he's dead, but then he shifts and moans. Blood bubbles out of his ragged lips.

Sigrud looks forward, through the blown-in windows. The bomb must have gone off about twenty feet in front of the nose of the car: the cables there are blackened and somewhat shredded, like unraveling yarn.

That's not good, he thinks.

He can see the next tram car fifty or sixty feet ahead. It appears to have stopped as well. He supposes he can't blame them: they don't have any visibility on what's going on yet, and they're likely doing systems checks to make sure their craft is still functional after the detonation.

But huddled in the hatch at the bottom is a pale figure: Ivanya. She's wide-eyed, shivering, but she appears uninjured, clutching the scatter-gun like it's a prized toy. Its muzzle is smoking, very slightly.

Sigrud sighs and waves to her, relieved. She waves back with one trembling hand.

Then she sits up, mouth open, and points. Not at him, he realises. But something behind him.

Then the knife sinks into his back.

Sigrud roars and brings his left elbow down, catching his assailant in the side – the Saypuri woman. She coughs and falls backward into the smoky cabin. He looks back at his shoulder, and sees a combat knife buried two inches into it. He reaches up and rips it out.

It should have gone in farther – hells, she could have cut his throat. She's had training, after all. It takes him a minute to realise why: as she struggles to stand, he sees she's bleeding freely from a wound in her belly. *Shrapnel*, he thinks. She's probably drunk with shock.

'You piece of shit,' she mutters. 'You . . . you piece of *shit* . . .'

He pulls out his pistol, intending to put her down. But she flies up with surprising strength and speed, and slaps the gun out of his hand. She delivers one quick strike to his neck, which nearly makes him black out, but he manages to block the next blow with his right arm before she can finish the job.

Sigrud grasps her wrist and swings his skull forward, soundly head-butting her on the cheek. She moans and stumbles back, but he's already advancing, brandishing her own knife at her. Growling, she assumes a defensive stance.

'You were going to kill Tatyana,' says Sigrud. 'You were the people who killed Shara.'

The woman spits blood on the ground. 'May that fucking bitch rot,' she says. 'May her and you and all you've done rot and fester.'

Sigrud nods, as if this is the answer he wanted. 'I'm going to kill you now.'

She spits more blood. 'And I'm going to make you work for it.'

They close in on each other.

She fights well, using his size and the small confines against him, trying to deliver quick, sharp blows to his joints, to his neck, to his face. But this is not her fight to win. She's in much worse shape than he is. And he has a hundred pounds on her, and a knife.

She dodges the knife as best she can, backing down through the crew's quarters, back through the pulverised door. She catches the blade on her underarm, then along her side. He opens up her ribs, and blood spatters onto the floor. She's good – she doesn't even cry out with the pain – but not good enough.

She finally stumbles. He steps into her stance, bumps his shoulder into hers, and buries the knife up under her ribs.

The slightest whimper. She tries to crush his nose with the heel of her palm, but he turns his face away and takes the blow on the side of his skull.

He pushes the knife in farther. Still she fights against him, trying to punch his throat.

He grabs her back with his free hand, pulls her forward, and shoves the blade in even deeper.

That should do it. She should stop fighting.

But then, to his surprise, she draws a deep breath and yells in a ragged voice, '*Now, Nashal! Do it now, do it now!*'

He drops her and turns. The bloodied, ravaged man in the cockpit has staggered to his feet. He's brought the mine-thrower up to his shoulder and is drunkenly pointing it through the broken windows.

Time feels like it slows down. He can't see Ivanya, but he knows she's there, still holding the scatter-gun. If she shoots another mine out of the air, it'll blow the cables apart and send both tram cars down.

Sigrud pulls the second pistol out of the holster on his thigh, and brings it up. But then, to his disbelief, the Saypuri woman's on him again, leaping onto his back and clawing at his face, trying to throw his aim off.

He struggles to hold the pistol up. The bloody Saypuri man is still trying to aim the mine-thrower out the window. The woman is punching Sigrud's face, digging her fingers into his cheek, and then into his eye . . .

Splut.

She rips out his false eye. This surprises her so much that she freezes just for one moment, holding the warm, white sphere. '*What?*' she says, bewildered.

Sigrud aims and fires.

The shot is true: the side of the Saypuri man's skull bursts open and he collapses, his weapon falling to the floor beside him.

With a shove, Sigrud tosses the Saypuri woman off. She falls to the floor, gasping.

He turns around, his chest heaving. He bends down, takes his false eye out of her hand, and stows it away in his pocket. As he stands, her other hand flies up to her mouth.

She slips something between her lips, a small, black sphere. Then she swallows it.

'Poison?' asks Sigrud. 'Why, if you're already dying?'

She laughs bitterly. 'I thought you knew everything about the Divine,' she says. 'They're all about resurrection.'

Sigrud chooses to ignore this. 'Why do you work for him? Why risk your life and kill innocents for him?'

'The game's rigged,' she gasps. 'Every system's broken. Saypuri, Continental, Divine. There are no innocents. He's going to burn it all down. Burn it all down and start over again.'

'And you? Will you burn as well?'

'No.' She shuts her eyes. 'When he starts over, I'll be right there with him.'

She opens her eyes. They're no longer the amber-gold colour he's familiar with: they're jet-black, like they're made of oil.

Sigrud says, 'What in the . . .?'

The woman lifts her left hand and plunges it into the wound in her side. Her face registers no pain: it's as if she's in a daze. Impossibly, she shoves her hand in deeper and deeper, the ribs crackling and crunching, until her wrist enters the wound, and then part of her forearm . . . and then she begins to pull something out.

It is long, and black, and gleaming. She pulls out a foot of it, then two feet, then she's using both hands to pull it out, more and more and more. Sigrud points the pistol and shoots her in the face, emptying the pistol into her skull. The bullets punch through her cheek and brow, but it makes no difference: her hands keep pulling, and pulling, and pulling . . .

And then it's out.

It's a spear. A huge, long, black spear, taller than he is, glimmering like oil. Though it makes no sense, he understands that the woman has just pulled this dark spear from her heart.

Still lying prone on the floor, her blank, black eyes staring up at the ceiling, the woman slams the butt of the spear down on the floor of the tram car.

The impact of the spear is rendered in silence: it's as if its touch kills all sound around it – and then after it, all light. The light from the windows, the fluttering lights in the ceiling – they all die the instant the spear makes contact, and all is dark.

Sigrud stands in the black. He pats his belt, pulls out more bullets, and begins reloading his pistol, thinking only, *This is bad*.

He feels vibrations in the floor: someone is climbing to their feet close to them. Someone . . . big.

Slowly, slowly, the lights return, the grey-white light of a snow flurry, and with it the rumble of the tram car. Then he sees the woman is not lying on the floor anymore.

There is something in the cabin of the tram car with him. Something very tall, something heaving with exertion, holding the spear.

It seems human-shaped, but it's difficult to confirm this: it looks like it's made of smoke and oil and sludge – a tall, thin creature whose long limbs speak of wiry strength. Its face, however, is blank, perfectly blank, like the face of a statue made of jet whose features have been completely sanded over.

The thing takes a breath – or it seems to, for can such things breathe? – and screams.

Its scream is silence: when it cries out all sounds die with it, as if Sigrud has entered a perfect vacuum incapable of transmitting sound.

Yet there are still words in that silence, an idea communicated in wordlessness:

<*Seneschal! Seneschal! I am seneschal! I am silence, I am void, I am silence!*>

Sigrud raises the pistol and starts shooting.

Shooting the thing, it seems, mostly succeeds in just pissing it off. He can hear the gunshots, though, which suggests sound still works – somewhat. The creature staggers back a little, but then lunges forward, its dark spear flying forward.

Sigrud ducks just in time. The shaft tears through the air just above him and sinks deep into the wall, slashing through it as if it were water.

Curiously, though, the impact makes no sound. If he hadn't seen it happen, he wouldn't have known it'd happened at all.

He reaches up with his right hand, attempting to grab the spear and wrench it out of the creature's grasp, but the merest touch of the shaft is like touching a glacier: his palm screams with icy pain, and he snaps it away, hissing.

He rolls away and scrambles back into the crew's quarters. He looks at his right hand and sees the flesh of his palm is bright red, like he dipped it in open flames. *Not good*, he thinks. The woman's fully automatic rifling is still lying on the ground. He snatches it up, checks to confirm it's loaded, and looks up just in time to see the creature dart into the quarters, the spear lashing out again like a black tongue.

Sigrud dives to the right, and once more the spear barely misses him. He can't hear its strike again – it's like its blows happen with no sound at all – but he watches as the spear slashes through the control panels of the tram car. Then the creature pulls the spear back, slaps its hands together . . .

And all sound dies. Seemingly permanently, this time.

Sigrud raises the rifling and opens up on the creature in a quick burst. The muzzle flare is bright, but the gun's chatter makes no sound. The creature flinches as the bullets spatter its face, its torso, and Sigrud uses its distraction to dive out the door, past it, and down the aisle, sprinting away with soundless steps.

His sense of gravity shifts, and he realises the tram car is now moving forward again, fast. The creature must have hit a lever or button when it stabbed its spear into the control panel – or perhaps it has mind enough to try to get close to Ivanya's car, close enough to jump aboard and slaughter everyone in it.

He whirls around to see the creature is much, much closer than he realises, and he falls back just as the spear blade darts out again, slashing open the chairs behind him.

He points the rifling up at the creature and fires, spraying it down with bullets. It recoils, tiny flickers appearing in its oily skin. Still the world is silent and soundless. The recoil, his own growls, the burst of the bullets – they're all totally silent, not even making a whisper. The effect is profoundly disorienting to him.

Sigrud stands and sprints farther down the aisle, then rolls behind a row of chairs to hide. This, he realises, was a bad choice: he never realised how much he was so dependent on sound to navigate combat, but now that it's like he's deaf, he can't hear if the creature's near or not.

He crouches and places his palm flat on the floor. He can feel vibrations, very slightly. The creak of the tram car as the wind and snow strikes its hull. The engine thrumming as the car blindly charges forward. And then, from somewhere near, rapid impacts . . .

Sigrud falls to the floor just as the black shaft shoots through the chair above him, punching through the wall of the tram. The spear retreats and white light pours through – it must have stabbed clean through the hull.

He rolls out into the aisle, only to find the creature stepping forward to straddle him. It raises its spear high, intending to run him through. This time there's nowhere for him to move to, no escape.

Then the tram car jumps and the creature stumbles back. Sigrud rolls over, rises, and springs back down the tram car – realising that his car has just collided with Ivanya and Taty's.

I do hope, he thinks as he flees, *that Ivanya has not been crushed* . . .

He has to think of a plan. There must be something to fight it with. Maybe not damage it, since bullets certainly don't seem to work, but if he can throw it out of the car somehow . . .

He cocks his head. It is, after all, very hard to stand up on the top of the car, since it's so icy. He's experienced this personally, of course.

He runs down the tram car, past the corpses of the three Saypuri men, back up the stairs, back to the waiting area where he came in . . .

Then the wall beside him seems to erupt. First comes the spear, shooting through the metal wall, and then the creature wriggles through the perforation, parting the metal effortlessly and shouldering through like some sort of bizarre birth.

Sigrud staggers back as he avoids the spear, falling to the floor. The creature whips around, the spear lashes out . . .

He has no time to lift the rifling in his right hand, no time to move. The creature will hurl the spear around and plunge it into his breast.

His instincts take over. With his left hand, Sigrud reaches up and snatches the shaft of the spear, just behind the blade, right as the creature swings it to point at his chest.

It should burn him, he knows. It should be like touching metal that's been submerged in the frozen depths of the ocean. It should rip his skin away, sloughing off the flesh of his hand like it's made of wet tissue paper.

But it doesn't. It doesn't hurt at all. His left hand holds the spear tight, and hard – and painlessly.

He feels a flicker of confusion from the black creature.

The point of the blade hovers just above his heart.

The creature quivers with rage, and tries its hardest to push through his grasp.

Sigrud clenches his jaw, turning his left shoulder into his hold on the spear, pushing it away from his heart. The point inches closer, and closer . . .

The tip pierces his sweater, nicks the flesh behind it on his right breast, close to the shoulder. The wound is like being shot through with ice.

He roars silently, leans forward, and pushes hard.

The creature's stance on the floor slips, and it falls back, surprised.

Sigrud – still operating completely out of instinct – shifts the spear in the creature's grasp so that the butt of it is pointed at its head, and shoves forward again, hard.

The butt of the spear slams into the creature's face – and this impact makes noise, a thick, loud *clunk*.

With that, all sound returns – the roar of the wind, the groan of the engines, and the creak of the metal as the tram car trundles forward along the wires.

Sigrud drops the spear and the rifling, climbs up onto a chair, and vaults up through the broken viewing dome in the roof.

The snow is even more intense now. The wheels grind and moan above him, and when he looks forward, he can see why: their tram car has slammed into the back of Ivanya and Taty's car, shoving it forward up the cables.

I hope this works, thinks Sigrud. He clambers forward, bear-crawling along the icy top of the tram car. He feels his grip slip once, twice, and then he's sliding face-first down toward Ivanya's car, down to the broken nose of his car and its shattered windows . . .

He can see Ivanya's face in the window ahead. She must have climbed back up through the shaft to their room. She's watching him, and he can see her mouth the words – *Oh, shit.*

Don't worry, he mentally tells her. *This was intended. Sort of.*

He keeps sliding down, down, faster and faster toward the nose of his tram car. Ordinarily either he'd go tumbling off the front of the tram car to be cut in half by the wheels as they zip along the lower cable, or he'd miss the cable entirely and go plummeting to his death. But as the front of the tram car has been opened up by the explosion, he instead falls headfirst into the open cockpit.

His landing is not graceful. The window frames are jagged and scratch at his chest, and though he breaks his fall somewhat his head still slams into the cockpit controls. It's enough to dizzy him, but he keeps his wits and crawls to the back of the cockpit.

Then things go silent again.

The creature must have done that . . . that *thing* it did earlier, casting that spell to kill all sound. But he can tell it's following his progress across the top of the tram car, because he can see Ivanya's face in the back window ahead of him: her eyes get huge and round, watching something above him, and she starts silently screaming.

Then there's another face beside hers – Taty's. The girl, he sees, has defied his orders, and come to watch. Her face goes blank with horror

– Sigrud thinks, *What must I do to get this damned fool girl to listen to me?* – but she doesn't scream like Ivanya. She just stares.

He can feel the vibrations in the tram car, feel the creature progressing across the top of the hull. It must be stabbing its spear down as it walks across the tram car, using it to hold on steady . . .

Sigrud narrows his eye. *I am ready. I am ready for you.*

The creature leaps down into the cockpit and swings the blade of its spear around it, slashing the walls in a 180-degree arc.

But Sigrud's not there. He's standing down the aisle just outside the door – with the mine-thrower ready and waiting.

Sigrud pulls the trigger.

The sticky bomb hurtles forward and smacks the creature in the face – hard. And sticks.

The creature stumbles back with the impact. Then it whirls around, clawing at its face. Though it doesn't seem to have any eyes, having a giant, adhesive glob stuck to its face appears to have blinded it.

Sound returns again – the gears, the crunch of metal, Ivanya's tinny screams ahead.

Sigrud lowers his shoulder, mine-thrower still in his hands, and charges forward.

His left palm hits the thing dead in the back. Once again, the contact causes no harm. He keeps shoving forward, pushing the creature up and out . . .

The creature flips forward out of the broken hull, bounces off the back of Ivanya's car, and falls, spear still clutched in its hands.

Sigrud almost breathes a sigh of relief. Then the spear stabs in through the bottom floor of the tram car, narrowly missing his crotch.

Sigrud leaps aside, looking down. The creature must have jammed its spear up into the undercarriage of the tram car – and is probably still hanging on to its end, somewhere down below him.

Sigrud looks ahead at Ivanya's tram car, which sits on the cables just beyond the ruptured cockpit of his own. The latrine hatch he originally climbed out of is still open.

He mounts the ruined control board, gauges the distance, and carefully steps across the gap into the open hatch on the back of Ivanya's tram car. He sets down the mine-thrower, grabs onto the top of the hatch for support, and reaches across into the open cockpit of the damaged tram.

He starts pushing levers until one of them works: the tram car stops advancing and instead begins reversing, crawling back down the cable away from him while Ivanya's car keeps moving forward.

As the car retreats, he sees he was right: the creature is holding on to the butt of its long, black spear, which is jammed into the tram's undercarriage. The creature twists in the wintry breezes as the tram car zips away, trying and failing to pull the sticky bomb off its face. It vanishes into the snow flurries.

Sigrud, groaning with pain, pulls out his pocket watch. Within a few seconds they should begin climbing to the next tower and the next set of cables. He snaps his pocket watch shut and waits calmly until they finally do so, proceeding safely and surely on to the next segment of the aero-tram line.

Then he picks up the mine-thrower and examines it. There's a small latch on the side, like a little door. He opens it up.

Inside the little door is a small red button.

Sigrud looks back down the cable. He pushes the button.

There's a *boom* from somewhere out in the storm as the radio-controlled mine detonates. He watches as the cables on the section they just left suddenly go slack and begin to fall, as if severed somewhere in the middle. Then there's a second sound, a loud crash like a hundred tons of metal have slammed into something hard, but this time it's from far below them.

Sigrud smiles wickedly, tosses the mine-thrower out into the wintry air, shuts the hatch, and climbs back up the shaft.

Sigrud lies on the loose pile of plumbing in the bathroom, trying to find a comfortable position. It seems impossible: all the pipes and the plates and the tools feel arranged to poke every bruise or scrape or pulled muscle on his body.

He hears a door open in the cabin beyond, and freezes. He can hear someone dart in, ask a panicked question. Ivanya's voice answers, along with Taty's. Sigrud stays perfectly still: it's likely a service crewman, and if he were to walk in and find Sigrud battered, bloody, and lying on a disassembled toilet with a lot of guns on his person, it would raise some questions.

But the door doesn't open. The crewman departs. Then, finally, the motor in the aero-tram springs back to life. He feels the world shift, and then slowly, slowly, they begin moving forward again.

Sigrud wants to exhale with relief, but he doesn't risk it. He must stay hidden. He waits for a few minutes longer, and then . . .

He awakes with a snort as the door begins to open. Apparently despite the uncomfortable plumbing in the very cramped bathroom, he fell asleep out of sheer exhaustion.

Ivanya's face peers in at him. The room is dark beyond – apparently hours must have passed. 'I thought you said you were going to put the toilet back together,' she says.

'I was,' he says, groaning as he sits up. 'But I did not realise how injured I was. She gave me quite a beating.'

'She? That thing was a she?'

'It is. Or was.'

'Is it dead?'

Sigrud pats his arm, feels the fabric on the sleeve of his sweater. It's crusty and sticky with blood. He's not sure where he got that laceration, but he supposes he had plenty of chances. 'I doubt it. It hardly minded getting shot in the face and chest many times,' he says. 'I am not convinced that having a mine detonated on its face and then dumping a tram on it finished it off. It is likely in a better state than I am, actually.'

'We have some time to clean you up,' says Ivanya. 'I told the crewman you were ill in here. Apparently they never planned for this sort of attack on an aero-tram – engineers are *so* brilliant, up until they aren't. They asked if the passengers wished to disembark at the next tram base, but as it's a frozen-over maintenance facility way up in the teeth of the Tarsils, very few passengers have agreed. So we just continue on our merry way – to Bulikov.'

Sigrud sits on the pile of plumbing, breathing hard and trying not to move too much.

'You look like shit,' she says.

'I look like shit,' he agrees.

'I know first aid.'

'You do?'

'Some. I had to learn medicine when taking care of the sheep.'

'I am not a sheep.'

'No. You smell worse.' She nods at his arm. 'You're still bleeding. You need stitches.'

'I need brandy,' he sighs. Wincing with pain, he begins taking off his boots, then his shirt. There's a black, unpleasant-looking nick on his right breast, where the spear stabbed him. The wound isn't open – it appears to have been fused shut, as if the spear blade was burning hot – but the blackness lies below his skin, like a bubble of oil suspended in his flesh just beside his shoulder. His right hand, however, simply looks burned – it's as if the tip of the spear did something . . . else.

He pushes on the black mark. It doesn't hurt any – but it doesn't go away, either. *That's concerning*, he thinks.

Ivanya fetches a bag from her trunk. Inside are needles, scissors, and bandages – almost a full kit.

'You are prepared,' says Sigrud, impressed.

She kneels and begins cleaning off the gash on his arm. 'We have forty-seven rounds left for the pistols,' she says, dabbing the wound with alcohol. 'And nineteen shells for the scatter-gun, and fifty-five rounds for the riflings. Though I have yet to count what you've returned with. I've already disassembled the scatter-gun and hidden it away. Let me know when you want to surrender your pistols. I'll clean them and do the same.'

Sigrud watches her as she works, threading the needle through his flesh. He suddenly feels terribly sad for Ivanya: he imagines her as she was, glittering and laughing, compared to this person she is now, stark and paranoid, casually discussing ammunition as she tends to ghastly wounds. She is still lovely, but there's a harrowed sense to it now, the fierce, fragile beauty of a wary hind on the slopes, ready to spring away at the snap of a branch.

She catches him looking. 'What?'

'You never stop, do you?' he asks.

'I can't afford to stop,' she says, looping her stitches back around. 'Neither can you. We're going to Bulikov, after all. That city is fraught with harm. I remember.'

'You walked away from civilisation, Ivanya Restroyka,' says Sigrud. 'I wonder if one day you can walk away from what happened to you as well.'

'Can I?' she says, tying off the stitches. 'Can you? You had, what, ten years to do something else with your life? You could have done anything else. Started over. But you didn't. You held on to it. You didn't let it go.'

Sigrud is silent.

'Perhaps I'm a fool,' says Ivanya. 'All I think of now is what will happen to Taty after all this. Maybe you're right, maybe she's Divine. But one can be Divine and also be a young, terrified, innocent girl.' She snips off the thread. 'And as we take her back to Bulikov, all I can think is – I will not let what happened to me happen to her.'

After Ivanya's done her work, Sigrud goes in search of Taty. Night has fallen, and the main cabin of the aero-tram is dark, but people are still awake, blinking owlishly in their berths as they wait to see if yet another explosion will come. Sigrud walks past them and climbs the stairs up to the viewing dome.

The viewing area is empty except for her. She sits at the far end, hugging her knees, staring up at the night sky. The moon is trying to free itself from a tangle of thin clouds, its pale luminescence stretched and distorted by the layers of ice on the glass.

Sigrud walks over and sits on the floor in the aisle. For a moment neither of them says anything.

'Are you all right?' asks Sigrud.

'Yes,' she says.

'Oh. Good.'

'Our tram didn't experience anything beyond a few bumps. It looked like you got the worst of it. Were you hurt?'

'I was. But I will manage.'

There's a moment of silence.

'So,' Taty says. 'That was the Divine.'

'Yes.'

'That was what you and Mother fought.'

'Yes.'

'And that's what the god you're fighting thinks I am.'

'Ah. Something like that.'

There's another long silence, punctured only by the *clunk* of the tram engine and the crackle of snowflakes on the glass above.

'It's not right, is it,' she says.

'What isn't?' he asks.

'It's not right that . . . that I could do what I did at the train station,' she says. 'That I could see something that . . . that was going to happen, or could have happened. I mean . . .' She laughs desperately. 'Of *course* it isn't right! How could it be?'

'No,' Sigrud says. 'It is not.'

'How am I supposed to live like this? How are you supposed to, to live with me beside you? I feel so afraid of . . .'

'Of what?'

'Of being someone *else*,' she says. 'Of changing. I don't want to lose me.' She blinks, and tears fall into her lap. 'If that happens, then . . . then I *really* lose Mother. I lose what she taught me. Who she raised me to be.'

Sigrud thinks for a moment. 'What do you remember of your time before Shara, Taty? Before the orphanage? Anything?'

'Little,' she says. 'I remember a lot about the orphanage, as I was four when Mother adopted me. But before that . . . I remember a woman. In the snow. We were in the woods. She was crying. And she was saying she was sorry. She was sorry she was going to have to give me over to these people, but she had no choice. And then a man walked out of the woods, and took me by the hand. And the woman ran over, crying, and kissed me on the cheek. And her lips felt so hot. It was so warm, that kiss.'

'Who was this man?' he asks.

'I don't know.'

'Where did you go?'

'I don't remember. I remember the orphanage, after that. But I dream about her, sometimes. This crying woman, her tears shining in the light of a fire. I think she is my mother. My birth mother, I mean. And in my memory, at least, she looks human. When I dream about her, I always wake up and feel a warmth on my cheek. It's as if her kiss is still there. It's as if that moment is still going on.' She sighs. 'It's unfair that the dead leave us,' she says. 'But it's worse that they never really go away.'

'Yes,' Sigrud says quietly. 'Yes, it is.'

'What can I do? What can *you* do, knowing I might be something . . . different?'

He takes a long, slow breath. 'In my operational days, there were three ways of thinking about things. There were things you knew. Then there were things you knew you didn't know. And then there were the things you didn't know that you didn't know.'

'No wonder we keep having so many international crises,' she says, 'if you lot are running around talking like that.'

'The rule was,' says Sigrud, ignoring her, 'that you only worried about the first and second things. The things you didn't know that you didn't know, you pushed out of your brain.'

'What do you mean?' she says. 'That doesn't help me at all!'

'It is about accepting a lack of control,' says Sigrud. 'Understanding that the situation you are in is complex and – how did Vinya used to put it? – fluid.'

'It's a little harder to accept this as a . . . a fluid situation when I might be Divine!'

Sigrud thinks for a moment. Then he pulls off the black glove on his left hand. He lifts the palm and shows it to her.

'Ugh,' says Taty, horrified. 'What is *that*? Did that thing you fought do that?'

'No. This was done a long, long time ago.'

'Who *did* that to you?' asks Taty.

'No one exceptional,' says Sigrud. 'Some ordinary sadists, though they used an extraordinary instrument.' He looks at his palm, feeling the lines of the scar with his thumb. 'A Divine instrument. But . . . ever since they did this to me, I have survived things I should not have survived. Urav, and our enemy, and Malwina's manipulations . . . And I could touch that strange, black creature aboard the aero-tram with this hand, and it would not burn me. It is . . . unnatural.'

'What are you saying?' asks Taty.

'I am saying, Taty, that . . . I think I am somewhat like you,' says Sigrud. 'There are things that I can do. I do not understand them. I do not know how they work or if they have affected who I am. I do not know how or if this scar has changed me. So I fall back on the things I know.'

'Which is what?' asks Taty.

'That there are those who mean us harm,' says Sigrud. He makes a fist and lowers his hand. 'And those who offer us shelter. We must flee from one to get to the other. The rest – that is beyond our control.'

Taty smiles sadly at him. 'This is what you know how to do, isn't it?'

'What do you mean?'

'When you were on the tram, with that thing, you looked . . . different. You looked *relieved*. Like you were playing a game you hadn't played in a long, long time. That's how you worked with Mother, wasn't it? She figured out what to do, and you made sure it happened. This is what you know. You were finally getting to do something you understood.'

Sigrud sits in silence.

'You want her here even more than I do, maybe,' says Taty. 'To tell you what to do again. To figure it all out. That's why you waited on her for thirteen years, isn't it? So she could tell you what to do next, how to make things go back to normal. To help you get home.'

He looks away. 'There is no going back to normal, Tatyana Komayd,' he says softly. 'There is no going home. I know that now. There is no way out of this, not for me. I have made my peace with knowing that my fight is lost.'

'But you've defeated such things before, haven't you?'

' "Defeat?" "Victory?" Those are words. What comes after them? What comes next?' He looks up at the moon. 'In Voortyashtan, after my daughter died . . . There were soldiers there, guarding her, trying to capture me. Young people, fresh recruits. Just following orders. I was in a rage, and when I found them, I, I fell upon them, and I . . . I . . .'

The tram *clunks* and *clinks* through the next tower.

'Your daughter had just died,' says Taty.

'What kind of an excuse is that?' asks Sigrud. 'I am old, Taty. All those things that one saves for, that one builds for, that one lives for . . . I have lost those things by now. I have only my grudges and grievances to keep me going now. They are my only guiding stars. And I suspect they shall not last much longer.'

'You live to hurt, then,' says Taty. 'And nothing more?'

Sigrud is quiet.

'I know I'm young,' says Taty softly, 'but it feels to me that . . . that death is but a thunderstorm. Just wind and noise. You can't ask meaning of such a thing. Not even of your own.' She shakes her head. 'I thought it would feel better. You killing them, hurting those people. But it feels like . . . like *nothing*.'

'Anger is a hard thing to live with, Tatyana. I think sometimes we are not punished for our anger – we are punished *by* it, I think.'

'Or perhaps,' says Taty, 'we just weren't punishing the right people.'

They sit in silence.

'Mother wouldn't have said that, would she?' says Taty softly.

'No. She would not have.'

'Perhaps I'm changing already, then. Perhaps I don't even know it's happening.'

Sigrud looks at her, his jaw set. 'If you really change, Taty . . . If something takes you and makes you different . . . I will not let you forget who you are. I will be there to remind you, Tatyana Komayd. Until you are you.'

'I didn't think you were quite the staying type,' she says.

'For you, I will stay.'

She looks at him questioningly – wondering, of course, if this time he's telling her everything.

'You're tired,' he says. 'Sleep here if you wish.'

'And you'll really stay?'

'Close your eyes,' he says, 'I'll be here in the morning.'

She closes her eyes.

II.
Dreamscapes

My definition of an adult is someone who lives their life aware they are sharing the world with others. My definition of an adult is someone who knows the world was here before they showed up and that it'll be here well after they walk away from it.

My definition of an adult, in other words, is someone who lives their life with a little fucking perspective.

— UPPER PARLIAMENT HOUSE MINORITY LEADER TURYIN MULAGHESH,
LETTER TO GENERAL ADHI NOOR, 1735

They come to the city late the next morning. The tram car crawls down the cables through the Tarsils, then to the foothills, and then, suddenly, there it is.

Bulikov. The City of Stairs.

The sight of it takes his breath away. Sigrud hasn't been here in twenty years, yet it's all still the same, this huge, massive, ancient metropolis, with its tremendous dark walls, hundreds of feet tall and dozens of feet thick. He can see strange, tiny, curling structures peeking past the tops of the walls: massive staircases, reaching into the sky to end in nothing at all. The staircases, he knows, are not the most disturbing of the distortions and damages left behind by the Blink. Those he's seen before, firsthand. Though probably they and nearly half the city were decimated in the Battle of Bulikov.

And yet, Bulikov survived. A city more than a thousand years old, still defiant despite the passage of time.

'It's so strange,' says Taty, joining him, 'to view a city from this angle.'

'I've seen it before,' he says lowly.

'What?' says Ivanya. 'You have? Ah. Yes. That's right. The flying ship.'

Ivanya and Sigrud's moods are significantly darker than Taty's: despite the conversation the night before, she's positively bubbling over with excitement as they approach Bulikov. 'See the walls there? I read *all* about those, they're having *immense* infrastructural problems because the city needs to expand, to site more industrial facilities, to just do more *stuff*, and because the walls are nigh impenetrable and also because they're, well, considered pretty holy, they haven't made much progress there. Oh! And look there, you can see the tip of the Brost Tower, Auntie! Aren't your firms the ones doing the financing for that?'

'Yes,' says Ivanya grimly. 'Though I frankly never hoped to see it in person . . .'

Taty ignores her, rattling off facts and figures about Bulikov that do little to impress the adults. Sigrud peers out the window as they make their final approach. He sees their destination is a huge train station, built right up against the side of the walls of Bulikov, an iron-and-glass-roofed structure that's just as large and beautiful and stately as the one in Ahanashtan. They certainly didn't have *that* when he was last in Bulikov – and now that he's closer to the ground, he realises he knows this location on the side of the walls.

'Is that . . . Morov Station?' he says, incredulous.

'Well, of course it is,' says Taty. 'What other station would it be?'

'That was the station Shara and I first used when we came to Bulikov,' he says. 'It was this tiny, grubby dump of a station . . . We had to use an old coal train to get here.'

'I keep telling you both that Bulikov has changed,' scoffs Taty. 'Everyone knows that!'

Ivanya rolls her eyes. 'The girl hasn't ever even *been* here before,' she mutters.

Sigrud narrows his eye. There's a large crowd waiting for them – no doubt due to the disaster on the tram behind them. He can see uniforms, and the odd badge. 'Police,' he says. 'And the press. They must be waiting to talk to all the passengers.'

'What do we do?' asks Ivanya.

'I'll find a way to break off from you two,' says Sigrud, 'and evade them.

Can you take the trunk and arrange for transportation, Ivanya, or should I steal a car?'

'I can get a car!' says Ivanya hastily. 'We don't need you breaking into things!'

'All right, then,' says Sigrud. He goes to the door. 'I'll go first. Meet me outside the train station in thirty minutes. Agreed?'

'Agreed,' says Taty.

Sigrud walks out into the cabin, where all the fretful passengers are gathering their luggage and lining up before the door. He tries to get close to the front. He can hear the crowd at the platform as they make the final stretch of the approach – the crowd must be big and anxious, which means it'll be difficult to handle.

The doors are flung open, and Sigrud finds his suspicions were right: despite the best efforts of the Bulikovian police, things devolve into total pandemonium within seconds. The passengers bolt out to be greeted by loved ones, lawyers, business associates, members of the press, all shouting, crying, laughing, screaming . . . Sigrud takes stock of the situation, slinks through the side of the crowd, and makes for the train station doors within seconds.

He keeps walking, doesn't look to the side, doesn't look anywhere. No one notices. Everyone's focused on the raucous chaos beside the tram car. With a slight sigh of relief, he slips into Morov Station.

Sigrud loops through the station, trying to spy out any more of Nokov's operators. He suspects there aren't any – after the Saypuri woman's sudden transformation, he thinks Nokov threw nearly everything he had at them – but it's best to make sure.

He sees nothing, to his relief. But while he looks, he can't help but marvel at what a different place Morov Station is now. He compares it to the last time he arrived: stepping off the train to find a trembling little Pitry Suturashni waiting for them, bowing low and mistaking him, impossibly, for Shara. This place had been abandoned, dark, and dingy, yet now it's full of light and noise and traffic, and shouted questions.

He waits until his time's almost up, then moves out to the front of the train station. There are no automobiles waiting, except for a thoroughly absurd black limousine. He stops behind a column, frowns, and pulls out his watch, wondering where the two women are. Then he hears a high-pitched whistle.

He looks up to see Taty leaning out the back window of the limousine, smiling and waving to him. Sigrud stares at her, then slowly comes over.

'This is . . . not quite what I meant when I said transportation,' he says.

'Get in,' says Ivanya crossly from inside. 'And stop scowling!'

Sigrud climbs in. The seats are large enough to allow him to sit comfortably. He looks back, befuddled, as the driver of the auto – a short, thickset Continental man in a shiny black cap – starts it up and pulls away.

'How . . . did we do this?' Sigrud asks.

'Auntie owns it,' says Taty happily.

'It's the estate car,' explains Ivanya.

'The estate car.' Sigrud flicks a thumb over his shoulder. 'And the driver is . . .'

'Choska,' says Ivanya. 'My valet.'

'Your . . . valet.'

'Yes.'

'You have a valet.'

'Yes. I had to have someone to look after the estate while I was away, after all. It's not a *completely* uncommon thing to have,' she says, nettled.

'It seems an uncommon thing for a sheepherder to have.'

'Yes, well, as you are the one who has dragged me back to Bulikov, I don't believe you have any right to criticise me. I was *happy* where I was.' She peers out the window. 'Or happier than I am here, at least.'

Taty pulls herself close to the window. 'I can't believe it. I can't *believe* it! We're actually in Bulikov! We're really here!'

Sigrud can't help but smile to see her reaction. When he first came here, Shara rode in the auto with her nose practically pressed to the glass, drinking in the sights of this mammoth, historic city – just as Taty acts now. Yet at the time Sigrud could have hardly cared a fig for any of it.

'Look at it!' says Taty in awe. 'Just look at it all . . .'

Sigrud has to duck low to look out. 'Yes,' he says, surprised. 'Look at it.'

He sees now how different it all is. There are bright, resplendent buildings where there used to be ruins, modern brick structures with large, glass windows – he remembers very few windows had good glass when he was here last. The auto putters through clean, squares and avenues lined with electric lights, all clear of rubble or blockades. The surfaces of the streets are smooth and unbroken, which is powerfully strange, as he recalls the concrete and paving was as cracked and creaking as a sheet of warm ice. People walk the streets with the casual air of pedestrians going about their daily routines, rather than the anxious skulking that Sigrud remembers.

It's all so modern, so organised. An elevated tram runs through the tall buildings, a face in every window of every car. Water fountains and shops and trees. An open-air market where people sell meat and fruit – actual, fresh fruit, something unobtainable in the Bulikov he remembers.

Every once in a while they come to some old warping of the world, a bruise in reality from the Blink. Yet they've gently papered over these as best as they could, turning these aberrations into small parks with a little sign next to them, stating: *This is what happened here, this is what we remember, and this is what we know.*

History – a thing so dreadfully suppressed and bickered over in the Bulikov he knew – stands unchallenged in the streets.

Finally they come to the Solda River. In his day this had been a field of frozen ice, with tiny fishing shacks and shantytowns clinging to its muddy shores; yet now there are docks, piers, millworks, refineries, industry. He watches as ships and barges slowly poke their way around the winding bends of the Solda. It's a thriving place, a place people go to toil and work and think, a place where one could live.

'I can't see the walls anymore!' says Taty. She laughs. 'It's amazing, isn't it?'

Sigrud turns to look back at the horizon. There's no hint of the walls in sight: he forgot that they grew transparent once you entered them. 'Oh. Right.'

'They're going to try to drill another aperture in the walls, you know,' says Taty, 'to allow passage to the planned industrial sites beyond. Factories and new housing and a larger rail yard.'

'Are they,' says Sigrud.

'Yes,' says Taty. 'It's all gotten too big. Too much is pouring into the city. These giant, Divine walls just can't hold Bulikov anymore, not since Voortyashtan and the opening of the Solda.'

Sigrud pauses. 'The opening of the Solda?' he asks quietly.

'Yes,' says Taty. 'It changed everything, you know.'

Sigrud sits in silence, looking out on this thriving metropolis, remembering the young Dreyling woman who once told him: *This is how civilisation progresses – one innovation at the right time, changing the very way the world changes. It just needs one big push to start the momentum.*

Signe, he thinks, *did you make this place?*

So much of the city is unfamiliar to him now – yet then they turn, and suddenly he recognises the sight ahead.

He knows this lane, and that alley. He remembers clinging to a speeding auto here once, long ago. The driver had tried to smash Sigrud up against the wall of a building, a fate that Sigrud barely managed to escape.

He looks up at the building ahead. He knows this too.

The Votrov mansion. It's still the same, from the bars in the gate out front to every brick in the walls. It's almost exactly as it was when he came here last, so many years ago, except it's day this time, and the house is totally empty: no laughing dinner guests, no parties, no chauffeurs – and no Shara Komayd to accompany him.

'This feels,' says Sigrud, 'incredibly weird. To return to find this one place unchanged, of all places.'

'I quite agree,' says Ivanya. He glances at her. She looks pale and ill, and she keeps pushing back one strand of hair that doesn't need to be pushed back at all.

Sigrud watches her as they approach. She pinches the skin on the back of her hand so hard that her fingers tremble.

He reaches across, grabs her hand, and squeezes it. 'It is all right,' he says.

'You say so,' she says. But she gives him the briefest of smiles.

Finally they pull up before the massive front doors. Sigrud tries to open the auto door, but suddenly Choska's there, opening it with a demure smile before hauling the giant trunk out of the back of the auto. Choska wheels it over to the manor entry and hauls open the front doors. Taty almost skips through them, and Sigrud slowly follows.

He skulks into the entry hall, which is just as grand and strange as he recalls: the chandelier of crystal slabs, the two huge hearths, and the hundreds of gas lamps, all of which are currently unlit.

He stares at one of the hearths, remembering how he glowered into the fire, drinking wine, thinking of his time in Slondheim. *Yet Slondheim*, he thinks now, *would prove to be only a slight misery compared to the years ahead . . .*

'It's amazing!' says Taty, staring around herself.

'You keep saying that,' says Sigrud.

'Well, it *is* amazing.'

'You used to live in a mansion,' says Sigrud. 'I'm not sure why this one is so amazing to you.'

'You two are no fun at all,' says Taty. 'Everything you see you have to glower at.'

'We are not on holiday.'

'You weren't stuck on Mother's estate for years,' says Taty. She walks up the mansion stairs, her nose in the air. 'I will make do with what's available. I'm off to find the library, and read something actually decent for the first time in *months*.'

Sigrud watches her ascend and shakes his head, exasperated. 'One must forgive the young,' says Ivanya's voice behind him.

He turns and sees she's standing at the threshold of the mansion. 'Must one?' he asks.

'Well. It's the polite thing to do.' She sighs deeply and walks through the door. 'Shara told me about this – something Mother Mulaghesh had, and other soldiers. Battle echoes, she called it.'

'Yes,' says Sigrud.

'When everything feels like it's still happening,' says Ivanya. 'Like you're still there, and it's still going on.' She looks around. 'And now I'm *actually* here. Did you ever have echoes?'

'Not of the Battle of Bulikov,' says Sigrud.

She sighs again. 'The espionage business is a horrid bunch of shit, as far as I say.'

'I agree.'

'Well. The hells with it. Let's unpack the guns. You and I have work to do, I expect.'

'We do,' he says. 'Tomorrow evening I will go to the Solda Bridge to meet Malwina, and I wish to be prepared.'

'And then what?'

'I have no idea. But I would prefer you and Taty stay here. I don't know what Malwina has planned. But I want Taty someplace defensible, and the bridge is not that.'

Ivanya laughs lowly as they open the trunk. 'The sheer silliness of preparing guns,' she remarks, 'when a volley of bullets means not one whit to your enemies.'

That night, after they've unpacked and washed up and eaten, Sigrud, Taty, and Ivanya sit on the upstairs balcony, looking out at the city. Taty, of course, wants to do nothing more than walk the streets and look at it all – but this Sigrud absolutely refuses to allow. So the balcony becomes something of a compromise, with Taty almost leaning over the railing, pointing out structures and asking questions while Ivanya and Sigrud do their best to answer.

'I remember Vo used to point things out to me,' says Ivanya, sipping wine. 'Over there, Ahanas's Well. And then over there, the Talon of Kivrey. Or, at least his father said those things used to be there.'

'It seems unlikely Vo would have known,' says Taty, 'since those things disappeared decades earlier, during the Blink.'

'What happened to those buildings over there?' says Sigrud, pointing. 'I remember there was some sort of big temple thing there . . .'

'It was destroyed during the Battle,' says Ivanya softly. 'I know. I watched it happen from this very balcony. The streets filled up with silver soldiers . . . and the very sky spoke words of wrath.'

Tatyana asks Sigrud about the Battle, about Pangyui, about Vohannes and Shara and all their work here. He does his best to stumble through an explanation, but he suddenly feels like he knows very little. Perhaps he forgot it all, or perhaps he never really understood it to begin with.

He remembers Shara walking alongside him through the snowy streets of Bulikov, pointing out all the relics and historical sites. He'd been so bored, grimacing as she talked, yet his heart aches at the idea of her beside him now, saying her mad things about history or politics, pushing her glasses up her nose, her hair tied back in its messy bun, her movements redolent with the aromas of tea and ink.

What a tremendous sin impatience is, he thinks. *It blinds us to the moment before us, and it is only when that moment has passed that we look back and see it was full of treasures.*

Taty chatters on about all the fabulous things she's read about Bulikov: all the plans, all the changes, all the developments, a brand-new world blossoming here on the banks of the Solda, things Sigrud and Ivanya barely understand.

'Could it all have been better?' asks Taty. 'Could Mother have done a . . . a better job?'

'I am not one to say,' says Sigrud.

'I wonder if she was too tolerant,' says Taty. 'Too indulgent. You have power but for a few brief seconds, and then . . .'

Sigrud frowns, remembering Taty's words on the aero-tram – *Perhaps the only way to clean a slate is with blood!* He understands these were the words of a furious adolescent, but still – they disturb him.

'Things could have been better,' says Ivanya. 'But things could also have been much, much worse.'

'Yes,' says Sigrud.

Taty looks out at the cityscape in silence for a moment. 'Will I ever stop hating them? For what they did to Mother?'

'To live with hatred,' says Sigrud, 'is like grabbing hot embers to throw them at someone you think an enemy. Who gets burned the worst?'

'Quoting Olvos,' says Taty.

'Oh. I thought Shara had come up with that one.'

'No. It was Olvos.'

'Well. Regardless. When will you lay down your embers, Taty?'

The girl stares out at the city. 'I don't know. Sometimes they're the only things keeping me warm.'

She falls silent again. Sigrud glances at her sideways, and sees she's passed out in her chair.

'She's asleep,' he says, startled.

'It's been a busy damned day,' says Ivanya. 'Come on. Let's take her to bed.'

Sigrud picks her up and carries her to a bedroom, then lays her on the sheets. She barely stirs. He realises she must have been terrifically exhausted.

Sigrud and Ivanya return to the balcony in silence. They drink plum wine and watch the dark cityscape, not saying a word, staring out at the faint, shimmering suggestion of the walls of Bulikov.

'The world is no longer for us, is it,' says Ivanya.

'No,' says Sigrud.

'I turned my back on it for a handful of years, and suddenly it belongs to her now.'

'Yes. Perhaps her generation will do a better job with it. If she can learn to forgive.'

'Perhaps. I thought we would do a better job, me and Vo, back before the Battle. We thought we'd change everything. A joyous revolution.'

'So did Shara, I think,' says Sigrud, 'when she returned to Ghaladesh.'

'A better world comes not in a flood,' sighs Ivanya, 'but with a steady drip, drip, drip. Yet it feels at times that every drop is bought with sorrow and grief. It ruins us.'

'You are not ruined, Ivanya Restroyka,' he says.

She looks at him, first questioning, then half-smiling. 'No?'

'No. I think you were asleep. But now you are awake.'

She turns back to the cityscape, bright and fiery in the sunset. 'I forgot about the walls . . . How *odd* they are. How impossible. How impossible all of it is.'

Sigrud isn't sure when they start holding hands. It simply happens, a movement as premeditated as a leaf falling from a tree. Her fingers are long and cold and wiry, yet they feel very hard, and real. He can't remember the last time he held someone's hand.

He's also not sure when she kisses him – and it's she that kisses him, very clearly so. It's a passionate kiss, yet also a desperate one, as if they were two refugees scrambling across disputed lands, uncertain what tomorrow might bring.

He does not protest as she leads him to a guestroom. Not the master bedroom, he notes – she avoids that space. But as she leads him into the darkened room, he's suddenly wracked with uncertainty: for so long, Sigrud has felt that his presence has brought nothing but woe to those he's loved. His efforts at civilisation, at domesticity, at intimacy, have all yielded the same result: tragedy and loss, followed by a retreat to the wilderness, to isolation and savagery, wishing that he'd never even tried.

But he doesn't fight her. He recognises that she wants to feel something, anything, besides what she's feeling. And he does not blame her. He feels the same.

Afterward they lie in bed together, looking at the moonlight filtering through the slats in the shutters.

'Today was a good day,' she says. 'I wouldn't have ever thought coming back here would be. Yet here we are.'

'Yes.'

She shifts closer beside him. 'We don't get to choose many things. What happens to us, if we live or die, or who we love. But we can at least choose to admit, sometimes, that things are good. And sometimes, that is enough.'

'Sometimes.'

He lies there, listening to her as she falls asleep, her breaths like the slowing ticks of a metronome.

Then Sigrud hears a *tap-tap* from downstairs – perhaps footsteps. He tenses, listening more, then rises.

'Oh, what a surprise,' says Ivanya, her voice muffled by the pillow. 'Leaving already.'

'I heard something,' he says.

'Sure you did.'

He puts on his trousers and shirt. 'I really did.'

'Hmph.'

'I will be back,' says Sigrud, opening the door. 'Stay here. And stay quiet.'

He pads outside, across the huge carpets, dancing from shadow to shadow until he comes to the top of the stairs. Then he peers out, and sees her.

Tatyana Komayd sits on the floor of the giant entry hall, wearing her white nightgown. Moonlight spills through the giant window above her, making her form indistinct in the soft illumination, a tiny, white splotch floating in a puddle of grey-blue.

Sigrud walks down the stairs. 'Taty?' he asks.

'Hello,' she says softly. Her eyes are open, but her voice is dreamy.

'What are you doing up?'

'I . . . I had a dream,' she says. 'About my mother.'

Sigrud cocks his head.

'Not my birth mother,' says Taty. 'Shara, I mean.'

'A nightmare? It woke you?'

'No, not really a nightmare. It was the strangest thing . . .' Taty sighs deeply. 'I dreamed of her here. In Bulikov. She was standing in the street, holding a black blade, and she used it to threaten a god that stood before her. It was all so *real* . . .'

Sigrud recognises it immediately. 'You dreamed of the Battle of Bulikov?'

'Mm. No,' she says. 'No, I don't *think* so. Because her hair was as I knew it, white as snow. And the god was not Kolkan.' She rubs her temple slowly, as if suffering a headache. '*A* battle of Bulikov, maybe. But not *the* Battle of Bulikov.'

'What are you saying?'

'What can one possibly say about such a dream?' She climbs to her feet, then stands there, thinking. 'I think my mother is dead, Sigrud,' she says. She rises and begins to climb the staircase on the other side of the entry hall. 'But I also think she's still here. It makes no sense. I *know* it makes no sense. I know it is impossible. Yet in what place could two totally opposite, impossible things be true, besides Bulikov?' She pauses at the top of the stairs. 'Maybe Auntie Ivanya was right.'

'Right about what?'

'Maybe we should have never come here. Maybe history weighs a little heavier here.' She looks over her shoulder at Sigrud. 'I hope Malwina has something good for you tomorrow night, Sigrud. I hope this all was worth it.' Then she slips away into the shadows, and is gone.

Nokov walks along the walls of Bulikov, alone and troubled. It's night now, true night, the moon pale and lonely above, wreathed with mist. He *could* make it night whenever he wished – to do such a thing is no more than a flexing of a muscle to him now – but he's at his most powerful when true night has fallen, when the shadows lengthen and the forests flood with darkness, and the brightest of bonfires is reduced to a miserable little pinprick. That's when he feels most at home, if he could be said to even have such a thing.

Winter will be here soon, he can feel it in the air. Winter, when the days grow short and the nights long. When he waxes strong, and encroaches steadily on the day like lines of infantry driving an enemy across a battlefield.

Yet when I succeed, he thinks (and he does not say *if* he succeeds, for there are no ifs to Nokov), *day will be but a memory, and the world will be something bold and new.*

But though he feels much at home now, in the depths of true night, he's not here for comfort: such darkness grants him power, and with such power he can walk the walls of Bulikov, and feel . . .

Miracles. Hundreds of them, thousands of them, all quaking and whispering within the walls. Miracles of a sort one doesn't see anymore, ones far beyond his means. The true Divinities wrought these walls long ago, when the world was still hot and fresh and young, as bright and bendable as metal at the forge. Nokov does not know if such miracles, such grand shiftings and warpings of the world, could even be possible nowadays.

He comes here often. Nearly every night, in fact, to walk the walls, and see, and sulk.

I could do it if I knew how, he thinks. *If they had taught me how. If they had given me the power that I ought to have.*

But he doesn't know these things. He himself cannot fashion miracles like this. So instead he walks the walls of Bulikov, fingers grazing the surface of these mammoth constructs, and listens to the whispering miracles trapped in their depths . . .

One day, he thinks to them, *you will be part of my domain.*

If the miracles hear him, they do not answer.

It's only because he's listening so hard that he senses her approach, speeding north out of the mountains. At first he's startled, even nervous, for her coming is furious and powerful and unmistakably Divine.

He wonders — *Is this another child? A sibling? Why would one dare to approach me?*

Yet then he realises what this is, why this feels familiar. It's a part of himself come to greet him.

She leaps down the mountaintops to him, dark and frantic. He waits at the bottom for her, and watches her approach, trying to understand what's going on. Finally she stops and stands before him, this tall, oily, faceless figure of a woman, and he slowly understands.

'Mishra?' he whispers, horrified. 'Is that you?'

The world stutters around him. Silence fills his ears. Yet in that silence are words:

<good evening sir how are you>

He stares at her, anguished and disgusted. He reaches out with one trembling hand, and she kneels before him. His fingers touch her smooth, featureless face.

'Oh, no,' he moans. 'Oh, no, no, no . . . This isn't what I wanted. This isn't what I wanted at all . . .'

A stutter of silence. Then:

<good evening sir how are you>

He reaches out to her, senses her mind, her spirit, and sees she is not truly Mishra anymore. Some thread of her intelligence remains, some piece of her that he knew and grew close to. But only a fragment. No more than that.

He shuts his eyes. He'd been waiting on her call, having heard about the disaster aboard the aero-tram. He assumed she'd been triumphant. Yet here she is, empty-handed, and so horribly malformed . . .

He gave her too much, he realises. Too much of himself, too much for any one mortal to bear. She is now Silence, an aspect of the true night, the dreadful silence in the blackest of nights. Yet she is not completely Silence, for some piece of Mishra is ground into this creature's being, so it exists in a warped half-state – not quite human, not quite Divine.

'I am so sorry, Mishra,' he says. 'I am so, so sorry.'

She bows her head before him. Although she says nothing, he senses that she knows something is wrong, but cannot identify or articulate what it is.

Another stutter of silence:

<good evening sir how are you>

The same words, over and over again. He moans once more, filled with loathing for this marred creature, and himself for making her.

A flash of a memory: Vinya Komayd, standing in the window, smiling at him, gloating. *You aren't a true Divinity, child. Nor will you ever be. You can't do the things they did. Give it up.*

Nokov trembles with fury. His fingers clench into fists.

'This is their fault,' he whispers. '*Their* fault!' He glances at the walls. 'And *her* fault, too. If they just . . . If she just . . .'

Silence looks up at him, head cocked.

'They're here in Bulikov, aren't they,' he says. 'That's where the tram was going. They aren't hidden in the mountains, they aren't in the depths of the sea, they're here, right *here*, under our noses!' Nokov turns to face the walls of Bulikov, eyes burning. 'I will find them. I promise, I will. And I'll make this right.'

Silence leans close, as if trying to say something.

<good evening sir how are you>

'What's that?' he says gently. 'What are you trying to say?'

Silence holds her spear out and points at its very tip. Then she taps her right breast, as if indicating an injury.

<touched him sir I touched him touched him>

She holds the spear blade out to him. Curious, Nokov reaches out and holds the point between his index and thumb.

The spear is as much a part of him as Silence herself is, wrought of his very heart and being. He feels it leap up to him, speak to him, tell him what it's done . . .

The spear tells him about how it almost ran the *dauvkind* through, how it poked its way through his clothing, licked just the slightest few drops of his blood, there on his right breast, and burned and blackened his flesh in turn, putting its own stain within his body . . .

It hurt him. It touched him. And its taint is still upon him.

Nokov opens his eyes. He realises that this tiny wound is still festering in the *dauvkind* somewhere: the spear remembers what it tried so hard to do, and desires to finish it. It's as if the spear has marked its territory like a dog marking a tree, and now it can catch the scent of its target on the slightest breeze.

'We can feel him, can't we,' says Nokov. 'We can feel the wound we gave him . . .' He turns back to look at Bulikov. 'And he's here. But where shall he go?'

The next night, Sigrud hunches low as he skulks along the Solda River. A few errant flakes float down to where he stands, as if the wintry clouds above are sending out scouts to enemy territory. The moisture and the cold create a heavy mist that clings to the lampposts in the warrens of Bulikov, making spectral halos among the streets.

But I suppose, thinks Sigrud, *it's somewhat better than how dark everything used to be.*

The riverside lanes are crowded with Bulikovians, Saypuris, and the odd Dreyling. How strange it is to see all three peoples here together, none of them attempting to throttle the others. The city facades, like the populace, are an interesting and diverse mix: sometimes there's a scarred old relic, almost certainly from before the Blink; next, a clean, fresh, brick-and-mortar shop front; then a glass-and-steel construct, something commercial and cutthroat; and then at the end some paved-over lot with a small sign before it, telling the onlooker of what once stood here before the Blink.

The Solda Bridge is just ahead, and what used to be a thin bone of a bridge is now a sprawling, two-hundred-foot-wide thoroughfare with thick concrete supports. He remembers the Saypuri cranes and machines setting up shop before the Battle of Bulikov – they must have done their work and done it well.

But how shall I find Malwina on such a thing?

He climbs the footpath up to the bridge. It's half auto roads, half market. Clattering autos and buses and limousines buzz past, the air behind them singed with exhaust. Little paper lanterns hang from the roofs of the market stalls. He sniffs: skewers of meat sizzle over bright red coals, coils of steam unfurl from the mouths of copper teapots. A warm, lively scene of a thriving metropolis.

Despite this, he shudders a little. The tiny cut on his chest from the spear aches curiously, burning hot or cold sometimes. He's considered opening up the wound and trying to squeeze out the blackness like pus, but it hasn't impeded his fitness yet, and with everything that he's trying to do right now, it's certainly not a priority.

He walks to the edge of the bridge and looks out. The waters of the Solda haven't frozen over yet. But he remembers how they were once, many nights ago, when the Divine horror slunk below the ice and terrorised Bulikov, and he, armed with but some spears and some rope, did his best to battle it.

He lost, though. Urav the Punisher consumed him. And when it tried to subject him to the many hells that dwelled within his belly, somehow he survived, uninjured and defiant . . .

He looks down at his gloved left hand. *And was that luck? Or something more?*

A voice behind him: 'You're late, asshole.'

He turns. Malwina Gogacz stands behind him, arms crossed. She's dressed like a boy, wearing an oversized brown coat, her mane of brown hair stuffed up under a small black cap. Her expression is familiar: impatience and acidic contempt.

'You said evening,' he says.

'Yeah, *evening*.' She points up at the night sky. 'It's fucking dark! That's way past evening. How did you ever get anything done with Shara?'

'I'm here,' he says. 'And it was not easy to get here. Many people could have died along the way.'

'Yeah, the aero-tram. I heard. It's all over the papers. So that was you? Were you followed here?'

'I do not think so.'

'You don't *think*?'

'I dropped a tram car on our attacker's head,' says Sigrud. 'She might have survived, but I do not think she was happy about it.'

'So . . .' Her mouth works as if chewing on this news. 'She was Divine, eh? Your attacker?'

'She wasn't at first; at first she was just human. But after I put a few holes in her guts, she panicked and she . . . ate something. And changed.' He describes the metamorphosis to her.

Malwina spits on the ground. 'Shit. That's bad news. Sounds like he fed her a piece of himself. Dangerous business, that. He's either desperate or insane.' She turns to look south. 'And there's something . . . out there. Something new.'

'What is it?' He looks south, but he can't see a thing. But of course he wouldn't, as the walls are invisible.

'I don't know. There's always pressure on the walls . . . perhaps *his* pressure, I suppose. But there's more of it now. A lot more. It's bad, whatever it is. And the walls are testy.'

'As in, the walls of Bulikov?'

'What other walls might I mean? There are miracles in them, bouncing through them, keeping them standing. A big, bright chain of agreements and strictures, all of them as flustered and nervous as a bunch of larks in a cage. It's bad news, whatever it is. I don't like it. But it's out of my hands. What about Restroyka and Tatyana? You didn't think to bring them?'

'I bring them to places that are safe,' says Sigrud. 'The last times I've seen you, I've been nearly set on fire or fallen to my death in an old shipwreck. So, the precise opposite of safe.'

'But they *are* somewhere secure?'

'For now. They have instructions if I do not return by morning.'

'Good. Your presence has been requested.'

'Where? By whom?'

She rolls her eyes.

'You cannot say,' says Sigrud.

'I can't speak of the place,' she says, 'or anything in it, unless I'm inside it. It's part of going to ground.'

'Fine. So how do we get there?'

Grumbling, Malwina pulls out a grimy pocket watch. 'We've got . . . Four hours to do this. I wanted more, but you were *late*. After four hours, the window closes, and we have to wait another period for it to open, which is time I don't want to spend in here with the walls chattering away. Can you still spot a tail in a crowd?'

'Some things,' he says, 'you don't ever forget.'

'Good.' She turns and starts pacing away. 'Then come on! Follow me. And watch the streets.'

Sigrud catches up to her. 'Four hours to do what?'

'To walk the walls of Bulikov,' she says, 'and unlock all the locks.'

What follows is a mad dash through the darkened warrens of Bulikov, keeping to the shadows, the gullies, the forgotten, peripheral parts of the world, the places denizens aren't supposed to see anymore. Sigrud and Malwina dart across alleys and ditches, slink through streets and gardens, dance along stretches of rusty piping, and, once, climb the supports of the elevated train and sprint a block down the line before climbing back down.

Finally Malwina points at a vacant lot ahead. 'There,' she says. She hardly seems winded at all.

They creep to the edge of the vacant lot. Sigrud goes first to check for assailants. Thorny weeds and broken glass litter the mud. Someone made their nest in the corner once, sleeping under an old bed frame that's been crudely converted into a tent. But they seem to be long gone.

Sigrud waves to Malwina. She hops up, trots across the lot, and walks down the far line of fence boards, all broken and splintered like a mouthful of ill-kept teeth.

She keeps looking back over her shoulder at the walls of Bulikov. They're quite close to the walls now, so the curve of the huge facades is a *little* visible, but just barely.

Finally Malwina stops, says, 'Ah!' and kneels at the wooden fence.

He watches carefully. She reaches out with her index finger and carefully strokes one insignificant-looking fence board. But her finger leaves a faint dark streak, like her very touch burns it, yet the burn fades quickly.

As she finishes, something . . . changes. Shifts. Moves. It's as if the entire city block has been jacked up one quarter inch: the tiniest change to the world, but noticeable.

Sigrud looks around, but whatever the change was, it doesn't seem to be visible. Yet he's been around miracles before, so he knows that felt like a very big one. 'What was that?'

Malwina stands and walks away. 'Come on. We've got four more to do.'

'*Four?*' he says. 'What, across the entire city?'

'What other city did you plan on visiting tonight?'

'Why not just get an auto?'

'What? I can't get an auto. I don't have a damned automotive permit, *or* money.'

'I mean steal an auto.'

'I don't know how to steal an auto.'

Sigrud throws up his hands in frustration and walks away down the street toward a seedy-looking office building.

'Hey!' cries Malwina. 'Hey, where are you going? We need to get moving.'

She peers down a dark alley, looking for him among the shadows. She frowns as there's a *clink*, then a *clank*, followed by a loud *clunk*.

'Sigrud?' she calls.

Then there's a roar of an engine, headlights blare to life, and a rattling, clattering, ill-maintained automobile comes shooting out of the alley. It screeches to a halt before her. Sigrud sits hunched up in the front seat, almost too big to fit.

He cranks down the driver's-side window. 'Get in. And please tell me where we are going.'

Malwina tenses up as Sigrud wheels the auto around a corner. 'How many autos have you stolen before?'

'A lot. They are the lifeblood of an operation. Steal a car, drive it somewhere, kill a man, drive it into the river, and so on, and so on.'

'Uh, how many times have you done that before?'

'What's this place we're going to?'

'The opera house. Three blocks ahead.'

Sigrud turns the corner and wheels the auto to a stop a few feet down from the opera house, its alabaster walls gleaming in the mist. The doorman at the front peers at them, wondering what such a junked-up vehicle could be doing coming to the opera, but Sigrud hasn't parked close enough for him to really care.

Malwina hops out, sprints across a splash of golden light from the opera house's windows, and examines the grey brick wall with the air of someone reading a newspaper. Then she finds one brick – one that seems no different from the rest – and carefully draws a symbol on it, some kind of loop with a streak through it.

Again, the brick turns dark at her touch. Again, the faint, distant feeling of things . . . shifting.

Sigrud glances out the window at the nearby walls of Bulikov, which again are hardly visible . . . except they seem to gleam or glisten very, very slightly.

Malwina hops back in the car. 'Let's go. Old Quarter next. Northwest.'

Sigrud pulls out and starts driving, careful to mind the speed limit. Malwina peers out the back window, watching the traffic behind her.

'There are no tails,' says Sigrud.

'Says you.'

'The streets of Bulikov were not built for autos. If someone was following us in an auto, it would be terribly obvious. We have no tails.'

'You worry about the physical realm,' says Malwina. She narrows her eyes. 'I'll worry about all the other ones.'

Sigrud glances sideways at her, trying not to feel too concerned about that comment.

'It is like tumblers in a lock, is it not?' he asks after a while.

'What?' says Malwina.

'Like tumblers in a lock, or a combination in a lock . . . A gesture you must make at the specific time and the specific place, using a specific device. And once you've done them all, then somewhere a door opens. Is that it?'

Malwina turns away, looking out the window. He expected that she couldn't discuss this – whatever the Divine strictures were placed on her are, they'd certainly prohibit discussing whatever mechanism she's manipulating – but it's still fun to needle her.

'This next stop,' says Sigrud, 'in the Old Quarter. Is it close to the walls?'

'Yes.'

'Does this mechanism you're activating *use* the walls somehow?'

She glares at him.

'Like you said,' he tells her, 'there are lots of miracles bouncing around in them. Maybe if one was clever enough, one could create other miracles to ride off their energy, just a little, to power something secret? Like resting a teapot upon a steamship's boiler. Not nearly as complicated as powering a whole boat, but it heats the water well enough.'

Malwina clenches her teeth. 'You're not stupid. I can see why she wants to talk to you.'

'Who?' says Sigrud.

She sulks in silence as they drive on into the night.

The auto jumps and quakes as its narrow wheels attempt to navigate the cobblestoned, pockmarked streets of Bulikov. In some places, the city's worked on the roads; in others, it's not quite there yet. *Though I hope*, thinks Sigrud as they hit another pothole, *that our vehicle survives the journey.*

Malwina sits hunched in the front seat, her pale face almost hidden behind the collar of her oversized coat. 'You know about our domains?' she asks.

'Domains?'

'The domains of us, the siblings. The children of the Divine. Our jurisdictions over reality.'

'Somewhat.'

Her queerly colourless eyes stare out at the road ahead, strobed by the lights of oncoming autos. 'It's like this. Some domains are inelastic. They are what they are. They aren't changing. They can't be interpreted to be other things, to contain other things. But other domains *are* elastic. They're expansive. They can grow. Like a sinkhole in the earth. You know what a sinkhole is? When a salt dome way underground gets penetrated by the tiniest bit of water, and then it just starts eating away at it? The sinkhole grows, and grows, swallowing up anything, everything. Cars. Houses. Whole trees. You name it.' Her face is grim and closed. 'That's what some of those domains are. We are our domains. And some of us are just hungrier than others.'

Sigrud wonders what sort of domain Taty might be. Perhaps something to do with maths, or commerce, since she's so good at economics – or predictions, maybe. 'And are you such a domain?'

She scoffs. 'Hells no. I'm the past, remember? The past is the past. It's fixed, unchangeable, unattainable. But our enemy . . . He's elastic. *Very* expansive, so to speak. His domain represents something primitive, something primal. The long night, the first night. That fear you feel when you're all alone in your house, and all the rooms feel so dark? That's *him*. That's him leaking into your frail little bit of civilisation, that first, dangerous night mankind spent out under the skies. You think you've walled him out, evolved past such savage peril – but you worry sometimes you haven't. That's what that fear is. He's still out there, circling your walls, trying to find a way in.'

'So how is he so expansive?'

'Because other domains fail before such a thing,' says Malwina. 'He's devoured the siblings that represent innovation, laughter, deep conversation, and many others. Because you don't laugh or think or talk when in such darkness. He's even devoured the siblings representing physical phenomena, like Mozshi, who was the Child of the Green Hill Grasses, or Vokayen, the Child of the Icy Mountain Streams. Because these concepts, these meanings stop *mattering* when eclipsed by the first night. The grass is still there, the streams are still there, sure – but what they mean to people doesn't matter anymore. Nothing matters when you're inside him. Not during the long night. Do you see?'

Sigrud grunts. He's always had a poor head for such abstractions – and these abstractions are about as abstract as an abstraction could get – but he understands the premise. 'He has an edge on all of you. And he is expanding, like an invader.'

'Yes. And with each one of us that he devours, each domain that is merged into his, he grows stronger. He is . . .' She looks out the window, thinking. 'He is reinterpreting himself. Reimagining his domain.'

'Into the last night,' says Sigrud. 'As you said.'

'Yes,' she says.

'And what will he do, once he has you all?'

She sits in silence for a long time. 'I worry the very skies will fail,' she says. 'All light will perish. And he will become creation incarnate.'

'And then?'

'And then, Mr. Sigrud, there will be no more *then*.'

They make three more stops, all close to the walls of Bulikov. Malwina runs her finger along the side of a lamppost by the front gates of Bulikov, the back of a bench in the park where the great Seat of the World once stood, and finally at one corner she scrambles out, lifts a manhole, and touches a single rivet in its underbelly. Each time, the world shifts. Each time, things grow a little more and more different. Until finally . . .

'It's done,' she says quietly. She looks up at the sky, and he does the same. 'Do you feel it?' she asks.

'Yes,' he says. 'It's like . . . like the skies are a little bit closer than they ought to be.'

'We've brought the gate close. But now we need to meet the gatekeeper.'

'Another step?'

'I don't know about you,' says Malwina as she climbs back into the auto, 'but I take security seriously. Come on. Take us back to the Solda Bridge.'

They ride in silence. Everything feels oppressively close, as if the air is too thick, or the streets too narrow. Even the people on the pavement seem to feel it, wrapping their coats tight and shivering.

'It's the walls,' says Malwina quietly. 'They have miracles in them that help people forget that they're there, miracles on top of the miracles that make them invisible or indestructible or what-have-you. Those miracles, the forgetting ones – they're getting strained.'

Sigrud pulls over and parks the car a few yards down from the Solda Bridge. 'By your locking mechanism.'

Malwina steps out and walks toward the underside of the bridge. Before she enters its shadow, though, she stops and looks up: at the streets, at the rooftops, at the windows and the alleys.

'You see anything?' she asks as Sigrud catches up.

'Nothing that alarms me.'

She crinkles her nose. 'Guess it's just nerves. But I feel like . . .' She shakes her head. 'Never mind. Let's get to it.'

He follows her under the bridge. There's a small shantytown of beggars and the destitute under here, taking advantage of the expanded bridge above. They mostly ignore Malwina and Sigrud as they walk through their ranks – but one man stands and walks almost in lockstep beside Malwina, a stooped old creature with rheumy eyes.

'Something's up,' he says to her in a rattling croak.

'I know,' she says. 'I feel it too.'

The old beggar looks back at Sigrud with a curiously keen stare. 'This the *dauvkind*?'

'Yeah. I hope he's worth it.'

'And you . . . are the gatekeeper?' says Sigrud.

He smirks. 'Something like that.'

They approach the far back wall under the bridge, a blank, dusty concrete surface covered with cobwebs. Sigrud isn't sure why the two seem to be heading straight for it, as there doesn't appear to be anything particularly special about it, but then the wall seems to . . . shiver.

Or quake, maybe. It's like the wall is the skin of a drum and someone on the other side has just given it a sharp tap, the concrete quivering and shuddering until it's no more than a blur to his eyes.

Then the wall stops quaking. And when it stops, there's a door in its middle – a very dull-looking wooden door with a beaten old doorknob.

'Ah. Oh,' says Sigrud.

Malwina lets out a long sigh. 'Good. It worked.'

'So we did all that work,' says Sigrud, 'for a door?'

'It's a lot more than just a door,' says the beggar, opening it. 'But your eyes see only what your eyes see, I suppose.' He bows low, as if they're guests at court, and they all walk inside.

Within is a narrow, bland concrete hallway, lit by a single electric light in the otherwise featureless ceiling above. The beggar shuts the door, mutters, 'Pardon me,' as he shoulders his way between them, and leads them down the hallway.

The hallway ends in a blank wall. Placed on the ground before the wall, though, is a solitary brick.

The beggar kneels before the brick, then glances back down the hallway, frowning as if he'd just heard something suspicious. Then he shakes his head, reaches down, and places his hands on the brick.

And then the brick . . . blossoms.

That's the only word for it. The brick seems to unfold from within itself, frames of brick bursting out from its depth with a chalky, clacking sound. The frames of brick fill the end of the hallway, and then they begin to expand *down* the hallway, extending it, floors and walls and ceiling appearing out of nowhere . . .

Though into what, Sigrud can't see. The end of the hallway is eclipsed by darkness.

'There we go,' says the beggar. Sigrud looks at him, about to ask what in the hells is going on. But then he sees the beggar isn't a beggar anymore.

Standing in his place is a short, young Continental man, with dark skin, a bald head, and bright brown eyes. His fingers are long and dexterous, and there's a curious cleverness to his face, as if he's permanently been struck by a wondrous idea.

'Oh,' says Sigrud.

'Sigrud, this is Voshem,' says Malwina. 'The embodiment of possibility.'

Voshem bows before him, again a strangely courtly gesture. 'How do you do.'

'Of possibility?' asks Sigrud.

'Yes,' says Malwina. 'Voshem's domain is not over things that are, but rather as they *could* be. The hallway ahead,' she says, gesturing forward, 'isn't really there, but it *could* be there. And as long as Voshem is with us, then it's as if it *is* there. Do you see?'

'No,' says Sigrud honestly.

Voshem smiles gently. 'It is a bit tricky. The touchstones awaken the door, and I connect the door to the sanctuary. A two-step security system. I'll take you as far as the stairs, and then I will leave you. Not wise to leave the key so close to the lock, one might say.'

The three of them continue on. The hallway doesn't seem to get any narrower, but suddenly he and Malwina are forced to walk in single file, as if the walls had closed in without their noticing. He had feet of clearance when they first walked in, but now he has mere inches on either side of his shoulders. He worries he'll have to start walking sideways to get through.

They keep walking. The hallway stretches on and on. He feels like they've been walking for ten minutes, maybe longer. Yet when he looks back over his shoulder he sees the door's still there, a mere fifteen feet behind them.

Yet they are moving, he knows that. Moving through something, under something . . .

'This is all in the realm of possibility?' asks Sigrud. 'So to speak.'

'We are passing through barriers,' says Voshem. 'Divine barriers. Barriers that are *almost* impossible to pass through . . .'

'Except we have you,' says Sigrud.

'Correct. Much can be done with the slightest shred of possibility.'

Sigrud shuts his eyes and continues walking forward at the same pace, listening to the fall of his footsteps and trying to focus on what this feels like rather than what it looks like. It feels as if he's walking through a sea of shifting sand, as if the material world is but an idea that hops into place when he looks at it, yet with his eyes shut there's actually . . .

He opens his eyes and sees only the hallway.

I am deep in the belly of something Divine, he thinks, *and I like it not at all.*

'We're close,' says Malwina.

Sigrud looks ahead and sees only the darkened end of the hallway. Then he looks back and sees they're still no more than fifteen feet from the door they walked in through. 'Are we?'

'Yes,' she says.

Something begins to emerge from the darkness ahead: a metal spiral staircase, which loops up past the ceiling into a blank concrete shaft.

The three of them stop at the foot of the stairs. 'I will let you continue on alone now,' says Voshem. 'I can't stay still for long. It's too dangerous.'

'Go, then,' says Malwina. She reaches out and squeezes his arm. 'There's something strange in the breeze tonight. Move quickly, find your safe places, and do not look back.'

Voshem nods, grim-faced, and turns and trots down the hallway. Malwina watches him until he slips out the door. Then the walls and floor of the hallway begin to quake and tremble . . .

'You'll want to step back now,' she says.

Sigrud does so. Then the hallway seems to collapse inward, the long, narrow passageway flooding with dark stone, as if the granite and loam were a liquid, and then . . .

There's nothing. Just a blank, dark wall where once there was a way out.

Malwina sighs heavily. She looks up the staircase. 'Now we go up.'

The staircase feels a lot more physical and tangible than the hallway did, but this is of little comfort to Sigrud. Mostly because, if he's gauging distance correctly, by now they've climbed enough stairs that they *should* be several feet above the Solda Bridge. But they're still in the tall, blank shaft, climbing and climbing. The staircase just keeps going.

Their steps echo on and on. Sigrud's calves start aching. He wonders if this place would deter Nokov just by how long it takes to get anywhere.

'You seem to be dealing with this all rather well,' says Malwina.

'It is not my first interaction with the Divine,' says Sigrud. 'And it is comparably better than what I am used to.'

'Jukov and Kolkan probably don't make the best impression of us, no.'

'He was the boy's father, correct?'

'Jukov? Yes. Good guess.'

'Was he your father as well?'

She gags at the idea. 'Absolutely not. That man, that *thing* was madder than a burning hare. No, no. My parents were Olvos and Taalhavras. Hope and order, you see.' She smiles. There's a touch of acrimony to it, but only the slightest touch. 'The past is a harsh, undeniable thing, like Taalhavras. It is what it is. Unrelenting, uncaring, just like all of his machines and devices. So I'm a bit like that. And yet people look back at the past, and in it they see . . . stories. Fables. Opportunity. Hope. Like her. So I'm a bit like that too.'

'I see.'

They keep climbing the stairs.

'Do you know what the worst part is?' asks Malwina.

'About what?'

'About being awake. About Jukov's plan to hide us among families, and one day wake us up.'

'No. What?'

'It's that . . . It's that you *remember*,' says Malwina. 'You wake up, and realise your true nature – you remember your Divine parents, the way things used to be . . . But you also remember your mortal parents. You remember what it was like to just . . . just be a *kid*, to be part of a family. You can't forget that. I don't think Jukov realised how damaging that would be.'

'Would you prefer to forget it all?'

Malwina sighs. 'I don't know. Sometimes.'

They keep climbing stairs.

'I have a question,' says Sigrud, now panting.

'Go ahead.'

'If Jukov died in the Battle of Bulikov,' he says, 'how is it that the Divine children are still asleep? Why didn't his miracle just vanish? Why didn't they all wake up, all at once?'

'Yeah, it's funny, isn't it?' says Malwina. 'I wonder about that myself.' Her footsteps have stopped. Sigrud looks up and sees the stairs have finally come to an end in an odd room.

The room is long but narrow. One long side is dominated by two enormous wooden doors, over ten feet tall, with giant iron handles and small flaming sconces on either side. When he looks at the doors he hears a high-pitched *eeeee* in his ears, a note warbling at some frequency that makes it almost impossible for him to think.

She smirks at him. 'Hear the noise?'

'Yes,' he says, wincing.

'Yeah. They don't want you here. You've never been here before. They don't trust new people. Anyways. You want to know what I think? About why some of the children are still sleeping, even though Jukov's dead?' She turns to the doors, then pauses, her hands on the iron handles. Her head is slightly bowed, her face concealed by shadow. 'I think they *like* it. They don't want to stop.'

'Stop what?'

'Being human. They like it. Subconsciously, they don't want to wake up. So they keep dreaming, and remain children. For as long as they can.' She looks at him over her shoulder. 'I wouldn't want to forget.'

'Forget?'

'Everything. You asked me if I wanted to forget. The answer's no. I want to keep it. Even if it hurts.' Then she hauls the giant doors open and steps inside. 'Come in. But *don't* touch anything.'

Sigrud steps through the big wooden doors and stares.

He's standing in a long, low, dark room, like a vast basement, perhaps six or seven hundred feet wide. The far wall is lined with windows, allowing in a soft, blue light, like the light of a distant moon. The ceiling is supported by short, fat stone columns marching in rows across the chamber. And between all the columns are beds.

Dozens of beds. *Hundreds* of beds. Maybe many hundreds, all spaced out evenly so that to his eye he's looking out at a huge grid of beds. The beds themselves are unexceptional, the sort of utilitarian cots one would find at a hospital or an orphanage, with plain white linens, plain white pillows, and next to each bed is a plain wooden table, on top of which is a small, flickering lantern.

Lying in every bed is a person. Or, more specifically, a young adult. The youngest occupant he sees looks around eleven; the oldest looks to be about twenty. But they all slumber softly, their dozing faces lit by the soft hues of their bedside lamps. He's so transfixed he barely notices the huge doors swinging shut behind him.

'Is this a . . . a hospital?' asks Sigrud.

'No,' says Malwina. 'It's our place of last refuge.' She lets out a breath. 'Oh, it's good to be here, to be able to talk about this now. You've no *idea* how many rules are bound up into this place, it's like taking off a particularly brutal undergarment . . .'

Sigrud walks over to one bed and peers at its occupant. It's a girl of middle teen years, her hair a dull gold, her eyebrows queerly yellow. She mutters something in her sleep and rolls over.

'*Don't* touch the bed,' says Malwina.

'Are these children . . . Divine?' asks Sigrud.

'Yes,' she says, walking over to join him. She looks out on the sea of beds and lanterns, and for the first time she looks vulnerable and uncertain. 'All of them. The ones who we could save, at least. Here they live unnoticed by *him*.'

Sigrud stares into the sleeping girl's face.

'Why do they sleep?' he asks.

There's a strange voice from behind him: 'It was the simplest solution.'

Sigrud whirls around, surprised. He glimpses someone standing in the darkness beside a nearby column and instinctively reaches for his knife.

Suddenly Malwina's on him, shoving his hand away. '*No!* No. Trust me, you don't want to do that.'

Sigrud looks closer at this new person. She steps forward, into the light. She's a short, teenage Continental girl, with big, wide-set eyes and a crooked mouth. She has no hair: she seems to have shaved it all off. She wears loose-fitting, white linen clothing, and though normally her appearance would cause Sigrud to think of someone in a mental ward, there is a calm, steady sanity in her gaze. Unnervingly steady.

She doesn't do or say anything. She just watches Sigrud with her big, calm, wide-set eyes.

'Who is this, Malwina?' asks Sigrud.

The new girl blinks, looks at Malwina in surprise, and smiles. '*Malwina?*' she says, incredulous.

'Shut up,' says Malwina. 'Some of us *like* our mortal names.'

'Some of the mortal names are pretty good. That one, though, is not.' She turns her unblinking stare back on Sigrud. 'So this is the *dauvkind*?'

'Everyone keeps asking me that,' says Malwina. 'Yes. Who else would it be? Sigrud, this is Tavaan, the spirit of slumber and dreams. She has control over this place.'

'Control?' he asks.

'This place exists within her reality,' explains Malwina. 'Within her mind, in a way.'

'That sounds very painful,' says Sigrud. 'I hope it at least has some benefits.'

Tavaan lifts a hand and snaps once.

Sigrud looks at her hand, curious, and sees it's gone. Actually, now that he looks, Tavaan and Malwina are both gone. He looks around himself and sees he's somehow been instantly transported to the other side of the chamber, far away from them, without his even noticing. Tavaan and Malwina are tiny dots in the distance, though he can see Malwina whirling around, looking for him.

Tavaan's voice echoes over to him: 'It has a few.'

Another snap, this one much fainter, and he's back where he was. Again, his senses report no change in the air or sound or gravity. It's as if the room moved around him without his being aware of it at all.

'I . . . see,' says Sigrud.

'She's trying to intimidate you,' says Malwina, glaring at Tavaan. 'Don't let her.'

'And yet you were the one warning him not to pull a knife on me,' says Tavaan.

'I didn't want you to put him in deep sleep,' says Malwina. 'That'd be hazardous for his damned health! That one woman fell over and broke her jaw!'

'But according to what you say,' says Tavaan, 'it might not work on him.'

Sigrud glances between the two young women. 'You know I can hear you — yes?'

Tavaan sighs and rolls her eyes. 'Did she tell you not to sit in the beds?'

'She said not to touch them . . .'

'Good,' says Tavaan. 'You'll pass out, and it'll be tricky for us to wake you up. They're intended to knock out someone Divine, so a mortal like you . . . it might make your heart stop.'

'So the beds are miraculous?'

'Yes,' says Tavaan. She walks down one line of beds, gazing at the sleeping occupants. 'When we use our Divine abilities, when we warp and change reality around us, our enemy *senses* it. He smells it. That's how he got the jump on us in the first place. For those who were awake, we could just sit around *existing* and he'd pick up on it. Those who slept, unaware of what they are, they could remain hidden from him, but those of us who knew ourselves . . . The very world changes as we merely walk through it. And when we congregated, meeting in groups of twos and threes, we were lit up bright before him, targets painted on our foreheads.'

'Are you not vulnerable here?' asks Sigrud.

'This place exists inside my domain,' says Tavaan. She taps the side of her head. 'Inside of *me*. It's not quite so attached to reality. So it's much harder for him to feel us here.'

'So it's like her domain,' says Sigrud. 'Like the shadow place the enemy pulled me into.'

'Not *quite* that intense,' says Tavaan. 'But close to it.'

'It's a dangerous play,' says Malwina, 'maybe a desperate one, but we've kept them alive for years doing it. The ones who didn't opt in to Tavaan's sanctuary . . . they didn't last long. He got to them quick. We take what victories we can get.'

'Yes, such a grand victory,' says Tavaan. 'You get to run around and make a mess of things out there, while I'm stuck in here all alone.'

'I *did* visit you,' says Malwina.

'Three times,' says Tavaan. 'Three times in the past year!'

'I brought you hot chocolate!'

'Yes, but no hot water to make it with.'

'I said I was sorry about that.'

'Sorries,' says Tavaan, 'don't taste nearly as good as hot chocolate.' Sigrud loudly clears his throat. 'Why am I here?'

'Why?' snorts Tavaan. 'To try something damned desperate.'

'That's because *we're* damned desperate,' says Malwina. 'Tavaan, listen to me – he tried to make a seneschal.'

Tavaan's eyes widen. 'He *what*?'

'You heard me. It sounds like it didn't go right, but the fact that he even tried . . .'

'He thinks he's as powerful as a Divinity,' says Tavaan.

'And he almost is. It almost *worked*. We're not winning this fight alone.'

'Is that why you asked for me to come?' Sigrud says to Tavaan. 'To help you plan a strategy?'

Tavaan looks surprised. 'Me? *I* didn't ask you to come here.'

Sigrud turns to Malwina, frowning. 'You said . . . You said *she* wants to talk to me. Who is this "she"?'

Tavaan's expression softens. 'Ah. He doesn't know.'

'No,' says Malwina darkly. 'He doesn't.' She sighs a little, then says, 'The Divine children . . . they're not the only people we've hidden here. Follow me. Just a bit farther.'

Sigrud follows her, still feeling bewildered. Between their strange journey to unlock the door under the Solda Bridge, then to travel through it to this bizarre sub-reality, and then to meet this mad-looking girl who claims to be slumber incarnate . . . He can't fathom what he's doing here or how they expect him to help, especially when he can hardly understand what's going on at any given moment.

He sees Malwina is leading him to the far wall, where the windows are. The windows look out on a navy-blue night sky, alight with stars, but situated before the one in the middle is a large overstuffed chair, facing away from him.

There is someone sitting in the chair: he can see a hand on the armrest, small and brown, with ink-stained fingers.

They get closer. And then he smells something . . . familiar.

Tea. Pochot tea, powerful and acrid.

Ink, lots of it, thick and dark.

And then there's the smell of very old parchment, and books, and dust, the scents of a library and all its musty tomes . . .

Sigrud stops walking.

'No,' he says. 'No. It cannot be.'

Malwina rounds the chair, then looks over its top at him. 'Come on, Sigrud,' she says gently. 'Come here.'

'I can't believe it,' he says. His face is trembling. 'I . . . I can't, I *can't*. It is a trick.'

Malwina shakes her head. 'No trick. Just come here. I'll only be able to wake her up for a short period. So hurry.'

Wobbling, Sigrud walks over to the overstuffed chair and slowly steps around it. And he sees her.

Though she has aged, she is still very much the woman he once knew: small, unassuming, with a closed face and large eyes, magnified even larger behind her thick glasses. Her eyes are closed, as if dozing. Her face has many, many more lines than he remembers, and her hair, done up in a hap-hazard bun, is the sort of white one can only get prematurely, a sort of snowy mane that contrasts brilliantly with her dark skin. She wears a plain blue dress and a white button-up sweater, and she leans against the side of the chair with her temple resting against the left wing, face pinched as if the position is slightly uncomfortable to her.

The woman who made his life as he knows it now. The person who saved him from the depths of prison after he'd lost everything, and given him hope.

'Shara,' whispers Sigrud. His mouth is dry. He looks at Malwina and swallows. 'How can this be? How . . . How can she be *alive*?'

Then Shara stirs, taking in a long, slow, rattling breath. She says in a croaking voice, 'I'm not.' She opens her eyes, blinking in the light of the windows. 'I'm not. I died, you see.'

12.
Ambassador

Sigrud stares at her. He simply can't process this. Her death was something he's lived with every day for the past month, something he woke up to in the morning and fell asleep to at night. To have it proved wrong, to have something he believed in so much blown apart like the head of a dandelion . . .

'Turyin . . . Turyin said she saw your body,' he says faintly.

'She probably did,' says Shara, soft yet amused. She sounds exhausted, though, the tone of a sick woman tolerating bedside visitors.

'They had a giant funeral for you in Ghaladesh,' he says.

'Yes, Malwina brought me the paper,' Shara says. 'Such lovely flower displays . . .'

'And they burned you,' says Sigrud, 'and put your ashes in a tomb.'

'That they did,' she says, nodding. 'I am not arguing with you about any of this, Sigrud.'

'Then . . . Then . . . Then who was cremated? Whose ashes are in that urn in that tomb?'

'Mine,' says Shara. She smiles faintly, and her eyes grow a little wider. 'Look at you, Sigrud . . . My goodness. You're just as I remember you. It's amazing, isn't it.'

'Shara,' says Sigrud. 'Shara, please – how . . . How did you survive?'

She sits up a little and gives him a level stare. 'Sigrud. Listen to me. I have said this repeatedly. I did *not* survive. I died. And I am . . . I am not really Shara Komayd. I am not the woman you knew.'

Sigrud looks at Malwina. 'So it *is* a trick.' He reaches out for Shara's hand — she does not withdraw — and touches it. It feels warm, though the skin is soft and loose, the hand of an old woman. 'But she feels real enough . . .'

'She *is* Shara,' says Malwina. 'But just a *moment* of Shara.'

'Specifically, the moment just after the bomb went off,' says Shara. She lifts the right side of her dress. He sees drops of blood along her ribs there, tiny entry wounds and perforations.

He kneels, shocked. 'Shara . . . You are hurt.'

'I am quite aware of that,' says Shara.

He reaches out to her wound. 'Here, let me . . . Let me take a look at it, we can find some bandages and —'

'There's no need. I've been dealing with it for weeks now.' She looks at Malwina. 'It has been weeks, right?'

'Just over a month since the assassination,' says Malwina. 'It's been five days since I last woke you.'

'Oh, good,' says Shara. 'Not too long, then.' She turns back to Sigrud. 'Listen, Sigrud. Sigrud?'

He can't stop staring at the wound in her side. He can't understand any of this, so he keeps focusing on this one thing he could fix, maybe, just maybe. 'I have a medical kit at the house, I could . . . I could . . .'

'Sigrud,' says Shara gently. 'Please look at me, and pay attention.'

He blinks, tears himself away, and meets her gaze.

She smiles. 'There. Just listen to me. The bomb *did* go off in Ahanashtan, yes. And I was right beside it, yes. But Malwina got to me *right* as the bomb went off. She couldn't save me from its blast, couldn't shield me from its damage — she could not stop me from dying, in other words. But she could preserve the tiniest sliver of time right as it happened. She took that tiny sliver and kept it going, perpetuating it long past when it would normally expire. And that is what you see before you now. I am not Shara, Sigrud, not truly. I am but a moment from her past, suspended here in the present, stretched out thin among all the seconds you're experiencing.'

'Which is a tremendous violation,' says Malwina. 'And a *real* pain in the ass to maintain.'

'Malwina bends the past around me, and through me.' Shara groans slightly, as if sensing such a bend. 'Certain parts of me progress at different rates – specifically the wounded parts of me, which go very slow. It is not a state I would ever recommend to another person.' She takes a rattling breath. 'Not to disparage Malwina's efforts, but dying is probably preferable. But she protects me, and wakes me at times for counsel. They've been kind enough to give me safe harbour.'

'Safe harbour,' scoffs Malwina. 'It was your idea to build this little pocket reality within Tavaan in the first place. We'd all be dead if you hadn't come up with it.'

'How much credit is owed to someone who says, "Do this," and does very little themselves is debatable,' says Shara.

'So . . . you can keep it going forever?' says Sigrud.

Malwina and Shara exchange a glance. 'Malwina – leave us for a moment, please,' says Shara. 'Sigrud and I have a lot to discuss. And much to do.'

Shara pulls her sweater tight around her shoulders. Sigrud drinks in how she sits, how she moves: she rubs her right wrist, which is slightly swollen with arthritis. Her legs are positioned awkwardly in the chair, placed as if to avoid putting further pressure on her back. And her eyes are so terribly sunken and tired, as if she hasn't slept since he last saw her, in the window aboard his tiny ship outside Voortyashtan thirteen years ago.

She smiles wearily at him. 'It is not *all* the effects of Malwina's miracle.'

'What?'

'How I look. What Malwina's done to me is taxing, yes, but . . . So was my life. I put my body through more than anyone ought to. I am old, Sigrud. Or perhaps I should say I *was* old. Who knows, with all this Divine trickery. But you . . . You are . . .' She searches his face, but unlike Mulaghesh, she doesn't seem surprised by what she finds. Rather, all the pleasant bemusement evaporates from her face, leaving behind an expression he knows well – *Time for business*.

'Malwina mentioned you found the *Salim*,' says Shara. 'Which means you must have talked to Turyin. So you must have received my message. Yes?'

Sigrud sits at the foot of her chair, feeling like a child listening to his grandmother tell a tale. 'Yes.'

She sits back, looking pained but pleased. 'Ah. Good. So satisfying when plans go right – even if you are making plans about your death.'

'You planned to die?'

'Oh, I've always planned to die,' says Shara. 'That's always been rather unavoidable. It's just *which* death I would meet – that required some thinking. How odd it is, to know what end I found. It seems deserving, doesn't it? After all our skullduggery, it's a Saypuri agent who topples Komayd. I'm surprised Khadse was able to get through.'

'Through the wards around the Golden?'

'Yes. How *did* he manage to do it? Did you ever find out?'

'Miracles in his coat, and shoes. I used them to help Malwina get out.'

'Ah. Well. There it is.' She looks at him, and her face is no longer half so humorous: she looks hungry, and worried. 'And . . . And Taty. You found her?'

'Yes.'

'And you and Ivanya kept her safe?' she asks quickly.

'Yes. The enemy has not been close to her yet. She's safe in the Votrov mansion now, here in Bulikov.'

Shara lets out a long, slow sigh. '*That* I would not have preferred . . . Just like in the past, all things gather to Bulikov, friend and foe alike. But there are so few safe places in this world anymore. We must all cling to our oases. How is she doing?'

'She is . . . grieving,' he says. 'For you, Shara.'

She sighs slowly. 'Yes. As she should. The things I have put her through . . .'

'She is strong,' says Sigrud. 'Or she is learning to be strong. But . . . Shara . . . Why did you not tell me who she was?'

'Who she was?' says Shara.

'Yes. That Taty was . . .' He looks at her. 'That she is Divine.'

Shara is silent. Her face is grave, and she suddenly seems terribly frail.

'She is related to Malwina, isn't she,' says Sigrud. 'She looks so *much* like her . . . Taty is her sister. Isn't she?'

Shara's mouth works, as if disliking the taste of the words she is about to say. 'Yes,' she says softly. 'Yes, clever Sigrud, you are right. They are twins, in fact. Not identical, but twins.'

There's a long, long silence.

'Malwina is the child of the past,' says Sigrud. 'And Taty . . . Taty is the Divine child of the future. Isn't she?'

Something in Shara's face seems to crumple at these words.

'It was something Malwina mentioned,' Sigrud says. 'About domains. That is how Taty can sometimes know what is about to happen.'

Shara is silent for a long time. When she finally speaks, her voice is again but a croak: 'I found her in Bulikov, you know. Just before Voortyashtan. I toured the Continent, seeing how my policies were being implemented. The press raved and ranted about it. Thought I was defecting from Saypur, going to the country I *truly* loved. Such mad stuff . . . But did you know, I found that things were not much better? Not really, I mean. Refugees everywhere. Starvation. Corruption. And the orphanages . . . By the seas, so many orphans. I went to one orphanage, and these little creatures were hardly more than skeletons. I could see the bones in their faces, in their shoulders. And then there was this one little girl, coughing . . .'

She bows her head. 'I was drawn to her. I didn't know why. We talked. She said she liked maths a lot. She talked on about it for a while, the way children do. And then she asked if she could come home with me. I said no, because I had to, of course – I was on a damned diplomatic tour, you see, one can't just swing by and pick up an orphan. But her request stuck with me. The way she looked at me, the way she pleaded to come home with me . . . It echoed in my head. So when I returned to Ghaladesh, I found myself compelled to put things in motion, and set up an adoption.' She looks at him, her dark eyes sharp and watchful. 'Malwina told you, didn't she? About Jukov's miracle?'

'Yes. Somewhat.'

'About how it puts the children in some kind of sleepwalking limbo? Drifting from one adoptive family to another?'

'Yes.'

She sits back in the chair. 'I worry . . . I worry if those actions I took, if those were truly *mine*. Perhaps I was miraculously compelled to adopt Taty, with neither of us knowing. What a dispiriting thought that is . . . That all your love could be founded on lies.'

'She worries the same of you,' says Sigrud.

'What? What do you mean?'

'She figured out that you have not . . . not been totally honest with her about your past.'

Shara's eyes grow wide. 'Ah. *Ah.*' She laughs lowly. 'You know, I hadn't thought about that. It seems obvious now that, when Taty fled Ghaladesh and went out into the wide world, she'd find out who I'd been in my past life . . . Was she angry?'

'Yes,' says Sigrud.

'Very angry?'

'Yes.'

'She has that right, I suppose,' says Shara quietly. 'It was . . . It was so pleasant, being a civilian. Being a mother. Being *just* a mother. I just . . . I just wanted that to keep going. I didn't want to spoil it.'

'But it did not last,' says Sigrud. 'Did it?'

'No,' says Shara. 'No. It didn't.' She licks her lips. 'Taty started . . . predicting things. She told the groundskeeper to go home one day, and it turned out the groundskeeper's husband was terribly sick, and if she hadn't made it home she couldn't have saved him. There were other incidents. She delayed the postman at the house once, just long enough for him to avoid a horrid automobile accident. And then there was her obsession with the markets . . . That was when I started getting worried. She was good. *Too* good. She wanted to start investing herself, but I put a stop to that. If people started getting suspicious . . .'

She shakes her head. 'Thank the seas I had her in Saypur. The powers of the Divine children don't work as well outside of the Continent. Who knows what could have happened if I hadn't taken her away. But it was around then that I started looking into the orphanages on the Continent, trying to understand if she'd been blessed or charmed somehow by some errant miracle . . . And that was when I discovered that Taty had been adopted before. *Years* before. By another family. And when I saw the picture from that adoption, she hadn't seemed to have aged at all since then.

'I was frightened. Terrified. I reviewed everything I knew about this girl. I asked her questions about her life on the Continent. She had no memory of another family, of another life. So I went looking . . . and I found more.

'More children. More children who had been drifting from place to place, being taken in by countless families. I resorted to a few Ministry contacts. And that was when I found I was not the *only* Ministry person who'd been looking into these Continental orphans.'

'Vinya,' says Sigrud.

Shara nods, her eyes steely. 'Yes. Vinya had stumbled across one of them before Bulikov. I found her paper trail. And that led me – very windingly – to the *Salim*. And what she had done there.' She sighs. 'He hates me, you know. Our enemy. I can't blame him. What my aunt did to him . . . It's a war crime, is what it is. But he is dreadfully driven, and dreadfully clever. You've met him?'

He nods.

'Really,' says Shara softly. 'I never have. He's always eluded me, that bright little boy . . . What was he like?'

'Young,' says Sigrud. 'He was like a teenager. An angry one. A furious child, lashing out. He was especially sensitive about his father – when I mentioned how you had killed him, he lost all control.'

'Did he,' she says. She cocks her head, as if making a mental note of this. 'Interesting.'

'Is he . . . Is he the maimed Divine child you were reading about in your books?'

She fixes him with a keen stare. 'How do you know about *that*?'

'I . . . I went to your house,' says Sigrud. 'I saw your books in your room.'

'Oh. Right.' She relaxes. 'Yes, I saw in the papers that my estate had burned down. You've lost none of your subtlety, Sigrud. But to answer your question . . . I'm not sure. I *thought* he was the maimed child, seeking to reconnect with all the pieces of him that were stolen away by the primary Divinities – yet I could find no evidence of such a thing. I think the primary Divinities resorted to one of their favourite tricks – they edited the past, edited the memory of the maimed child, so he would never remember what he was. So if he is this child, he himself may not know it.'

'But if trauma can make a child remember they are Divine,' says Sigrud, 'perhaps the torture in the *Salim* made him remember much, much more.'

Shara nods slightly. 'Perhaps so. I've done my hardest to find out more about him, with no success. And he was prepared. After the *Salim*, I started searching for him. I suppose he must have figured me out, because he staged a minor incident – a minor manifestation of the Divine that was reported back to me through my own channels. I should have known it was a ruse, since only *my* people heard about it, and no one else noticed. But I investigated, worried it had something to do with him. And I made one critical mistake – I brought my black lead with me.'

Sigrud nods, suddenly understanding. 'Which he then stole. Didn't he? *That's* why you never used it on him. I had wondered about it so much.'

She smiles bitterly. 'Yes. I hadn't realised the extent of his powers by then. Anything that is eclipsed in darkness, he controls. And I was hardly going to keep the black lead sitting on the top of the cupboard in total daylight, was I? When I realised it was gone, I discovered the danger we were in – myself and the rest of the Divine children. That was when I tracked down Malwina. And then we really started to organise. But then, unfortunately . . .' – she smiles sadly – 'I died. Which rather complicates things.'

'And . . . now what do we do?' asks Sigrud.

She thinks for a moment. Then she says, 'Here. Help me up.'

'You can stand?'

'With help, yes. I'd like to do something I haven't done in a long time.' She smiles brightly at him. 'I'd like to go on a walk with you, Sigrud.'

They walk along the wall of windows, Shara clutching his right arm, her steps tottering and uneven. Yet there is a queer peacefulness to it all, as if they are a long-married couple in their later years, strolling through a park. Though he can't quite match it, he senses Shara is . . . content.

The beds stretch out on their left, the dark room shimmering with soft snores and sighs.

'There are so many,' he says.

'Yes,' says Shara. 'Three hundred and thirty-seven, specifically. Only four of the six Divinities were procreative, but . . . they did get up to rather a lot. Got to do something to fill the time during those thousand or so years, I suppose.'

'Why did you take up their cause?' asks Sigrud. 'Why them, of all the wretched people who need help right now?'

'Because they had no one to speak for them,' she says. 'No ally, no protector. People either want to control them or kill them. And I suppose living with Taty for so long . . . I saw what she could have become, had I not been there for her. What if it had been her that Vinya had captured, so many years ago? Though I'm not always sure I've done a better job with her . . . Lying to her, about myself, about the world . . . Perhaps we Komayds are simply poison for the Divine.'

'She loves you, Shara,' says Sigrud.

Shara looks away. 'Does she?' she says.

'Yes. She asked me many questions about you. About who you had been. It was as if I'd done a magic trick for her.'

Shara smiles weakly. 'All parents are dull to their children, I suspect. I suppose I was no different from any other parent. I'd watch her sleep, and I'd just wonder – Who's in there? Who will you be one day? Will you remember me? Or will I be no more than a pleasant shadow, faint and indeterminate, skulking at the borders of your memories as the years stretch on before you?'

'If one were to protest all the injustices of life,' says Sigrud, 'great and small, one would have no time for living.'

'Using my own words against me. How cruel of you.'

'They are good words,' he says. 'I think about them a lot. More and more, recently. But I do wonder . . . If Taty believes you've died – and she does, as far as I am aware – then why has she not . . . remembered? Why has she not remembered her Divine power?'

'I've debated this endlessly. I suspect that Taty, being Divine, has a lot of senses we don't. And though these senses are repressed, just like all of her Divine nature, they feed her information subconsciously. And one of those senses knows or understands that . . . that I am *not* truly gone from this world. She senses that I have been extended, and stretched, far past my actual death. She knows I am still here. So she knows not to truly grieve.'

'I think you are right,' says Sigrud. 'She's said as much to me. She feels like she's going mad.'

Shara sighs. 'What a trial I've put her through . . . It sounds odd, to feel guilty just for being alive. Even though what I am right now is not technically alive.'

Sigrud looks across the room and sees Malwina and Tavaan sitting side by side on the ground, facing away from them. They're seated very close. He watches as Malwina puts an arm around Tavaan, and Tavaan leans into the embrace, resting her head on Malwina's shoulder. Then Tavaan reaches up and grasps Malwina's hand and holds it tight – a deeply familiar gesture, one so common that neither girl notices it happening.

'Are they sisters as well?' asks Sigrud.

'No,' says Shara.

He thinks for a moment. 'Oh. I see.'

'It's good that they have this,' she says. 'Malwina, of all people, deserves a quiet moment of solace.'

'Malwina said she remembers much of the old days . . . the Divine days, I mean.'

'That she does. Malwina is one of the oldest and most powerful of all the children. She has been fleeing our enemy for some time. But out of all of the children, she is the one who poses the most threat to him.'

'Then why does she not remember her twin sister?' he asks. 'I asked her if she thought Taty was Divine, and she said she didn't think so.'

There's a brief pause. 'I think,' Shara says quietly, 'that it is because of their nature. Their domain dictates so much of how they act, you see. Malwina is the spirit of the past, and Taty the future – and the past and the future never seem to acknowledge one another, do they? Certain Divine children and even proper Divinities repelled one another. Voortya and Ahanas certainly hated each other to bits, as one would expect of life and death.'

Yet then Shara does something that's deeply familiar to him: she reaches up, pushes her glasses up, and rubs her thumb and forefinger along the bridge of her nose, where the nosepiece of her glasses sits. He's seen her do this a few times in their careers, always in difficult meetings: Shara was terribly good at lying, but when she was quite nervous that her lie would be detected, she'd perform this odd little tell.

'Shara,' he says. 'Are you holding anything back from me?'

'Always,' she says immediately. 'And for your own good.'

'I . . . I have fought hard to come to you here . . .'

'And I have fought hard to keep my most desperate plans at bay,' she says curtly. 'There are things, Sigrud, that I would never wish to do. Yet in the future, I may have to do them. And when I do them, I cannot let you stop me. So you cannot know about them. Do you understand?'

'Like the old days.'

'Yes. Just like the old days. And we are in desperate need of some of your old talents.' Shara looks across at the two girls, smiling. 'What riddles children are. How time changes them. That's the real enemy, time. We race against it, then try to slow its arrival.' She sighs. 'And time is against us. We can't win against the enemy alone, not anymore. We need to call in help. And that's where you come in, Sigrud. You're good at getting into difficult places. And I need you for one last operation, to go somewhere very difficult indeed, and be our ambassador.'

'Where's that?'

'Into the Divine sanctum of the Divinity Olvos,' says Shara. 'Where you will beg her to help us.'

Voshem walks along the Solda River, disguised once again as a tattered transient, a small smile on his face and a bounce in his step. He is, of course, aware of the gravity of the situation, but it's very difficult for him to be anything but positive. As the spirit of possibility itself, he tends to feel optimistic even in the direst of situations.

Right now, as he walks past a street full of wine bars and cafés and salons, where women wearing trousers (a very recent development) walk arm in arm with young men in their bright blue coats and fur caps, his mind is absolutely bubbling with potential. Most of those potentials are purely sexual: the fervently wished-for possibility that this night could maybe, just *maybe*, go right for once, and perhaps you could convince this person to sneak away with you back to your apartment, or at the very least somewhere private and soft and dark, where your fingers could entwine, your shoulder bared and hot breath on your neck . . .

There are other potentials, of course. Bad ones. The possibility of a drunken word, blurted at the wrong moment. The possibility that you might miss that person who could help you transform and know yourself more than you ever could alone.

All of these possibilities course through Voshem like tributaries pouring into a river. There are certainties too – the certainty of death, for example, the certainty of age, the certainty of the seasons. Some people have deeper fates, events their lives can't possibly avoid – but Voshem can't really see any of these. Certainties are almost invisible to the spirit of possibility. They are not his realm. He focuses only on the possibilities, thrumming with their energy, watching these events burst and fade like fireworks in the night sky.

Voshem shuts his eyes. He reviews them all, one by one, dreaming them.

But then one possibility drips into his mind . . .

He opens his eyes. He watches as the walls of Bulikov ahead turn black – absolutely, perfectly black – and then they begin to . . . unscroll. They blossom, like a flower petal reaching for the light, but the walls keep reaching up and up, twisting around him until they form a tower, huge and black, rising into the sky . . .

Voshem blinks. The possibility is gone. The tower vanishes. The walls of Bulikov remain distant and translucent as always. He keeps walking.

Voshem knows of a lot of very strange possibilities floating around out there. This being the Continent, anything is possible.

But that one . . . That one felt like it just got a little *more* possible.

It disturbs him. It almost makes him forget that odd feeling he's had since he walked away from the Solda Bridge: the feeling that he was being watched. He's looked, of course, and stayed careful, and he's even searched the possibilities before him. In all cases, he's found nothing. So he should be safe. Right?

Right?

Voshem keeps walking.

Sigrud walks Shara back to her overstuffed chair. 'How can I possibly talk to a Divinity?' he asks.

'I went there once,' says Shara. 'Long ago. Toward the tail end of the events in Bulikov. She reached out to me, contacted me, asked me to come. And I did.'

'You didn't tell me that,' he says, resentful.

She waves a hand. 'It was when I was setting up Vinya's coup, and then *your* coup in the Dreyling Republics. There was little time for idle chat.'

'Being whisked away by a god sounds like it is well more than idle chat!'

'Suffice it to say,' she says forcefully, 'it would have been a complicated subject to broach at the time. But there is a place in the physical world that is connected to her sanctum – just like how this room connects to the physical world beneath the Solda Bridge. But she has set up defences – Malwina and others have tried to penetrate them, but have had no luck. She is far, far more powerful than they are.'

Sigrud helps ease her down into her chair. 'And how will I be any different?'

'That's a good question. And one that worries me quite a bit.' She groans as she adjusts her side, then sits back. 'You are no fool, Sigrud,' she says. 'You know you don't look . . . wait, how old are you? Fifty? Sixty?'

'Sixty-three,' he says.

'By the seas . . .' She adjusts her glasses and blinks at him. 'Well. You know that you have not aged appropriately – don't you?'

Sigrud hesitates, then nods.

'And you are of course aware that you have successfully defied the effects of the Divine an *extremely* unusual number of times? And each time . . . Each time it was your left hand, wasn't it? It played some part in your survival?'

Sigrud nods again. To hear his fears and anxieties spoken aloud is deeply alarming to him.

'Let me see it,' she says. She holds out her own hands, small and brown and wrinkled.

He rests his left hand in her palms. She looks at it, taking in the scars that haven't changed in decades: the scale of the Divinity Kolkan, waiting to weigh and judge.

'I don't understand it,' says Shara quietly. 'And I've no idea how it works. It shouldn't do anything at *all*, with Kolkan dead. But . . . something changed when you were tortured in Slondheim, Sigrud. It's not that you are immune to the effects of the Divine – otherwise Malwina and the others couldn't transport you or protect you – but it's like you can survive them, defy them, dampen them.'

'I don't understand,' says Sigrud.

'I don't either,' says Shara. 'I've never encountered anything like this in the literature before.'

'But you think . . . you think I could use this to penetrate Olvos's defences?'

'Perhaps. It's a chance we have to take. Our enemy wishes to become a Divinity in his own right. To have our own Divinity on our side . . .'

'Another Divine war,' says Sigrud darkly.

'I hope to cut it off before that,' says Shara. She sighs. 'Perhaps this was unavoidable. Perhaps I should not have been so careful, so cautious. Perhaps I should have made open war upon our enemy immediately. But how many times have we seen children march to war in the garb of soldiers? I look back through the years, and all I see . . . all I see are maimed children striking out blindly, trying to avenge past misdeeds. I can't bring myself to perpetuate this, Sigrud. I won't be a part of that history I know so well. I'll do whatever I can to avoid it.' She adjusts her glasses. 'I hope this is the last battle. One big push.'

Sigrud's face clouds over. He looks away.

'What's wrong?' asks Shara.

'It's nothing.'

'It's clearly not nothing.'

'It's . . . That was something Signe said to me once.' He looks at her. 'One big push.'

She smiles sadly. 'Ah. Quoting Thinadeshi, I expect. I wish I could have met her. She sounds like my kind of person.'

'She was.'

Malwina and Tavaan, perhaps sensing the direction of their discussion, stand and walk over, holding hands. 'Are we getting to the desperate part?' asks Tavaan.

'Yes, dear,' says Shara kindly.

'You know I'm several times your age, right?' says Tavaan. 'You don't have to talk to me like you're my grandmother.'

'Age is just a number, dear,' says Shara in the same maternal tone. 'I've informed Sigrud of what we need of him.'

'But I still don't know what I'm *doing*,' says Sigrud. 'You want me to go to this place where Olvos is, and overcome her wards using – what? This thing in my hand that I hardly understand? And what am I even supposed to use it *on*, exactly?'

'The tethering point is in the woods,' says Malwina. 'Just outside of the polis governor's quarters.'

'A place you know well, Sigrud,' says Shara. 'Since you recuperated there after Bulikov.'

'There are layers there,' says Malwina. 'Worlds within worlds within worlds. Bands and striae of varying realities. Whatever charm or glamour or miracle you carry with you, you must try to use it to break through them.'

'This is just like the plans you've always made, Shara,' says Sigrud, frustrated. 'Always lacking the most important part.'

'And yet, in the past, we've been triumphant,' she says. Then she adds, 'Mostly.'

'We must act now,' says Malwina. '*Tonight*. I think . . . I think he is aware of us, somehow. The air outside, in the city, it's all wrong. We must act before he has time to prepare.'

'Will you do it?' asks Tavaan. 'We have no other option.'

'And you are quite talented at improvising,' says Shara.

'Improvising with knives, guns, bombs, yes,' says Sigrud. 'But improvising with a god . . . That is much less certain.' He hesitates, then says, 'There is one question you have not answered yet, though.'

'Which is?' asks Shara.

He looks at Shara. 'Can Malwina keep this going . . . Can she keep *you* going . . . indefinitely?'

Tavaan and Malwina glance at each other uncomfortably.

Shara smiles at him, her eyes sad. 'No, Sigrud. Of course not.'

'But . . . then what will happen?' he says.

'Then this will end.' She waves at her body. 'And it will be as if this thing before you had never been at all.'

'You'll just be gone?'

'Yes. Gone.'

He bows his head. 'But . . . But that's not fair.'

She smiles desperately. 'I know.'

'It's not *right*. It's not right to lose you and get you back and then lose you again.'

'I know, Sigrud. I know. But it will happen. It *will* happen.' She reaches out and grasps his hand. 'All things must end. You knew that. Even the gods must end eventually. And so I will as well.'

He wipes tears from his eye, ashamed of his weeping. 'After you, and Mulaghesh, and Hild and Signe . . . I . . . I don't want to be alone *again*.'

'I know. I know, Sigrud. And I am so sorry. But listen to me. We are all of us but the sum of our moments, our deeds. I died, Sigrud, and I died doing something I believed in. I will die doing it again. But if I lived my life rightly, what I did during it will echo on. Those I helped, those I protected – they will carry my moments forward with them. And that is no small thing.'

'You say this to me,' says Sigrud, 'a man whose moments are little more than slit throats, and sorrow, and skulking in the dark.'

'And if you had not been there to do the things you did,' says Shara, 'I certainly would not have lived as long as I did. And I, personally, would not have liked it that much.'

He sniffs. 'I hate arguing with you. You always win.'

'Well, console yourself with the fact that this is probably the very last request I make of you,' says Shara.

He nods, sniffs once more, and straightens up. 'So. Olvos. She's at the polis governor's quarters – yes?'

'Something like that,' says Malwina.

He shakes his head. 'How absurd it is to go lurking at a Divinity's doorstep, as if she were hiding from creditors. How will I get there? Are there any magic doors or stairs that can take me?'

'There's a secret back exit there,' says Malwina, pointing at a distant, dark fireplace along the far wall. 'One only I use and know about.'

'Only you?' says Sigrud. 'Not . . . what was his name . . . Voshem?'

She shakes her head. 'No. Wouldn't be smart to put so much power into one person's hands. The exit only leads to a tollbooth in the park next to the Seat of the World, nowhere fancier than that. We'll use it, as we can't leave by the Solda Bridge door again – too much traffic there might give watching eyes ideas.'

'And what shall I do once we're out?' asks Sigrud.

'Well,' says Malwina. 'You said you were good at stealing cars, yes?'

'Steal a car and drive it through all those checkpoints to the polis governor's office . . .? I will be shot before I get outside the walls.'

'Bulikov isn't as you remember it anymore, Sigrud,' says Shara. 'Those checkpoints are gone, mostly.'

'I'll get you through the exit,' says Malwina, 'and then I'll stay at the tollbooth in the park, waiting for you.'

'How will I get word back to you if I succeed?' asks Sigrud.

'If you succeed, you'll have a damned Divinity on your side,' says Tavaan. 'She'll probably drive you across the sky in a chariot pulled by swans.'

'And if I fail?' he asks.

'If you fail . . .' says Malwina. 'If you knock on the door, and there's no answer . . . then you just come back, I suppose. And we try to think of something else.'

Sigrud rubs his face. 'And do we have any other backup plans?'

Tavaan looks to Malwina. Malwina looks to Shara.

Shara sits very still, staring into space, as if deciding something. And then she does it again: she raises her right hand, lifts her glasses, and wipes the bridge of her nose with her thumb and forefinger.

She looks at Sigrud. Her eyes are hard and cold. 'No,' she says firmly.

He knows she's lying. He can see she knows that he knows. She has some other trump card she's holding back. But he can see that she desperately, desperately does not wish to play it.

'All right,' he says. 'I'll do it.'

'Good.' Shara turns to Tavaan. 'Then we need one final thing.'

'What's that?' asks Sigrud.

'This is war,' says Tavaan. 'A poor war, yes, a lopsided one with the odds against us. But this will be the one real strike against our enemy. So if it's to be war, it's best to outfit you appropriately.'

Sigrud waits for more. 'Meaning we need . . .'

Malwina gives him a faint smile. 'A seneschal.'

Sigrud kneels on the floor of the room, feeling both awkward and confused. Malwina and Tavaan stand before him, holding hands, while Shara looks on from the comfort of her chair. Though no one's done anything yet, he feels something's changing in the room. It takes him a while to notice it: the snores and mutterings and gentle sounds of slumber are all fading. The hundreds of sleepers are growing still.

'Are we sure this is necessary?' asks Sigrud.

'It's likely our enemy knows Olvos's location too,' says Malwina. 'He can't get to her, just as we can't, but he'll know the region. He could have prepared it against you. So you need to be prepared in turn.'

Tavaan looks down at him, her wide, strange eyes filled with a curious light. 'Are you ready?'

'And you're sure I won't become a monster,' says Sigrud, 'like the woman on the aero-tram?'

'You won't be a true seneschal, Sigrud,' says Malwina. 'That's what the enemy tried to make – a mortal with a piece of a god in them.'

'We aren't that powerful,' says Tavaan. 'Unfortunately.'

'But we do have gifts to impart to you. Yet in order for these gifts to be used to their full effect, they must be transferred with an agreement.'

'These gifts are a part of us,' says Tavaan. 'So the gift can only be given to a part of us – an aspect, a facet.'

'Which means what, exactly?'

'A lost child,' says Malwina quietly. 'That is our communal domain, so to speak. We are refugees. We can only give these gifts to someone of a similar state.'

Sigrud sits in silence.

'Are you ready?' Tavaan says.

'I don't know,' he says. He looks to Shara. 'Am I?'

Shara shrugs. 'This is likely the first time such a thing has been attempted in global history.'

'Which means what?' asks Sigrud.

'Which means I've no idea what could happen. But I've never known you to turn down a weapon, Sigrud.'

He grimaces and scratches his neck. 'Fine,' he says.

'Shut your eye, Sigrud,' says Tavaan.

He does so. One of them takes his left hand – Tavaan, maybe. Then he feels cold, hard fingers pressing upon his brow. Then there are voices. He thinks he hears Tavaan's loudest among them, but he's not sure – he hears many voices wrapped up in it, like it's not one person but many speaking at the same time.

'Do you hear us?' ask the voices.

'Yes,' he says.

'Do you feel this?' ask the voices.

A juddering in his skull. He feels like the fingers are penetrating his brain, reaching into the deep, dark caverns in his thoughts, to scrawl upon a secret wall there . . .

He tries not to gag. 'Yes.'

'Good,' say the voices. 'Now, listen. You must find a memory in yourself, Sigrud. A memory of desperation, of loss, of hope eclipsed by sorrow.'

More voices chime in: 'When you fled. When you ran. When you fought not for pride or for purpose, but simply to live.'

'When you were like us,' the voices say, swelling. 'Alone. And forgotten.'

Dozens of voices flit through his mind, whispering: *Please. Please, help us . . . Please, we've wandered for so long . . .*

Then he feels them: feels every year, every hour, every minute of their purgatory, the miserable, dispossessed mass of Divine children, all lost, all aimless, mindlessly seeking shelter and warmth.

And then he remembers something: a moment long, long ago, when he was a young man, barely twenty. Returning from a sea voyage to find his parents murdered, his home reduced to ashes. He remembers sitting on the blackened hillside, staring into the empty, frigid vale before him, and feeling a powerful aloneness, a wordless isolation in whose shadow he has lived his entire life.

If there had been someone there for me then, he thinks, *would I be who I am today?*

And then he realises that there had been someone to help him, though it took some time for her to find him: Shara Komayd. Though his life has been far from perfect, it would have been much worse without her chance intervention.

And now, perhaps, he can finally repay her.

'That's it,' say the voices.

There's a tremendous pressure in his skull, as if the two fingers there have paused, suspended in his head, waiting to hear his answer.

Then one voice stands out, very slightly. 'Is this you, mortal man? Is this memory you? Is this what makes up your heart?'

'Yes,' he whispers. And he knows this is true. 'Yes, it is.'

With these words he feels a warmth flooding into his left hand, like he's holding it close to a fire.

'In your hand is a sword,' say the voices. 'Do you feel it?'

Sigrud frowns. At first he felt a hand gripping his own, perhaps Malwina's or Tavaan's, but now it feels very . . . strange. There is something new in his hand, and it is not another hand. It is something hard yet warm, with a slight give to it, like that of wood.

'Do you feel the blade?' the voices whisper. 'Do you?'

'I . . . I think I do,' he says, but he's not certain.

'Do you see it, Sigrud?' asks Malwina, her voice quiet and close. 'Do you see it in your mind?'

Sigrud furrows his brow. He's not sure what they mean – see in his mind? He doesn't see anything with his mi –

Then he sees it.

A flicker of gold-white light, just to his left, like the flicker of a candle flame. A golden ribbon, whipping about brightly in a stiff breeze. A blade like the wing of a yellow butterfly, flitting through shafts of sunlight in the forest.

He feels it being bound to him, not to his hand but to *him*, the idea of him, the thing that makes him who he is.

'A tool,' the voices say, 'to find a path in empty shadows. Will you use it wisely and well, to protect us and guide us to a new home?'

'Yes,' says Sigrud. 'Yes. I will.'

'Then take the sword,' the voices say. 'Take it an –'

Then there's a sharp cry of pain. The warmth in Sigrud's hand suddenly vanishes, the pressure in his skull evaporates, and his eye snaps open.

It takes him a moment to get his bearings. Tavaan is kneeling on the floor, cradling her right hand like it's been burned. Malwina crouches beside her, helping her sit up. His hands are empty, and the sleepers groan quietly.

'What . . . What happened?' asks Sigrud.

Tavaan swallows and shakes her head. Then she glares at him like he hurt her. 'There is something *nasty* living inside you,' she rasps.

'I felt it too,' says Malwina. She glances back at him, her face troubled. 'Whatever it was, it didn't want us to bind the sword to you. But we did. I *think* we did.'

'How can you be sure?' asks Shara.

'Ask him if he can find it,' says Tavaan. 'Ask him if it's there.'

'Can you reach out and feel it, Sigrud?' asks Malwina. 'Can you find it near you?'

Sigrud's not sure what they mean. Feeling absurd, he reaches out and paws the space in front of him like someone trying to find a doorknob in a dark room. But then his hand feels magnetically drawn to a spot in the air . . .

And then it's there, as if he'd always been holding it: a short, thin blade that looks like it is made of gold or bronze. Its handle is warm, even somewhat hot, as if it were sitting near an open flame.

Malwina and Tavaan let out a breath of relief. 'Thank goodness,' says Malwina. 'For a moment I thought we'd done all that work for nothing . . .'

'What . . . is it?' asks Sigrud, examining its edge.

'*Flame*,' says Malwina. 'That's the name it chose for itself, when we made it.'

'Like we said,' says Tavaan, 'it's a tool. It won't harm the enemy, but it can destroy his works.'

'He is here, and he is anxious. The stronger he gets, the more he'll send at you,' says Malwina. 'And us.'

Sigrud tosses the blade back and forth between his hands. It feels solid enough, not at all like how it felt in his mind, where it was an idea rather than a physical object. 'How did you two make it?' he asks.

'*We* didn't,' says Malwina. She waves at all the sleeping children in the beds. 'We *all* did.'

'In our minds,' says Tavaan. Then she taps her temple. 'In our slumber. We dreamed it, you see. There was a reason they put me in charge of this place, after all.'

'Put it away,' says Malwina. 'Hide it away again. The more it's out in the open, the easier it is for him to sense it. It's Divine, after all.'

Sigrud waves the sword around, trying to feel for that pocket of air again, as if it was an invisible sheath he could just slide it back into. But then something in his mind kicks in, as if he's remembering a motion he did long ago: it's not like he's sheathing the blade, but rather like he's pressing it into soft mud, submerging it into a pocket in the reality beside him. His hands begin the motion, and then suddenly it's gone.

Though Tavaan still looks weak, she nods, pleased. 'Good.'

'Will it cut flesh?' asks Sigrud. 'And metals? Or merely the Divine?'

'It will perform like a very good sword, I suppose I should say,' says Malwina, 'and it won't break. But its primary use will be against the enemy. And it won't do shit against Olvos's defences. She's far more powerful than we are.'

'What happens if I drop it?' asks Sigrud. 'Or someone steals it?'

'It won't leave you or work for anyone else,' says Malwina. 'Unless you give it to them. It's bound to your will.'

Sigrud nods, impressed. 'I could get used to Divine trinkets.'

'Don't,' says Tavaan. She sits up, shaking her hand like the pain is lingering. 'There won't be any more where that came from. It's time to go.'

Together the four of them walk to the fireplace, which is huge and old and dark. As they walk, Sigrud realises how much this exchange has drained Shara: she seems faint, and she blinks repeatedly, as if fighting back a stupor.

'Do you know . . . I wonder if this will make a difference,' she says.

'Why else would we do it?' asks Sigrud.

'I mean in the lives of average people,' says Shara. 'We do our backstage skullduggery in the halls of power . . . but little changes for the people in the streets. They live their lives at the mercy of people like our enemy . . . and people like me. I worry Vinya was right.'

'About what?' says Malwina.

'That power doesn't change. It just changes clothes. The Divinities formed reality for their people. And when they were gone, government picked up where they left off. Few have any choice in how they live. Few have the power to decide their own realities. Even if we are victorious – will that change?'

'We focus on the tasks at hand,' says Sigrud. 'Such grand problems are beyond us.'

'You're right, Sigrud. Of course you are.' Shara sighs as they approach the fireplace. 'I don't know how you do it, Sigrud.'

'Do what?'

'Keep going,' says Shara. 'There are some crimes that you don't understand the awfulness of until you're older. I sit here now, separated from Taty, knowing that . . . knowing that it is likely I will not see her again. I won't hear her voice, smell her hair, feel her fingers in mine. And it is as if someone buried a thorn deep within me, and I feel it pressing on my heart with every breath. And then I worry you were right.'

Malwina climbs into the fireplace and gestures to Sigrud to do the same. He does so, but looks back at Shara, confused and concerned. 'Right about what?' he asks.

'When you said to me that the fight could not ever be worth it,' Shara says, 'when it asks us for our children.' She looks at him, her tired eyes burning in her lined face. 'I'm sorry about Signe. I regret so many things. But that I regret more than any other.'

They share one moment longer, each looking at the other across the boundary of the fireplace, separated by years and sorrow and death itself. Sigrud tries to think of something to say, but the words do not come.

Malwina touches the side of the fireplace. The world twists.

Sigrud finds himself toppling out of the shadows and into the night air. He manages to catch himself before he falls, staggering forward a few more steps. He stops and looks around – they're in the park, just as Malwina said they would be. He looks back to see a small, abandoned tollbooth standing by a little concrete path. There's a shiver in the shadows in its doorways, and then Malwina steps out, looking grim.

She looks him up and down. 'Are you ready?'

Sigrud walks over to the tollbooth to find it's a simple, empty wooden structure. He feels the walls with one hand, perhaps wishing he could reach through them, find Shara, and touch her once more, just one moment longer with his friend.

'I said, are you ready?' says Malwina.

Sigrud drops his hand. 'Yes.'

'Good. Then listen.'

Voshem slips through the streets of Bulikov like a mote of dust through a sunbeam. He moves cautiously now, listening to the crackling hum of electric lights and the *honk* and *putter* of distant automobiles. He's walked these paths many times before, and everything seems the same, but that vision lingers in his mind: the walls turning into the dark base of a tower, which stretched toward the skies . . .

He shivers as he comes to his apartment building – one of them, at least, as one must stay mobile to stay safe – but pauses before the door.

He looks up and down the street. He searches the possibilities afloat in the air.

Being stopped by police. A stray question from the old woman who lives downstairs. Corroded plumbing causing a cave-in, the couple next door violently fighting, a beggar spilling an oil lamp in the alley two blocks over . . .

Could any of these midnight wanderers threaten him? Is such a thing possible? If so, he doesn't see it. And if it was there, he would.

He enters and walks quickly down the hallway. He comes to his door, slips in the metal key, and also wipes his finger along one piece of brown veneer. It grows slightly hot under his touch, recognising him, welcoming him. The door falls open before him.

Voshem looks in at his apartment. The rooms are empty, but he prefers it that way: sometimes he sits back and bathes in the possibilities one could do with such an empty place. He smiles, takes a relieved breath, steps in, and flicks on the light.

It doesn't come on.

He looks at it, confused.

Then the door slams shut behind him.

Voshem whirls around. Though it's dark, he can dimly perceive a black, female-like form standing behind him, her arms long and stringy, her face as blank as a piece of polished stone. One dark, clawed hand digs into the wood of the door, and the thing stands up to its full height, several feet above Voshem's head.

Voshem stares at her. He can't understand it. 'How . . . How . . .'

'How did you not see,' says a soft, cold voice behind him, 'that this was possible?'

He slowly turns. A young man stands in the centre of Voshem's empty apartment. His skin is pale, his hair is dark, and his eyes are like crude oil. His right hand is hidden in the folds of his dark robes, which quiver and quake with the sound of distant cheeping and rustling, like the forest at midnight.

Voshem searches the air for possibilities, and finds that there are none. There are only inevitabilities – which, to his eyes, are almost invisible.

'We watched the Dreyling,' says Nokov, stepping close. 'Saw where he went. And who should come out of that same door but merry old Voshem, who laughed so gaily so many years ago?' Nokov attempts to smile, but it's as if he's not quite sure how to do it. 'From that moment, there were no possibilities, Voshem. Only certainties.'

He steps closer. Voshem realises he has to keep looking up to see Nokov's face, as if he's suddenly terribly, terribly tall.

'I'd ask you where they are,' says Nokov, 'and how to get to them. But I don't need to.'

The stars begin to fail above them.

'Once you dwell within the night,' whispers Nokov's voice, 'it will be as if I've always known.'

The shadows close in like crumbling walls.

'And all your safeguards, which should be almost impossible to penetrate . . .' Nokov's face dissolves into the shadows. 'Well, when I have *your* talents at my disposal – that won't matter at all, will it?'

Darkness fills Voshem's mind.

13.
The Man Without Hope

And Olvos said:
'Nothing is ever truly lost
The world is like the tide
Returning, for an instant, to the place it occupied before
Or leaving that same place once more
Celebrate, then, for what you lose shall be returned
Smile, then, for all good deeds you do shall be visited upon you
Weep, then, for all ills you do shall return to you
Or your children, or your children's children
What is reaped is what is sown.
What is sown is what is reaped.'

— BOOK OF THE RED LOTUS, PART IV, 13.51–13.61

Sigrud pilots the clanking automobile into the hills outside of Bulikov, where the low, rambling forests threaten to overtake the road. Ordinarily such a journey would have taken hours, but there were barely a handful of checkpoints on his way out of the city. It seems Bulikov now uses its roads for transportation, rather than as a security system.

Finally he sees the polis governor's quarters on the hill in the distance, and he's oddly relieved to see it's more or less the same, though the guns on the walls are more advanced than he remembers.

He comes to an intersection and slowly pulls over. The road is dark, abandoned. He remembers what Malwina said: *You'll come to a crossroads, a little winding road leading off to a farm. On the northeast side of the intersection is a copse of trees. There's a ravine on the other side. Pass through that, keep heading east, and you'll come to it. I'll be waiting for you at the tollbooth when you're done.*

But come to what? Some wound in reality itself? He doesn't know. But he steps out of the auto and starts off.

At first this feels like many operations he's done in his time: creeping through the woods with his torch in his hand and the fortifications on his left, guard towers black and skeletal in the night. He comes to the ravine, and he passes over that, and into the woods on the other side. He walks, and walks, and sees no problems, and certainly nothing extraordinary.

But then things feel . . . strange. The space between the trees gets bigger – very slowly, but eventually he notices it. The brush on the ground gets sparser, as if it's been deprived of sunlight. But that shouldn't be, as the trees this high up in the hills should be short, stubby, crinkly things . . .

He looks around, flashes his torch on a few nearby specimens, and sees that the forest is now very different. The trees are now tall and straight. Quite tall, in fact. He looks back, and though he can see the polis governor's quarters in the distance, it feels as if he's passed into someplace very far away.

That is . . . very odd, he thinks. Though perhaps this is a good sign, suggesting he's headed in the right direction.

Sigrud walks on through the woods. The air changes: it grows drier, cooler. The trees continue to get bigger, and bigger, and bigger, though he steadfastly ignores this alteration.

Finally he comes to it.

He had thought that the boundary Malwina mentioned would be subtle, unnoticeable: so many Divine works are invisible tinkerings with all the rules that underpin reality. But what is in front of him is decidedly not invisible, or subtle.

A blank, rough-hewn, black stone wall abruptly splits the woods in two. It is about twelve feet high, too tall for him to climb, continuing north and south as far as he can see. It bears no mark or insignia or suggestion of who made it or why it's here.

Sigrud scratches his chin, thinking. He reflects that this forest could be very similar to the sanctum for the Divine children, in that it might not be a part of normal reality. The idea is not comforting to him.

He walks along the walls, but sees no way in. Finally, reluctantly, he holds the torch under his left arm and pulls the glove off his left hand. The scars on his palm shine in the light. He looks at it, remembering Tavaan's hurt face – *There is something* nasty *living inside you* – and wonders if he really wants to try this.

He sighs, and realises he must try something – even if he has no idea what that something is.

Feeling absurd, he walks up to the wall, holds his breath, and places his left palm against the stone.

He expected (or perhaps hoped for) some burst of energy or Divine ripples in reality – but instead there's nothing. The wall remains the wall, implacable and indifferent, cool to his touch. His hand is just a hand.

Sigrud frowns at his palm, like the scars there might hold instructions as to what he needs to do. But of course they say nothing, just as they have for so much of his life.

He grumbles. He reflects on how this was really a very bad plan; his response to the Divine has always been to hit it with something very durable as hard as he can, preferably in the face – if it has a face.

He slams his hand on the wall, hoping brute force could make a difference. It doesn't. The wall remains solid.

Sigrud sits back and rethinks his approach. He reaches out into the air, concentrates, feeling for it . . .

Then suddenly the sword is in his hand again, the short little golden blade – Flame, they called it. He knows they said it would do nothing against Olvos's works, but perhaps the sword could tell him the nature of the wall. It's the only Divine thing he has access to.

He is immensely loath to test the blade against stone – dulling a good edge is a tremendous sin to Sigrud – so he gently pokes the surface of the wall with the sword. There is no reaction whatsoever, no indication that the two items are in any way Divine. He considers hacking at the wall with the sword, or perhaps testing it on a tree branch – but, again, he can't bring himself to mar the blade.

Growling, he puts the sword away, placing it into that curious pocket of air that seems to be hovering around him. Then he presses his palm against the wall again, hoping in vain that it might do something – but of course it doesn't.

Sigrud stands in the darkness, feeling foolish and frustrated. He knows the seriousness of the predicament, knows that lives rest upon whether or not he succeeds here. But what could they have expected from him? Why send the most primitive creature in their ranks up against what is likely the most advanced being in the world? It was all so idiotic, and now here he is, with a blank wall and a torch and not much else.

Something inside Sigrud begins to simmer and churn. He rubs his mouth with the back of his hand, glaring at the wall. He hates this, despises this – feeling so helpless, unable to affect the lives of those who so desperately need him.

This is what I have always been, he thinks. *A savage alone in the wilderness, fearsome but worthless.*

Sigrud lashes out, striking the wall with his left hand, a blind, stupid gesture of pure frustration. His hand aches with the impact, and he turns away, shaking out the pain. Then he glares back at the wall as if it's muttered a personal insult at him – and stops.

There is a very small crack in the wall. Right where he hit it. The impact mark is slight, like someone threw a pebble at a thick pane of glass – but it's there.

He peers at it. 'How . . . How did I . . .'

A voice behind him: 'What are you doing?'

Sigrud turns, expecting an assault. He reaches for the sword, fumbling at the air, but he can't manage the trick under pressure. Instead he's left facing the intruder – who, now that he sees her, doesn't seem to be intruding at all.

A small, bald, oldish Continental woman sits on a stone bench under the trees, smoking a crude pipe. She's short but broad, bordering on tubby, and she watches him with a look of quiet, detached contentment.

Sigrud sheepishly begins to realise that she might have been sitting there all along, and he simply missed her. (Though a voice in the back of his mind pipes up, saying: *Shouldn't you have smelled her pipe? Noticed its flame? Noticed the bench?*)

Sigrud says, 'What?'

The woman puffs at the pipe. 'What are you doing?'

Sigrud looks at her, looks back at the crack in the wall, and turns back to the woman, mouth open as he wonders what to say.

'It looks,' says the woman, 'like you were hitting the wall.'

'Uh,' says Sigrud.

'Is that what you were doing? Hitting the wall?'

He scratches his neck. 'Yes.'

She nods, as if she's heard of this quaint pastime before. 'Doesn't seem like a very productive activity. But perhaps productivity isn't the point. Is it?'

'Is what?'

'Are you hitting the wall,' says the woman, 'because you *want* something?'

'I . . . suppose.'

'Oh. Well then, no, hitting it doesn't seem productive.' She puffs on her pipe, contemplating the issue. 'At least, not to *me*.'

'Who are you?' says Sigrud.

'I am an old woman,' she says, 'wondering why this big man is out here in the dead of night hitting a wall as if it kissed his mother on the mouth.' She looks at him keenly. 'What are you here for?'

'I . . . I want to get through the wall?'

'Oh.' She sits up. 'Well then. Why didn't you try knocking?'

'Try what?'

'Knocking,' she says, but this time much slower, as if trying to explain a maths problem to a student. Then she points down the wall with the stem of her pipe. 'At the door.'

'There's a door?'

'I hope so. Otherwise something is wrong with my eyes.'

He shines the torch in the direction she was pointing in and sees that, yes, there is indeed a door: a short, round, wooden door, one low enough he'd have to duck to get through.

That is odd, he thinks faintly. *I was sure I looked there and saw only more wall . . .*

Sigrud looks back at the woman. Some part of his mind is vaguely wondering why he doesn't feel pressed to ask her more questions, such as what she's doing here, why she stayed quiet for so long, or how she knew where the door was. But though he wonders these things, he feels a curious but powerful urge to simply accept the woman's presence, much as he would a tree or a rock in this landscape.

'Just . . . knock on the door?' he says.

'It seems easier than knocking on the wall,' she says. 'Less painful. And louder, so someone inside can hear. Come. Let's try it, shall we?'

She hops off the bench and walks with him over to the door. Feeling quite awkward, Sigrud lifts his hand and knocks at the short wooden door three times.

Silence. Nothing.

'Oh,' says the old woman. 'That's right. I forgot. I'm supposed to be over there . . . Whoops! One moment.' She clears her throat, twists the knob, opens the door – Sigrud glimpses nothing more than dark woods on the other side – steps through, and shuts it, leaving Sigrud alone.

Her voice comes floating through the wood of the door: 'All right – try again.'

Sigrud blinks, feeling confused and very stupid. He lifts his hand and again knocks three times.

The door opens just a crack. One bright eye peers out at him. 'Yes?' says the old woman.

'Can I . . . come in?' he asks.

'Why?' demands the old woman. 'Why do you want to come in?'

'I . . .' He awkwardly looks around, like he's worried he might be over-heard. 'I need to speak to Olvos.'

'Is that so?' The eye narrows. 'Why?'

'It's . . . It's a matter of great importance.'

'That is a tremendously subjective term. What would you hope for? What do you hope to accomplish?'

Something in her voice changes. It sounds deeper, more resonant. There's a glimmer of firelight through the crack in the door. And her eye gains a curious orange sheen to it . . .

Things feel strange. Dreamy. Odd. Sigrud blinks, trying to focus. 'We need her help,' he says. 'To save us. To save everything.'

'You say these words,' says the old woman's voice. 'And this might be what you feel obliged or compelled to do. But is this what you *hope* for? If so much were not at stake, would you still be doing it?'

'Are you going to let me in?'

'In the sanctum,' whispers the old woman, 'what did they name you?'

'Name me? What do you mean?'

'They gave you a gift. They made you think of a memory. And in doing so they named you.'

He frowns as he tries to remember. Everything suddenly seems very thick and close and very loud. Thoughts drip through his mind like they're made of molten lead, and his tongue feels swollen and hot. 'They did?'

'That they did. There was a name that went with that memory. What was it?'

'A . . . A refugee,' says Sigrud. 'A lost child.'

'That is what you were,' says the voice. 'But it is not what you are.' The door begins to open. 'Not what you truly are, in your deepest heart. You know that name, mortal creature. You are the man without *hope*.'

The door swings open. There is no one on the other side. All he sees is a small glen. In the centre of the glen is a huge bonfire with four logs serving as benches around it, and beyond that a stone table. Shadows leap and caper in the trees with the flick and flash of the flames.

Sigrud walks in. The door shuts behind him. He barely notices.

He keeps walking toward the fire, drawn to its radiance, its warmth. He must go to the fire, because it's suddenly so cold in here, isn't it? Yes, it is – he can see snowflakes pouring through the trees in the distance, turned into shifting white pillars by the light of the distant moon.

Sigrud steps over one of the log benches and holds his hands out to the fire, eager for warmth. His right hand grows hot, yet he notices his left does not.

A voice echoes through the glen, low and purring and warm, coming from no specific place as much as from everything, as if the glen itself is speaking: 'Welcome, Sigrud je Harkvaldsson. I've looked forward to meeting you for some time – the man who has been touched by darkness twice, the man who lingers without hope. This, I think, will be a most interesting discussion.'

Sigrud looks through the flames and sees there's a woman sitting on the log bench across the bonfire from him. She is short and thick and bald, naked from the waist up, wearing a skirt of firs and nothing else. She smokes an old bone pipe, long and skinny, which she lights by holding it over the fire.

'And it *was* nice of you to knock,' she says. She sniffs and takes a puff from the pipe. 'None of the others did.'

Ivanya Restroyka tries to stifle a yawn as she stares at the mirror before the window. It's a trick Sigrud taught her before he left: you put a light veil over a window, set up a mirror before it at an angle, and that way you can look out the window while making it very hard for anyone outside to see you. Currently the window faces the main path up through the Votrov estate – but this is but one of many ways of accessing the main house, which might be why Ivanya is gripping the rifling in her lap very tightly.

Taty sighs across the room as she reads her book. 'I can't bear it.'

'I know,' says Ivanya.

'What are we waiting for?' she says. 'It's been hours. Will he call? Will he send a messenger? How long should we wait?'

'He said he didn't know. I believe him.'

'Believing him isn't the problem. The problem is that he hardly knows what he's getting into any better than we d –'

She pauses. Ivanya keeps her eye on the mirror, determined not to look away. 'Taty?' she asks.

Silence.

Ivanya looks over her shoulder at the girl. Taty is seated in the chair in the corner, book in her lap, but she's not reading it: she's staring straight ahead, eyes dull, mouth open.

'Taty?' Ivanya says again.

Still nothing. The girl slowly blinks.

'What's wrong? Taty? Say something!' Finally Ivanya stands and walks over to the girl. She kneels before her and shakes her shoulders. 'Are you all right? Taty? Come on now, girl, don't do this to me now . . .'

Taty takes in a rattling breath. Then she softly says, 'Fox in the henhouse . . .'

'Fox? What?'

'There's a fox in the henhouse,' she says again. Another slow blink. Her eyes widen, her pupils dilate, and suddenly Ivanya gets the feeling that Taty is seeing something she herself cannot.

Ivanya's only seen this once before: in the train station in Ahanashtan, right before Taty somehow predicted that they were being watched.

'He's going to get in,' she murmurs slowly. 'He's found a way in. They can't stop him. He's going to gobble them all up.'

'What?' says Ivanya. 'Who? Who's they?'

'And Mother,' Taty whispers. 'Mother . . . She's going to die. She's going to die *again* . . .'

'*What?* Taty . . . Taty, you . . .' Grimacing, Ivanya rears back and slaps the girl. She's not sure if she's doing it to wake Taty up or because she's scared as all hells and wants Taty to stop it.

Taty blinks rapidly, her eyes now focused, and touches her cheek. 'I . . . I . . .'

'Taty,' says Ivanya. 'Can you hear me?'

Taty looks around like she's surprised to find herself here. Then she looks at Ivanya, terrified. 'There's a park!' she says. 'A big park, here in Bulikov! A girl's there, and . . . We have to go there, now!'

'What? What are y —'

'I don't understand it, so don't ask me to explain!' cries Taty. 'Just *listen*! There's some big park, and a tollbooth there, and a girl outside it — we have to go there, to warn them to get them out, *get them out*! They're not safe and he's coming for them and we don't have much *time*, Auntie!'

'A big park? There's so many that could . . .' She pauses. She knows that's not true. There's only one really big park in Bulikov. 'The Seat of the World,' she says. 'But who's there, Taty? Who are we going to try to save?'

'Everyone!' screams Taty. 'All of them! We still have a chance, but we need to go now, now, *now*!'

Deep in the sub-reality of their sanctum, Tavaan walks down the rows of beds, looking out on all her sleeping siblings. Some look peaceful while others look concerned, dreaming with faint expressions of pain on their faces. Tavaan looks at all of them with some sense of wonder — for though she is the Divine spirit of slumber, she herself never truly sleeps, or dreams. Much as a fish does not understand water, Tavaan has no concept of rest.

She walks up to Shara Komayd's overstuffed chair and sees the old woman is awake, sitting slouched with her eyes half-open. She somewhat resents Komayd: it was Komayd's idea to build this place, and while Tavaan is in many ways the god of this sanctum, she is also its prisoner, babysitting her sleeping siblings as well as this half-second of an old woman's life that Malwina has twisted and distorted well past its expiration.

Tavaan watches Komayd for a moment. 'Will it work?' she asks.

Komayd draws a rasping breath. 'Olvos can be unpredictable. But she is also resolute. It will not be easy.'

'Resolute?'

'She is principled,' says Komayd. 'I suppose a god can afford to be principled, if no one else ca – '

Komayd never finishes her sentence. There's a noise from the other side of the huge wooden doors on the far side of the room: a tremendous, dreadful clanking, like some massive machinery has just irreparably broken, gears being stripped and rods snapping in two.

The noise echoes through the room. The sleepers all stir in their beds, shifting and moaning.

Komayd and Tavaan sit still, listening. No other sounds come.

'That doesn't sound right,' says Komayd. 'Is . . . Is that right?'

'No,' says Tavaan quietly. 'It isn't.'

Sigrud looks across the fire at the woman. She is the exact woman who met him outside the walls, yet now she looks strangely different. Besides her change in garb, looking at her feels queerly dizzying, like walking up to the edge of a cliff and looking down.

'You are . . . Olvos?' he says.

She smiles at him. 'I am, dear. Would you like some tobacco? Or some tea?' She gestures at the stone table behind her, on top of which are a number of strange items he can't see well in the firelight.

Sigrud considers the consequences of consuming something offered to him by a Divinity. 'I think I am all right.'

She shrugs. 'Suit yourself.'

'You just let me in? Just like that?'

'What, you thought you'd have to break through every barrier, piece by piece? I suppose you *could* have, if you were willing to spend a few decades at it. Though I *am* impressed. Most intruders never get to the wall. Most never even get to the glades. They get turned away well before that. Yet you barged right in, totally unaware of any hazards.' She glances at him, her bright, copper-coloured eyes shining. 'Curious thing, isn't it? Here. Let me get a look at you. Why don't you come around to my side of the fire? I don't bite, I promise.'

He hesitates.

'I understand your previous interactions with a Divinity have not been positive,' she says kindly, 'but while I am not wholly pleasant, nor kind, I have no ill intentions for you at this palaver, Sigrud je Harkvaldsson.'

Sigrud reluctantly walks around the fire, and though he still doesn't want to sit beside the Divinity, he allows himself to sit on the log to her immediate right.

'You *do* have the look of the kings of old. I remember,' she says. 'Bold and fierce and merciless. Had the life spans of a marsh fly too. Made lots of babies, though only a handful were produced consensually. I'm glad we're *well* clear of those days.'

'Olvos,' says Sigrud, 'I . . . I feel I must tell you the nature of my visit, which is extremely urg – '

She waves a hand. 'Yes, yes, yes. You're here to ask me to wade into your ongoing war and establish peace, yes? Swat your enemies down like flies, yes? I'm aware of all that, and you'll get my answer in due time.'

'You knew why I was coming?'

'Oh, yes,' she says mildly.

'How?'

She looks at him like she's suddenly worried about his intelligence. 'You *know* I'm a Divinity, right?'

'Well, I mean – '

'I keep an eye on things, at a distance,' she says. 'I'm aware of your situation. It also helps that the second you come here you're in my place, in *me*, so I see quite a bit about you.'

'So you know about the children?'

She nods.

'And the enemy . . . He is – '

'You can say his name here,' says Olvos. 'He's not getting in here. Not yet, anyway.'

'Nokov,' says Sigrud. After days of dreading its mention, it's odd to say the name aloud. 'You know of him?'

'I do.'

'But . . . But if you know that, if you know how dire things are, then why haven't y – '

'I told you you'd get my answer in due time,' she says. 'I rather think I hold all the cards in this particular negotiation, dear. Please don't rush. Are you *sure* you don't want any tobacco?'

'No,' says Sigrud, frustrated. 'No, I do not want any tobacco. So my coming here was your intent?'

'Not quite. I've been watching events unfold for a good bit now,' says Olvos. 'And I must admit, things have gone largely the way I expected they would – not exactly utopia, but not another Blink. Not very good, but not very poorly either.'

'If you know about all this,' says Sigrud, 'if you knew all this would happen, then . . . when you met Shara here, after Bulikov . . . why did you not warn her?'

'Why didn't I tell someone that there was a small army of incredibly powerful, very malleable people that could be snatched up at any moment? Why didn't I tell the one person who was about to speed to the top of the government, the one person who had the *one* tool that could control and destroy this army?' She laughs scornfully. 'I did *not* think that would go well.'

'You didn't trust her.'

'Shara is one person,' says Olvos. 'One person who was going to have to engage with many large institutions of people. Not all of whom, as you've learned, are benevolent. I thought it wiser to let things get sorted out on their own, rather than give any ambitious up-and-comers their own little Divine army.'

'And do you think that has gone well?' asks Sigrud.

Olvos is silent. She takes a deep breath and exhales, smoke pouring out of her nostrils. 'Going well or poorly isn't the point,' she says quietly. 'Those are short-term standards for short-term goals.'

'The deaths of so many Divine children? So many people? These are short-term goals?'

She looks at him. For a moment her eyes aren't right: they don't look so much like eyes as distant flames, burning somewhere deep within her face. 'I have been in existence for a very long time. I have seen many horrible things. As much as it grieves me to say it, *yes* – I would permit a few small tragedies to avoid catastrophe. I have sat here and watched many things being woven out in the world, many ways the future could go. I think there is a chance, just a *chance*, that the way of least damage could win out. But it depends on many things. One of which is you.'

'I have done my piece,' says Sigrud. 'I am here speaking with you. The rest depends on you.'

She slowly shakes her head. 'No. You, Sigrud je Harkvaldsson, are a person of – how shall I put this? – great momentum. You do not stop. You *cannot* stop. You bowl forward, charge on, wrecking many things in your path. And now here you come, rolling to my doorstep – but you won't stop here either. You know this. I know this. I have watched you. Very, very closely.'

Something quivers in Sigrud's stomach as he hears this. 'You have watched me?'

'Oh, yes,' she says.

'Why?'

'Because you are a remarkably odd creature, Sigrud. Even if you weren't so intricately wound up in this, I'd still watch you – that's how fascinating you are.'

'What do you mean, "remarkably odd"?'

'Do you even have to ask? You have lived through circumstances almost none could survive. You have conquered things many would consider unconquerable. If this were the old days, and were I to look out on my domain, and see some strange, errant mortal carving a path of destruction through the world such as you do now – do you know what I would think?' Olvos leans close. 'Why, I would think they were touched by the Divine. By another god. A person miraculous or blessed, twisting reality around them as they moved through it. I would be very suspicious indeed of this mortal. *Very* suspicious.'

'I was not touched by a god,' says Sigrud slowly. 'I was tortured with a Divine tool, but no more.'

'Yes, that's true. But can you think, Sigrud,' says Olvos, 'if your torturers ever used that Divine tool again after you overcame it? What was it called, the . . . the . . .' She snaps her fingers.

'The Finger of Kolkan,' says Sigrud.

'Yes, of course. Awful thing. Did you ever see them force other prisoners to hold it after your brutal session? Maybe not. Slondheim was an awful place, a shifting nightmare, and it must be hard to remember how things were. But I don't think you saw it used again – did you?'

He stares into the fire.

'It's almost as if that little stone stopped working,' says Olvos offhandedly. 'Almost as if the miracle that was in it . . . left. But of course this makes one wonder – where did it go?'

Sigrud's left hand is clenched in a trembling fist.

'Such a curiosity, you are,' says Olvos. 'Never directly touched by a Divinity, yet you seem strangely blessed. But – not *quite*. You defy the Divine, you defy death, you defy pain and suffering. That's the cycle of your life, isn't it? You throw yourself into dangerous, hopeless situations. These situations punish you mercilessly. Yet you overcome them, and live. But at the end of it, after all your trials and tests, you are left alone. A lone savage in the wilderness, helpless and frustrated. A creature of powerless power is what you are, strength rendered impotent by rage. And you've lived these past forty years like a man with one foot nailed to the floor, walking forever in circles. That's been the pattern of your life – ever since that stone kissed your palm, that is.'

'What are you saying?' whispers Sigrud.

She smiles. The expression is far from wholly pleasant. 'Do you know, back in the old days, when one of your kind showed up, we all killed it immediately? Me and the rest of the Divinities. We didn't agree on much, but one thing we agreed on was that such things had no right to live. Things like you were too dangerous.' She stares into the fire. 'We did that a lot back then. When something threatened us, we met, held a vote, and usually put it down. Odd how power has that effect on the mind, even the godly mind. Some of those choices I regretted. But for things like you – why, I had no qualms at all.'

'What am I?' says Sigrud softly. 'What are you saying that I am?'

'You, Sigrud je Harkvaldsson,' says Olvos, tapping out her pipe, 'are a man that a miracle mistook for a god.'

Tavaan stands before the huge wooden doors, head cocked, listening. There's silence from the other side, but . . . that tremendous crash and clattering couldn't have been nothing. She places a hand on the doors and shuts her eyes, trying to feel it out.

'What is it?' calls Komayd from the other side of the room.

'I don't know,' says Tavaan. 'I'm working on it.' She searches the many paths and devices that lie outside the doors, all the Divine constructs that, invisibly or otherwise, admit or deter entry.

She feels them falling away, one by one. Someone is blowing through all their security measures as if they were no more than smoke.

They know how to get in, thinks Tavaan. *They knew how to open the hallway. Could it be Voshem? Could he be returning?*

But this troubles her. If it were Voshem, he should have contacted them and told them he was returning. And moreover, why would he be returning unless something was wrong?

Tavaan grits her teeth. She is, in essence, the Divinity of this little piece of sub-reality. Its walls and floors and windows all give to her touch. If she wished, she could bring the ceiling down with but a thought, or make the furniture dance. But despite her control, there are only two means of exit and entry to the sanctum: the doors before her, and the secret exit on the far side.

She looks at the secret exit, thinking long and hard. They've rarely used it, since it's far less protected than the main entrance. She could open it up if she wanted to – but what if this is a feint? What if this is the workings of the enemy, and that's what he *wants* her to do?

'What is it?' asks Komayd. 'What do we do?'

Then the doors start to whine and hum like cages full of nervous birds – which they only ever do if someone new is approaching them, someone who's never been to the sanctum before.

Tavaan turns to look out on the many beds. 'We start waking people up.'

*

Sigrud stares at Olvos, who stuffs her pipe and holds it out among the flames again. He swallows. 'What do you mean?'

'Do you know what a miracle is?' asks Olvos. 'I mean, what one *really* is. Very few do. Most Continentals didn't even know back in the days when the world was practically swimming with them.' She puffs at her pipe. 'It is like a living thing, a tiny, thoughtless Divine creature, working away below reality like a termite under your floorboards. It lives its life in cycles, just as you do. You wake, you eat, you defecate, you sleep, and so on, and so on . . . Just like the flora and fauna of a great forest, the background of the world was once thriving with tiny Divine creatures feeding one another, doing things, making things. But the thing about living things is that they change. Rapidly.'

She stands with a grunt, walks over to the stone table, and begins preparing what looks to be a rudimentary pot of tea. 'We'd see it occasionally,' she says. 'A rogue miracle, one might say. Usually these just showed up as mistakes in reality, sometimes colossal ones. There was one miracle Taalhavras made to create roads, only it got overexcited and overlaid thousands upon millions of roads in *one place*, just a giant tangle of roads hovering in the air. But other times . . . Other times, it was dangerous. Like when a miracle got a hold of a person.'

She walks back over, and delicately hangs the crude pot over the fire. 'What do you know about the Finger of Kolkan?' she asks.

'I know it hurt,' says Sigrud.

'Besides that, I mean.'

'I . . . I think it was a test of some kind.'

'Yes. It was just like most of Kolkan's miracles, which were usually quite punitive. Through pain, through pressure, the miracle was meant to coerce human beings into becoming strong, and pure – but the standards were set so high that no human ever actually *passed* this test. The pain was too much – they either failed, or perished. Until you came along, that is.

'When you touched the stone, Sigrud je Harkvaldsson, it was a curious moment in your life. You hated yourself. You hated your failures, your impetuousness, your brutish thoughtlessness. These things, you felt, had cost you everything. So you did something the Finger of Kolkan did not expect – you *embraced* it. You invited it. You felt you had earned its pain. And in doing so, you defeated it.

'The horrid miracle in that stone was not prepared for this – when Kolkan made it, in his utter ignorance, he did not tell it what to do if a mortal actually passed the test. So the miracle, being small and simple, made an assumption: the being that had just defeated it had to be no one but Kolkan himself. So it *changed*: it migrated to you, thinking you to be its maker. And ever since, it has been bound to you, worshipping you, giving you many things and altering your very reality. And it has changed in turn.'

She sits, reaches out, and snatches Sigrud's left hand. Though he's much larger than her, he finds he can't resist her strength.

She points to his palm. 'Do you see? Do you see this part?' He can't see what she's pointing to, but she keeps talking. 'Punishment. Excoriation. Despair. And through these elements, power. This miracle takes what pain is inflicted upon its bearer, and transmutes this into furious, desperate, righteous anger. A mechanism of terrible retribution. But you knew this already, didn't you?'

Sigrud sits hunched on the log. The warmth of the fire is a distant memory.

The pot of tea begins to bubble. Olvos reaches forward, plucks it off its hanger, and places it on the log beside her. 'Sigrud je Harkvaldsson, you are a person who has held his torments very close to his heart,' she says. 'You believe, somewhere deep inside of you, that such pain gives you power – perhaps the power to inflict a crude justice on the world, retaliation for all the wrongs that have been done to you. From suffering comes might. And the miracle, which slavishly worships you, rewards that hunger for suffering with all the tools it has available. It is trying so very hard to give you what you want. And the miracle will allow *nothing* to violate this – not death, or age, or the Divine itself. The miracle is like a jealous lover, preventing all others from touching you – and you encourage it.'

'You're lying,' says Sigrud softly.

'Am I? How many times have you been injured yet recovered? How many times in your life have you fled civilisation? How many times in your career with Shara did you hide in isolation, drifting at the edges of society? And why do you know how to do a great many nasty things, Sigrud, more than anyone else alive?' She smiles bitterly. 'I know. It is because everyone else *died* learning them. Perhaps it's luck that Shara found you, or maybe it's fate. Working with her put your dark blessing to somewhat good ends. It made you the perfect operative. Such people live very short lives – except for you, of course. What an exception to every rule you are. And at what terrific cost. You survive, yet have no hope. Only torment.'

'It . . . It rewrites reality,' he says quietly, 'to punish me?'

'Yes. That is its nature. That is what it thinks you want. In your secret heart, Sigrud je Harkvaldsson, you think yourself terrible and pure in your despair. You believe you reflect the cruelty of the world back upon it, and you think this just. This dark blessing is simply giving you the fuel you desire.'

There is a long silence.

'Then . . . my daughter, Signe . . . Was her death . . .' He looks at her, trembling. 'Was it natural? Or was it yet more punishment?'

Olvos is quiet. Then she finally rumbles to life, saying, 'It is . . . difficult for me to see that. The miracle often nudges reality very, very slightly. And there were many Divine currents alive and raging in Voortyashtan. But you *feel* it was punishment, don't you? You feel that, because you are a man who has done so many wrongs, it was justice for you to lose the best thing you had ever produced. Don't you?'

Sigrud stands. He's too furious to do the trick with the sword, so instead he pulls out his knife. He holds it just above his left wrist, which he extends above the fire. 'I'll . . . I'll cut it off!' he snarls. 'I'll cut it off and be done with it!'

Olvos shrugs. 'Then do so.'

Sigrud lowers the knife. He grits his teeth, readying for the blade to bite into his flesh, to saw at the bone – yet he hesitates.

'You can't do it,' says Olvos. 'The miracle will not be gotten rid of that way.'

Sigrud shuts his eyes, weeping. 'I'll do it. I will. I will!'

'You won't,' she says. 'This is not a matter that will be resolved with the marring of flesh. You are a creature of constant warfare, Sigrud. You have made a weapon of your sorrow. You have put this weapon to terrible use for many, many years. Only when you set it aside will this miracle release you. Only then will you have any chance of freedom. Freedom to live and die as a normal, mortal man.'

Sigrud bows his head and lowers the knife. 'So until then . . . I am cursed to keep living, keep suffering.'

'Probably. You are very hard to kill, Sigrud. You can take abominable punishment. But you are *not* immortal. If you were to, say, jump off a cliff, or catch a bullet in your skull, I doubt the miracle could do much to save you. And a true Divinity could kill you if they really wanted to. I could do it now, for example. But I won't. I try very hard not to intervene in such things. It's not prudent, not anymore.'

'Can you remove the miracle?' he asks.

She glances at him. 'I could.'

'Then . . . will you?'

She lifts her pot of tea and takes a long slurp. 'I just said why I would not. Because my interference is not prudent.'

'Not . . . Not prudent?' says Sigrud. 'Not *prudent*? This, this curse is ruining my life, destroying me! Will you not give me aid, will you not save me?'

'No,' she says firmly. 'No, I will not. You are asking a very dangerous thing of me, Sigrud. For me to flex my Divine will is no small thing. It would make me vulnerable to a number of mortal influences. When I intrude into the world, when people notice me, pay attention to me, believe in me, I . . . change. Shift. Conform to their beliefs. That is extraordinarily, extraordinarily dangerous, especially right now. One sole Divinity on the Continent, with nothing to keep me in check? I won't allow that. That is why I left the mortal world in the first place.'

'But it is just one little miracle,' says Sigrud. 'Surely it would be no more than swatting a fly?'

'To destroy the work of another Divinity takes great effort,' says Olvos. 'Almost as much work as it would take to harm or even destroy another Divinity. And the greater the effort, the more vulnerable I become.' She slowly looks up at him. 'And that is partly why I will *not* intervene to help Shara and Malwina.'

It takes him a moment to process what she said. 'What?' he asks.

Olvos sips at her cup of tea again.

'You will not help?' he asks. 'You won't fight him?'

'No,' she says. 'No. I will not.'

'But . . . But he's killing them,' says Sigrud. 'Nokov wishes to *destroy* them. He wishes to, to bring final night to all the world!'

'I know that,' says Olvos softly. 'He's done horrible things. Many, many horrible things. And I've told you one reason why I will not intervene. But you of all people should understand the other.' Her orange-red eyes are wide and sad. 'You've lost a child. Even if they had done horrible things – could you bear to take your child in your own hands, and destroy them yourself?'

Sigrud stares at her. 'You . . . You mean . . .'

She sighs deeply, and suddenly she looks very old and tired. 'Yes,' she says. 'He is my son. Nokov is my son.'

Ivanya tries to focus as she pilots her auto through the streets of Bulikov. She hasn't driven in the city in years, so she jumps the occasional curb. Taty sits beside her in the passenger seat, grimly staring ahead.

Every block or so, Ivanya asks the same question – 'You're sure?'

Every time, Taty gives the same answer – 'No. But I know it's true.'

Finally they come to the Seat of the World. It's a mostly empty space, as the original temple was completely destroyed in the Battle of Bulikov, and the remaining park stands as a monument to the tragedy.

Taty and Ivanya park and climb out. 'Where?' asks Ivanya. 'What do we do now?'

'This is it,' Taty says, staring around herself. 'This is what I saw, just for a moment. But I'm looking at it from the wrong angle. It was . . .' She spies something, some landmark, and her eyes light up. 'There! Over there! To the right of that tree, I'm sure of it!'

They sprint off, running through the park, dashing over the concrete paths until finally, just ahead, they see a small, shabby, abandoned toll-booth. Someone is standing outside it, hands and face buried deep in their coat, and they keep glancing over their shoulder at the two women running over.

As they get closer, Ivanya's mouth drops open. Because the person standing outside the tollbooth is Taty.

Well, not quite – this girl isn't as well fed and her hair is longer, though it's stuffed up under a boyish cap, and she has an angry look on her face that looks somewhat permanent. But her face, her mouth, her size . . . all of it is so much like Tatyana it's dumbfounding.

Ivanya stops walking. 'What in *hells*,' she gasps.

'What?' says Taty. 'What is it?' Then she looks up and sees. 'Oh . . . *Oh*. Ohhh, my goodness . . .'

The girl glances sideways at them suspiciously, then turns away, as if trying to avoid attention. Taty simply stares at her, thunderstruck by the sight of this girl.

'Hey!' shouts Ivanya. 'You! Hey, you!' She struggles in vain to recall the girl's name, then blurts, '*Malwina Gogacz!*'

The girl freezes. Ivanya can tell she's debating whether or not to run.

'You're in danger!' says Ivanya. She glances at Taty, wishing she would say something, but she's still staring at the other girl, openmouthed.

The girl turns around, eyeing them suspiciously as they stagger up. 'What? Who in hells are you? What are you talking ab – ' Then she sees Taty. Her jaw drops. 'What the fuck?' she says softly.

The two girls stare at each other with expressions of faint horror for a very long time.

'It's . . . It's like looking in a carnival mirror,' says Taty softly.

'Enough,' says Ivanya. 'Tell her what you told me.'

Taty licks her lips. 'He's . . . He's going to get in,' she says. 'He's going to get into your place you made, and kill all of you, *all* of you. And Mother.'

Malwina goes pale. 'How did you . . . You can't be serious . . .'

'We are,' says Ivanya.

'That can't be right, that *can't* be,' says Malwina. 'He can't . . . Wait. "Mother"? Who?'

'Komayd,' says Ivanya. 'This is Tatyana Komayd.'

Malwina's eyes couldn't possibly go any wider. She steps back and rubs her temples as she tries to take all this in. 'This is . . . This is all too much . . . How do you know that? How do you *look* like me?' She keeps rubbing the sides of her head as if the sight of Taty has stupefied her.

'What do we do?' asks Ivanya.

Malwina keeps rubbing her head. She looks like she's about to be ill.

'*Well?*' says Ivanya.

Nothing still.

Ivanya stamps her foot. 'Listen, you,' she snaps. 'I've got no idea what in hells is going on here, but I *know* you. You were a patron of my organisations for years. I've probably personally paid for your trousers and your bed and your meals and your damned toilet paper *dozens* of times over. So as bewildering as all this is, you *owe* me. Why don't you return the favour and focus a bit, and do whatever it is we need to do to start saving some damned lives, eh?'

Malwina shakes herself. 'How can she know that we're all in danger? I mean, how?'

'She just does,' says Ivanya. 'Apparently. Trust us on this.'

Malwina's eyes dance around as she thinks. 'We could go in the back way. It's dangerous, I don't want to draw attention to it, but . . . There's no other choice.' She sighs. 'Fuck it. Let's go.'

'Go where?' says Taty.

'Don't you know?'

'Not . . . not *really* . . .'

Malwina points at the tollbooth. 'In there. Come on. Are you with Sigrud? Is that what this is?'

'Something like that,' says Ivanya.

'Well. I hope you have some experience with the Divine. If not, this is going to be really weird for you.'

'This is already pretty weird for us,' mutters Ivanya as they walk into the tollbooth.

They keep walking. It takes Ivanya a moment to realise they seem to be walking far farther than they ought to be – the tollbooth was only six or so feet wide, wasn't it?

Then she sees it ahead. A small square of blue light, not the right size for a door. But beyond it are . . .

Beds. And windows. A huge, grand room that just seems to be hanging there, suspended in the darkness.

'Okay,' Ivanya says. 'That's weird.'

Tavaan feels it before it happens. With her eyes shut and her hand on the door, she feels it flying up the stairs outside, hurtling through the air, rocketing toward the doors with all its strength . . .

The boom is like a crack of thunder. The force of the blow reverberates all the way up Tavaan's arms and into her shoulders. She doesn't need to see the doors to know they were nearly blown off their hinges.

'Shit,' she says quietly. She opens her eyes. '*Shit.*'

She can hear the sleepers muttering behind her, the ones farthest from the door sitting up and rubbing their eyes. Being lifted from such deep sleep is no easy thing, and she could help them return to full consciousness – but she knows she won't have the energy to spare, not now.

She summons up all of her strength and presses against the doors, holding them in place. She does it just in time, as the second blow comes hurtling at her even stronger than the first.

The doors crack and splinter, very slightly. Tavaan focuses, using all of her mind to keep them whole. But she knows it won't last.

It's him. He's here. And he's stronger than I ever imagined.

'Can you imagine what it's like?' asks Olvos. 'To watch from a distance as your son drifts from family to family. To watch him get captured, tortured, driven mad. To watch him escape through murder and bloodshed, and go on to do terrible, awful things . . .?'

'But you could have stopped him,' says Sigrud. 'You could ha –'

She turns to him, eyes burning and fierce. 'Look at me. Look at me *now*. Look upon the burdens of power. Imagine what it's like to know that if you flexed your will and saved your child, then the belief of this Continent might drive you mad, and so much *more* would be lost. Power corrupts, Sigrud. It has its own gravity. The only thing you can do is disperse it or isolate it. That's what I've tried to do for so many years. If things go right tonight you will know this full well. But oh, you mortal man . . .' Olvos shakes her head. 'You cannot know how I despise myself. Both for what I am, and for what I'm forced to do.' She wipes her eyes. 'It'll be over soon, though. For me at least.'

'What do you mean?' asks Sigrud.

She keeps talking as if she didn't hear him. 'The last night of hope. It's been long coming, and long deserved. But such a thought is no solace to me, though, not really.' She shuts her eyes. 'Not since I know what Nokov is about to do.'

*

When Ivanya, Taty, and Malwina all walk into the giant room of beds through what appears to be a large fireplace, Ivanya notices two things right away.

The first thing she notices is the tremendous rumbling and clanging coming from one side of the room, where there are two large wooden doors that seem to be trembling like they're in an earthquake. There's a small girl standing before them, dressed in sleeping clothes and with a shaved head, her hands pressed against the doors like she's desperately trying to keep them shut – but it's clear it's a losing battle.

The second thing Ivanya notices is that there are people in all the beds in the room, all very young people, and several are stirring and sitting up with an air of a drugged person trying to remember where all their limbs are.

Malwina looks to the doors. Her face goes from pale to a light green colour. 'Tavaan!' she cries. 'What's wrong? What's going o – '

The girl at the door shouts over her shoulder, 'Malwina! Get them out, get them out, *get them out*! He's here, he's coming through!'

'*What!*' screams Malwina. 'He's here? I'll help you!' She starts running over to the doors, but she halts in midair, as if she just slammed into an invisible wall.

'No!' cries the girl at the doors. 'I won't let you closer! I can't hold him for long, just get them out, get them out of here!'

'Tavaan!' cries Malwina. 'Please, I can help y – '

There's another blow to the doors, which almost seem to shatter, though some invisible force shoves them back together. '*Do as I say, damn you!*' bellows the girl at the door. Her voice seems to come from everywhere in this place, from the stones and the beds. '*Get them out!*'

Malwina falls to the floor, shaken. She begins blinking rapidly. Her face stays stoic, but tears start falling from her eyes. She stands and turns to Ivanya and Taty. 'You, and you,' she says, her voice shaking. 'Get these kids up and get them over to the door. *Now.*'

Ivanya sprints over to the closest bed, where a young boy of about twelve with curiously scaly skin is rubbing his eyes in a stupor. She doesn't bother introducing herself: she just grabs his arms, drags him out of bed – muttering as she does, 'You are a *lot* heavier than a sheep' – and trots over to the fireplace, where she dumps him down like a sack of flour. She looks to Taty, who's still dumbfounded by the sight before her. 'Taty! Focus and *help* me, now!'

Taty shakes herself and goes to the next bed with Ivanya, while Malwina hauls one of the drowsy children out of bed like someone trying to get drunken friends home from the bar.

Another crash, another bang. The doors tremble. There's an awful sound coming from the other side, the sound of creaking trees and cheeping insects and a high, cold wind. Ivanya's not sure why, but she begins to feel like she's lost somewhere deep and dark, waiting for morning . . .

It's him, isn't it, she realises. *The thing Sigrud's been fighting all this time.*

She shakes herself as they haul another child out of bed. As they carry the child away they walk by a chair, which is strangely out of place in this odd room: it's tattered and overstuffed, and it sits with its back to them, facing the windows, like a chair at a convalescent home.

As they round the side of the chair, she sees it's occupied.

And it appears to be occupied by a dead woman. Or, at least a woman who *should* be dead.

Ivanya gasps and nearly drops the sleeping child. In the chair sits an ill-looking Shara Komayd, craning her head around the other side of the chair so she can see the doors better. She seems wholly unaware that there are two people in front of her, and only turns around when Ivanya gasps. She blinks owlishly at the two of them. Then her mouth drops open.

'Oh, no,' she says. '*Taty?*'

Tatyana Komayd stares at her. 'Mother? Mother! You . . . You . . . You're *alive*? You're really *alive*?' She drops the child's feet and almost bursts into laughter. 'I *knew* it! I don't know how but I knew it, I knew it, I *knew* it!'

Shara tries to stand, but she doesn't seem to have much strength. She swallows, panicked. 'You can't be here, dear, you *can't*! Not here, not now! He's coming through, he'll kill you! You're not safe here!'

Ivanya looks up at the doors, which shudder again with another fierce blow. 'I'm starting to think,' she says, 'that we might have gotten here too late.'

*

Tavaan's arms and legs scream in pain as she tries to hold the doors up. *How many more blows can I withstand?* she thinks. *One? Two? No more than that, certainly.*

Her ears are filled with the sounds of night: the crackle of leaves under invisible feet, the soft cry of distant birds, the shifting of tall grasses. It's hard to focus now. She uses all of her power to survey the sleeping children behind her.

Twelve awake, only twelve. The rest still struggle to rise from their slumber, the one she herself placed them in.

How did it go so wrong? How did he get in? How did we let it all come to this?

Another blow. Tavaan is knocked back from the doors and sent sprawling onto the stones. The doors break open the slightest bit.

'No!' she screams. She makes the floor come rising up, shooting her back at the doors, slamming them shut and forcing all the pieces to stay where they are.

Twelve awake. And Malwina, Komayd, and the newcomers.

She grits her teeth in rage and despair. Tears fall from her eyes and patter onto the stones.

What a damnable choice to make, she thinks, *and what a damnable end this is*.

Tavaan focuses her energy, takes a breath, and screams.

Ivanya, Shara, and Taty all jump when the girl at the doors begins screaming. 'What in the world?' says Ivanya, but she doesn't have time for another thought, because then Shara's chair begins moving of its own accord, sliding toward the fireplace and scooping up Ivanya and Taty with it, who both fall on Shara with a *thump*.

Ivanya cries out in surprise, but she sees the chair isn't the only thing moving in the room: all the beds bearing children near the fireplace are drifting toward the exit as well, as if the whole room has been tilted up, dumping the furniture to that one corner, and taking Malwina with it.

As they slide toward the exit, Ivanya can't help but notice that many beds are staying still. These seem to contain children who are still asleep – so it's only the ones who are awake who are moving.

Ivanya thinks, *But what will happen to the others?*

She doesn't have time to wonder, because the next thing she knows, the chair is dumping her and Taty and Shara out through the fireplace, sending them tumbling down the strange passageway, back through to the tollbooth, until . . .

Ivanya lands on the grass outside the tollbooth, followed by Taty and Shara, who each land on top of her, knocking the breath from her. They roll to the side just as a handful of children come tumbling out, all of them ones they managed to waken.

Malwina refuses to stay down. The instant she strikes the ground she rises back up and staggers back toward the passageway, seeming to fight against an invisible wind. 'No!' she cries down the passageway. 'I won't let you! Not like this, *not like this*!'

Ivanya can still see the distant blue square of the fireplace entrance down the passageway. The light within seems to quiver, like a candle flame brushed by the breeze. Ivanya isn't sure how she knows this, but she can tell that something is leaking into the distant room, flooding into it like poisonous gas through the frame of a door, something invisible and terrible . . .

A screaming voice comes echoing down the passageway: '*Tulvos! I love y—*'

There's a tremendous crash. The distant room floods with shadow. Then comes a horrible sound, a sound that carves itself into Ivanya's mind: the sound of dozens of children all crying out at once.

The passageway goes dark. The screams are cut short. Malwina is blown backward like ten tons of explosives have gone off in her face, and she lands on a heap in the grass.

Then there's silence.

Malwina coughs, then claws herself to her feet. 'No,' she whispers. 'No, no!' She runs back to the tollbooth, but is dumbfounded to find it is only four blank, wooden walls – no more, no less. 'No!' she screams. 'No, no, no!'

She begins hammering on the walls of the tollbooth, sobbing hysterically. Ivanya rises and physically restrains her, pinning the girl's arms to her sides. 'Stop,' says Ivanya, firmly but gently.

'She shut the door!' screams Malwina. 'She dumped us out and shut the door and trapped him in there with her!'

'Stop,' says Ivanya again.

Malwina keeps struggling. 'I have to go back! I have to help her! I have to, I *have* to!'

'*Stop*. You'll hurt yourself.'

'Shut up!' cries Malwina. 'Shut your mouth, shut your fucking mouth!' She kicks at the walls once, twice. 'Let me go, let me go! Let me go, let me go, let me go!' Then she dissolves into tears.

Everyone sits in silence, trying to understand exactly what happened.

'M-Mother?' asks Taty, sitting up. 'Are you all right? Are you . . . Are you really *alive*?'

Shara snaps up into a sitting position with a surprising amount of strength. Then she grabs Taty's arms and pulls them towards her, frantically looking at her wrists, her arms, her neck and face. 'Are you all right?' Shara says. 'Are you hurt? Taty, tell me, *are you hurt*?'

'Mother, stop!' says Taty. 'I'm fine, I'm fine! I should be asking you if *you're* hurt, since you're the one who di – '

Taty never gets to finish her sentence, because then Shara throws her arms around her, hugs her tight, and bursts into tears. 'I never thought I'd see you again,' she whispers. 'I never, never, *never* thought I'd see you again.' Even though she's weeping, her arms don't stop searching Taty's back and neck, still seeking any hidden injury.

'I'm fine,' says Taty, who sounds torn between terror and bewilderment. 'But . . . But what just happened?'

One of the children, a boy of about fifteen, stands and walks to the toll-booth door. 'Malwina?' he says. 'What's going on? We were asleep, and then . . . And then he was coming . . .'

'What's going on?' says Malwina savagely. '*What's going on?*' She makes a noise that's halfway between a sob and a laugh. 'We fucking *lost* is what's going on! We lost! He got everyone else, *everyone else*!'

'What do you mean?' asks the boy. 'What . . . What do we do now?'

'What do we do? There's nothing *to* do,' says Malwina. 'Don't you see? We're the only ones left now.' She blinks as if realising what she just said. Then, quieter, 'We're the only ones left.'

*

Alone in the little room, mighty Nokov eats his fill. He eats greedily, lustily, with a fervour he's never known before. To think he'd ever have such a victory, such a complete and total victory, with hundreds of his siblings laid out at his feet . . .

He grows and grows and grows. With each death, a new domain. With each new domain, a greater power.

Nokov changes.

He is a serpent, vast and terrible.

He is a great raven, his wings made of purest night.

He is a long, lean wolf, whose jaws devour light and life itself.

He is a tremendous volcano, pouring ash into the dawning sky.

He is many things, many ideas, many concepts all merged into one, all lost within the night.

Nokov eats. His hunger is insatiable and his vengeance merciless.

All your happy lives, he thinks as he pounces from bed to bed. *All your days free of torment. I will show you what they showed me. I will share with you my pain.*

When the last whimpering child vanishes into the endless abyss of the first night, he finds he is still not full, still not complete.

He needs more. He must have more.

He hears footsteps behind him. He turns around, which takes some time – he is no mere child anymore, but a creature of terrible, rippling bulk. He sees his servant at the door, his distorted seneschal.

'Silence,' he says to her. 'We have won. We have won, Silence, we have won.'

There is a rippling silence in the room, and with it comes the words:

<he has moved sir he is gone sir sir sir he is gone he has left>

It takes him a moment to realise what she means. Then he understands – the *dauvkind*. He came here, that Nokov knows – he sensed the taint in the man's body, felt its shadow dwell here. But where is he now?

Nokov reaches out, rifling the darkness for the man's scent. Finally he finds it.

If Nokov still had lungs – and he never did, but he certainly doesn't now – he would gasp.

Because the *dauvkind* now stands in a place Nokov himself could never find, never penetrate, never see. Yet now it seems Nokov is strong and great enough to do so.

And perhaps, he thinks, standing straight and tall until his head touches the ceiling, *great enough to challenge her.*

14.
The Twilight of the Divine

I keep coming back to Voortya, and her afterlife. It seems a running theme in this world that a Divinity must defeat themselves in order to accomplish something great and beautiful.

Death, as you know, had to die to understand death. War had to lose in order to understand victory.

If Kolkan had been punished, and confessed, would he have been different?

If Olvos had lost hope, and despaired, would she have been different?

— FORMER PRIME MINISTER ASHARA KOMAYD, LETTER TO UPPER PARLIAMENT HOUSE MINORITY LEADER TURYIN MULAGHESH, 1734

Olvos opens her eyes. 'There,' she whispers. 'It's done.'

'What's done?' says Sigrud.

'The last stages of the end,' says Olvos hoarsely. 'You and I, Sigrud, you and I and Shara, we all have a part to play in this. In what began when the Kaj first crossed the South Seas and made war upon these lands. Saypur thought that was the end, but it was just the beginning of the end. The first hour, perhaps, of our twilight.'

'What do you mean?' asks Sigrud, now anxious. 'What . . . What has happened?'

'Your sword,' she says. 'Flame. Can you still find it?'

Sigrud fumbles for it, focuses, then grabs it in the air. It's there still, waiting in the space before him, and though it feels firm in his fingers he notes the blade is now queerly insubstantial, as if it were but a piece of golden tulle.

'What's wrong with it?' he says.

'Most of the people who made it are now gone,' says Olvos. 'It is just a shadow of what it once was.'

He stares at the blade. Then he slowly puts it away and turns to look at her. 'Gone? What do you mean?'

Olvos bows her head.

'What . . . What are you saying?' he asks, horrified.

'That's the problem with a power vacuum,' she says, smiling sadly. 'Something must swell to fill the gap. It's . . . It's just nature, I suppose. But though one may weep, one can't fight nature.'

'They're gone?' he asks. 'The children? They're really gone? He's . . . He's won?'

She does not answer.

'And this . . . This is how you justify your cowardice?' he says. 'With talk of nature? This is how you rationalise allowing *children* to be lost to the most dangerous thing walking this earth, the thing that wishes to devour the world?'

'Nokov is not the most dangerous thing walking this earth,' says Olvos. 'He never was. None of the six Divinities ever were. That title is reserved for a player who has yet to make their appearance. Though you will come to know them in due time.' She stands and looks down at him, and once again her eyes are like distant flames. 'Listen to me, Sigrud. Do you hear me?'

'I wish I did not,' says Sigrud bitterly. 'Such is my disgust for you.'

'Your disgust is well earned,' says Olvos. 'And I share it. But listen – this was born in blood. It always was. It was born in conquest, born in power, born in righteous vengeance. And that is how it means to end. This is a cycle, repeating itself over and over again, just as your life repeats itself over and over again. We must break that cycle. We *must*. Or else we doom future generations to follow in our footsteps.' She stabs a finger out at him. 'You have a choice, a choice I never did. You have a choice to be *different*. You, who have defeated many by strength of arms, you will have a moment when you can choose to do as you have always done, or you can choose to do something new. You, a man who has never forgiven himself, who believes he deserves all his ills, you will have a moment to reconsider. And in that moment, the world will teeter upon a blade of grass, and all will be decided thereafter. Walk it carefully.'

'What are you talking ab –'

She cocks her head as if she hears something, though Sigrud's ears catch nothing but the crackle of the fire and the sigh of the snowflakes.

'He comes,' she says, her voice low and full of dread. 'He comes to me now, my prodigal son.' She smiles slightly. 'What is reaped is what is sown. And what is sown is what is reaped. You must go, Sigrud. Soon he will be here, and he cannot find you. Soon the walls will grow and the dawn will be threatened. And time, as always, will remain our deadliest foe.'

Sigrud stands. He sees her jaw is trembling. To see a god so anxious fills him with terror. She notices his glance, and smiles and reaches out to touch his face, a strangely reassuring gesture. 'Quiet now, child. All things end. Just as the stars fade and mountains fall, all things end. But that does not mean there is no hope.'

'What is it you wish me to do?' asks Sigrud. 'What is there to do?'

'Fight, of course. And, if we have luck, live.' Her smile fades, and hot tears spill out to hiss upon the ground below. 'When it comes to it, when you have that chance . . . please don't hurt her. She didn't deserve what we did to her. And she loves you so. Please be there for her when she needs you to be, as I never was.'

'Who do you mean?' asks Sigrud. 'Why must you speak in riddles?'

Olvos points over her shoulder. 'There,' she says. 'Your auto.'

He turns to look. He sees she's right: his automobile is just behind him, parked next to the road – but wasn't the wall there just a bit ago?

He turns back only to find she's gone: he's standing on the grass beneath the trees, facing the dark forest below the polis governor's quarters. There is no bonfire, no walls, no sight of Olvos.

Sigrud looks around, seeking any sight of the Divine, anything that could possibly suggest this last interaction really happened. But there is nothing. He is alone.

Nearly all the children are gone? Can she be right? He feels a Divinity is probably a reliable source, but . . . What about Malwina? Tavaan? And Shara? Could he have lost her again?

He climbs into his auto, starts it up, and begins the short journey back to Bulikov.

*

He comes to her like a thunderstorm, like a pack of wolves charging through the forest, like a great, dark wave pouring up on to the shore. Her barriers and protections are nothing to him, mere spiderwebs he can bat aside with but a flick of his hand. He is drawn to her, he finds, drawn to her light, drawn to the shadows dancing around the bonfire.

How he despises those who have the light, who enjoy the warmth. How he despises her.

He leaps forth from the shadows and stands at the edge of the bonfire, tall and proud and regal. A child no longer, certainly not. He stares down at her, smiling, waiting for her glance to fall upon his form – her eyes will widen, surely, and she will be overcome with awe and terror, and beg forgiveness . . .

But Olvos does not do this. She just sits at the edge of the fire, lights her pipe, and puffs at it.

'Hello, Nokov,' she says absently, as if he just walked in. 'I see you're still struggling with the idea of doors.'

Nokov's smile turns into a scowl. He walks closer to his mother, his footfalls heavy on the earth. He walks over to the fire to show her what he can do, to show her how the light means nothing to him anymore – but she still doesn't look at him, doesn't behold the wonder of his presence. She just keeps fiddling with her pipe.

'Look at me,' he says.

She glances up at him. She meets his dark gaze for but a second, her fiery eye blazing bright.

'*Look* at me!' he snarls.

She sighs slightly, then sits up straight and faces him. Her face does not fill with awe and horror as he wished; instead there is only a contemptuous resignation.

'Do you see me?' he asks. He tries to smile. 'Do you see?'

'I see you full well, Nokov,' says Olvos.

'Do you see how strong I am? Do you see how I have conquered? Do you see how I have grown mighty?'

Olvos says nothing.

'I did this *without* you,' he says. 'Just as I have lived my whole life – without you. I found a way to survive, to grow strong, to prosper, all without you.'

'It seems sad to live one's life,' says Olvos, 'defined by the absence of another.'

Nokov is speechless for a moment. 'Sad?' he says, furious. '*Sad?*'

'Yes,' says Olvos. 'I think so.'

'How sad it was when they captured me,' he snarls. 'How *sad* it was when they *tortured* me! For days, for months, for years! I don't even know how long it was. And you, a Divinity, a god who could hold the whole of the world in her hand if she wished – you did nothing to help me. *Nothing*. If I were to choose a word for this, it would *not* be "sad", oh, no.'

'If I said I was sorry,' says Olvos softly, 'would that mean anything?'

Nokov pauses. 'W-What?'

'If I said I was sorry. Would that mean anything?'

'Sorry? Could . . . Could that mean anything to *what?*'

She shrugs. 'To you. To everything, I suppose.'

Something hisses on the ground at her feet. It takes Nokov a moment to realise they're tears.

Olvos, to his disbelief, is weeping.

The sight of his mother crying fills him with confusion. He wished for his mother to be haughty and proud, or perhaps cowardly and quailing, but . . . but, perversely, he did not wish her to weep so.

'Your . . . Your tears mean nothing to me,' he says. His voice shakes. 'You were gone from my life well before the Kaj. You were gone from *all* our lives, long before then. You left us.'

'I had to,' says Olvos. 'I knew how this would end.'

'You could have taken us *with* you!'

'Could I have?' she says. The pipe is trembling in her hands. 'Could I? I wasn't sure . . .'

'You should have tried!' says Nokov. 'You could have at least *tried.*'

'Do you know what I was trying to avoid, Nokov?' asks Olvos. 'Do you know what I feared most, my child?'

'The Kaj,' says Nokov. 'The purge. The Blink.'

'No. I feared what power would do to me. I feared it would change me. I feared it would make me dangerous.' She looks up at him. 'I feared, my son, that I would become what you are now.'

Nokov hesitates, confused. 'Mighty,' he says. 'You feared strength.'

'No,' says Olvos. 'I feared being *alone*. To be the *one* Divine thing, with all the beliefs of all mortals leaning upon me . . . I knew that would be unbalanced, and unwise. A lone celestial body, spinning out of its orbit . . . The damage would be catastrophic. But I know a way out. For you. And for me.'

'Do you.'

'Yes. So now I ask you, Nokov – will you let me give you what you've wanted most of all for these long years?'

He is silent.

'I will give you myself,' says Olvos. 'I will be here with you, mother and son, forever. We will be together forever. But you must stay here with me. You and I, the two strongest Divine creatures in this world, we must stay here, alone, isolated. We must not allow ourselves to spill into the world. We *must* not.'

She looks at him, her eyes wet with tears. But her words echo in his ears, and he begins trembling with fury.

'You . . .' he whispers. 'You want to *trap* me.'

'No!' she says, alarmed.

'You want to put me in a box,' he says. 'To stuff me in a box out here, all alone!'

'No, I don't! Nokov, Nokov, I don't!'

His face twists in anguish. 'You're just like her . . . Why are you people *like* this? What did I *do* to you?'

'I am trying to help you!'

'*That's what she said!*' He rises up, a vast, dark spike shooting into the sky. '*That's what she said to me before she trapped me! And look at me now, look at me now!*'

Olvos pauses, stunned, then bows her head in defeat.

Nokov looks down at her. 'To be alone,' he says. 'That is a thing I have *always* known. Whatever madness this world could do to me, Mother – it won't be anything I haven't already seen.'

'It breaks my heart,' says Olvos, 'to see what all this has come to.'

'A chance to begin again,' says Nokov. 'A chance to start over bright and fresh and anew.'

'No,' says Olvos. 'No, it will not be that. You are doing nothing new here, my child.'

He cranes his head down to look at her. 'What do you mean?'

'I mean I think this is not the first time this has happened,' she says. 'Not by far. Imagine this, child – a world is born, and mortals and Divinities are born into it. Some mortals get access to the gods, others don't. Conquest begins, enslavement, until there is a great war, and someone finds a way to slay the gods. The old Divinities are overthrown, and their children inherit the world – and rewrite it. They erase reality and rewrite it, birthing a new world, with new mortals, new gods, new origins, new conquests, and new wars. The old ways and the old gods are forgotten, as if they'd never happened. The world doesn't even remember they were ever alive. And it all starts all over again.'

Nokov is grave and silent for a moment. 'I don't believe you.'

She shrugs. 'It is what I believe. Believe what you like.'

'You're saying you . . . That you had . . .'

'Do you know what they say of Olvos?' she says softly. 'They say she was born when all the dark of the world became too heavy, and scraped against itself, and made a spark – and that spark was she. She was here from the beginning of this world.' She shuts her eyes. 'She and her siblings, perhaps. And then the mortals changed what they believed, and she listened and overwrote her own reality, and forgot it.' She looks up at Nokov. 'You are here to do, my son, what I suspect I myself once did long, long ago. To overthrow your parents. To take power from them and make your own world. You and I are just separate incarnations of this long dance, child. There have always been Divinities. Always been mortals. Always been slavery and war and revolution. There is blood upon your hands, just as there is on mine – the only difference is that you will remember it.'

Nokov strides forward through the fire, the flames licking his black skin. 'I will be *different*.'

'How many tragedies follow those words,' says Olvos quietly.

'Shut up. Shut up! *Shut up!* You're using me, you're just *tricking* me, just like *she* did! You're just like her. *Just* like her.'

Olvos takes a deep breath and sets her pipe down beside her on the log. 'Perhaps you're right, dear,' she says wearily. 'But now you must ask yourself the hardest question.'

Nokov is breathing hard. 'And what is that?' he says.

She smiles at him, tears upon her cheeks. 'Will that make what you're about to do any easier?'

Nokov shuts his eyes, twists up his face. He doesn't want to cry now, not during his greatest triumph.

He desperately shouts, 'Yes!' and springs on her.

When he's finished, when she's still and cold and he's dragged her into the first night, he realises that though she looked like a small woman by her campfire, she was much, much, *much* more powerful than he ever knew. More powerful than he could have ever understood.

She could have struck him down where he stood. She could have killed him in an instant. Yet she didn't.

He wonders why she didn't. He can't understand why she didn't.

Ivanya Restroyka feels a little ridiculous as she makes four pots of tea for her guests. It's not that she's unused to making a lot of tea for company. It's just that she never expected to be entertaining a bunch of godly children and a dead woman – or at least, not all at once.

The Divine children sit in stunned and despairing silence, especially Malwina. The consequences of what's just happened haven't truly sunken in, Ivanya can tell. She's been through this before, after the Battle of Bulikov, when people sat dumb and dreamlike in the streets, babbling about inconsequential things. If they live to see tomorrow, she knows, the morning will bring countless horrors as they try to force a normal life on the shattered remnants around them.

But that day is tomorrow. And right now, today, there is at least a hot cup of tea.

She sets the first tray down before them. 'Drink up,' she says gently. 'Get something warm in you.'

The only people who don't seem to be crushed with despair are Taty and Shara. And though Ivanya feels it's Taty who has a right to have countless questions, it's Shara who's doing the interrogation, asking about her daughter's travels, how she's been sleeping, any rashes or cuts or bruises, and so on, and so on, and so on. Taty gives her answers in a tone that seems both bored and familiar to her, and Ivanya can't help but feel a little heartened to see that mother and daughter have, impossibly, resumed their relationship with barely a hiccup.

Though one thing has changed: Shara's eyes, which seemed so tired at first, are drinking in her daughter's every movement, every word, every gesture, every sound. It's as if she's trying to record all of this, to capture everything, and keep it locked somewhere safe deep within her.

'Now what?' asks one of the Divine children.

'What do you mean, now what?' asks Malwina.

'Now . . . what do we do?' a boy asks. 'Do we run? Regroup?'

'Regroup?' asks Malwina. She laughs caustically. 'And if we were to regroup – let's see here – the Divine spirits of glassblowing, clocks, hearths, elderly maiden aunts, the Ahanashtani spring, and the rest of us – exactly what could we then do?'

There's a long silence.

'I don't know,' one of the girls says. 'Something.'

'Something,' grumbles Malwina. 'But not enough.'

Ivanya's bringing the third tea tray over when Taty glances at Malwina, and whispers to Shara, 'Is . . . Is that my . . . sister? Could it be?'

Shara thinks for a long time. 'Yes,' she says finally. 'She is.'

'And she's . . . she's . . .'

'Divine,' says Shara. 'Yes.'

'And I . . . I . . .'

Shara looks at her daughter levelly. 'You are.'

Taty's face flushes bright. 'I'm D-D . . .'

'You are *lucky*, Tatyana,' says Shara. 'The main difference between you and that girl across the room is a great deal of sorrow.'

'That's not an answer!' says Taty, frustrated. 'And you know it!' 'Isn't it?'

'No! You . . . You should have told me, you should have *helped* me understand this, about . . . about what I am, or what I'm going to be!'

'Are you so sure,' says Shara, quietly sipping tea, 'that I didn't, my love?'

Then the sound hits them. It's a deep, terrible, reverberating sound like someone has just struck an impossibly large bell, a bell the size of the moon. It's so loud that, despite her efforts, Ivanya can't help but drop the tea tray, sending it clattering to the floor.

'What in the hells is *that*?' says Ivanya.

Shara sits forward. 'Could someone help me over to a window?'

Ivanya obliges her, helping her to the big bay windows that look out the east side of the mansion.

'Ah,' says Shara, peering out the window. 'Then it's as I thought.'

'What is it?' asks Ivanya.

Shara nods ahead. 'The walls. They're there. Don't you see them?'

Ivanya looks and does a double-take. As a former citizen of Bulikov she's often forgotten that the walls are even there, since they're invisible from the inside. But now they most certainly *are* there – and they've changed colour. They aren't the slate-grey colour that the outside walls so commonly are.

Rather, these walls are black as jet.

There's another deep *gong*. It's so loud it sends curls of dust swirling up in the streets. As the gong keeps going, the walls seem to get darker and darker, until they're a shade of black so deep they almost hurt the eye.

'What in the world is going on?' gasps Ivanya.

'It's him,' says a voice behind them.

They turn to look. Malwina is standing there, her face pale and her eyes bloodshot from tears.

'It's the enemy,' she says. 'He's taking over the miracles in the walls.'

'What?' says Ivanya, shocked. 'But . . . But that means . . .'

'Yes,' says Malwina. 'She's dead.' She goes back to her seat and sits staring into space. 'It means Olvos is dead.'

Nokov stands in the forest outside Bulikov.

Dawn is near. He can feel it. Ordinarily he would shrink from the world, his power waning as light floods the countryside. But not now. Not with so much Divine power thrumming inside him.

He feels Olvos's countless miracles, all the ones she built thousands of years ago, the ones still working away in the background of reality . . . and the thousands of potent, churning creations working mere miles away from him, in the walls of Bulikov.

Old miracles, *real* miracles. The stuff of legends. The sorts of things he ordinarily wouldn't ever be able to make. Yet now they are his.

Nokov breathes and takes a step.

In an instant he's inside Bulikov, standing at the gate before the sheer black walls, which curve around him in a huge embrace. Silence is there with him, standing at his side, staring around in total confusion, unable to comprehend how she got here. The few mortals awake at this hour stare at the two of them for a moment before running away, screaming incoherently.

He gazes up at the walls. 'The gates of Bulikov,' he says quietly. His voice is like the voice of the stars in the sky and all the bones of the earth were whispering at once. 'Once the gates were so tall, so mighty, so glorious . . . A monument to the old Divinities, to their power, to their ordering of the world. Yet I shall dash it all aside shortly.' He looks at Silence. 'I'm going to start it now.'

Silence is about to speak, but she doesn't need to: he can see into her mind, see what she's about to ask.

'Dawn is coming,' says Nokov. 'But I will not let it come. I will ascend to the skies and kill them, kill the heavens above. I will slay the light before it falls. This is what I will, this is what I wish. And then the whole of reality will be but a blackboard for you and I to write upon.'

Silence nods, awed and dazed.

'I will be vulnerable during this,' says Nokov. 'I will work behind reality, under it, over it. This is a vast act that will take all of my concentration. Do you understand?'

She nods again.

'Good.'

Nokov focuses, narrowing his eyes slightly. The black walls of Bulikov tremble, shift, groan. They tremble more and more until they should fall apart, yet they do not.

And then they begin to . . . unwind.

It's as if the walls had been just the tip of a circular, hollow tower all along, and now the tower begins to sprout up and around the city, slowly, slowly extending into the sky, adding layer upon layer upon layer. The ground quakes and rattles and rumbles, but the tower keeps growing into the sky with a powerfully dispiriting silence. Running along the inside of the growing tower is a tremendous black staircase, curling around and around its interior in a helix. The end of the staircase just happens to fall before Nokov's feet.

Nokov looks up, watching as his tower keeps climbing into the sky. 'Do not allow anyone upon the staircase,' he says to Silence. 'I will ascend, and no one must follow.'

Silence bows low and watches as her god departs, starting up the stairs that will soon end at the sky itself, the firmament above – which Nokov will destroy with but a touch.

As he climbs the stairs, looking down on the vast city below, he can't help but laugh.

And they thought it was the City of Stairs before . . .

Sigrud stomps on the brakes as the earth begins to shake. The sky is lit with faint predawn light, but he can see that something is definitely wrong with the sight ahead of him: for one thing, the walls of Bulikov have just turned black, which isn't normal. And also they are . . .

'Moving?' he says.

The walls of Bulikov shake and tremble . . . and then start growing into the sky, forming a vast, black tower that shows no signs of slowing down. It's half a mile tall now, and getting taller by the second.

'Okay,' says Sigrud. 'That is probably bad.'

He steps on the accelerator. The wheels of the old auto shriek, and he speeds off toward the gates of Bulikov – which, he can't help but notice, don't seem to exist anymore. The entry is now just a solid black wall, leaving him no way into the city.

I will figure that out, he thinks, *when I get there.*

'What in hells?' says Ivanya, staring out the window at the growing walls. 'What in *hells*?'

Shara looks over at Malwina. 'Malwina? What's happening? Can you tell us?'

Malwina, still pale and red-eyed, screws up her mouth like she's doing maths in her head. 'If I had to guess,' she says in a hollow voice, 'he's remaking all the miracles that hold up the walls into one big staircase. Which he'll then climb. Up to the sky.'

There's a long, loud silence. The other Divine children slowly look at one another in horror.

'And then what?' says Ivanya. 'Then what happens?'

Malwina tosses back a cup of tea. 'Then he poisons the sky with darkness. And the endless night begins.'

'Endless night?' says Taty. 'What does *that* mean?'

Malwina laughs. 'Who the hells are you, girl? You look like me, but I don't remember you, I don't smell a whiff of the Divine about you – or, not *yet* at least – and you *obviously* can't tell the Divine from a hole in the ground . . .'

'She is the least of your problems,' says Shara sternly.

Malwina looks at Shara. 'She isn't awake yet, is she?'

'Malwina.'

'But you know what it's going to take to do that.'

'*Malwina.*'

Malwina smirks. 'Endless night means that he dilates completely,' she says. 'Nokov – I mean, let's go ahead and say his name, since it's obvious he's won – once the world falls under endless night, he controls *everything*. All of reality becomes a plaything in his hands.'

'How do we stop him?' asks Ivanya.

'We don't,' says Malwina. 'He's devoured so many of the children, and Olvos. He's unstoppable now, or close enough that it doesn't matter.'

'Unstoppable?' says Taty, horrified. 'Is he really?'

'Not . . . Not necessarily,' says Shara. 'This thing he's doing, this grand act . . . He's exposed himself. He's bent on doing this one, massive thing. He won't have the attention for anything else. He's like a surgeon in the middle of an operation.'

'We could attack him,' says one of the other children. 'Gang up on him. Slow him or even stop him.'

'Slow or even stop the most powerful Divine being in all of history?' says Malwina. She laughs again. 'Sure.'

'We have Sigrud's guns, don't we?' says Taty.

Ivanya nods. 'We do. Three pistols, two riflings, and a scatter-gun.'

'And I can see the foot of the stairway from here,' says Shara. She points toward the gates in the walls, or where the gates used to be, at least. 'That's got to be the way up.'

'Are you *hearing* yourselves?' asks Malwina. 'Go after what's now a Divinity with, what, some fucking guns? Chase him up the stairs? That's madness!'

The room goes quiet as they try to think.

'Sigrud would try it,' says Taty quietly.

There's a long silence.

'Sigrud,' says Malwina, 'is just a *man*.'

'He's never let that stop him,' says Taty.

'He's just a man, and he *failed*,' says Malwina. 'He was supposed to get Olvos on our side! And now she's dead. There's nothing left, nothing left!'

'There was nothing left for him either,' says Taty softly. 'He lost everything. Everyone. But he still travelled across the world to help me. I know. He told me so.'

'So what?' snaps Malwina. 'Are we supposed to launch an attack on Nokov himself with nothing more than sheer, bloody-minded stupidity in our pockets?'

'The alternative, Malwina,' says Shara, 'is doing nothing. And I know your heart is broken, my dear. I know you feel bruised and lost. But you and I have been comrades in this fight for a long time now. Tavaan fought and died to make this fight last a little longer. Will you abandon it now?'

Malwina falls silent. The snarl fades from her face. She bows her head. 'I . . . I didn't ever think it'd be like this, Shara. I really didn't.'

'I know,' says Shara. 'But it is.'

Malwina takes a breath, then grabs another cup of tea, and tosses it back just like the first. 'All right. Let's gear up and get ready to go get ourselves killed.' She smiles a grin full of mad despair. 'Maybe we'll give him a split lip doing it.'

Sigrud slows the auto as he approaches the solid black wall surrounding Bulikov. He has no doubt that this has something to do with Nokov: this is the same colour black as he saw in Khadse's jacket, the same black as that odd sub-reality he tumbled through after he nearly broke Nokov's hand. An extraordinarily dark blackness, a colour that has never known light.

He steps out of the auto, leaving it running. He looks the wall up and down. It looks solid, but . . .

He stoops, picks up a rock, and throws it at the wall. It bounces off with a *clack*, but leaves no mark.

He thinks, then places his bare left palm on the black wall. The wall is cool and hard, as if made of obsidian, but despite everything Olvos said, his touch appears to do nothing. But then, she said the thing living in his palm exists mostly just to beat the hells out of him and make sure he survives.

Then he stops, and remembers.

It's a tool. It won't harm the enemy, but it can destroy his works and machinations.

Sigrud focuses and reaches into the air, concentrating . . .

Suddenly Flame is in his hand. And though its blade is but a dim flicker now, he can't help but notice that it seems to project a radiance that makes the wall look very . . . thin.

Sigrud holds the sword out at the wall. As he does so the wall seems to recede, like shadow before light.

'Hm,' he says.

He walks toward the wall. It falls back, as if the sword is projecting a perfect bubble of light around him – much like Malwina did back at the slaughterhouse.

'Hm,' he says again. He looks at the bubble of light around him. It looks to be ten or fifteen feet across in diameter. Large enough for his small, ramshackle auto, in other words – and who knows where he'll need to get once he's inside?

Sigrud climbs back into the auto and sticks his left arm out the window, holding the sword forward like he's leading a cavalry charge. He presses the accelerator very, very slightly, sending it puttering forward into the wall, which draws back like a curtain, allowing the auto through.

Sigrud smiles, delighted that at least one thing has gone right tonight, and speeds up.

Ivanya and the others trot through the streets of Bulikov, with she and Taty supporting Shara between them. Ivanya's happy she did so much walking about and stayed fit when she was a shepherd, because between Shara's weight and the scatter-gun and rifling on her back, she's sure she'd be dead otherwise.

The city, unsurprisingly, is in complete uproar. *Flashbacks of the Battle, no doubt*, thinks Ivanya as they trot through the remains of a street market, its tents and booths overturned, the cobblestones covered in smashed potatoes and shards of porcelain. The city is lit with a queer grey light as the rising walls block out all hint of the dawn. The atmosphere feels so close and thick it nearly chokes the air from her lungs. Someone has turned on a few of the streetlights, but they don't do much to fight back the pervading darkness.

'You and I,' says Ivanya to Shara as they help her over a curb, 'are going to have a chat once we're done here.'

'Oh, are we,' says Shara.

'Oh, *yes*,' says Ivanya, panting. 'I fund all your war games for years, and you don't even tell me what you're up to? And now you've cheated death? *And* I'm carrying you all the way across Bulikov?'

Shara groans, cringes, and pales a little. 'I can guarantee, Ivanya . . . I have *not* cheated death.'

'Well then, how in hells am I carrying you right now?'

Shara swallows and takes a shallow breath. 'Think of it,' she says, 'like a loan I've had taken out against it. Which is being paid back with great interest.'

Ivanya shakes her head. 'I fucking hate this Divine nonsense.'

'I sympathise heartily,' says Shara.

They turn the corner. The black staircase is only a few blocks ahead. It's enormous, jutting at least a hundred feet out from the walls.

'We need a plan of attack,' says Malwina quietly.

'We'll have to think of one,' says Ivanya, 'once we know what we're attacking.'

Shara looks up, and Ivanya does the same. The giant black cylinder is still rising above them, curling around and around at the top. It's several times taller than the tallest skyscraper Ivanya's ever seen, and she swears she can see wisps of cloud near the top, like it's about to breach the bottom of the overcast skies.

'There he is,' says Shara. She points up.

Ivanya squints. It takes a while for her to see what she's pointing at, but then she spots it: a dark figure quietly walking up the stairs curling around the interior of the walls, its movements slow and ceremonial, like a monarch approaching their throne. He looks like he's nearly a quarter of a mile up by now – which means that the black figure must be very, very, very big.

'Why doesn't he just fly up and do it?' asks Ivanya. 'I mean – he's basically a god now, right?'

'This is heady stuff he's getting into,' says Malwina. 'He's got to form a connection point with the skies themselves. This is a vast, symbolic act, overlaid on the countless miracles, dead or living, that still function behind the firmaments above.'

'If you say so,' says Ivanya. 'How are you going to get up there?'

'Using that,' says Malwina. She points to the bottom of the stairs. 'The gates of Bulikov used to have towers on either side of them, before the Blink. The towers were Divinely made, so they were incredibly, *incredibly* tall. They had a chamber inside them that could zip you up to the top in a split second, faster than any elevator in Ghaladesh.'

'How could *that* help?' asks Taty.

'Because it's in the past,' says Malwina, glaring at her.

'What?' says Ivanya.

'Malwina is the Divine spirit of the past,' says Shara. She coughs, her face twisted in pain. 'She knows many things that have happened, if not all of them. And she can access the past, and utilise things there to our advantage.'

'Which I can do now,' says Malwina.

'So . . . you take your war party into the past,' says Taty, 'put them in that tower, zip them up to the top, then bring everyone back to the present – hopefully on top of the stairs. Is that it?'

'Yes,' says Malwina. She looks reluctantly impressed with Taty's deductions. 'If I'm in luck, we might actually wind up in front of him, blocking his path.' She looks toward the gates, and her eyes seem to shimmer a little, like they're filling up with smoke. 'Yes, I think so . . . I can see what the tower was like. It was about halfway up the walls – or at least as tall as the walls are now.'

'That must have been some tower,' says Ivanya.

'It was,' says Malwina. They start moving ahead again. 'But the problem is that I *have* to get my people to the base of the stairs, where the tower existed in the past.'

Ivanya pants as she and Taty haul Shara around an overturned sausage stand. 'And what's the problem with that?'

They come to a wall alongside a street corner. Malwina holds up a hand, peers around the corner, and quickly draws back. 'The problem is,' she whispers, 'as I thought, that the base of the stairs is guarded.'

'Guarded?' says Ivanya. 'Guarded by who?'

Malwina opens her mouth to speak, but nothing comes out. It's not that she can't talk – she *is* talking, her lips moving, but all the sound is gone.

Ivanya frowns. Now that she notices it, the sound seems to be gone from . . . everywhere. As if the whole city has gone silent.

Ivanya turns to Shara. She tries to say, 'What's going on now?' but the words make no sound.

Nothing makes sound. Not the wind or the screaming people or the automobiles hurtling in panic down the street.

Nor the huge black spear that comes plunging through the stone wall behind them.

The spear punches right through the chest of one of the older Divine children, who goes as limp as a rag doll, blood pouring from his mouth. Ivanya blinks in shock as the warmth patters her face and side. The spear passes right behind her head, so close she can see its oily, shifting surface.

She screams. She can see Taty screaming next to her, but there's no sound. Everyone turns and begins to run in all directions, with Malwina and her Divine children falling back down the street.

The spear slides back through the wall. The corpse of the Divine child silently falls to the ground. Something huge and dark steps around the corner.

It is . . . feminine, somewhat. Seven feet tall, black as coal, with long, distorted limbs and a totally featureless face. It carries a black spear in one hand, which drips with the blood of its victim. And as they scatter, the thing lifts its head, and appears to scream . . .

There is no noise. Just a pulsing silence. Yet in that silence is a message:
<run! run run all of you all of you run run I will cut you down cut you down>
The next thing she knows, Ivanya's in motion. She's reaching over her

back, pulling the scatter-gun from over her shoulder, and lifting it up. Time seems both stupendously slow – slow enough for her to think, *Am I really doing this?* – and stupendously fast, so fast she can't stop herself.

All the years spent training in the ranges come back to her in an instant. She opens fire at the creature, falling back. The shots seem to stun it and irritate it, but little else than that.

'Shit,' she snarls, though she can't hear the word. She can see Shara and Taty cowering just to the creature's right, and realises it could spear them in a second if it but wished.

Without even comprehending what she's doing, Ivanya runs forward, right in front of the creature, trying to draw it away from the corner and across the main road. The creature gives chase, picking its way across the streets like a stork among the reeds, its long, delicate spear slashing through the air.

As she reloads and runs, Ivanya understands right away that she is not up to this task. Despite all her paranoia, despite all her training, all her worrying and preparations, she is still little more than a farmer with a firearm. She's shot a few foxes and wolves in her day, but she's never done anything like this.

She darts among a parking lot of autos, screaming in silent terror as the creature tears through the vehicles behind her, thinking, *Why did I ever come back to Bulikov? Why did I ever, ever come back to Bulikov?*

She turns right, trying to cut around the creature. Yet then the black thing lifts up an auto and overturns it, blocking her exit and trapping her in the middle of the street.

Ivanya whirls, raises the scatter-gun, and unloads it into the creature, but it's clear it's hopeless. The thing raises its spear, preparing to run Ivanya through . . .

Which is when something very strange happens to the black walls at the end of the street.

Something bursts through – an old, rattling auto, with what appears to be a shining flame atop its canopy. And below it, behind the windshield, is Sigrud's face.

When Sigrud's auto finally makes it through the black walls, he's struck by how different the city now feels: the black tower blocks out the dawn, so the light within has a queer, flimsy quality to it, like an evening storm threatening to turn into a tornado.

Then he notices his right shoulder hurts, a strange ache just like he had in the aero-tram, when the point of the seneschal's spear penetrated his skin.

Then he sees why: the seneschal is in front of him, *right now*. And unless he's mistaken, it looks like it's about to spear Ivanya like a snail on a platter.

I do not really know what's going on, he thinks. He stomps the accelerator and buckles his safety belt. *But I hope I live to find out*.

The seneschal turns to look at him, surprised. Sigrud points the auto at its knees.

Then the world leaps, and he's hurtling into the steering wheel of his auto, and glass is flying around him. He catches sight of the seneschal tumbling backward, smashing into a lamppost, but he's snapped around too fast to really see.

Finally, things stop moving. The world seems to have reorganised itself: the auto is now lying on its passenger side, Flame is gone from his hand, and his chest aches like he took a fierce punch to the solar plexus. Sigrud blinks, coughs, unbuckles himself, and kicks the driver's-side door open. He tumbles out to see the seneschal lying sideways in the street, slowly gathering itself.

Ivanya sprints over to him and helps drag him away from the scene. 'What in hells!' she says. 'What in all the *hells*! Did you *plan* that?'

'No,' says Sigrud. 'What is happening?'

'The end of the world,' says Ivanya. 'As far as I understand i —'

All sound fades before she can finish her sentence. Sigrud shoves her aside just as the black spear comes hurtling down, effortlessly piercing the road where she stood. The black seneschal leaps over them, pulls the spear out, and turns to face Sigrud, twirling its weapon like a baton.

Sigrud rolls over, then stands, Flame leaping to his hand. He grins at the seneschal. 'Hello again,' he says, though the words make no sound.

The seneschal shudders in rage and slashes the spear out at him. Sigrud dodges it and flicks the sword up at the shaft, batting it away. The sword doesn't destroy the spear, as he hoped it would, but it does seem to have an outsized impact on it, striking it with a force several times greater than he intended, almost knocking the spear from the seneschal's grasp.

He looks at the faint, golden blade in his hand. *So it still has some bite left*, he thinks.

The seneschal looks surprised by this, but quickly recovers, whirling around and sending its spear shooting at Sigrud's right shoulder with a strange speed, as if the point is magnetically attracted to him. Sigrud just barely dodges the attack, bats the spear aside again, and darts inward, into the seneschal's stance, where he flicks the blade up.

The creature tries to move back, but the blade slashes its right forearm. The silence shudders and quakes, and he knows the thing is screaming in pain. It falls back as Sigrud advances – but he sees that the thing's arm is healing right before his eyes, the black wound fusing shut. Whatever damage Flame can do to the seneschal, it doesn't seem to last.

This is bad, thinks Sigrud.

Yet the seneschal is learning, and it doesn't want to be hit again. It assumes a defensive stance, crouched low with its spear point extended a few feet from its body, preventing Sigrud from getting close. He feints left, right, back and forth, but the seneschal isn't buying it: it wants him to gamble and try something stupid, at which point it'll run him through. They're stuck in a stalemate there in the street, two combatants crouched low, shuffling back and forth.

Ivanya runs around behind the seneschal, waving her hands to get Sigrud's attention. She's shouting something, though he can't hear her. He focuses, trying to read her lips, then understands:

Get it close to the auto.

The seneschal takes advantage of the distraction and strikes at him again. He falls backward, barely evading its thrust, then rises and swings Flame – a miss, not even close. The seneschal leaps back and resumes a defensive stance.

Sigrud glances at his auto, which is still lying on its side. He slowly begins to strafe around the seneschal, positioning himself so he can back it up toward the overturned vehicle.

He takes a risk, flicks his blade at its spear. It deftly dodges the attack and nearly guts him, but he leaps out of the way and brings his sword down hard on the shaft of the spear. The seneschal roars silently in frustration and backs up. Sigrud feints forward once, then again, until the thing's back is mere feet from the auto . . .

Sigrud drops to the ground.

The seneschal pauses, confused.

Then Ivanya – who has been hunched down across the street with a rifling trained on the auto's exposed petrol tank this entire time – finally pulls the trigger.

There's a blast of wild heat. The silent spell vanishes just as a loud *whump* batters Sigrud's ears. The seneschal is blown sideways into a shop front, its writhing black form smashing through the wood and glass.

The heat scalds Sigrud's feet and legs, which were closest to the car. He sits up and sees his pants are on fire, and dumbly swats at them. Then someone grabs him by the underarms. He looks up to see Ivanya straining to lift him up.

'Come on, dumbass!' she shouts. 'Run!'

He flips over and staggers to his feet. He looks over his shoulder as they run away and sees the seneschal stirring in the blown-in shop front.

It isn't dead, he thinks. *Not by a long shot.*

Once they're around a corner – where, he notes, the bloody body of a young boy lies with a hole through its chest – Sigrud hears the screaming. He wonders who else is under attack when he realises it's the entire city: the citizens of Bulikov are screaming in naked terror of what's going on around them, and Sigrud can't really blame them.

Someone stands and waves a hand from a building front ahead. They sprint over to find Taty crouched in the doorway. 'In here!' she whispers.

They run inside. On the first floor, Shara, Malwina, and some young people Sigrud doesn't recognise are all crouched below the windows, out of sight.

Sigrud lets out a long breath. 'Okay,' he says. 'Thank goodness. You are all alive.'

'All? Not all,' says Malwina grimly. 'Only a fraction of us. I take it your meeting with Olvos didn't work out?'

'I am not quite sure,' says Sigrud. 'She told me many things. But it's . . . it's true what she said, then? The children? Are they . . .'

'I don't know what she told you,' says Malwina. 'But . . . yes. We're all that's left.'

'I . . . I did not think she was lying,' he says, shocked. 'But to hear it's true . . . She would not help, and she spoke in riddles. She seemed to suggest we would still have some way to triumph, though.' He looks out the window at the walls of the black tower that surround the city. 'But . . . I am not sure exactly what the battle is.'

Malwina looks at Shara and sighs. 'Do you want to try to explain this, or should I?'

'Let Shara do it,' says Sigrud. 'She knows how to explain things to me.'

Shara coughs. 'We have to get Malwina's team to the gates,' she says, gesturing to the children behind her, 'or where the gates used to be. That thing, the seneschal, is guarding the area. We need to penetrate the enemy's position, eliminate it, or draw it away. Then it's in Malwina's hands.'

'I see,' says Sigrud, nodding. 'Then it is very simple.'

'What!' says Malwina. 'You didn't say anything about Nokov killing the skies, or the tower, or the world ending, or anything else!'

'That is because I do not give a shit about that,' says Sigrud. 'And we don't have time for it anyway. Not with that tower getting taller and taller by the second. So – what to do?'

'Bullets didn't seem to work on it,' says Shara. 'Not from what I saw.'

'No,' says Ivanya, 'but Sigrud's sword sure seems to make a dent in it.'

Taty looks at him, bewildered. 'Sword? What sword?'

Sigrud sheepishly reaches into the air and produces Flame, which lights up the room with its golden luminescence.

'How did you learn to do *that*?' says Taty, bug-eyed.

'Never mind that,' says Sigrud. He looks at Malwina. 'The sword isn't as strong as it was, is it? But can it kill the seneschal?'

Malwina grimaces. 'It'd have to be a lethal blow. To the heart, to the head. Nothing else will do it. Lop off a limb and it'll hurt it, sure, but it'll just grow back.'

Sigrud scratches his chin. He dearly wishes he had his pipe with him, but he seems to have lost it somewhere. 'And she does *not* like me at all . . . Since I'm the one who originally killed her and everything . . .' He looks at Taty. 'I taught you how to shoot.'

'What?' says Taty, startled.

'I taught you how to shoot,' he says. 'And back aboard the aero-tram, you wished to fight. Now is that time. Do you think you can?'

'Sigrud . . .' says Shara. 'She *is* my daughter, after all. Are you sure that you should b –'

'With all due respect, Shara,' says Sigrud firmly, 'I did not ask you.'

Shara blinks. Then she sits back and looks at her daughter with a slightly shocked expression, as if to say – *Well. Never mind, then*.

'Can you shoot now,' Sigrud asks Taty, 'as I taught you?'

'I-I think so,' says Taty.

'Good,' says Sigrud. 'I will draw the seneschal away from the stairs and lead it on a chase. Shara, I will need you and Taty to take up a position in the window on the third floor in the building across from the gates. Taty, once it starts chasing me, I need you to shoot it and *keep* shooting it. It is much faster than I am. I will need you to slow it down as much as you can.'

'Hold on,' asks Ivanya. 'Shouldn't I be the one doing the shooting? I've already tangled with the thing.'

'Which brings me to my next question,' says Sigrud, turning to her. 'It is not your skill with firearms that I'm thinking about.'

'What do you mean?'

'You said fencing was a time-honoured ladies' sport in Bulikov,' he says. 'You said your mother drilled you mercilessly. Do you think you remember what she taught you?'

After checking their gear, they all troop back out into the street in single file, with Sigrud and Ivanya in the lead. Their procession is silent and solemn, warriors young and old trying to come to grips with their situation. Sigrud has seen it before. True fights, real fights, are rarely calculated, choreographed things: they are chaotic, ugly, unpredictable, and quick – lives saved and spent in a handful of screaming seconds. The inexperienced fall first, unprepared for the flurry of action. Today, he knows, will be no different.

Battle never changes, he thinks. *Always about territory and terrain. And now, if we are lucky, to take some from our enemy.*

Taty and Shara split off from them as they approach the apartment building on the corner. Taty pauses in the empty street, looking back at Sigrud uncertainly.

'Remember to breathe,' says Sigrud. 'Remember it is a machine. Remember it does but one thing.'

She nods. Shara, wheezing, locks eyes with Sigrud. 'Did you *really* teach my daughter to shoot, Sigrud?'

'It seemed the right thing to do. I knew nothing else worth teaching.'

Shara smiles. 'I don't think that's true.' Then she turns and limps toward the apartment building. Sigrud watches as Taty helps her mother into the door and up the stairs.

How much she's grown up already, he thinks, *in what feels like but a handful of days*.

Sigrud, Ivanya, and the Divine children wait as they get into position. 'Have you had much success fighting that thing before?' asks Malwina.

'Some,' says Sigrud. 'But mostly luck.' He glances down at his left hand, looking at the scars there. *I wonder*, he thinks, *will you save me again?* Yet he remembers what Olvos said – he is not immortal. If he takes that spear through the throat, no miracle in the world can keep all his blood inside him.

'That thing has the most powerful Divinity in existence behind it,' says Malwina. 'Do you know what that means for you?'

Neither Sigrud nor Ivanya say anything.

Malwina looks up, narrowing her eyes as she tries to find Nokov climbing the stairs. 'It means the same thing for you as it does for us,' she says softly. 'It means we're dying here today, friends.'

Sigrud shrugs.

'Do you know what I thought when I first met you at the slaughterhouse?' asks Malwina. 'I thought you looked like a suicidal person. Throwing yourself into danger with a mad gleam in your eye. I guess you're getting what you want today.'

'No,' he says. 'That day I was fighting because that was all I knew to do. But now I have a reason to fight.'

'Oh, do you?'

Sigrud looks up and sees Taty set up the rifling in the window above, her small, pale face serious and grave. 'I have failed so many in my life,' he says.

'So many people I was not there for, so many missed opportunities, and so much lost because of it . . . I will not miss another chance. Not now. Not today.'

'Even if it kills you?' says Malwina.

'We are not dead yet,' says Sigrud. He holds out a hand, concentrates, and finds Flame, its yellow-gold light leaping forth in his hands. 'We spend every second fighting, until we have none left.'

He looks at Malwina. She looks back, her eyes fierce. Then she nods. 'Okay,' she says quietly. 'Okay.'

He squints back up at the windows above. A hand waves out the third-floor window. 'Let's get in position,' he says.

Tatyana Komayd fights a brief thrill of guilt as she clears the floor around the window in the empty apartment on the third floor, shoving aside a desk and knocking over a vase. She opens the window and peers out on the group assembling in the street below, grey and tiny in the queer, faint light. Then she looks at her mother. 'I need something to kneel on.'

'I'll get some pillows,' Shara says.

They set up her nest silently and carefully, like maids arranging the table before everyone comes down to breakfast.

'Is this normal for you, Mother?' asks Taty.

'Normal?' says Shara. 'How could it be?'

'Urban warfare,' says Taty, inserting a clip into the rifling. 'Fighting street by street from people's homes. You never did this?'

'I . . . would say I did this very, *very* rarely, my dear,' says Shara.

'*Very rarely*,' says Taty bitterly. She shakes her head as she loads the rifling. 'You hid all this from me. You *lied* to me.'

'You are right to be angry with me,' says her mother, loading an extra clip. 'But I would hardly be the first parent to present themselves to their children as they wished themselves to be, rather than as they are.'

'But why?' says Taty. 'Why not tell me the truth? Why not be honest with me?'

'Because . . .' Shara hesitates.

'Tell me now,' says Taty, 'because soon we won't have another chance.'

'Because I grew up in the shadow of hard truths,' says Shara. 'I was a child who was raised for war and governing. And I did not like it much. And even though I knew the stakes, I thought . . . Is it so much to ask that my daughter have a normal life? I just . . . I just wanted a moment alone, a moment *apart* for you. A moment when we didn't have to worry about the outside world, all that history and sorrow waiting for us.' She looks at her daughter, and her eyes are full of tears. 'I just wanted you to be what you are now.'

'What's that?'

'You,' says Shara. 'You. A thousand times you. I'm prouder of you than anything I've ever done before, Taty. I'm so, so happy that I've had the opportunity to say so.'

'I . . . What?' Taty frowns in confusion. 'But . . . But you killed gods.'

'I am aware of that.'

'And saved the world.'

'That is debatable.'

'And . . . And opened the Solda River.'

'That was the effort of many,' says Shara. 'But it was all as forgettable as teatime to me, in comparison to having you in my life.'

Tatyana Komayd looks at her mother, frail and old and injured. Then, feeling slightly absurd, she places the rifling on the dusty bed beside her. 'I'm . . . I'm sorry for being angry at you.'

'You don't need to say you're sorry,' says Shara. 'Not ever.'

The two embrace, Taty squeezing her mother very, very lightly.

'Oh, Mother,' says Taty. 'What are we going to do?'

'Well,' says Shara. 'You're going to shoot. And I'm going to reload. All right?'

In the street below, Sigrud begins to move.

He sprints across one lane, pistol in his hand, then leaps behind a short brick wall. He waits, rises carefully, peeks over the top, and surveys the scene.

The foot of the black staircase is about three hundred feet away. The seneschal crouches before it like a huge, black beetle laying eggs. Just before the seneschal is a short complex of tenement apartments, low and rambling and disorganised, lots of alleys and passageways. Decent cover, then, and it seems to be evacuated, which is good but expected – waking up and seeing the seneschal out your window would make anyone abandon their property.

He looks back in the direction he came from. Malwina and the other Divine children are slipping through a back alley, sneaking toward the black wall. Once he's drawn the seneschal away – *if* he draws the seneschal away, as that thing isn't stupid – Malwina should be able to get to the gates, and do whatever Divine trickery they need to transport themselves several thousand feet up the wall to face Nokov.

He looks up and sees Taty hunkered down in the window of the apartment building. She's got the rifling aimed at the seneschal and ready, with Shara crouched beside her with a fresh clip.

He watches her, thinking. Taty, he knows, is an unknown variable. If Malwina dies – which sounds extremely likely, considering what she's about to do – then she won't support Shara anymore, and Shara will, as far as he understands it, blink out of existence. And then Taty might 'elevate', ascending to her Divine state – and he has no idea what in the hells that could mean for everyone. Nothing good, probably.

He focuses back on the job. He can't see Ivanya anymore, which is good. She seemed to accept his task without hesitation. Hopefully she's ready.

Hopefully they all are.

Sigrud watches the streets. Everything is silent. Everything is still.

He raises a hand. Then he drops it.

Taty opens fire, letting off six quick shots at the seneschal, emptying the rifling. She does a good job, with three shots striking the creature in the chest and shoulders, and one in the head. The seneschal recoils, surprised and irritated: Sigrud suspects that, for the seneschal, being hit with rifling rounds is a bit like being stung by a wasp.

As she fires, Sigrud sprints along the street, firing his pistol up at the seneschal, which infuriates it further – but he makes a point of running around it, toward the stairs, as if trying to take advantage of its confusion.

The seneschal, however, is having none of it: it shakes off its pain and frustration, dives to block his path, and lashes out at Sigrud, forcing him to leap back and roll away.

The creature then does what he expected it to do: it hesitates, assuming he'll summon Flame to force it into a duel again.

But he doesn't. He keeps rolling, then stands up, fires a haphazard shot at the seneschal, and runs.

Now to see, he thinks, *if it will do what I hope it will do.*

He tries not to look over his shoulder to check – to do so would give the game away – but he can't help but sense that the seneschal is keeping its position by the stairs, not at all willing to pursue this irritating man who's just attacked it even though the man doesn't *appear* to have his sword with him anymore . . .

Then the world goes silent.

I knew you couldn't resist, he thinks, smiling. *You hate me so . . .*

He feels the reverberations in the soil behind him as the creature pursues him, and turns into the warren of tenements just as the seneschal's spear licks out at him, its point slashing through the wooden walls behind him.

The chase is on, he thinks, sprinting down the alley. *Now for Malwina to make it count.*

Malwina waits, watching the seneschal. At first she's sure it won't take the bait – it's fairly obvious bait, in her opinion – but the thing apparently hates Sigrud *that* much, because it springs after him with a silent roar.

Its aura of silence fades as it gives chase. Malwina waves a hand to the other children. 'Come on! Now!'

They run down the black walls toward the staircase. It's a motley crew, that she knows. Malwina doesn't understand exactly what these Divine children could hope to do against Nokov, but they have to do *something* – don't they?

Her eyes cloud over as she reviews the past. She can see the huge towers that once stood at the gates in the old days, and the giant, moving chamber set in the interior of the closest one – a splendid, gorgeous, white-and-gold structure that makes her think of swans in winter.

'Stand right here,' she says to the other children, pointing at the ground. 'Are we ready?'

No one says yes, but no one says no either.

'Hold tight,' she says.

She builds a bubble of the past around them, and pushes them *back* . . .

Suddenly they're standing in the chamber, surrounded by tall, broad men in flowing, golden robes, their faces hale and hearty, their teeth white and clean – not at all the Bulikovians Malwina grew up seeing. They talk amongst themselves in hushed tones, debating the will of the Divine, the warp and weft of creation. They are creatures of optimism, and ignorance: ignorance of what is happening in Saypur in their era, all the misery and slaughter their luxury breeds, and ignorance of the destruction it will bring down on their heads.

The men ignore Malwina and the other Divine children, creatures of the past blind to the chaos of the present. The white chamber begins hurtling up, up, up through the tall spire.

The Divine days of old, she thinks. *Would I wish to go back to this, and live only here, living the past over and over again?*

One thousand feet. Two thousand feet. More.

No, she thinks. She shuts her eyes. *Because then I would have never met Tavaan.*

She opens her eyes. *Now. Now!*

She pops the bubble of the past around them. For a moment they all keep continuing up, just a few feet – but then they begin falling, crashing into the broad, black staircase that's suddenly appeared below them. As they recover, Malwina looks up and takes stock of their circumstances.

They seem to be about a mile or two above the city, whose buildings are a clutch of grey architectural anarchy below. It's freezing cold up here – she can see ice forming on the walls.

Then she sees Nokov.

It's hard *not* to see him. Tall as a tree, eyes like holes in space, a broad, swaying, shadow-flecked figure slowly advancing up the stairs toward them, his every movement thrumming with power.

'Oh, man,' whispers one of the children next to Malwina.

'Quiet,' she snaps. 'Stand up. And get ready for him.'

'What are we supposed to *do*?' asks another.

'He's distracted by building the tower,' says Malwina. 'He won't be as strong as he could be, in other words. Knock his ass off these stairs. Anything we can do to keep him from taking another step is a victory.'

A nervous silence falls over them as they take their positions. Malwina's hands won't stop making fists, her knuckles white with strain.

Nokov slows as he sees them, his black, glittering brow wrinkled in puzzlement. 'Oh,' he says quietly. His voice doesn't seem to come from his mouth, Malwina notes, but rather from the walls, as if the entire tower is speaking.

'We're not going to let you do this, Nokov!' says Malwina.

He takes another step. 'There's little you can do against me.'

'Little it may be,' says Malwina. 'But we're going to do it anyway.'

'Do you wish it to end this way?'

'If it has to, yes.'

He cocks his head. 'Were your lives just? Content? Happy? I will remake reality now. I will make it *better*. I will *fix it*. All the wrongs we lived under will be righted. I promise you this.' He extends a hand. 'You can join me, you know. Be a part of me. Come into the night, and I will show you greatness.'

'You're not some saviour, Nokov,' says Malwina. 'And you're not some justified rebel, avenging past wrongs.'

'No?' says Nokov.

'No. You're just some fucking selfish kid who thinks his misfortunes are bigger than everyone else's, and you're taking it out on everyone around you. You're not special. If I lined all the people like you up, you'd go around the world twice. We're just unlucky enough that *you* happened to be able to actually *do* something about it, and unluckier still that you were stupid enough to try!'

Nokov blinks, outraged. Then he begins to tremble. 'I'll kill you last,' he hisses. 'I'll kill you *last*.'

Malwina smiles. 'Try it.'

He leaps at them.

As Sigrud sprints through the alleys the sky above erupts with thunder, or something a lot like thunder – it sounds a little louder and sharper than the thunder he's used to hearing, and it doesn't seem to echo as much. But the really odd thing is that with the seneschal chasing him, everything *should* be silent – yet that particular sound breaks through.

He knows he should be focused on trying to avoid the seneschal, but he takes a moment to glance up . . .

The space at the top of the tower is flashing with light. Light of many colours – reds, blues, greens, and some other colours that his eye can't quite interpret correctly.

So that's what a Divine battle looks like, he thinks. He's glad he's several thousand feet below it – though he does hope nothing comes raining down on them.

He can feel the seneschal behind him, feel its feet pounding the concrete alleys. Sigrud takes a gamble and dives through a window in one of the tenement homes, breaking through the glass and the frame. He crouches next to the wall, waiting. He can feel the seneschal's footsteps; he knows it's close. His right shoulder starts hurting again, aching powerfully . . .

The spear smashes through the wall of the home. Sigrud drops to the floor, but it's not fast enough: the spear comes hurtling at his chest, and stops only a few feet away. He sees that the seneschal happened to break through a tenement wall with a lot of plumbing in it, and has been slowed down by the pipes. If it had completely broken through, it would have managed to extend its thrust a handful of feet farther, and probably run him through.

Sigrud doesn't wait to see more. He rolls over, scrambles through the bedroom door, and flies out the front window, turning east down the street toward the trap they laid.

But this is bad. It's bad because it seems like the seneschal can *track* him, somehow, like it can sense where he is, which means eluding it will be impossible. And he's starting to think that he knows how it's tracking him: the spear point was speeding toward a certain spot on his right breast, the spot that aches terribly whenever the seneschal is near . . .

The distant skies echo with crashes, bangs, cries, and shouts.

Whatever Malwina is doing up there, he thinks, *I hope she wins, and soon*. He turns down the next alley, hopefully leading the seneschal onto the final leg of their trap. *Because I am less and less certain this will work.*

Taty narrows her eyes, watching the tops of the tenements down the sights of her rifling. Her right shoulder aches from the recoil, but then she sees the seneschal pop up, and forgets all her pain.

She puts the sights on it and fires. She hits it in the shoulder and it seems to stumble very slightly for a fraction of a second – but hopefully a fraction of a second that Sigrud can use.

'He's headed toward Ivanya,' says Shara. 'I think.'

'Yes.' Taty fires again, this one a miss. 'Will he make it?'

'I don't know,' says Shara.

Taty fires again – the last round in the clip. The empty clip comes shooting out with a *ping*. 'Next one,' she says, extending a hand.

Her mother passes a full clip over. Taty pushes it in until the bolt smoothly slides into place, chambering the top round. She raises the rifling to her shoulder, but then pauses, noticing her mother's gaze and her broad smile.

'What are you looking at?' Taty asks.

'Nothing,' says Shara. 'I just . . . I just want to remember this. To keep this. We lose so much. I hope I keep this.'

'Keep it until what?' asks Taty.

Shara looks away, face now clouded. 'Nothing. Nothing.'

Sigrud makes another corner, now sprinting down the main street that runs along the black wall, back toward the foot of the staircase. He needs to get into position before the yellow brick tenement on the corner, and soon – but the seneschal isn't running the route he needs it to. He was hoping it'd take the alley running through the tenements, but because it seems to know how to track him, it's not bothering with this complication, and is instead making for the main road, looking to cut around and through.

He eyes the brick tenement on the corner, its sides painted bright yellow, and the window on the second floor. The seneschal rounds the corner, its spear low, its silence thrumming.

Sigrud considers his options – maybe lead it back down into the warren of tenements? – but he knows there's no time. He sprints toward the yellow brick building, knowing full well he won't make it.

Not even with Taty shooting will he make it.

Taty sits up straight. 'Something's wrong.' She aims and fires, hits the seneschal in the belly, but it keeps coming.

'I know,' says Shara.

'He's too exposed!' says Taty.

'I know!' says Shara.

Taty pulls the trigger, and there's a click. She blinks and looks down at the rifling. 'Misfire!' she cries. 'Shit!' She watches in horror as Sigrud sprints down the street, small and tiny before the black form of the seneschal.

'Oh, no,' she says. 'Oh, no . . .'

Shara sits up and looks out the window, her face calm and watchful.

A hundred feet from the tenement. Fifty. He feels the ground shaking with the steps of the seneschal behind him

Please, Ivanya, he thinks. *Please be ready . . .*

Impossibly, he makes it to the yellow brick wall, but he can see from the shadows over his shoulder that the seneschal is going to cut him off, keeping him from escaping down the next alley.

He whirls around, hoping he can perhaps leap aside and dodge under the seneschal's stance, but . . .

A flash of darkness.

It's close, he sees. Too close.

The spear flies at him.

There's a *crunch* sound. His right side goes numb.

Sigrud tries to stumble back, but finds he can't. He can't move.

He stupidly looks around for the source of the sound, and sees that it came from behind him, where the spear has penetrated the brick wall.

He looks down.

He sees that the spear hit the wall after passing cleanly through his right breast, beside his shoulder. Right where it left that dark little spot just a few days ago.

Sigrud tries to breathe and finds he can't. His chest is bright with pain.

The seneschal crouches low, its featureless face staring into his own. He can't help but get the sense that it is wickedly gleeful in its victory.

And it is victory, he knows. Sigrud je Harkvaldsson has seen enough mortal blows to know that this is one.

*

'No!' screams Taty from the window. 'No, no, no!' She drops the rifling, going white as the seneschal impales Sigrud, pinning him to the wall.

Beside her, Shara Komayd silently stands and begins walking downstairs.

The seneschal leans close to him, its silence now an odd purr he can feel in his bones.

He coughs and manages to laugh. He grins at the thing. He hopes she can read his lips as he says, 'Don't get too close. I don't want to get nicked when she guts you.'

The seneschal cocks its head and looks up . . .

Just in time to see Ivanya leap from the second-floor window of the tenement, Flame in her hands.

The strike is strong and true. The edge bites through the seneschal's neck as if it were but a switch of straw.

The head of the seneschal strikes the ground with a loud *thump* – which means, he dimly realises, that sound has returned.

The seneschal's tall, spindly body follows, collapsing before him like a suspension bridge. Ivanya falls beside the carcass, rolling as she lands, but he can tell the fall was rough, maybe spraining or breaking an ankle. She turns to look at him, sees him impaled on the wall, and her mouth opens in horror.

Sigrud tastes blood in his mouth. He tries to smile. 'You . . . You did a very good job,' he says. His voice is a whisper.

'Oh, no,' says Ivanya.

Malwina lies on the black staircase, beaten and bloody and faint. She knew it would be hard. But not this hard.

She looks up to see Nokov run through one of the Divine children with nothing more than a finger, as if his digit were a rapier, then turn and snatch another Divine child out of the air and stuff it into his huge, black maw. Malwina slowly realises that she is now the only one left – Nokov has proven too strong, too shifting, too mutable, too powerful for them to even make a mark on him.

'I thought I would enjoy this more,' says Nokov. He lifts his finger, the

Divine child hanging limp from his knuckle, and stuffs her into his mouth. 'But none of you are even much of a challen – '

Then Nokov sits up straight like he's just heard a terrible sound. He whirls and stares down at the city below. 'No,' he whispers. 'No, no! Not Mishra, *not Mishra*!'

It's at this moment that Malwina summons up all her strength and uses the trick that she's been sitting on for a while. She'd wished to do it before, but Nokov was too slippery, too fast – yet now he sits stock-still, peering over the side of the staircase in dismay.

Lightning is a curious thing. Most lightning is cloud-to-cloud lightning, dancing through the air. If one were to look back through history, picking a random spot in the skies, and wonder how many times, say, one cubic foot of atmosphere had lightning course through it, the number of instances would be quite extraordinarily high – and the cumulative amount of electricity would be nothing short of inconceivable.

Malwina focuses, and tracks down all the lightning that has ever passed through the spot of air that currently happens to be occupied by Nokov's head.

She focuses more, and makes past and present *twist*, just slightly.

Nokov's skull lights up with a luminescence brighter than a million suns. The force is so great that it blows him forward, shooting him down off the staircase like he's been fired out of a cannon, leaving a trail of black smoke in his wake.

Malwina leans over the edge and screams, '*That was for Tavaan, you piece of shit!*'

Nokov hurtles down toward the city, but his black form slows after about three or four hundred feet. She can see him righting himself, floating above the city, and he turns to look up at her, his face still smoking.

When he speaks, the walls and stairs vibrate with each word. 'That,' he says, 'was quite tricky.'

Sigrud tugs at the spear lodged in his right breast, but it doesn't move. He knows this is the wrong thing to do anyway, since removing the spear will likely cause him to bleed out, but he can't stop himself from trying. It's as if he has a piece of food stuck in his teeth and he can't stop tonguing it.

Ivanya rises and comes to him. 'No, no . . . Don't. Don't, Sigrud, you'll just make it worse.'

'It . . . It doesn't hurt that much,' he says to her, his words thick and slow.

'You're in shock. You don't know what's happening.' She looks at his back, where the spear protrudes and enters the brick wall. 'Oh, by the seas . . . Oh, no, Sigrud, oh, *no*.'

He tries to say, 'I saw a man get impaled with a tree when I worked as a logger, and he survived for six hours with the trunk lodged in him,' but he briefly blacks out, and the words are lost to him.

There's a tremendous boom from above and the world fills up with bright, white light. Sigrud blinks in confusion, wondering if this is what dying feels like. But then the light recedes, and the world coalesces into sense again, though it bursts and warps with blue-black bubbles as his eyes adjust.

Though something has changed: he sees there is someone standing across the street from him. It's Shara, watching him with solemn eyes.

She limps across the street to him. 'I'm so sorry, Sigrud,' she says.

'What was that?' he asks her. He coughs. 'Shara, what was that noise? Did we win?'

She shakes her head. 'No. I . . . I thought maybe they'd find a way. But no, we have not won. Not yet.' Her face crumples as she gets close. 'Oh, Sigrud . . . Oh, *Sigrud*. Look at you.'

'It's . . . It's not as bad as it looks,' he says, trying to smile. He feels his face trembling. His legs are giving out, which means he's leaning more and more on the spear, causing terrible pain.

Shara is standing before him now. How old her face looks, how weary. Yet there's a resolve there he never saw before.

'It's time to do my part. The last step in this long dance. But the most dangerous one by far.' Shara reaches forward and takes his black knife from his holster on his thigh. Ivanya moves forward to say something, but stops herself, hesitant.

Sigrud coughs. Blood comes spilling from his lips. 'What do you mean?'

'I let Vohannes sacrifice himself to a god for me once here, long ago,' says Shara, 'and now I stand before yet more sacrifices. It's not right, is it?'

Shara looks up, the lenses of her glasses reflecting the light of a nearby lamppost. 'No. It's not. Now it's time for me to give.' Her head moves very slightly as she looks at the window above, where Tatyana watches them. 'To give the last thing I have left.'

'What are you doing, Shara?' he whispers.

She kisses him on his brow. 'She'll need guidance,' she says. 'She'll need help. Don't let her do anything too rash – if you can, Sigrud. If you can.' Then she walks to the foot of the black staircase.

She stands there for a moment, gathering herself.

She says, 'We are all but moments.'

Then she raises his knife and screams, '*Nokov! Nokov, son of Jukov! I demand you come to me!*'

Nokov, smoking and furious, begins to fly up to Malwina, surely to crush her like a bug. Yet then he freezes, head cocked. He turns around and looks back down at Bulikov.

'No,' he whispers. 'No, no, it can't be . . . I had you killed, I *know* I had you killed!'

He whirls and streaks back down to the city in a bolt of darkness.

Taty goes sheet-white as her mother begins screaming to the sky. 'What is she doing?' she asks faintly. 'What is she *doing*?'

She turns and dashes down the stairs.

His coming is like black lightning, like all of the wrath of a thunderstorm channelled into one being. The streetlights of Bulikov flicker and blink, struggling against the sea of darkness brought by his coming. The shadows tremble, quake, and shiver – and then he is there.

Nokov, great and terrible, standing in the streets of the city with a confused look on his face as he stares down at the small woman with snow-white hair, knife in her hand.

Shara Komayd looks up at him, her gaze fierce and steady. 'Nokov,' she says. 'How long I have wished to meet you face-to-face. After all these years, I find you don't look much like the picture I found in Vinya's files. Not *too* much, at least.'

'This . . . This isn't possible,' says Nokov faintly. 'I had you killed. I-I had you killed just like I did your aunt . . .'

'I've been learning,' says Shara. She steps closer to him. Nokov glances at her black blade and steps back a little. 'I've been learning from your father, specifically.'

'My *what*?' says Nokov, stupefied.

'Jukov was a clever creature,' says Shara. 'His backup plans had backup plans.' She takes another step forward. 'We thought he was dead. We thought *you* and all your siblings were dead. Wise to learn from him, then, and trick you into assuming the same of me.'

Nokov takes another step back, away from Sigrud, and Ivanya and Taty's nest. 'This doesn't change anything,' he says. 'I'm . . . I'm still the last Divinity, I'm *still* going to kill the skies.'

'*And* you thought my black lead was gone too,' says Shara. She holds up the knife. 'You thought you'd stolen it from me.'

'I-I did!' says Nokov. He stares at Sigrud's black knife. 'I know I did! That's not . . . It's not – '

'But you never knew how much I had in the *first* place,' says Shara. She takes another step forward. 'This is the problem with you and your family – Jukov was so damnably clever that he was actually quite *stupid*.'

Nokov's face twists, and suddenly he's no longer a fearsome, powerful Divinity, but an adolescent trying to control himself after a playground insult. 'Shut up!'

'He trapped himself with Kolkan,' says Shara. 'And he went *mad* . . .'

Nokov falls back another step, but now he's shaking with fury. 'You shut up!'

'And when they emerged, twisted together, and I faced them, seeing them broken and bitter,' says Shara, 'do you know what they asked me?'

'Leave me alone!' says Nokov.

'They *asked* me,' says Shara, her voice growing, 'to take my black lead, and draw it across their throats. They *begged* me to kill them.'

'You and your aunt, you . . . I hate you so much, I hate you *so much*!'

'They said they didn't even want to be Divinities anymore.'

'You're lying!' cries Nokov.

'I'm not,' says Shara. 'You know I'm not.' She takes another step. 'It's fitting, then, that you're going to die the same way.' She lifts the knife. 'Just as pathetic as your father. He imprisoned himself in a box of his own making. And now, Nokov, I'll put *you* in a bo – '

Nokov roars with fury and lashes out at her in a desperate, wild strike.

Shara whirls around. She stands still for a moment.

There's a dim *tink* as Sigrud's knife falls to the ground. Shara follows, falling to her knees.

The top of her dress grows a dark, dark red, stained by the blood flowing from her throat.

She looks up, smiling faintly, looking first at Sigrud, then down the street, beyond him. It's a curious expression, both apologetic and encouraging, regretful but hopeful, wistful and yet full of sorrow.

She collapses – and then she's gone. She vanishes as if she'd never been there at all.

Nokov stares down at where she was, bewildered. 'What?' he says. 'What . . . What was that?'

Then comes the sound of screaming down the street, the high, tinny shrieks of a young woman in horror.

Sigrud looks up as he hears Taty screaming. He can see her, he thinks, standing in the street just a block down from him. Even though he feels faint, he can't help but feel the urge to go to her, to run to her, to comfort her in her moment of grief.

But then her shrieks . . . change. They grow deeper. Older.
Stranger.

As if it weren't one girl screaming, but hundreds of them, thousands of them, all overlaid on top of one another.

Then the streets fill up with a bright, bright white light, as if a star has burst into life right there in the middle of the road.

He hears Ivanya screaming nearby, shouting, 'What in hells is going on?'

The screaming continues, but the light fades. He opens his eye to see Taty floating there, hanging above the street, arms and legs splayed out and her face lifted to the sky. Even Nokov seems astonished by this turn of events, looking on with a confused expression.

The screaming stops. Taty slowly, slowly floats down to the ground.

She crouches there for a moment, head bowed, hair falling in front of her face.

Then she speaks, whispering, 'I . . . I . . . remember.'

And for some reason her words hurt Sigrud's ears, or perhaps his mind. At first he thinks they seem to come all at once, but that's not quite right – rather, it's as if the words he's hearing haven't been spoken yet, like he's hearing words that *will* be spoken, perhaps in the next second, or the second after that, and this queer, schizophrenic feeling is breaking him.

Ivanya leans toward her. 'Taty?' she asks nervously. 'Taty, is that you?'

The girl stands, her face still obscured by her hair. 'No,' she says. 'No, it's not.' Then she raises her head and screams up at the tower above, '*Tulvos! Tulvos, daughter of the past, do you remember? I remember! I remember everything now!*'

Nokov's jaw drops. Then he snarls and springs at her, 'I know you now! I know who you are, *I know who you've been all along!*'

He's too late, too far away. Taty – or whomever she is now – springs up into the air and shoots up, flying straight for the far wall, right for where the Divine battle was taking place just a few seconds ago.

And as she nears it, things . . . slow down.

Nokov, who was a shadowy streak mere feet behind Taty, slows until he hangs in the sky, a black insect trapped in amber.

Ivanya, who was turning to look up, slows until she's stationary, her hair frozen in a peculiar position, like the hair of a woman swimming underwater.

Sigrud looks around, panting. It's very hard to stay conscious now, but he can see specks of dust hanging in the air, distant Bulikovians frozen in mid-stride as they sprint away, even a nearby moth suspended below a streetlight, its delicate white wings caught in mid-flap.

'Ivanya,' he whispers, choking. 'Ivanya, what . . . what is going on?'

She doesn't answer. She hangs in space, suspended and still.

Taty's voice rings out above him, as loud and furious as thunder, '*Daughter of the past, do you know me? Do you know me, Tulvos, do you know me? Do you remember when we were one? Do you remember what they did to us? Do you remember who we were?*'

And instantly, Sigrud understands.

He understands why Shara was lying to him in the sanctum. He understands why she wished to stay alive, why she wanted to delay her daughter's elevation.

He understands who the maimed Divine child was, the one whose domain was so vast it threatened all the original Divinities.

He remembers Olvos saying to him: *Soon the walls will grow and the dawn will be threatened. And time, as always, will remain our deadliest foe.*

Sigrud's mind whirls. *What if the maimed Divine child wasn't just maimed?* He twists his head up, ignoring the brutal, horrible pain, and tries to look at Taty as she grows close to Malwina. *What if it was split in two? Split into two different people, who were never permitted to be close to each other, forced to forget about each other, otherwise all of creation would be threatened . . .*

'They're time,' he says weakly. He blinks, growing faint. 'Past and future, each halves of a whole. They're time itself.'

His head is too heavy. He lets it fall. Then he shuts his eye, and things grow dark.

15.
One Big Push

I keep waking up in the night, panicked, and thinking only — what if they're just like us?

What if our children aren't any better? What if they're just like us?

— FORMER PRIME MINISTER ASHARA KOMAYD,
LETTER TO UPPER PARLIAMENT HOUSE MINORITY
LEADER TURYIN MULAGHESH, 1734

Malwina recoils as the figure comes shooting up to her, thinking it to be Nokov — but it isn't. The way this new arrival moves is . . . strange. They flick across the skies like a bat, and it takes Malwina a moment to realise they're dancing across the seconds, gracefully hopping from moment to moment — but they're moments that haven't *happened* yet. Which Malwina always thought was impossible. It's antithetical to her very being.

The figure leaps up and lands on the steps before her. It's a girl, she sees, about her own age, and she looks . . . familiar.

Malwina sits up. 'T-Tatyana?'

'No,' says the girl. She looks at Malwina, and Malwina sees her eyes have changed. They're now queerly colourless, yet as she stares into them Malwina gets the strangest feeling: she can't help but imagine that in this girl's eyes she's seeing all the things that will happen in the next few moments.

Malwina watches what she sees in the girl's eyes. Then she gasps and looks away, horrified.

'You know me, Tulvos,' says the girl slowly. 'You know me, daughter of the past. Don't you?'

'I . . . Yes,' says Malwina reluctantly. 'Yes. I . . . I think I do.'

The girl's face is fierce and terrible. '*Say it.* Say my name.'

'You're . . . You're the future, aren't you?' says Malwina. 'I am the daughter of the things that have been. And you are the daughter of the things that will be.' Malwina shuts her eyes, and slowly understands she knows this girl's name. 'You . . . You're *Alvos*, aren't you?'

The girl nods. 'You remember now. So do I, finally. That was what they named me. But I am more than that. As are you.'

'What?'

'Don't you remember yet, Tulvos? They made us so that each would always repel the other, and we could never be in the same place at the same time . . . And now I know why. Because they knew that if we got too close, we would remember. Now that I am myself, now that I am close to you, I remember everything.'

'Remember . . . what?' asks Malwina.

Alvos steps closer. 'You don't remember because you don't *want* to remember. Do you recall the last time you saw your mother? Your true mother – Olvos. Do you remember?'

'What in hells does it matter to you?'

'You were young,' says Alvos. 'Very young, in the forest, at night . . . Olvos was there. She was weeping. And the other Divinities were there, all six in one place. And they took you, and led you away from her, to the darkness . . .'

Malwina's eyes widen. 'How do you *know* that?'

'Because I have this same memory,' says Alvos. 'Because it *is* the same memory.' She crouches to look into her face. 'Because at that time we were not two people, but *one*.'

Malwina stares at her for a long time. Then she whispers, 'No . . .'

'Do you remember our name?' asks Alvos. 'The name of the person we used to be?'

Malwina shuts her eyes. 'Stop. Please stop talking.'

'I do,' says Alvos quietly. 'We were *Sempros*. Past and future melded together. Time itself. All things that have been, all things that will be, and all things that are, in one being, one mind.'

'No.'

'Listen to me, Tulvos. Haven't you always felt a curious hollowness in you, as if some part of you was empty, or incomplete?'

'No!'

'Do you remember what they did to us? How they split us, tore us apart? Maimed us and remade us in the darkness as we wept and struggled?'

'Stop it!'

'They changed our memories,' says Alvos. 'Broke us open and reshaped our personalities . . . Do you remember our father, Taalhavras, saying that it had to be done, and it had to be done while we were young, and weak? How if we grew up and grew too strong, none of them could resist us?'

Malwina buries her face in her hands, weeping.

'Taalhavras,' says Alvos. 'And Kolkan. And Ahanas. And Jukov, and Voortya. And Olvos, our mother . . . She just wept. Wept and watched. Watched as they brutalised her child, all so that they could rule unthreatened . . .'

'What do you want?' shouts Malwina. 'What do you want from me?'

Alvos sticks out her hand, her face grim. Malwina stares at it for a moment before she realises what she's suggesting.

'No,' says Malwina softly.

Alvos's stare is fierce, but her cheeks are wet with tears. 'You know you must.'

'No, I won't . . . I won't do that, not *that*.'

'It wasn't right, what they did to us,' says Alvos. 'It wasn't right, what Jukov did to us. Wasn't right that we lived and loved as mortals, and then lost those that we loved so dearly. Me, my mother, Shara . . . And you, Tavaan. None of this was right. These people, they keep hurting us, taking things from us . . . And now we can do something. Take my hand. Take my hand, and become one again with me.'

'And then do what?'

'Fix this,' says Alvos. Her face is a mask of grief and despair. 'Fix what has been done to us.'

'You sound like Nokov.'

'Take my hand,' says Alvos, 'and we can defeat him. No one else can. That's why they cut us in two, because together we could grow stronger than all the gods combined. Don't you remember why they feared us so?'

Malwina bows her head. 'Because . . . Because all things are subservient to time.'

'Yes,' whispers Alvos. '*Yes*. All these plots, all these schemes. See what sort of world the powerful few have built. See how they fought to retain that world. So much pain, so much sorrow, all so they could rule for a handful more years.'

'And what would you do about that?' asks Malwina.

Alvos leans close. 'I would wipe it clean,' she says savagely. 'Wipe away all that sorrow, all that pain, all that *history*, and start over again.'

Malwina sits in silence.

'The only way to truly clean a slate,' Alvos says, 'is with blood. Many have tried to convince me otherwise. But now I know it is true.'

Malwina slowly turns to look out at Bulikov below. She sees that the world has recognised the two of them coming together: as the past and future grow close, the present is unsure how to advance, and simply waits. She can see Nokov suspended in the air below them, his face twisted in fear and fury.

She likes it. She likes seeing him afraid and weak. After what he did to Tavaan and the other children, this sight is maybe the one last thing she could enjoy.

'He deserves it, doesn't he?' she says quietly.

'Yes,' says Alvos. 'He took away my mother. He took away the love of your life. And all because he was angry and frightened. He deserves it. And we deserved none of this pain. No one in this world has deserved any of the pain that it has brought them. No one.'

Malwina turns to look at Alvos's outstretched hand. She is silent for a long while. Then she says softly, 'I never liked being me much, anyway.'

She takes her hand.

Several hundred feet above Bulikov, Nokov is very aware that something is very wrong.

For one thing, he can't move. But it's more than that.

He's powerful enough to understand that something has gone wrong with time. He keeps reliving the same split second over and over and over again, a piece of time so small that it's almost insignificant. To the outside observer – if someone could resist these effects, that is – he would appear frozen.

But he's not. Nokov is powerful enough to know that – and he should be powerful enough to overcome what's happening. He really *should*. Yet for some reason he can't resist.

I am the strongest Divinity to have ever lived, he says in vain. *What is wrong? What is happening?*

And then he begins to move.

He is pulled upward, up toward the far edge of the tower, where someone, he sees, is now walking down the stairs.

It's a woman. Tall and noble, bloodless and alien-looking, arrayed in . . .

Moments. Seconds. Bands of fate, streams of time. From her arms hang all the tides and all the storms of all the seas, and all the dawns and sunsets; from her back there hangs a cape of all the births and all the deaths, both those that have come and those that have yet to be; and about her waist is a skirt composed of all the frantic desires that time would not pass by, the wish that all these moments, however beautiful or brutal, would persist, and linger, and continue. And at the bottom of this skirt is a broad, black hem, cutting all these wishes short.

The woman turns to face him, and he understands she is pulling him to her.

A familiar sensation floods Nokov's mind: the old terror of being trapped by a very dangerous and very pitiless woman.

He wants to say, '*Who are you?*' but the words will not escape his lips.

Yet the woman responds as if she heard him. 'You know me, Nokov,' she says. 'You know me, son of darkness, son of night.'

When she speaks, it's as if he knew what she was going to say, as if she had already said it.

'I don't,' he tries to say. 'I don't know.'

She pulls him closer. Her eyes are filled with dying stars.

'You do,' she says. 'I am the sea in which the night swims. I am the country in which all other Divinities frolic and play their little games. All things you do, all things you have been, they have all happened in my shadow. I am *time*, Nokov. I am every dawn and every dusk. And so your will and wish means nothing to me.'

She pulls him yet closer. Her eyes are now filled with graves and forest fires and babies born bereft of breath.

'But I am also the woman whose mother you slaughtered,' she whispers. 'I am the woman whose love you devoured. You stole everything from me. You stole my brothers and sisters from me.'

'I . . . I had to!' Nokov tries to say. 'I had to! It wasn't right, it wasn't right what they did to me!'

'But the thing I *most* despise about you,' says the woman, 'was that you made me the thing I am now. I was *happy* being mortal. I was *happy* being in love. I was *happy* being small. But you have forced my hand, and made me shed all the things I love like a snake shedding its skin.'

She draws him closer. In her eyes are all the seconds that have passed in between the stars, the limitless stretches of time that unspool in the vast abysses of the world.

'No one saved me!' Nokov tries to scream. 'No one helped me! I was alone, I was alone!'

'I will relieve you of your burden,' says the woman. He's now so close she can whisper into his ear. 'All things end, Nokov. I have seen it. I have seen the end of everything.'

She extends a single finger to his face.

Nokov tries to writhe and scream and sob, but he cannot.

'And yours,' she says, 'hides behind the next second . . .'

Her finger grows closer.

'. . . like an insect below a stone.'

She brushes his cheek.

Instantly, Nokov vanishes.

Sempros, goddess of time, stands alone upon the stairs.

She looks around. If she wanted to she could bat away all the miracles Nokov left behind him: the walls, the stairs, the dead seneschal and its spear below. But she doesn't.

Because it doesn't matter. She's going to shut it all down.

She closes her eyes and begins.

In one sense, Sempros still stands upon the stairs. But in another, she expands and grows and slips behind reality, ascending it like a vast bird, until she finds the sea of moments upon which all things float, a near-limitless ocean of things that have happened, things that are happening, and things that are waiting to happen.

Sempros stands upon the sea of time, her pale feet firm upon the gentle waves.

She crouches. The seconds are tiny, but her eyes are sharp. She can see them all.

She reaches out and brushes one with her finger. It unspools, unscrolls, and there is a tiny, wordless cry – a cry of pain, a cry of sorrow, a cry as this second suddenly simply never was.

She looks up at all the other seconds. And then she starts her work.

On the stairs above Bulikov, Sempros clenches her fists and walks across the air to float above the city – a city that both brought and lived through indescribable pain, a gorgeous capital founded upon slavery and misery, a city plunged into holocaust and bloodshed in a half-second.

Time is frozen below her. It's frozen everywhere, in all things. Yet she still wants them to hear her, to hear her sorrow, to hear her grievances.

Sempros cries out, '*I have been in this world since before its birth! And I will be here after it fades from this reality! And I say to you now, now at the end of all things, that this world is unjust! That it was born in chaos and inequality and pain, and every second after was shaped by that pain! And I say no more! I will not allow it to continue any longer! I will not allow this injustice anymore! I shall wipe it clean! I shall wipe it clean, wipe it away, and relieve you from this punishment that none of us deserve!*'

The world stands still below her. Bulikov stands frozen, as does Ahanashtan, and Voortyashtan, and far across the seas, even Ghaladesh. Every molecule, every atom, every speck of light and dust, all of it stands in attention as Sempros begins her terrible work, dissolving the supports upon which reality stands, dissolving reality itself. The world is her frozen audience to her first, last, and greatest act.

Except.

Except, except, except.

In the streets of Bulikov, a single hand trembles.

The hand is bruised and bloody. Its fingernails are cracked, its knuckles raw. And on its palm is a lurid scar.

Two scales, waiting to weigh and judge.

Sigrud je Harkvaldsson takes a rattling, painful breath.

In his ears he hears the seas. They beckon to him, asking him to walk away from the shores of his life, and be swept away. But for some reason he just . . . He just . . .

I told her I would stay.

His eyelid flutters. The spear is a lump of ice in his shoulder.

I told her I would remind her of who she was.

His left hand, still trembling, slowly rises.

Shall I fail her as well?

He opens his eye, focuses, and stares at his left palm and the gleaming scar upon its flesh.

The words of Olvos echo in his ears: *You defy time . . .*

Sigrud takes another breath. His ribs scream in pain at the effort, but he does so anyway, filling every available part of his body with air. Then he exhales, and in doing so says a single, whispered word:

'Tatyana.'

Sigrud grabs the spear with his left hand and begins to pull. Then he plants his feet on the ground and leans forward, pushing away from the wall.

The agony is unlike anything he has ever known. He can feel the queer metal grinding against him, against some tendon or bone inside his body. He can feel the flow of his breath quake and shiver with each effort.

But he keeps pushing. Until . . .

With a *crack,* the spear is free.

He nearly falls forward into the street, which would be disastrous, but despite the agony thrumming through his body he manages to stay upright. The spear is still lodged in him, huge and heavy, putting downward pressure on his wound.

He stands there in the street, whimpering, quaking, the spear in his breast, his left hand gripping its shaft. His right arm, he knows, is useless. So this will not be easy.

He takes a breath. Then he begins to pull the spear up.

The torment is indescribable. He can feel every ripple in the shaft of the spear, every bend and buckle in its dark surface. He feels it twitch and shift, grinding his bones and tissues and muscles throughout his body.

He screams, long and loud, a ragged scream he didn't know he was capable of. But he keeps pulling, sliding inch after inch of the spear shaft out of his shoulder. He feels the weight of the spear change and shift, feels it bobbing as he pulls the tip close.

He shivers, swallows, and pulls harder, until . . .

His eyes streaming tears, Sigrud je Harkvaldsson slides the black blade of the spear out of his right breast. Then he collapses to the ground, vomiting blood, his right arm growing both cold and warm at once as blood leaves his body and floods out of his wound.

He lies there on the street, coughing, his breath crackling and bubbling.

He hears waves. He hears the ocean. And he catches the distant, salty fragrance of the sea . . .

He blinks lazily. Lying here on the ground, he can see the figure above him: a woman glowing bright white like a firework, floating in the air before the stairs along the tower wall.

His body is shuddering. Everything feels very cold now.

Then the building on his right vanishes.

Sigrud, trembling and faint, lifts his head to look. It's not just that the building is gone: where it stood is now a black hole in . . . well, not space, but *everything*. It's difficult for his mind, as fatigued as it is, to make sense of this sight.

He slowly understands. It is not just that the building is gone. It's that it never was. Its time in this existence has been erased.

He looks to his left and sees Ivanya disappear as well. More and more buildings disappear behind her.

Sigrud looks up at the bright white figure, then eyes the stairs leading up to her.

It's a long way. He lifts his left hand and stares at his palm. *Will you keep me alive until then? Shall I persist?*

The scar says nothing, as it always has.

Sigrud shuts his eyes. He feels colder and colder. His arms won't stop shaking.

I who have waited so long in the halls of death. He looks up. *Yet now, of all times, I wish only for a few seconds more.*

He summons his strength, shifts his weight, and rolls over onto his face. He coughs madly, his wound bright and hot with each convulsion. Blood leaks out of his mouth and nose. His left hand flails until he manages to press it flat against the street. Then he slowly, slowly pushes himself up until he's on his knees.

He grasps the black spear. Then he places its butt against the street and, grunting in misery, leans against it until he lifts himself to his feet.

He leans against the spear like a drunk against a lamppost, gasping and panting. His lungs beg for oxygen, but only one of them seems to be working properly.

Sigrud takes a step forward. His foot holds fast.

He chokes, spits out a mouthful of blood, and takes a breath.

Slowly, slowly, using the big spear as a crutch, Sigrud hobbles to the foot of the giant black staircase, and begins to climb.

Each inch is a struggle, every step a war. His breath is shallow and ragged. Each time he hauls himself up one step, he's convinced he won't be able to do so for the next.

Yet he does. Leaving a trail of blood behind him, Sigrud climbs the endless staircase, lifting one foot after another.

And as he does so, he begins to see things.

The first is his father, sitting atop the stairs ahead, nonchalantly chewing a piece of bread and cheese, young and fresh and clear-faced – far younger than Sigrud is now. His clever eyes are bright with joy, and he looks at Sigrud and smiles. 'If you want a bite of what I'm eating,' he says, 'you'll have to stand and walk to me. Come on! No crawling!'

Sigrud walks on past his father, staggering up the stairs. He's sure he's hallucinating, that this is a sign of his brain failing – yet then he realises what this was.

My first steps, he thinks. *How is it possible for me to remember this? How young was I?*

Sigrud keeps climbing.

At the next twist of stairs, things shift, and change – and he sees Slondheim, dark and dingy and miserable, and the face of his chief tormentor,

Jarvun, leering at him from rusted bars, his teeth brown as old coffee. 'You're a plum, ain't you?' the man says, cackling. 'A plum, I say. Soft, soft. Just as I likes them.'

Sigrud staggers on. The vision fades.

More stairs. More and more.

Things grow soft and strange around him again – another vision.

This one of the burned hillside where his house once sat, where he lived with Hild and raised his children. He sees, of all things, himself, young and clean and slender, kneeling in the ashy mud and weeping, holding a handful of charred bones. This younger Sigrud tips forward until his forehead touches the black, sodden earth, and he howls, a cry of unspeakable grief.

He knows what this young man believes – that his family is dead and slaughtered, and he is too late to do anything about it. He doesn't know that his family has been secreted away. Doesn't know that his suicidal wrath will win him nothing but woe, and set himself upon the path that the elder Sigrud walks now, wounded and bleeding as he climbs the stairs.

Sigrud walks past this younger version of himself and continues up the stairs.

She's doing something to the past, isn't she? he realises. *Unwinding it. Destroying it. And with each stroke, the past quakes like wheat before the scythe.*

He glances to his left, out over the edge of the stairs. He's far up now, farther than he would have ever imagined he could make it, approaching where the tips of the taller buildings would be – but many of them are gone. Much of the world below is gone, wiped away by the Divine machinations occurring above.

He looks up at the glittering figure above him. He's not even halfway there yet.

Can I make it?

Another step.

Can I?

Sigrud keeps climbing.

Things flicker and change, and he sees another vision.

Himself, asleep with Hild on some leisurely morning, his hand thoughtlessly strewn across her naked belly. He watches her sleeping, pushes one strand of hair from her face, and gently kisses her temple.

He and Shara, setting up an antenna atop a rail yard in Ahanashtan. She, young, laughing, delighted in their exploits. He, grim, silent, cruel.

He and his daughter Carin, seated on the floor of his old house, she cradling a cloth doll in her arms. He listens as she explains the doll's complicated, heroic origins in tones of tremendous gravity.

His father, older, graver, sadder, seated at a long table. 'The high-minded rhetoric men will use,' he says, 'to justify the basest of their instincts . . .'

Then he sees himself, in Fort Thinadeshi in Voortyashtan, sobbing and screaming as he grabs a terrified Saypuri soldier, hurls them against a wall, and plunges his knife into their neck. Blood fans out and splashes his face, his chest, his arm. Then he drops the dying soldier and charges down the hall.

As Sigrud staggers through this memory, his eye lingers on the dying soldier. This one a young man not yet twenty-five.

How many years did I take from people that night? he thinks. *How many years have I stolen from others throughout my life?*

He sees Olvos, standing by the fire, pointing at him and saying, 'This was born in blood. It always was. It was born in conquest, born in power, born in righteous vengeance. And that is how it means to end. This is a cycle, repeating itself over and over again, just as your life repeats itself over and over again. We must break that cycle. We *must*. Or else we doom future generations to follow in our footsteps.'

Sigrud walks on and on, his blood sprinkling the stairs. The ground grows smaller below him. His body is cold, faint, distant.

I have lived as a wounded animal, he thinks, *seeking to inflict my pain on the world.*

He grips the spear tight in his left hand as he hobbles up the stairs.

I thought my pain was a power of its own, he thinks. *What awful foolishness this was.*

More stairs, more and more.

Will I let the same thing happen to Taty? Will I let her make my mistakes all over again, before my very eyes?

Then he sees it.

Himself, not yet seventeen. And in his arms, an infant child.

Young, tiny, perfect, frowning in discomfort.

This younger Sigrud lowers his head to the infant's ear, and whispers: 'Signe. That's your name. Signe. But I wonder – who will you be?'

Sigrud shuts his eye as he tries to move past this moment. Then his toe catches the edge of a stair, and he stumbles.

He crashes to the stairs, the spear falling from his grasp. His breast howls with pain. Everything hurts, every piece of him is torment, and though he tries he can't push himself back up.

Sigrud sobs, weary and miserable. 'I can't,' he whispers. 'I can't do it. I can't.'

He shuts his eye, knowing that he's failed, knowing what it means. The world will not simply vanish – it will be as if it never was.

He opens his eye to see it coming, to see the world dissolve and the abyss take him. And he sees he is not alone.

There is someone standing on the stairs above him.

Sigrud looks up.

It is a woman, mid-thirties, dressed in leather boots and a sealskin coat. On the breast of this coat is an insignia – the insignia of the Southern Dreyling Company, accompanied by a small gear. The woman looks down on him, her blonde hair bright in the light of the figure above her, her blue eyes passionate behind her glasses.

She says something. Sigrud is now so faint he can't hear what she says. But he can see it's three words, and he knows they're words she spoke to him long ago, when she declared her life's purpose to him, a bold statement of grim, determined hope:

One big push.

Sigrud nods, weeping. 'All right,' he says. 'All right.'

He gathers himself, rolls over once more. Then he works his left hand into position and pushes himself back up onto his knees. He reaches down and grasps the shaft of the spear, which luckily has not fallen the rest of the way down. Then he hauls himself back up to his feet, one last time.

One step more. Then another, and another.

In each moment, I thought of what I'd lost, he thinks.

Another step, another.

Of what was done to me, and how to inflict my own justice on this world.

Another, another, another.

But I know better now, here at the end.

And then finally, he comes to her.

The woman who hangs in the air has the look of Tatyana Komayd to her, and a dash of Malwina Gogacz: there is the small nose, the weak chin, the pugnacious mouth. She floats about twenty feet past the edge of the staircase, her hands lifted, her eyes turned to the heavens. Her eyes shine brightly, their pure white luminescence lancing up past the top of the tower. Yet her face is twisted in sorrow and grief, and her cheeks are wet with tears: a creature, however Divine, overwhelmed with despair.

He knows that look. He looked the same way when he lost his father, his family, his daughter, his friend.

And then he understands: it's a loop, an endless loop of injured children, growing old but keeping their pain fresh and new, causing yet more injury and starting the whole cycle over again.

He looks at the goddess, and sees only the young girl who stared up at the moon a few nights ago, and declared the dead a mystery to her.

'Death is no place to look for meaning, Taty,' he says to her. He tosses the spear away, letting it roll down the stairs. He slowly walks back along the stairs, until he backs up to the wall of the tower. 'You told me that.'

He looks at the gap. Twenty feet from the stairs to her. Can he make it? Even in such an injured state?

I will have to.

He crouches down, positions his feet, readies himself.

'I will remind you,' he whispers.

He runs along the step, a hobbling, drunken, halting run, but still fast, still strong.

Sigrud comes to the edge.

He leaps.

He soars out, arm extended, the frozen city of Bulikov below him, the endless dark tower stretching above.

He flies to her, reaches out, touches her shoulder, grabs her and holds her close, and then . . .

All the moments crash in around him.

*

Sigrud sits upon a white plane.

The plane is vast and never-ending, and though he doesn't understand it, he knows the plane stretches in all directions, all at once. Yet still, he sits upon it, nude and cross-legged, his scarred, bruised, wounded body bared to the light that seems to come from all directions.

Something shifts around him. He realises that this plane, this place, exists in the palm of someone's hand – someone inconceivably vast.

'HOW DARE YOU,' says a voice.

Things keep shifting. And then she raises him up to her eyes.

Sigrud sees the goddess before him, holding him before her gaze, all of time swirling in her grasp. Her eyes are filled with dying suns and the howl of a thousand storms, with a thousand raindrops falling upon a thousand leaves, a thousand whispered words and a thousand laughs and a thousand tears.

Her face twists in naked fury. 'HOW DARE YOU INTERRUPT ME,' says the goddess. 'HOW DARE YOU DEFY TIME.'

Sigrud looks at the goddess, and blinks slowly. 'I do not defy it,' he says. 'I am simply fulfilling a promise I made to a young girl not that long ago.'

'I AM NO LONGER SHE,' thunders the goddess. 'I AM MUCH, MUCH MORE THAN SHE EVER WAS, THAN SHE EVER COULD BE.'

'And yet,' says Sigrud, 'she was far wiser than you are now.'

The goddess stares at him, outraged. 'YOU KNOW NOTHING OF WHAT YOU SPEAK. I WILL REMAKE TIME, REMAKE THE WORLD. I WILL MAKE A JUST WORLD, A MORAL WORLD, A WORLD FREE OF VIOLATIONS AND WRONGS AND PUNISHMENTS.'

'Tatyana,' says Sigrud softly, 'Malwina . . . How many times have we been here before?'

'THIS HAS NEVER HAPPENED BEFORE. NEVER HAS TIME AWOKEN. NEVER HAS TIME ITSELF REFORGED CREATION.'

'Perhaps not,' says Sigrud. 'But how many times has one person performed an unspeakable atrocity, all in the name of making the world better? The Divinities, the Kaj, Vinya, Nokov . . . And now you? Will you join their ranks?'

'I AM FAR MORE POWERFUL THAN THEY EVER WERE!' shouts the goddess. 'I WILL DO IT RIGHT THIS TIME!'

'I am sure they said the same.'

'YOU DO NOT UNDERSTAND ANY OF THIS,' she says.

'You are wrong,' says Sigrud. 'I have done the same. I have done what you are about to do.'

The goddess hesitates, confused.

'When my daughter died,' Sigrud says quietly, 'I was filled with fury and grief, and I killed those soldiers. It felt righteous. It felt just. But it was monstrous, beyond monstrous. For all my righteousness, I made the world worse.'

'PERHAPS THEY DESERVED IT,' says the goddess. 'OR PERHAPS THEY DIDN'T. THAT IS BUT ONE OF MANY SINS THAT I WILL RIGHT. I WILL MAKE A WORLD WHERE WE GET WHAT IS JUST, WHAT WE DESERVE.'

'You cannot,' says Sigrud. 'You are as powerless as I was. The world is written upon your heart just as it is mine. Pick up all the weapons of all realities and use them all as best you can, Taty, but you cannot inflict virtue on the world. You cannot.'

The goddess stares at him. 'YOU WHO HAVE SUFFERED. YOU WHO HAVE BEEN WRONGED AND VIOLATED. YOU WHO HAVE KILLED AND MURDERED AND MADE WAR UPON THIS WORLD. YOU SAY NOW THAT THERE IS NO JUSTICE?'

'Not like this,' he says. 'Not like this. And I should know. I lost precious things in my life. I suffered. And I thought that suffering made me righteous. But I was wrong, Taty. I tried to teach you this. But how could I teach you this if I had not learned these lessons myself?' He bows his head. 'I . . . I saw my life laid out upon the stairs,' he whispers. 'I gave so many of my own years to wrath, and I stole so many years from other people. How selfish I was. How many wonders I ignored . . . If only I had looked beyond my pain. If only I had laid aside my torment, and chosen to live anew. But I did not, and I lost so much. Yet you will lose so, so much more if you do this.'

The goddess hesitates. He can see it in her face, just a flash of it – a look reminiscent of one he saw on Taty's face, and Malwina's: of anguish, of sorrow, and yet the desire to do right.

'Tatyana, Malwina,' he says. 'Let go of your embers, before you are burned too deeply.'

'I WANT TO MAKE THINGS RIGHT,' she says.

'Shara Komayd once had this chance,' says Sigrud. 'A chance to draw from her pain, and force her will upon the world. She chose instead to give people the tools to make their own worlds better. She lived, and died, to do this. I know she taught you this, Tatyana Komayd. And I know you do not wish to lose what she taught you.'

The goddess looks away, thinking. She trembles. 'I . . . I JUST WISH I COULD HAVE BEEN THERE FOR HER,' she says.

'I know,' Sigrud says.

'I WISH I COULD HAVE SAID GOOD-BYE,' she says.

'I know,' says Sigrud. 'I know. I know, I know, I know.'

The goddess raises her other hand, and things begin to change.

The vast white plane begins to blur and whirl and shift, collapsing in on the point just above the palm of her hand. As it does, the goddess transforms: she is no longer the tall, towering being adorned with all moments of all things. She shrinks, she grows younger, imperfect, until finally she is a small Continental girl who is not quite Malwina Gogacz, and not quite Tatyana Komayd either.

The white plane collapses until it is a bright, bright star in her palm. She looks at him, her eyes full of tears, and looks at the star.

'I don't want this,' she says quietly. 'I don't want to be this anymore.' She lifts the star to her lips and gives a tiny puff.

The star dissolves like the seeds of a dandelion and goes dancing through the air, all these tiny, soft lights scattered to the winds.

The girl bows her head and bursts into tears. 'I miss her, Sigrud,' she says. 'I miss her *so much*.'

Sigrud says, 'I know.'

Everything vanishes.

Sigrud falls.

He's falling, but not at the speed of someone tumbling through the air: rather, he senses he's being carefully lowered.

He opens his eye.

The girl – Taty? Malwina? He's not sure – holds him in her arms as if he were a child. Together they slowly float down to earth, and as they do the black tower unravels around them, dissipating and dissolving.

He's weak now, terribly weak. He's shivering, he's so cold. Yet he manages to look at the face of the girl holding him.

She's weeping, her cheeks covered in tears. 'Go away, go away,' she whispers. 'All of this can go away.'

They land as light as a thrush upon a branch. Suddenly Ivanya is there, staring at them.

'What in hells?' says Ivanya. 'What . . . What just happened? Where's Nokov?'

Sigrud tries to smile and say, 'Ivanya – you're back,' yet he has no air for it.

The girl gently lays him on the ground. As she does, he looks at his left hand and the scar there, the miracle that's dominated his life.

The scar is fading away, the lines unraveling like the threads of an old sweater.

I thought my sorrow was a weapon, he thinks, watching it.

It is just the barest whisper of a line now.

Yet all this time, it was simply a burden. And how I suffered because of it.

The scar is almost gone.

Pain seizes him. He begins convulsing. He feels the blood flow from his wound double, triple, a waterfall of blood from his right breast.

'What's going on?' says Ivanya, alarmed.

Sigrud is trembling, so he can't answer her, but he knows: the miracle that kept him alive for so long is abandoning him. He's becoming a common, mortal man, as susceptible to wounds as any other.

'No!' cries the girl. 'No, no!' She snatches at his left palm like he's got some treasure hidden there, then rips something out – something black and fragile, like a spiderweb. She crushes it, and slaps it to the wound on his right breast. His wound screams in pain, and he feels something slip *inside* him, writhing under his skin.

Then things go dark.

16.
Close your eyes,
I'll be here in the Morning

The older I get, the more I think human history is just combinations and recombinations of inequalities.

For over a thousand years the very, very few on the Continent had absolute control not just of the world, but of reality.

The Kaj changed that, of course. But then Saypur held all the purse strings of all the world, and a wealthy Saypuri elite had the most say over who loosened or tightened them.

I like to think I helped loosen the purse strings, just a little. But freedom and human happiness has a direct relationship to the number of people who have power over their own world, their own lives. Far too many people still have no say in how they live.

The more that power is dispersed, the more that will change.

— LETTER FROM FORMER PRIME MINISTER ASHARA KOMAYD TO UPPER
HOUSE MINORITY LEADER TURYIN MULAGHESH, 1732

Far away from Bulikov, in one of the provinces surrounding Ghaladesh, Sharma Muhajan stops and looks up.

Sharma is not rich, so she was in the middle of churning her own butter, a long, exhausting process. But then things seemed to ... *pause* very strangely. Like things froze, just for a second. Yet now it's gone.

A slight breeze wafts through her house. It's curiously warm. But it makes her shake herself, and remember what she's doing.

She goes back to her work, then fetches more milk for the churner. She sighs as she looks into the bucket of milk. It's a pitiful amount, not enough to make what she needs, but she supposes it'll have to do.

Sharma begins pouring the milk into the churner, staring into space and thinking about how, or rather if, they'll make it through the month. Then she jumps, alarmed by the feeling of coldness in her sandals.

She looks down. The churner has overflowed. Milk is spreading across her floor in a dingy puddle.

Sharma frowns, bewildered, and looks into the bucket of milk. It's the same amount – the same small, pitiful amount at the bottom – yet somehow it has overflowed her big churner.

Curious, she thinks, then walks over to a big pot, and tries to pour out the milk.

But she can't pour it out. Because the milk just keeps coming. And coming. And coming.

And coming.

In Voortyashtan, far to the north, Mads Hoeverssen frowns as he tries to figure out what in the world is wrong with his automobile. Something somewhere is not draining right, he's sure of it, which is blocking one of the fuel lines. But it's just a matter of trying to figure out *what* is not draining right. If only he could get past that damn shaft here, on the side of the engine block here . . .

Then things pause for a moment. An odd little stutter, it feels like. And it's gone.

A warm breeze flows across his face. He shakes himself and returns to his work, trying to get that shaft to budge, but it . . .

Squeak.

Mads stares. The shaft gives way to his touch as if it were made of soft cheese, bending perfectly.

He peers at the shaft. He realises that what he's done – however in the *hells* it is that he's done it – is very bad, bad enough that the whole damn auto might not work.

Then, as if it heard his very thought, the shaft pops back into its original form with a *squeak*.

Mads peers at it again. He rubs his eyes. Then he slides out from under his auto, and thinks.

He looks at the dent at the edge of the driver's door, which he's never taken the time to get rid of.

With a *clunk*, the metal pops out and smooths itself over.

'Oh my word,' whispers Mads.

In Taalvashtan, in the southwest region of the Continent, a young boy chasing a ball accidentally runs up a wall, pauses as he realises what's happened, and bursts into tears, terrified. His parents, baffled, will have little idea of how to get him down, but they will eventually succeed. They may regret it later though, when their son realises he can also run across ceilings.

In Navashtra, in Saypur, a young girl obeys a strange impulse and sings a song to the stones at the nearby quarry. She and the rest of her family, who are picnicking nearby, stare in fear and confusion as the stones slowly roll down the slopes to spell the words: THANK YOU, THAT WAS LOVELY.

In the Dreyling Shores, an old woman looks up and nearly has a heart attack as she sees her niece casually walking across the empty sky above the seas, laughing hysterically, waving her arms in mimicry of the nearby sea-gulls, who are no less alarmed than the old woman.

All of these aberrations – these and the thousands of others occurring across Saypur, the Continent, and the Dreyling Shores – are preceded by two things: the first is the strange pause, as if the world was frozen for a fleeting second; and then a warm breeze flooding through, touching people's faces.

As one very young boy who has just discovered he can walk through wooden walls puts it, 'It's like there were stars in the breeze. And then the breeze put them in our heads.'

In Ghaladesh, the Military Council's meeting with Prime Minister Gad-kari and her cabinet is not going well. Mostly because the Military Council, despite being the Military Council and thus being very well informed, has very little understanding of what's going on.

First there were the reports about the tower around Bulikov, and the giant black Divine thing that walked up the stairs inside. The Military Council had thought this was another Continental insurrection – except that the Continentals seemed just as surprised and terrified by it as everyone else.

Then there were the reports of former prime minister Ashara Komayd being sighted multiple times in the streets of Bulikov, which was very puzzling, as everyone knew she was quite dead.

And then there were the reports that the black tower, along with the famous walls of Bulikov, had simply disappeared. As if none of this had ever happened.

At first they were relieved. But then all the other reports came flooding in.

The prime minister's aide rattles off the latest flurry: '. . . a woman in Ahanashtan can read poetry to wooden fences and make them rearrange themselves; one child, male, in Jukoshtan, leaves flower petals in his wake when he runs very fast; an elderly gentleman in Brost can make glass directly from sand just by having an argument with it; and now there are two or possibly even three – this is rather unconfirmed – women in Ahanashtan who can heal injuries of all types simply by holding the injured person in their arms and taking a long nap with them.' Her aide checks the figures once more. 'In total, this is seventy-three reports in the last two hours.'

'And those are the ones we *know*,' says General Noor, ancient and grey but still wielding his steely stare. 'There must be countless ones we *don't* know about. Either because these people have hidden themselves away, or their . . . *abilities* function in an unseen manner.'

Prime Minister Gadkari considers this. She is known for being a quiet contemplator, not the sort of prime minister to rock the boat – a great contrast to Komayd and, after her, Gawali. 'So,' she says eventually. 'These are . . . miracles.'

'They *would* be, Prime Minister,' says General Noor. 'Yet these are happening *everywhere*. Most miracles were restricted to the Continent.'

'And none of these people were known to have these miraculous qualities before,' says General Sakthi. 'They've just . . . come from nowhere.'

There's a snort from the back of the room. Everyone along the table slowly turns to look at Minister Mulaghesh, who is absently peeling a cigarillo.

'Do you have something you wish to say, Minister?' asks Gadkari.

'I am cursed,' says Mulaghesh, 'with an abundance of things I wish to say, as we are well aware, Prime Minister.'

General Noor studiously looks away, as if trying to hide a smile.

Gadkari glares at Mulaghesh, who is minority leader of the opposition party and an eternal pain in her ass. It is only due to decorum that Mulaghesh is a part of any such cabinet meetings, though Gadkari has found that Mulaghesh does more talking than nearly all the people who actually have a right to be here.

'Do you, Mulaghesh,' says Gadkari icily, 'have any opinions on the matter at hand? You do have some experience in . . . these matters.'

' "These matters," ' snorts Mulaghesh. 'By which you mean these insane horrors.' She sucks her teeth. 'Komayd once said that the Divine might have been like any other energy – there's a fixed amount of it, all being used by various . . . I don't know, machinations.'

'Miracles,' says Noor. 'Gods.'

'Yes,' says Mulaghesh. 'Things like that.'

'Would this have been Komayd the elder?' asks Gadkari's aide. 'Or Komayd the younger?'

'I mean the one who wasn't a scheming fucking bitch,' says Mulaghesh.

'Kindly cut to the point, Mulaghesh!' snaps Gadkari.

'The walls of Bulikov, the biggest miraculous thing ever, are now gone. That big black Divine thing that appeared out of nowhere, that's gone too. All those things were using that Divine energy. And now maybe it's just . . . dispersed. Like a plume of gas from a refinery flare.'

There's a long silence as the room understands what she means.

'Dispersed,' says Sakthi, stunned. 'You mean . . . Everyone, everywhere . . . could be a *god*?'

'Probably not,' says Mulaghesh. 'These are just little things, little miracles, in comparison to what a Divinity can do. But they can still do them, apparently.'

'But . . . But you are saying that average, *everyday people* can now shape reality,' says Gadkari. 'You are saying that anyone, anywhere, can take the world around them and make it what they want!'

Mulaghesh shrugs. 'Somewhat. Sure. But at least it's not just the Continent sitting on this. It's everywhere. Now people everywhere can do it.'

Another long silence.

Noor turns to the prime minister. 'I suspect we will need to set up some kind of an organisation,' he says, 'responsible for identifying and regulating such peoples.'

Gadkari, still bewildered, blinks. 'I'm sorry?'

'Some kind of . . . temporary police bureau,' says Noor. 'An emergency agency of some kind.'

'And if these effects are not temporary?' asks Sakthi.

'Then . . . perhaps a Ministry of its own,' says Noor.

Someone at the end of the table laughs bitterly. 'A Ministry of Miracles,' they say. 'What a nightmare!'

'The real question,' says Sakthi, 'is who shall spearhead this effort?'

'True,' says Noor. 'Ever since Komayd died – and it sounds like she's *actually* dead this time – we have very few people in government with any experience with the Divine.'

Another silence. Then, for the second time, all the heads in the room slowly turn to look at Minister Mulaghesh.

Mulaghesh's brow wrinkles as she realises she's the centre of attention. She drops the cigarillo in shock. Then she sighs and says, 'Ah, *shit.*'

Somewhere deep within Sigrud's mind, sentience slowly blossoms.

He is alive. He is aware. And he is in terrible pain.

Everything hurts. Everything. It's unimaginable how his body could hurt so much. Just thinking about drawing breath pains him, let alone actually drawing breath.

His mouth is dry. He moans.

Someone nearby says, 'He's awake. He's *alive!*'

He opens his mouth. Someone dribbles water into it. The water is a blessing and a curse: his body hungers for it, yet it's so difficult to swallow. He manages to do it once, twice, but can't handle a third.

He cracks open his eye – this barest of gestures is like lifting two hundred pounds – and sees he's in an opulent bedchamber, probably Ivanya's. He trembles and looks to his right. Ivanya is sitting on the bed next to him with a bowl of water and a rag. His right shoulder is a huge mass of bandages. She looks tired, like she's been working on him all day, if not all night.

She smiles at him sadly. 'Can you hear me? Are you all in there?'

He exhales softly through his nostrils.

'Good. That's good!'

He can't speak the question, so he tries to use his eye to communicate it.

'You're been out for three days,' she says. 'I didn't believe you'd make it. But you did. Barely.' She blinks rapidly. Sigrud realises she's trying very hard to hold her bedside manner together, which means his condition might look as bad as it feels.

He tries to speak, but he can't get further than, 'T-T-'

'Taty. Yes. She's . . . Well.' Ivanya steps back.

Another person walks into view. A girl.

It is not quite Malwina, not quite Tatyana. She is a mix of the two: she has Taty's wide, soulful eyes, and Malwina's truculent mouth – and, oddly, the way she carries herself still reminds him of Shara. Unlike Ivanya, she doesn't bother trying to smile. Her eyes look haunted and hollow and miserable.

Again, Sigrud tries to use his eye to communicate what he wishes to say.

'Hello,' says the girl. She takes a moment, wondering what to say. 'We've . . . I've asked everyone to call me Tatyana. I guess because Taty had Shara in her memories. More of her, at least. And I wanted to keep that.' She tries to smile. 'I couldn't go back to being two people. Not after everything I did. Some things . . . Some things you can't take back.'

Though Sigrud doesn't have the strength to lift his hand, he crooks a finger. She sees it and crouches beside his bed, holding her ear up to his cracked lips.

'Weren't you a god?' asks Sigrud, his voice a rattling whisper.

'I was,' she says. 'I was . . . powerful. Quite powerful. Powerful enough to give it all away.'

He frowns at her.

'I gave it to anyone,' she says. She waves at the ceiling. 'Anything.

Random, perhaps. It wasn't right for me to make such decisions about reality. It wasn't right for me to make decisions about *who* should make such decisions. So I just . . . scattered it, sent it to wherever it all wanted to go.'

'A lot has changed since you've been out,' says Ivanya. 'People are showing some . . . unusual talents as a by-product of what Taty here did, to say the least.'

He frowns at her, confused.

'*Miraculous* talents,' Ivanya says. 'Everyone. *Everywhere.* The Ministry's in an uproar. Everything everywhere is in an uproar. It's a new world overnight.'

Sigrud crooks his finger again. The girl – Taty, he supposes – leans close. 'Why am I alive?' he whispers.

She sits up and smiles weakly at him. 'I gave it away, but I couldn't give it *all* away. I can't change what I am. I am still a creature of the Divine, still the daughter of time – just not as strong as I used to be. But I could still snatch that miracle living inside you, and break it open, and use all the time it'd stored up. Specifically, I . . . I used it on your wound.'

'Your shoulder's knitted faster than anyone's should, from what happened to you,' says Ivanya. 'You should have died within minutes of pulling that spear out.'

He shuts his eye, deflated.

'What's wrong?' asks Taty. She leans close.

'I was ready to die,' he whispers. 'You should have let me die.'

She sits up. She looks at him, her dark eyes large and sorrowful. 'You're all I have left,' she says. 'You're the only person who was there when I needed you. You're all I have left now.'

Sigrud shuts his eye and sleeps.

He awakes in the night. He coughs and someone is again there beside him with the water, the rag, the drops in his mouth. Again he struggles to swallow.

'There, there,' says Ivanya's voice. 'There, there.'

When he opens his eye he sees she's watching him with that curious, strained light in her eyes again, like she's struggling to keep smiling.

He finds he can speak – but just barely. 'Is Taty here?'

'No. Something's wrong with her. She's been having terrible headaches, and has nearly been as bedridden as you a –'

Sigrud shakes his head. 'We have to get her off the Continent.'

'Why?'

'The Divine . . . it is shaped by the beliefs of the people around it. She's still Divine, still being affected by the Continent. Olvos was terrified of it. Terrified of belief changing her.'

'You really think that's what's happening?'

'Olvos stayed cloistered away for fear of it happening to her,' he whispers. 'She couldn't even stop the torture of her own son.'

'But what can we do?' asks Ivanya. 'Where can we send her? Saypur's in a state of disarray, but I don't think she could last there, not with the Ministry trying to make lists of everyone miraculous.'

Sigrud coughs. The movement sends daggers shooting into his chest. 'The Dreyling Shores,' he says. 'We never had gods, never had the Divine. I can take her there.'

'What! You? You're not in a state to sit up, let alone take a voyage by boat!'

'I must speak to my wife. To Hild. She can make arrangements for me.'

'Your . . . Your wife?' Ivanya's sidelong glance speaks volumes.

'She was my wife the last time I saw her. That was thirteen years ago. I believe she has remarried since.'

'This is the only way to save Taty?'

'I think so.' He coughs. 'Shara asked me to protect Taty. I will do so until I am certain she is safe. Even from a bed.'

'I'll make the arrangements,' she says. She tries to smile again, but it doesn't quite meet her eyes.

'There is something you're not telling me,' says Sigrud.

'What?'

'When you look at me. You see something. What is it?'

She hesitates.

'Is it my injury?' he asks.

'No. Not just that.'

'Then what?'

She looks at him, cringing, then goes to her vanity and fetches a mirror. She holds it up to his face for him to see.

The face of an old Dreyling man looks back at him. It takes him a moment to realise it's his own. His face is lined with wrinkles, he has faint brown spots at his temples, and veins riddle the edges of his nose. His hair and beard are silver-grey. His eye is faded, no longer the bright, glacial blue he's used to seeing.

'She said she pulled the miracle out of you,' says Ivanya, 'and all the time it had stored up. But it seems it had . . . stored up quite a bit of time. And when she put it back into you . . .'

Sigrud chuckles weakly. 'Oh, goodness me. Goodness me.'

'You seem to be taking this well.'

'It would be foolish of me,' says Sigrud, 'to dance with time itself and expect to come away unscathed. I thought I would be dead now. But I live on to help deliver Taty from danger. I hold no grudge against this.'

'I do,' says Ivanya sadly. 'A little.'

He looks at her and smiles. 'It was good while we had it,' he says.

'One evening,' says Ivanya, 'does not seem to be enough, Sigrud je Harkvaldsson.'

'Yet it was what we got,' says Sigrud. 'Will you help me, Ivanya? Will you help bring Taty to my homeland?'

She bends down and kisses him on the forehead. 'Of course. Of course, of course, of course.'

Ivanya hires an ambulance for their procession to the Solda River the next day. Between Sigrud, who still looks ravaged, and Tatyana, who leans up against Ivanya with her face pale and sweating, they look like a bunch of plague victims being shipped off to quarantine.

Sigrud is only half-conscious, but no one bothers to glance at any of them. Mostly, it seems, because Bulikov has gone insane.

A woman builds a staircase out of a low cloud in the sky. A man passes by riding what appears to be a deer made of vines, laughing delightedly. A child sitting on a staircase draws something on the wall with his finger. A small, round door appears. The child opens it, steps inside, and shuts the door, which promptly vanishes.

This is the world we have made? This is what Shara and Taty and Malwina and I made with all our striving?

They finally make their way down to the Solda. Their vessel proves to be a dingy old yacht, and their captain a shifty-looking Saypuri man who quickly states his desire to get the living hells out of Bulikov at full haste, since it's gone mad. 'But the whole world's mad now,' he says hollowly. 'The whole *world's* gone mad.'

'Get us to the Dreyling Shores quickly,' says Ivanya, 'no questions asked, and you can buy a little piece of the world that *hasn't* gone mad.'

They help Sigrud and Taty get stowed away in the passenger cabin. Ivanya quickly sets up shop beside their beds, unpacking boxes and boxes of medical equipment. Sigrud can tell already that it will be a difficult journey for him: this is much, much less comfortable than Ivanya's beds.

He stares up at the ceiling, trying to remain conscious. He fails, and falls asleep again.

One day passes, then another. It's a drifting world for Sigrud. Each time he sleeps it feels like an eternity. Sometimes it's a handful of minutes. Other times it's more than a day. His breath is shallow and quick now, always wheezing. He's not sure if he'll ever regain full use of both lungs.

Once he awakes to hear someone weeping in the night. He turns his head and finds Taty lying on her berth, eyes wet with tears.

'What is wrong?' he asks.

'I miss her,' she says. 'I just miss her. That's all.'

He isn't sure if she means Shara or Tavaan. Perhaps it's both. Perhaps it doesn't matter.

He looks out the porthole. They're well north of Bulikov now, passing through the western arm of the Tarsils. Snowflakes twirl down from the moonlit skies.

'Does it get any better?' asks Taty. 'Does it?'

'Eventually,' he says. 'Yes.'

She looks at him, her eyes burning. 'Don't you leave me too. Not you. Not after all this.'

He tries to smile at her. 'Close your eyes. I'll be here in the morning.'

She frowns at him, suspicious.

'I'll be here for a while,' he says.

She rolls over and falls back to sleep.

As Sigrud, Ivanya, and Tatyana continue their long, slow journey north-west along the Solda, the greater world begins its own journey into strange new lands.

In Taalvashtan, all those with the ability to produce or manipulate raw materials – iron, wood, stone, sand – begin to gather and meet every other night. They're crafters, they've decided, workers and labourers, so perhaps it'd be wise for them to join forces. Create a guild or association of some kind. Make what they like, for a fee.

The next morning they start on their work, just to see if they can do it.

By evening, they've built a third of a skyscraper.

By the next day, word will spread of what they can do, and others will carry on the idea.

By the week after that, global real-estate markets will begin to collapse.

And by the end of the month, the finance markets will begin to do the same – just after the newly formed Alchemists Guild of Ahanashtan officially opens for business.

In Jukoshtan, a man who can sing songs that send listeners into a delirious, joyous daze travels through the outskirts of the city, sending audiences into rapturous, joyful trances – for a fee, of course. It won't be until just after he's gone that people begin to notice the sharp rise in teenage pregnancies – pregnancies originating in sex that the girls cannot remember, and certainly didn't consent to.

Within days, a bounty will be put on the musician's head. But this will do little to stem the outrage, the shame, or the grief over the eventual suicides.

In Bulikov, a woman sets up as a street vendor: she sits in a chair beside a nondescript door, and over the door hangs a sign reading, ANYWHERE – FIFTY DREKELS. Curious people ask exactly what this means, and she simply says, 'Anywhere. I can take you anywhere.' They soon find out she's right: for fifty drekels, the woman will open the door on a desert island, the top of a mountain, or someone's mansion.

By evening the queue for her business stretches all the way through Bulikov.

By morning a railway company puts a price on her head. But any would-be assassins will find it's very difficult to catch a woman who can open doors to anywhere.

More and more. More and more miracles.

More and more changes, more and more and more.

In Tohmay, in Saypur, there is talk and mutterings of a militia, or even an army. Some of these talents, it's clear, are more aggressive and harmful than others. 'Round them up,' one belligerent minister says, 'start drilling them, and prepare for what's coming. It's going to be war now, got to be, war between us and whoever gets their troops ready first. If men can do anything, anything in the world, they'll do war first, and we'd be fools not to strike hard and fast.'

In Ghaladesh, Minister Turyin Mulaghesh ignores these mutterings of war, and instead stays awake for four straight days, barking orders, answering messages, and planning with her own personal cabinet. 'They may be miraculous,' she says to her employees, 'but they are still citizens, and we will treat them justly.' She notices one sceptical glance, and snaps, 'This changes *nothing*. They will still act like people, for better or for worse. And we shall be there to watch them.' Her employees and representatives salute her and scurry to work, making phone calls, running off to police stations.

On the dawn of the fifth day she stares out her office window at the Ghaladeshi skyscape, chewing an unlit cigarillo. They haven't figured out a name for her yet, not who she is or what department she's running, but she has to admit – it feels *damned nice* to be back in charge.

And on the outskirts of Ghaladesh, a curious procession is taking place: Saypuris slowly gather at the Saypuri National Memorial Grounds, where the remains of Saypur's most honoured heroes are interred. The dozens of people wind through the paths until they come to the Komayd section, where one monument is still fresh and new – a recent addition.

The Saypuris stare at the memorial to Ashara Komayd, the benevolent but defamed prime minister who suffered in silence, died tragically, and yet was somehow resurrected to fight for her nation one last time.

They place candles and flowers at the foot of her monument, solemn and silent. In a few years they will begin calling her a name that will grow in popularity until it becomes the common way to speak of Komayd; and though they could not possibly have known it, the name they will choose is curiously fitting for her last days.

They will call her Mother of the Future.

Sigrud awakes and smells the cold winds drifting through the cabin. 'Are we in Voortyashtan?' he croaks.

Ivanya, tending to his bandages, looks taken aback. 'We're quite close. How did you guess?'

'Take me on deck when we pass through,' he says. 'Once we're free and through.'

'That's not happening, my dear. You can't sit up, let alone stand and walk upstairs.'

'I will do it,' says Sigrud grimly. 'I welcome your help, if you can give it. But if not, I will still do it.'

Ivanya and Taty exchange a glance, but remain silent.

Their shifty captain has to do some quick talking and perhaps even quicker bribing to get them through the port of Voortyashtan, but after a few tense moments, the dingy old yacht continues on. Ivanya, grimacing and reluctant, helps Sigrud sit up in his bed. The pain is tremendous. The world spins about him, and he feels nauseous. He sweats and quakes, and is not at all sure he can get his legs to do what he needs them to do.

Yet he succeeds. With Ivanya and Taty's help, he comes to the deck, stands underneath the dark night skies, and looks east as they leave Voortyashtan behind.

He smells the cold north breezes and the salty air. *How long has it been*, he thinks, *since the winds of this place have passed through my lungs?*

The shore is alight with construction, with industry, with life and commerce and movement. It is no longer the miserable, brutal hovel he remembers, not the crude, lethal place it once was. It is a place people travel miles to come to, not one they avoid.

'My daughter did that,' says Sigrud weakly, nodding at the lights on the shore. 'She did that. She made all that happen.'

The two women support and embrace him as he watches as Voortyashtan fades into the distance.

'She did that,' he whispers, as if wishing that the world would hear, and notice. 'And I am very proud of her.'

It won't last forever, he knows. Not even that will last forever.

But it will last a while.

Sigrud awakes to the sound of clinking pots and pans, someone humming cheerfully, and the smell of smoke.

Where am I?

He opens his eyes and sees a grey stone ceiling above him. He smells pine in the distance, and he can hear something – the hush of waves, not far away.

It takes him a long, long while to remember. He's in the Dreyling Shores, he realises, back in the homeland he left so, so many years before. It was hard for him to follow, to understand everything that happened when he was feverish aboard the boat . . .

'You've got that confused look again,' says a voice from the door.

He looks over and sees Taty standing there, smiling uncertainly at him.

'Do I?' he says. His voice is terribly hoarse.

'Yes. Are you going to ask me where we are again? Ask me where the boat is? What day it is?'

'I don't know what day it is,' he says. 'But I remember – we are in the Dreyling Shores. Yes?'

'Yes. In the house your . . . ah, your wife got for us.'

He frowns. This memory is a little hazier for him. He remembers Ivanya going ashore somewhere, coming back with news of some kind – apparently the two of them must have arranged it all. A memory of this house calcifies in his mind – spacious, even palatial, and secluded in the hills. A safe place for three refugees to hide while the world sorts itself out. 'Where is Ivanya?' he asks.

'She's cooking. She's very enthusiastic about it. But not yet, ah, very good at it.'

'Yes. I remember the broths she makes for me now . . .' He pulls a face. 'It is very taxing, trying to be polite about them.'

Taty sits beside him on the bed and smiles. 'You're getting better, though. You remember more. You must be stronger. Aren't you?'

Sigrud smiles weakly at her. 'I remember *this* now.'

'Do you?'

'Yes. Now is when you come in and tell me what you've seen in the woods outside.'

Taty laughs. 'I do! Very good. And this time I won't tell you the same story again and again. I'll tell you something new.' She tells him about her explorations in the forest, in the hills, along the shore, and especially about her new acquaintances. 'There are all kinds of kids from the village down the road,' she says, excited. 'They come to the shore every day and fish, and they showed me a cave, Sigrud, a real *cave!*'

Sigrud smiles as he watches her. *I forget so easily*, he thinks, *that she is still but a child.*

'I would like to see that,' he says.

'What, a cave?'

'No. To see you on the shore.' He thinks about it. 'I will do that tomorrow, I think. Yes. I will come with you tomorrow.'

She looks at him, uncertain. 'Are . . . Are you sure about that?'

'You said I was getting better.'

'But . . . Can you really get out of bed?'

'I have never been surer of anything. Find me a cane, and you and I will stroll together tomorrow.' He smiles. 'I'll be here in the morning, waiting for you. Do not let me down.'

Taty grips his arm as Sigrud, wheezing and wobbling, limps down the garden path to the forest edge. 'Auntie is going to skin me alive for this,' she says. 'She's absolutely going to skin me *alive*.'

'Let her skin me instead,' he says. 'I will be easier to catch.' He coughs, swallows, sniffs, and focuses on his next step.

'Are you sure you want to do this? Really?'

'I grew up with the sea. It is my right. And it is my right to see my friend enjoy it. Do not deny an old man his wishes. That is rudeness.'

Taty helps him slowly, slowly mount the hill before the shore, each step taking nearly a minute at times.

'Are you sure you can make it?' Taty asks.

'I have climbed higher heights,' he says. 'After all. You were there.'

'I wasn't paying much attention then.'

'Nor was I, really.'

They continue up the hillside.

'Did I do the right thing, Sigrud?' asks Taty suddenly, troubled. 'In the tower, when I was someone . . . else. I worry about it. I could have, I could have . . .'

He remembers Shara saying: *Few have any choice in how they live. Few have the power to decide their own realities. Even if we win – will that change?*

'You did something few could have ever done, Taty,' says Sigrud. 'You walked away from power, and gave people choices where they'd never had any before.'

'But now what will they do with them?'

'I think,' says Sigrud, 'that they will be people. As they have always been. For better or worse.'

His cane sinks deep into the earth, it's so rich and moist. The air is cold and splendid. The trees tower above them.

'I used to cut these things down, you know,' he says, gesturing at them. 'A foolish way to make a living, isn't it?'

'We're almost there,' says Taty. 'Almost.'

'I know. I can hear it.'

They crest the small hill, and Sigrud sees.

The sea is the same. The sea is always the same, as is the wandering, white shore before it. His heart is glad to see this, yet also saddened.

'It's beautiful, isn't it?' says Taty, awed.

'Yes, it is,' he says. 'Perhaps the most beautiful thing. But it could be more beautiful yet.'

'What do you mean?'

He waves at the shore. 'Go and play. That is just what this scene needs.'

'Are you sure?'

Sigrud, grunting and wheezing, slowly sits to lean against the tree, facing out to sea. 'I will be here for a while. Go on. Do not waste your seconds on me.'

'They aren't a waste, Sigrud,' she says reproachfully.

He smiles at her. 'I know. Go.'

'You won't be cold?'

'I won't be cold. Go and have fun.'

'All right. I'll be back soon! I promise!' She lightly steps down the stones to the shore. He watches as she races along the waves to be met by three children he doesn't recognise. By their gestures and demeanours, though, they seem to be very familiar with one another.

'A social butterfly, then,' he says, sniffing. *Good. She needs more people in her life.*

Sigrud leans against the tree. The forest rings with the distant sound of birdsong and the echo of the waves. It's late morning now, the sun reaching the spot in the sky where its beams no longer pierce the pines at that striking angle, but it is still a gorgeous day.

A peaceful day. One bereft of threat or danger.

I did it, Shara, he thinks, gazing out to sea. *We did it.*

He looks up at the tree above him. A piece of time itself, calcified and slowly accrued, stretching toward the bright blue skies on this beautiful day.

He reaches to the side and feels its rough bark, its roots digging down deep into the soil.

And what have you seen, I wonder? What have you seen? And what will you see yet?

He tries to imagine it. Tries to imagine the world that's passed, and the world yet to come. The one he had some small hand in making.

He looks down. A girl is walking up the shore to him. The sun is bright, reflecting off the waves behind her, and it's hard for him to see, but he thinks her hair is blonde. And is she wearing glasses?

A woman's voice in his ear, perhaps Shara's, whispering, 'Can you believe it?'

Sigrud closes his eye.

*

Tatyana Komayd dances up the hill, shimmering with delight. 'Seal babies!' she cries. 'There are seal babies up the coast, Sigrud! I *saw* them!'

She climbs up to the top of the hill and looks around, trying to remember where she left him. Then she sees him, his broad form leaning against the biggest tree, one hand on his cane and the other touching the trunk, a curiously wistful touch, as if touching an old lover.

'They were tiny!' she says, running through the trees to him. 'They were tiny and perfect and they were playing and I just couldn't *believe* it! Are seals common here, Sigrud?'

He does not answer.

She walks over to stand before him. 'Sigrud?'

Silence.

She peers closer at him, then her eyes widen.

She covers her mouth.

'Oh,' she says, in a soft, crushed voice.

The waves crash and crackle on the shores below.

She stares at him for a long time, hands on her mouth, tears silently running down her cheeks, the sound of birdsong in her ears. Then she sniffs and nods.

'All right,' she says. 'All right.'

She sits beside him. Then she takes his hand in her own, fingers woven tight in his, and she watches the waves in the evening light.

Acknowledgements

Many thanks to my agent, Cameron McClure, and my editor, Julian Pavia, who both helped me keep the ship aright during this (somewhat accidental) journey.

Many thanks as well to my parents, my family, and to Ashlee, who helps me work every day as if we live in the early times of a great nation. The future is indeed a bloom worth tending to.